Critics Applaud *The Reckoning*

The Reckoning is a bold story of gripping suspense and mortal conflict. Critics and readers alike praise Byron Huggins' writing as ACTION-FILLED, GRIPPING, SPELLBINDING AND PIERCING TO THE VERY MARROW.

> Shirley J. Updyke
> —*WRGN Radio, PA*

From the first page, Huggins RIVETS READERS to this INTERNATIONAL ESPIONAGE ADVENTURE LACED WITH SUPERNATURAL, PROPHETIC OVERTONES. The suspense never falters but continually builds until the final shattering climax.... Both well-written and orthodox, this novel may well slake the literary and spiritual thirst for high-quality Christian fiction.

> Mark Horn
> —*Bookstore Journal*

James Byron Huggins' *Reckoning* is a brooding, SUSPENSE-FUL novel.... [Protagonist] Gage, as adept at shedding blood as any character in a Don Pendleton novel, is more fully realized than Mack Bolan, and the malevolent powers he's up against *are* scary.

> —*Booklist*

RIVETING...POSITIVELY RIVETING. For the male reader who enjoys Jack Higgins and Stephen Coonts high-adventure novels, *The Reckoning* comes close to being *A MUST READ*. It's next to impossible to put down....

> George Allen
> —*The Christian Advocate*

...A THRILLER, CHARGED WITH CONFLICT AND INTRIGUE. and masculine spirituality. Gage, a man reconstructed by the rigors of his combat training, draws us into his struggles to understand himself in light of his newfound faith. Huggins manages to develop Gage's spirituality without preaching or romanticizing his faith.

> Charles Garland
> —*The Decatur Daily*

THE RECKONING

A NOVEL

JAMES BYRON HUGGINS

HARVEST HOUSE PUBLISHERS
Eugene, Oregon 97402

Also by James Byron Huggins
A Wolf Story

THE RECKONING

Copyright © 1994 by Harvest House Publishers
Eugene, Oregon 97402

Library of Congress Cataloging-in-Publication Data

Huggins, James Byron.
    The reckoning / James Byron Huggins.
        p.   cm.
    ISBN 1-56507-181-6 (Cloth)
    ISBN 1-56507-367-3 (Trade Paper)
    I. Title.
PS3558.U346R4   1994
813'.54—dc20   94-10717
                                                           CIP

Printed in the United States of America.

95   96   97   98   99   00   —   10   9   8   7   6   5   4   3   2   1

*Dedicated
to
Bill Jensen*

the best there is

THE RECKONING

A NOVEL

I am in blood...

Stepped in so far that, should I wade no more
Returning were as tedious as go o'er.

MacBeth
Act III, ii

Prologue

Dusty tomes of ancient manuscripts rested upon the marble slab where he worked, all but concealing his cloaked and hooded shape. Shrouded in silence and subterranean darkness, he wrote, holding the pen in skeletal fingers.

In the subdued glow of a single candle he bent over the stone. Aged Egyptian pictographs and cuneiform tablets lay heavily across the granite floor and the wall to his back, only to disappear in the stygian gloom, where light surrendered to night.

Intent upon his task, he did not seem to notice the soundless steps of the man who emerged from the nearby shadows to stand before him. Separated by the burdened slab of stone, the intruder seemed to hold a cautious distance.

Robed in imperial splendor with bronze armor glinting dully in the candlelight, the lordly figure stood without words. One hand, crowned with a monarch's ring, was clenched at his side, while the other nervously gripped the short sword at his waist. Beneath the long white hair and aristocratic face, the crimson cloak that flowed from his shoulders waved in the dark wind. His ice-blue eyes narrowed, focusing coldly on the spectral shape.

"Are you so drunk, priest, that you do not know the presence of Vespasian, Emperor of Rome?" he said, sullen.

His words were absorbed by the gloom.

With a slow, dying scrawl, the quill fell silent. And, hauntingly, the scribe raised his head to reveal what the shadows had hidden: a haggard skull of a face, unnaturally narrow and white, that melted strangely into the darkness of the blackened hood. Pale eyes, opaque and unblinking, settled upon the Emperor of Rome.

"I know infinite mysteries of the cosmos, proud Vespasian," he whispered in a dry, mocking rasp. "I know the future, and the past. I speak with unseen dominions of the earth, so surely I know your presence..."

With a trembling hand Vespasian removed his black and silver ring, tossing it quickly to land upon the marble slab. It rang against the stone, rolled, and fell silent on the manuscript clutched reverently in the pale, taloned hands.

"Seal the prophecy yourself, priest," he said, his voice quaking.

"But finish it! I am returning you to Egypt. My personal legion waits outside Rome to insure your safe passage to Alexandria."

Somberly, the scribe gazed at the ring.

"No, Vespasian," he rasped. "I am far too old for such a journey. Far, far too old. And it has been revealed to me that my time ... has passed. I will not look upon sacred Alexandria again. And yet the manuscript must, indeed, return to Egypt. For my masters must know ... the *name*."

"Do *not* ..." Vespasian began sharply, hesitating, before his teeth clenched. He glanced nervously into the shadows. "Do *not* speak of these things, priest! I did not come here to witness any ... infernal conjurings! I came only to tell you that Jerusalem has fallen and Herod's temple is in flames. Israel can threaten you no more. It is safe for you to return to Egypt under protection of my legion."

A slow grin spread across the skull-like face.

"Foolish, foolish Vespasian, you deem yourself powerful because you command the legions." Pale fingers spread upon the manuscript. "But *here* is power, Vespasian. Here is power you only dream of. Power that will resurrect from the dust what your glory cannot hold in the centuries to come."

Dark laughter echoed in the shadows.

"Then finish it, priest!" Vespasian stepped forward with the words. "If you will not leave Rome, then *it* must leave Rome! I dream of things I cannot bear! The Nazarene, the one they called King of the Jews, has been dead for forty years, but I have *seen* him! I have seen him in my dreams! He has cursed me since you walked these halls!"

"No, Vespasian, the Nazarene is not dead ... not truly dead ..."

Laughing, the hooded skull bent again and taloned hands caressed the manuscript.

"Yet *this* shall be his undoing," he whispered, laughing again. "So summon your mightiest centurion, Vespasian, and an escort to guard him. For it is time to bear the prophecy to Alexandria. Yet advise him his journey shall be long and dangerous. For the Jews would still claim the manuscript, if they could. And they are not yet destroyed ..."

Turning his head as if listening, the dark priest paused.

"Yes, Jerusalem has fallen," he rasped finally. "This much I knew before messengers returned from the siege. But Jerusalem will arise twice more, before it falls forever." He laughed through a hideous grin. "No, Vespasian, there is only *one* who is powerful enough to destroy Israel, even as there is only *one* powerful enough to truly destroy the Nazarene. And we must wait for his ascension."

Dark wind vanquished the candleflame.

"Yes, only *one*..."

. . .

Wounded and burning in his bronze armor, the centurion staggered upon the crest of the dune and turned, glaring wildly through the desert sun at the wounded warrior who pursued him. In the distance, the savage shape advanced, striding across the wasteland, still holding a broken sword in a bloody hand.

Enraged and clutching the precious manuscript wrapped tightly in black leather and sealed with the ring of Vespasian, the massive centurion angrily cursed his pursuer through dry, cracked lips. He turned again and moved down the mound, fleeing further into this oppressive desert. Weakening in the scorching heat that seared his skin, he began to sense death upon him.

Soon, he knew, he could go no further. Soon, he knew, he must finish this brutal battle with the savage warrior-Jew, or die in this cursed Hebrew desert.

For a moment, as he staggered down the dune, the centurion remembered the battle as it had begun in that mountain pass of Megiddo, again saw the conflict that had erupted when the powerful escort of Rome was ambushed by the barbaric attack force of Judah. A raging collision of unyielding sword and spear had continued from dusk to dawn until, in the merciless end, there remained only the two of them: a wounded centurion and a wounded warrior-Jew, each standing in a tide of blood, each glaring at the other over their dead.

Sensing himself overpowered, the centurion knew that survival lay only with escape. So he had leaped atop his horse and fled, descending the mountain to storm into the desert beyond. Through the day he had forever glanced back with wide eyes to see the Jew pursuing him on a Roman horse. Pursuing, always pursuing.

Stung by a vivid fear, the centurion had raced over the scorched sands, leaping from his horse when it had stumbled at last in a frothing death throe, to continue running. The Jew's horse had also died beneath him, ridden to death in the blazing heat; when the horse fell, the Jew also leaped from it, to finish the battle on foot.

Gasping, breathless in the airless heat, the centurion wearily staggered to another crest and stared back once more, seeing the Jew closer now, much closer, closing on him. Frantically, his massive head twisted, fierce eyes glaring desperately for a path of escape before locking on a dark opening that entered a nearby slope.

Blinking, the centurion focused through half-blind eyes.

It was a cave, disappearing into a mountain slope marked with ragged heaps of white stones; overturned walls that marked the ruins of a long-lost and long-forgotten city, now a long-forgotten grave, half-buried by sand. He wondered at what Jew civilization might have inhabited this rock, before deciding he did not care.

It was enough; the darkness of the cave would give him a chance for ambush, a chance to strike the last blow in this fight.

With crumbling strength he stumbled down the dune, white sand scalding his sandaled feet, only to collapse in heated exhaustion as he reached the entrance. Groaning sickly, he staggered up again, turning wildly only to see the terrible warrior of Judah atop the bleached dune, following, always following.

Enraged to madness and cursing vengefully, the centurion drew his sword and whirled the blade over his head in a challenge. Then, laughing maniacally, he turned and fled into the tunnel, still clutching the precious manuscript.

The warrior watched the Roman vanish into the darkness.

And after a moment, with the Roman gone, he suddenly swayed in the conquering heat, almost falling into the blood beneath his sandaled feet. Yet his somber face, burned black by the sun and scarred with wounds, recovered quickly to reveal only grim determination, a fierce resolve to finish this fight.

He did not fall.

His bloody hand tightened on his sword, and with a supreme effort, he focused on the cavern entrance, brutally indifferent to his own life, death, or pain. And then, accepting the challenge, he descended the dune and entered the darkness.

Westchester, New York

"Is he dead?"

Father Stanford Aquanine D'Oncetta shook his head patiently, casually removing a cigar from the darkly illuminated Savinelli humidor.

"No, Robert, he is not dead," replied D'Oncetta calmly. "But there is no need for emotion. He will be dead soon enough."

"Not soon enough for me."

Stately and imperious, D'Oncetta laughed. Drawing steadily upon a vigilance candle to light his cigar, the priest leaned back against a mahogany desk, slowly releasing a stream of pale blue smoke.

Separated from D'Oncetta by the length of the library, Robert Milburn regarded the priest in the dim light. Reluctantly impressed by D'Oncetta's authoritative appearance, Milburn noted the deeply tanned hands and face of a man who had actually spent little of his life in dark confessionals or chapels.

The face of this man commanded true power and feared nothing at all.

Above the clerical collar and the black, finely tailored robe, D'Oncetta's straight white hair laid back smoothly from his low forehead, lending him the demeanor of an elder statesman. Everything about the priest was richly impressive, dignified, cultured and refined; an investment banker wearing the robe of a holy father.

"What are you so afraid of, Robert?" D'Oncetta laughed in his voice of quiet authority, a voice accustomed to controlling and persuading. "How many men is it that you have stationed outside?"

"Eleven." Milburn met D'Oncetta's steady gaze.

"And is that not enough to guard a single, isolated mansion in Westchester, especially with the noble assistance of New York's

vaunted police force, who even now have a priority patrol on surrounding streets?"

D'Oncetta smiled reassuringly and exhaled again, savoring.
Then he looked down at the cigar, turning it in his fingers with
familiar approval.

"A Davidoff," he remarked fondly. "Rich and complex, always
the result of superior breeding. And it's not even Cuban, as one
might presume, but a product of the Dominican Republic."

D'Oncetta's satisfied gaze focused on Milburn. "Would you like
to try one?"

"No."

Turning his back to the priest, Milburn moved to the uncurtained picture window. He stared past the mansion's carefully
manicured lawn and into the shadowed night beyond.

"I just want that old man upstairs to die so we can all get out of
here." Control made his voice toneless. "I don't like this, D'Oncetta.
If Gage is really out there, like your people say he is, then we should
just leave the old man alone. Because if Gage claims the old man as
family, if he's put Father Simon under his protection, then he'll be
coming for him. And if that happens . . ." Milburn paused, turning
coldly toward the priest. "You don't have any idea what you're
dealing with."

"But that is why you are here, isn't it, Robert?" D'Oncetta
responded tolerantly, and Milburn suspected a faint mocking tone.
"It is your solemn responsibility to deal with such matters. And
there is much that remains, for this is simply the beginning. There
are even more delicate tasks which will require your skills in
the near future. Tasks which, through the centuries, have always
demanded men such as yourself. Men deeply inured and intimately
familiar with the higher arts. Men who can insure the success of
our plans while simultaneously protecting us all from this individual that you seem to respect, or fear, so profoundly."

Milburn's face was stone.

"Yes, Robert, that is why we need superb field operatives such
as yourself. And that is why you and your men will remain here,
guarding us all so efficiently, until Father Simon is dead. We do not
want him . . . *disturbed* . . . in his final, tragic hours, do we?"

Milburn took his time to reply. "I'm retired," he said, finally.

D'Oncetta nodded magnanimously. "Of course." He smiled.

Milburn looked again out the window. Shadows completely
cloaked the darkened woodline, untouched by the security lights
illuminating the surrounding lawn. Training told him not to look
for the faint outline of sentries concealed within the obscured trees,
so Milburn allowed his gaze to wander, unfocused, receptive to

discerning movement where shape could not be seen. But there was nothing.

He turned nervously toward D'Oncetta. "How much longer will it take?"

Black and stately, the priest shrugged. "An hour," he said, with supreme composure. "Perhaps less. The chemical is quite painless and, I might add, undetectable. Not that we shall have to worry. Validating documents have already been executed. There shall be no confirmation of peculiarity. So it will be tragic, but natural. For, as you know, Robert, all of us are destined to die."

D'Oncetta released another draw from the Davidoff and smiled again, this time plainly amused. And Milburn made a decision, releasing some of his tension by taking a slow and threatening step across the library.

Toward D'Oncetta.

The priest watched Milburn's measured step with calm detachment. And when Milburn was face-to-face with D'Oncetta he stopped, as if he had always intended to stop, emotions tight once more. But as Milburn stood close to the priest he felt a sudden strangeness in the moment, in the tension, and he heard the question coming out of himself before regret could silence it.

"Who are you, D'Oncetta?" he asked quietly in a voice of unbelief no matter what the answer.

D'Oncetta laughed indulgently.

"I am a priest, Robert."

Milburn's face was a rigid mask. Slowly, he turned away and lifted a small radio from his coat.

"Command post. Perimeter check."

One by one, unseen guards responded.

"Position one, Alpha clear . . . Position two, Epsilon clear" until finally the code words "Position eleven, Omega clear" emerged from the radio with startling clarity.

"Command clear." Milburn lowered the radio to his side, refusing to look at D'Oncetta again. But he knew the priest maintained his air of amused calm.

"There, you see, Robert. We are all quite safe."

The pale figure lay silently beneath the white shroud that stretched, thin and veiled, from the vaulted ceiling.

Darkness cloaked the room, leaving the dying man within a single white space claimed by the lampstand, a separate light that removed the old man from the shadows with a deep and glowing authority.

He laid with eyes closed, as motionless as he would lay in true death. But he was not dead, for the ashen face would sometimes tighten, stirred from within some abysmal pain, to release a low moan.

Watching in silence, the stranger stood in the shadows, far from the dying man, sweat glistening on his darkened face. Only moments after the priest had departed the room, he had stepped from the curtained balcony, moving without sound to shut the wide double doors behind him.

Now, he studied the room. And after a few moments he slowly removed a thick, black visor from his waist-length coat and raised it to his eyes.

His head turned with a mechanical, trained precision as he scanned the room, concentrating longer on areas that separated him from the dying man. Then he placed the visor again within his coat and eased into a crouch, feral, wary; an animal approaching a trap baited with what could not be resisted.

A long time he poised, as if searching for something that should be feared but could not be seen. Then, in a slow, fluid movement, he rose and stepped lightly upon the floor. At home with the darkness, he threaded a careful path through the shadowed furnishings to approach the dying man.

With reverence, with tenderness, the stranger reached down to clasp the man's trembling hand. The dying man weakly turned his head to behold the ghostly image and through clouded eyes, he smiled. Then he returned the stranger's grip with a strength that made death seem suddenly more distant. For the briefest of moments the hands held strong, encouraging, delivering and receiving with the familiar measure of firmness known only to old friends. And the weakened eyes looked up warmly into the shadowed face.

"I knew you would come. My son...I knew you would come..."

Silently the stranger nodded. Then he lowered his head even more, his face close to the dying man, a strong hand on the white softness of the bed.

"I'm taking you out of here," he whispered.

The old man shook his head. "No, no...It is too late for me. Far too late..." He drew a painful breath. "Quite effective...this pestilence. And," he laughed softly, "I am too old to run."

The stranger searched the fading eyes. Then he shook his head and moaned softly.

"I know..." The old man squeezed the stranger's hand. "But you will do well without me...You are strong, now... *Strong*... You are not the man you were..."

After a moment the stranger raised his head, but his countenance was changing with each breath, eyes narrowing slightly with a bitter frown turning the corners of his mouth. He gazed upon the pale hand held within his.

"What is happening?" He leaned closer to the old man, eye to eye. "Why have these people done this to you?"

The dying man shifted suddenly, remembering something that resurrected horror in the unseeing, widening eyes.

"It has been *taken!*" he rasped. "They have stolen...the *prophecy!*" He rolled his head from side to side, grieved. "I cannot believe they would commit...such sacrilege! Surely it is mortal!" Trembling, he paused. "Clement would have destroyed it in time. He scorns their secrets and has always stood against them." A mournful breath escaped the sunken chest. "They will destroy us all!"

"Who? Tell me! Who are these people?"

The old man stared blindly into the surrounding darkness. "No, no, I do not know who they are...But I knew you would come..." He focused again on the stranger. "Yes, it was ordained long ago...And now the hour...has come..."

The stranger's brow hardened in concentration. "What would you have me do?"

"Destroy the prophecy!" the old voice hissed. "Destroy it! It has cursed us all...too long!"

With compassion, the stranger's hand settled on the old man's chest. "Rest, old friend," he said.

"No, no, there is no time," the dying man whispered. "And I wish...I could tell you more. But there is no time...no time. But I knew you would come...so I prepared a letter for you. It is hidden in the cathedral...You know where to look." A sudden thought, and he found a defiant strength, struggling to rise. "Ah, only know ...*this*, my son. Their victory is not *complete*! For Santacroce has repented of his sin! He...repented! And he has buried it again in the tomb of his father!...You can find it! You can destroy it before the evil ones claim it once more!"

The stranger gently pushed the old man to the bed.

"Rest. I'll know what to do."

The dying man hesitated, staring, and was quiet. The stranger watched as the thin, dry lips moved in an unknown supplication, before the prayer fell still.

"I've loved you like a father," the stranger said.

Old eyes laughed. "And I have loved you as a son. I am sorry that I did not tell you more...I feared that this would come...But I wanted you to forget...that world. To forget...I know you have seen...too much..."

"I have forgotten," the stranger said.

The old man shook his head. "I know better...I know the faces still come to you...in the night. But you are *not* what you were! The Dragon is dead, my son...He is *dead*."

Abruptly the old man stiffened, face pale with pain.

A frown hardened upon the stranger's face.

"Do what you can...for Sarah," the old voice whispered, and the stranger perceived that he heard a faintness behind, or within, the words, as if they were spoken from within some invisible mist. "Malachi is prepared to die. He is a good man...But Sarah has done nothing! She does not even know their secrets!" He shook his head. "She was there when we found it...But she does not know what it contains!"

"No one else will be hurt, my friend." The stranger placed a hand upon the old man's brow, gently pushing back the wispy, white hairs now damp with sweat. "I'll bring an ending to this."

Nodding, the old man began to speak again, but the thought was lost as the clouded eyes saw something in the surrounding shadows. The stranger didn't turn; he knew there was nothing there that he could see.

"Yes...an ending," the dying man whispered softly. "At last ...an ending."

It happened quickly, peacefully. The stranger knelt in silence, waiting, holding the weakened hands until softness faded from the pale face beneath him and a brittle coldness settled upon the brow. Then, breathing deeply, he slowly rose, stepping back from the light to gaze mournfully upon the still shape.

A long moment passed before the first, violent shudder stiffened him, and his fist clenched. Though his gaze remained focused on his silent friend, his fist clenched tighter, trembling, bloodless, a force struggling to find release, and he shut his eyes, fiercely resisting a hated passion.

Then, after a moment, the cold gray eyes opened again and turned to gaze, malevolent and measured, upon the bedroom door that led to the hallway, and to the stairs, beyond, that led downward.

To the library.

And finally, though the stranger continued to stare at the door, the trembling fist slowly relaxed, was lowered to his side. Frowning, breathing heavily, he turned back to the still form on the bed.

He nodded, whispering, "An ending."

Shattering the solemnity, static emerged from the radio concealed within the stranger's coat. An authoritative voice, tense and harsh, requested yet another perimeter check, and unseen guards responded with clearances and codes.

Impassive, the stranger reached into his coat and removed the radio, along with the bloodied headset that he had chosen not to wear during the final, cherished moments with his friend. And he remembered the shocked expression of the guard now lying coldly beneath the shadowed woodline.

When it was the guard's turn to respond, the stranger engaged the device, speaking softly.

"Position eleven, Omega clear."

"Command clear," came the reply.

The stranger waited, gazing quietly upon his friend. Then he slid the radio into his coat, wearing the small, wireless earphone for silent monitoring. From his side pocket he removed a pair of black gloves and put them on, tightening a strap at each wrist. When he finished he was again completely cloaked in dark, somber hues.

He crossed the shadowed room with movements made profound by sadness, solid with purpose, until he reached the balcony doors.

Was lost in the night.

Shadow in shadow, the stranger crouched on the balcony outside the room, opening his mind to the night to search by sound, sight, or scent. But he sensed nothing beside him in the dark. There was only the cool breeze, the sound of wind rustling the autumn leaves, distant transversing of traffic.

Moving slowly, carefully, the man reached back and removed the continuous circuit device that had bypassed the contact alarm on the double doors, placing it again within his coat. He turned, allowing his gaze to wander across the estate.

Almost completely concealed behind the balcony wall, he studied the surrounding grounds. He didn't center his gaze, but scanned vaguely, knowing that in the darkness he would recognize shape by peripheral vision before he could discern it from middle focus.

He wondered if the slain guard, or the dog, had been quietly discovered and a trap set. He suppressed the violent urge to rush; it was always a mistake.

Soon.

He took a slow, deep breath and repeated the procedure to slow his pulse, waiting until the trembling stopped.

He shook his head.

Three years. A long time.

Too long.

Cautiously he took out the nightvisor, a compact device resembling welding glasses that intensified ambient light sources for nightvision, and slid it over his head. Starlight luminosity registered 64 percent, easily allowing him to penetrate shadows of the distant treeline. He could also discern the faint outlines of three sentries, still holding the standard separation of one hundred feet.

No movement.

Suspicious, always suspicious, he attempted to scan along the treeline for other guards hidden behind the foliage.

He hesitated. Cautious. Uncertain. He initiated a switch on the upper right side of the visor, and the green-tinted screen was doubled over a thermal imaging detector that registered differences in air temperature.

Able to read through fog, windows, curtains, and rain, the heat sensor could detect heat variations as minute as one degree Fahrenheit. Instantly the three sentries were outlined in a reddish-yellow glow of body heat, while the remainder of the field was projected on the green rectangular screen in starlight, everything clear.

With the thermal imaging-starlight synthesis, he again scanned his field of observation. But he saw only the three sentries. He knew that the rest would be stationed to the west and north of the estate, or roving.

That would make it more difficult.

Through an internal gauge in the nightvisor he saw that the batteries were nearly depleted and calculated that the double readout mode was quickly exhausting remaining power. He switched off the heat index, leaving only starlight for visibility. Once more he scanned the layout of the surrounding terrain and streets, drainage pipes, hedges, and other areas that allowed limited visibility. And as he had done for the past night, he mentally familiarized himself with the architecture and landscape of the sprawling manor, preparing his mind for the instant rejection of any escape plan and the immediate selection of another.

Before entering the estate he had predesigned three various lines of retreat, with the last and most desperate being the initial line of entry. But he had never been forced to leave an objective along the path of entry. Never. It was an unbreakable rule, though desperation in past missions had taught him no rule was truly unbreakable.

On penetrating the security he had noted the roving patterns, the equipment, of the teams. He knew that whoever controlled the grounds had also hired military expertise for the job. Even after only a single night of surveillance he had determined that everything was done by the manual: listening posts directed outward, nightvision equipment and microwave transmitters for communications, patrol teams two by two roving interior grounds with dogs on the inside and perimeter.

Standard Operational Procedure.

Night concealed his dark frown.

None of you can stop me.

Automatically his mind locked into a familiar mode—fiercely focused, emotionless, concentrating his fear and rage and pain into physical strength and skill. A thousand calculations were formed, all turning intuitively in simplifying combinations: the mechanics of movement, light variations, background and cover, sound factors and noise discipline, tactics of evading detection while maintaining observation.

Then, remembering and ruled by the knowledge, he closed his higher mind. His training, sharpened and alive with instinct, would direct him. The science, the art would automatically select the tactic that his physical conditioning would reflexively execute.

Black gloves absorbed the moisture on his palms, but he wasn't accustomed to wearing gloves and unconsciously shook his hands, as if the cool night air would dry the sweat. Scowling, he noted the wasted movement, and his abrupt anger broke him from his heightened state.

Three years.

I've lost my edge.

Shut it down, he thought, shutting his eyes tight.

Concentrate on what you have to do.

He expelled a slow, quiet breath, focusing.

Opened his eyes again.

No movement in the treeline. All visible listening posts faced outward.

Clear.

Silently, careful to keep his profile low, he moved slowly over the balcony, descending a thin rope he had lashed to the stone railing. When he reached the ground he eased against the most advantageous background, a trellis of broken ivy and high shrubs that profoundly compromised security, partially concealing him from even ambient light devices. Then, patiently, he moved forward, coldly channeling feverish adrenaline and raging emotion into silent stalking.

An instinct, hot and fresh, that was the center of him, flowed through him. And he was hot with it; thirsty, predatory, finding a familiar way with it.

But he knew he would not surrender to it.

Not like before.

Wild, frantic strides hurled Father Nicholai Santacroce along the shadowed corridor of the cavernous cathedral; reckless strides that threw him past deeply carved images of the dead, cruel images that marked his passage with stony stares, untouched by the panic that propelled his desperate flight.

Yet as the priest emerged from a hallway and into the cathedral, he halted. Frozen in place, he was suddenly struck by a terrible, overpowering presence, a presence that caused fear to thicken in his chest, his arms and legs, making him clumsy, awkward. With wide, distraught eyes he quickly scanned the sanctuary, his unseeing gaze passing over shadowed recesses, confessionals, and alcoves.

Santacroce's labored breathing and pounding heart seemed to echo in the hall. He eased stiffly along the wall, chilled by an instinct of death.

He reached out to touch the wall, attempting to brace himself. But the movement only increased his fear, for the cold lifelessness of the stones reminded him even more of how truly alone he was within this former sanctuary of God, now a sanctuary of secrets, of pain. The stony chill continued to embrace him, overpowering his will, making him weak, transferring itself from the lifeless stones to invade the center of his being with alien force.

Blinking sweat from his eyes, fear dominating all reason, Santacroce crept slowly, stiffly, along the wall. His frenzied gaze darted between shadows, and he prayed against what he knew was there. But his faith became thinner, more distant with each cold moment of deathly silence. He knew that beside him in the darkness they were there.

Even though he had fled across three continents in four weeks, Santacroce knew that he had only barely eluded their grasp. For he had ceaselessly sensed their haunting, chilling presence that would awaken him from terrifying nightmares to life, a nightmare

even more terrifying. Until now, in the end, when they had finally
cornered him in this ruined rectory.

Tormented by the fear that his sin was mortal, unforgivable,
Santacroce prayed for absolution. But even as he began a supplication his mind returned to that darkened night when he had finally
cast down his vows, had defiled the Secret Archives of the Church of
Rome.

Sweating, trembling, Santacroce remembered how it had
ended, saw again how he had sacrilegiously violated the Archives
to retrieve the apparently meaningless document. He remembered
the bright promise of career advancement for his sin, the promise
that would forever end his disillusionment and pain.

And yet when his sin was full-born and he stood alone in the
dusty light of the Archives, holding the ancient prophecy, Santacroce realized that he could not resist the need to know, the need
to fully understand the true purpose of his betrayal. So he opened
the manuscript and read the prophecy.

He could not, even now, recall the events following that dark
hour, but he had not forgotten the horror, the terror, that had
paralyzed his reason and broken his mind. Dimly he remembered
leaving the Archives, numbly clutching the yellowed pages of the
dusty manuscript against his robe. Narrowly avoiding the silent
ones awaiting him, he ran blindly through the Vatican's midnight
corridors, sightlessly watching the brilliant, brightly colored tap-
estries that swept past—incomprehensible images of war and
suffering and Apocalypse.

It was his hour of madness.

For only in the last moment of night did he finally calm, knowing he could not return the book without suffering penalty of death.
So he buried it in the one place worthy of holding it and then fled as
before, using what few funds he thought to remove from the office
of the Archives. But no matter how far he fled or how desperate his
flight, Santacroce knew they would punish him for his failure. He
was a dead man, as dead as the cold stone images surrounding him
now.

As he crept stealthily forward along the wall, Santacroce shook
his head, still amazed that he had been so deceived, amazed that he
had believed their lies.

No, it wasn't theological prejudice or the eclectic, soul-stealing
intolerance that caused Pope Clement XV to suppress the prophecy. No, it was something far worse, something evil, final, and
terrible; something Santacroce could not fully comprehend even
with the knowledge he had gained in that haunting moment of
translation.

He had tried desperately to redeem himself, the guilt of his second crime swallowed unfelt within the overpowering condemnation of the first.

Santacroce smiled wanly as he remembered the ancient tomb where he had re-hidden the manuscript, content that it would never be found again. He had called the old man, the ancient priest who *knew* what to do.

Yes, old Father Simon would protect him, would save him.

Shocked again by the deathly silence of the cathedral, Santacroce moved a shuffling step, breath catching, releasing, catching with the fear that clutched his chest. But almost as soon as his movement began, he halted, sensing even before he heard the terrifying image emerging without visible movement from the shadowed corridor before him.

Livid, the priest whirled to behold a second shape emerging, also without perceptible movement, from the hallway he had just fled. And though they moved as one, the darkly cloaked men did not speak, did not communicate, but coordinated their approach with a precision and skill that scorned the need for words or signs.

Santacroce turned to run, but they seemed to anticipate the priest's thoughts and enclosed him against the wall. And as the two men moved toward him, Santacroce realized that they were, indeed, what their conquering ancestors had claimed to be: consummate in skill, inhuman in patience, makers of their own destiny and the destiny of all those less perfect in power.

As he was.

Then from other, darkened regions of the cathedral, four additional, somber forms revealed themselves, illuminated by the candles of communion. In his horror Santacroce saw each impassive face, each image was vague and unremarkable but for a black, gigantic shape that stood cloaked in the distant shadows. And then they were standing fully in the light as they had always stood in the darkness; waiting, confident, knowing from the beginning that they would win, in the end.

A pale fear, white and trembling, made Santacroce light and faint with each quick gasp. And then the first man that he had seen, the tall man wearing a long, brown tweed coat, moved closer with effortless poise, closer, closer, a graceful smile appearing upon the impassive face as the man closed the final few feet.

The tall, commanding figure was before him, and yet the man seemed to exhibit neither threat nor threatening intent. Santacroce looked into the good and kindly face, a face that might have belonged to a pastor, a father. And for a moment, with his reason defeated by fear, a thin hope flamed in the priest's heart. But then he remembered, and he knew that he would receive no mercy, not from any of them.

Santacroce paled as the man leaned slightly forward.

"Nicholai, my dear friend, why do you do this foolishness?" he whispered in a faint British accent. "Truly, you have nothing to fear. All is forgiven. Come, let me help you."

A second man appeared beside Santacroce; an Oriental, young, in his mid-thirties, his heavily muscled frame apparent even through the loose-fitting clothes. Santacroce perceived vaguely that the massive Oriental was Japanese. His dark hair was cut close above an impassive face that seemed somehow unnaturally hardened, the image of brown skin drawn tautly over chiseled granite. When Santacroce looked into the man's blackened eyes he momentarily forgot his fear, or his fear increased even more; he could not be sure. For the implacable gaze revealed a cold force that did not seem to know life; a force of absolute, pure strength, merciless and cruel.

"Nicholai." The tall man was speaking again. "This misunderstanding is not important. Remember, soon you will have wealth that most men only dream of, and as you so richly deserve. I only ask that you let me help you. Now, tell me, where is the manuscript?"

Icy sweat beaded Santacroce's brow.

"I won't tell you!" he whispered, unable to prevent his pleading tone. "Kill me if you will, but I won't tell you!"

Santacroce tangibly felt the sinister sensation that emanated from the tall man. The smile remained but no longer reached the kindly eyes. With a barely perceptible movement the man leaned forward.

"Nicholai, all games must end," he said quietly. "And this game must end now. I will help you, but you must tell me where you have hidden the manuscript."

Distantly Santacroce heard himself speaking. "You cannot have it! Don't you understand? He will destroy us all! You must . . ."

A sudden movement by the Oriental twisted Santacroce's shoulder and arm into an unbearable position. It was a movement so swift and cruel with cold skill that the priest was more shocked by the merciless indifference than by the pain that pierced his shoulder. Santacroce surged with hysterical, adrenaline strength, whirling to break away. But he felt as if he had been seized by a force of nature.

Absolute and controlling, the Japanese moved with him. The man's steel grip seemed to obliterate the flesh of Santacroce's forearm; remorseless, destroying for the pleasure of destroying, fingers dug deeply into his bones.

The Japanese held Santacroce for a moment more, with the priest struggling for balance on the balls of his feet. Then the Oriental moved again, and Santacroce felt something deep within his shoulder tear away, lancing pain through his neck and face. He screamed, but he knew that it would make no difference, no difference at all.

"*Sato!*" The tall man's commanding voice shattered Santacroce's screams. "No!"

The Japanese turned Santacroce toward the tall man, effortlessly holding the priest upright. He lightened the pressure on the injured shoulder, and Santacroce felt a wave of agony flow out from the joint.

Santacroce swayed, jerking involuntarily at the knifing tendrils of electric pain that sparked along his ribs, neck, and face. Shocked, he blinked sweat from his eyes while a groan escaped his lips.

The tall man's face was compassionate, and he leaned forward intimately to speak again.

"Nicholai, forgive me." He lightly placed a hand on Santacroce's injured shoulder. "That was not my wish. I assure you that Sato will be punished. Please, my friend, allow me to help you. I will take you home. Only tell me where I can find the manuscript. I promise that you will not be further injured."

Santacroce shook his head. "No!"

Another figure stepped forward and through a white mist Santacroce saw a broad, tanned face, shaggy blond hair. But when the leader half turned his head, the man stopped silently in place. Though no words were spoken, the blond man stared at the taller, and seemed to understand. Then he moved forward again, and with the Japanese, lifted Santacroce, dragging the priest towards a nearby corridor.

Santacroce only dimly saw lights and shadows as he was dragged swiftly along the darkened hallway. His pleading eyes swept the doorways, the adjoining rooms for someone, anyone, to intercede for him. But there was no one, even as he had known in his heart that there would be no one. He was pushed into a large, unidentifiable vehicle. A needle was thrust into his arm. And then darkness.

With a trembling hand, Professor Malachi Halder shut the massive and unyielding oaken portal and methodically rearmed his alarm system.

The code activated a security circuit that cloaked exterior entrances and carefully selected interior rooms with a sensitive combination of ultrasonic and microwave frequencies, providing a defensive field that could detect the slightest intrusion or movement of life.

In truth, the system meant little to the professor, for he placed no confidence in his own feeble abilities to preserve his life; he had long ago reckoned himself a dead man. But the alarm had been purchased with the Manhattan townhouse, and he had used it steadily, possessing no desire to make it easier for his enemies to destroy him.

And, yes, he knew fear, as any man doomed to a violent death would know fear. So he finished the code that initiated the alarm and wearily set his heavily laden briefcase on the lapis lazuli floor.

Disheartened by the chilled sweat that soaked his shirt, the professor removed his overcoat and stood for a moment in the entrance, lost in dark thoughts. Then, remembering, he held his breath and turned to look behind him into the brightly lit entranceway.

He exhaled slowly. Yes, he was alone.

Across the expansive hall was his study. The professor's gaze rested on the distant wall, passing over the carefully catalogued books that lined his library; hundreds, thousands of works, many of the volumes lost to the world but for these few and ancient remaining editions. They reminded him of the long forgotten secrets that he had resurrected and studied for half a century. Yes, exploring the age-old mysteries hidden within those dusty tomes had consumed his life and awarded him far-reaching acclaim.

Over fifty years ago, as a young archeologist for Harvard University, Malachi discovered the lost tombs of the kings of Ur. Then, in swift succession, he had uncovered cuneiform tablets that documented the biblical journey of Abraham. He had verified the story of Joseph through Egyptian pictographs, fixed the date of the Exodus to 1220 B.C., in the reign of the cruel Egyptian ruler Merneptah. And in 1965 he had worked with the British Museum to uncover two clay tablets from the ruins of Shuruppak, tablets written in 1646-1626 B.C. which testified to a phenomenal flood that had inundated the Mesopotamia long ago.

In his long life Malachi had excavated the underground desert civilizations of Be'er Matar. And he had, with his own hands, uncovered the bone and stone and temples that revealed the secrets of Solomon and David and those less revered, searching out over 4,000 years of history between the Hebrew God and the people of Israel.

It was his life's work, and he had done it well.

Remembering, Malachi could not suppress the coldness that embraced him, even within the sanctity of his home. They had long threatened to avenge his interference with their plans. For, in truth, once he fully understood their continuing existence, it had become his life's work to defy them. He hoped to ultimately reduce their measure of influence in the modern world by destroying the validity of their beliefs.

As an adjunct professor in Harvard's School of Archeology and Ancient Languages, a distinguished scholar at Princeton Theological Seminary, or in his current post at Saint Matthew's Hall of Theology and Philosophy in New York, he had forever challenged those who claimed moral sovereignty by natural superiority, supernatural right, or intellectual might. Yes, he had challenged them all, scholar and student alike, upon their own ground, the high ground of critical reason, and he had never been defeated.

For years he had listened respectfully, patiently, to their arguments, allowing the metaphysicists, nihilists, existentialists, and anarchists to build an aggressive defense. And then, when their arrogance was complete, Malachi would begin to speak, comprehensively and authoritatively, minutely dissecting their ideas as a physician might dissect a rotting corpse, by clinically folding back the surface to reveal the rotting logic concealed within.

And when he was done, and no reply could be found in his listeners, Malachi would begin to speak again. He would speak of mysteries that even he did not comprehend, true mysteries that had eluded the mind of man since the beginning of time. And then he would leave them to ponder foundational questions of truth that their shallow philosophies could not begin to fathom.

And though he had won every argument, Malachi knew that he had failed. As he was doomed to fail, from the beginning. For he discovered that they weren't searching for anything so humbling as truth. No, it was power they had sought, and they had finally found it, in the end. Fears for his own life faded into nothing when Malachi remembered that, in all the long centuries, those evil masters of ancient Mesopotamia had never stood closer to uniting the kingdoms of the Earth than they stood in this hour.

Malachi's tired eyes continued to study the wall, and then his gaze rested upon the cherished plaque displayed prominently behind his desk:

Presented to Malachi Josiah Halder, Ph.D., Th.D.
Professor of Archeology and Ancient Languages
Saint Matthew's Theological Seminary
From Sarah

Sarah, his beloved child.

Wearily, feeling the frailty of his 72 years, Malachi turned and beheld once more the reassuring presence of the massive door. He placed a trembling hand against the rough-hewn timbers, comforted by its solidity, noticing once again how deeply the iron bolts were set into the frame, appreciating the unbending bars that held the stout beams in place.

And as his weakness sometimes prompted him in times of personal suffering, his mind returned to centuries long past for comforting thoughts. He remembered the noble history of the door, this very door, that now stood between him and his enemies. Ironically, in 1656 this portal stood between a small force of persecuted Italian Christians and a merciless, mercenary army.

Though it cost Malachi a small fortune to have the door restored and transported from the long abandoned sanctuary of Saint Constantine, it was worth the sacrifice because it never ceased to remind him of that lost and noble age, an age of heroes.

The portal's history had begun on April 25, 1655, in the village of Rora, a tiny community once located high in the Italian Alps, where the Marquis de Pianessa had issued a proclamation forcing all Protestant believers to swear allegiance to the Church of Rome or suffer execution. Throughout the villages and provinces surrounding the township, thousands of Protestant men, women, and children who refused to submit were beheaded in an orgy of wholesale murder, survivors fleeing into the mountains. In the end, only Rora remained, besieged as the last surviving Protestant stronghold.

An army of 500 experienced soldiers attacked in the early morning. But the impoverished villagers of Rora, inspired by a Protestant captain named Joshua Gianavel, organized and fought with their families to their backs, defiantly holding the Catholic army at bay for six months. Until, in frustration, the Marquis de Pianessa, dark commander of the expedition, hired mercenary forces that increased his army to almost 8,000 men.

Enraged to insanity and vowing to see indomitable Rora razed to the ground, the Marquis ordered the entire Militia of Piedmont to the field beside his mercenary troops, and with a combined force of 15,000 men launched a three-front attack. In the long and savage end, Rora's defenders died holding their positions or were captured and burned at the stake, father and son holding each other upon the pyre.

Some, however, including Gianavel, slashed a path through the mercenary troops and escaped into the mountains where, in time, they reorganized to launch merciless and cunning counterattacks against the Marquis's army. Until the winter of August, 1656, when the diminutive force was cornered in the monastery of St. Constantine.

And it was there that the final, bloody battle ensued.

Lost to a past that he knew as well as the present, Malachi ran his hand across the scarred wooden timbers of the door, wondering at what savage conflict had passed this portal in that doomed and defiant last stand.

"Yes... an age of heroes," he whispered softly, his fingers touching a smooth, deeply carved cleft that was once slashed into the wood by ax, or sword.

Slowly, the memory moving him, Malachi lowered his hand and ascended the staircase that led to his bedchamber. But he knew that he would not sleep tonight. Indeed, with the sad news that he had received in recent days, he was uncertain that he would ever sleep again. For Simon, wasting away beneath that malignant illness which physicians could still not fully diagnose, had returned to the Vatican, presumably to die.

Malachi knew that this malady was not the bane of nature; it was the hand of man. And he suspected that soon he, too, would fall to this mysterious and unseen foe. For he had stood beside Simon deep within that ancient grave in the Negeb, had seen what was unearthed, and witnessed the testament that stretched forth from the tomb in that skeletal hand...

Feeling anew the initial sensation of the unexpected discovery, Professor Malachi Halder, revered Harvard archeologist and man of science, saw once more in his mind the spectral scene: the sight of the long-dead messenger, still armored in rusted iron, locked in a mortal embrace with his slayer.

Long buried within the subterranean corridor beneath ancient Horvat Beter, skeletal arms intertwined, the dead men had lain for two millennium, each the victim of the other. Each warrior still held the iron blade of the era buried deeply through the petrified ribs of his foe. Malachi could only imagine what hideous drama had unfolded in the tunnel during that distant, desperate hour. But he believed that he knew. Even as he had retrieved, shoulder to shoulder with Simon, the all but obliterated parchment from the armored hand and initiated the thrilling translation, he had begun to understand.

As Malachi reached the top of the stairs, walking heavily towards his bedchambers, he cursed that unexpected discovery and swore sorrowfully that the crumbling manuscript had not been buried deeply enough.

"No," he whispered, and he felt the plague of the abomination darken him within, "it could never be buried deeply enough."

Rome itself, the Citie del Vaticano, had financed the archeological dig on the ruins of Horvat Beter, just as the Vatican had financed many of Malachi's expeditions over the years. And faithful Father Simon, longtime friend of Malachi and himself a respected archeological scholar within the Catholic hierarchy, had accompanied Malachi on the excavation, just as he had accompanied the professor on a hundred similar expeditions over the last half-century.

As always, Malachi was grateful for the wise company. For he had long ago found a valuable and faithful friendship with old Simon. Mutually beneficial, Malachi provided the higher understanding of science, the more technical reference of knowledge, while Simon personified the more sensitive spiritual acumen, and also commanded the power and protection of Rome.

More than once, to Malachi's astonishment, Simon's quiet, humble voice, with his fearful evocation of the Roman Catholic Church, had preserved both their excavations and lives in countries as diverse as Iran, Syria, and Egypt. Though, for the most part, they executed their last expedition in the Negeb of Israel without incident until that day of remarkable discovery, when the horror was unearthed, and the terror began.

Fulfilling his solemn responsibility, even as his duties required, Simon immediately sent a dispatch to Rome, alerting Pope Clement. Then, Malachi and Simon began an immediate translation.

Malachi remembered how they had worked ceaselessly through the next 48 hours, carefully completing a Latin translation of the ancient book that was long ago sealed with the emblem of Titus Flavius Vespasian, Emperor of Rome. By the time they finished the translation, the scorching desert air had almost obliterated the original writing, leaving only isolated lettering and the faintest swirlings on the crumbling parchment. But by that solemn hour, both he and Simon had realized, with the most profound regret, what they had truly discovered. And, as reluctant brothers in a horrible crime, they planned to burn the parchment.

It was an act that went against everything Malachi knew and believed, for his was a life dedicated to the discovery and preservation of lost artifacts and texts and civilizations. But the manuscript was not part of history, he told himself. No. It was part of death itself, and had no place in the world of men. Before the dark deed could be completed, however, an official emissary from Rome arrived, demanding the manuscript under the authority of Clement. Always loyal, old Simon reluctantly surrendered the parchment.

Malachi never saw it again.

Awakened from his memory, the professor found himself in his bedchamber. He touched the lamp upon his desk, and the room was instantly bright. But he sensed a presence beside him in the chamber, and his heart skipped a beat as he turned, gasping and livid, towards the still form sitting in the chair at his bed.

Malachi froze, unable to run, unable to shout, and struggled to meet death as he had always intended, with dignity, his faith defiant to whatever painful end was forced upon him. Yet the stranger did not move, did not speak, and the professor squinted, peering, to discern the form.

The stranger was dressed in subdued clothing, a vague array of gray and black. Yet the athletic build was evident, muscular but lithe, like the body of a professional boxer. Not overmuscular, it was hardened and powerful, even in stillness presenting an impression of explosive power and swift agility.

Recovering with each moment, Malachi studied the stranger's features. Though only in his early thirties, the man's deeply tanned face betrayed the weathered signs of long exposure to sun and wind; it was lined and toughened, aged beyond his years. His collar-length dark brown hair was raggedly cut, providing a shaggy frame to the lean face. The faint image of a thin white scar descended from an area beside his left eye, drawing a line past his cheekbone. It was almost imperceptible, as if the wound had occurred long ago. Smaller scars crisscrossed the weathered face: the white trace of another cut, a long, scarred burn mark, narrow as a man's finger, on the left side of his neck.

The face reminded Malachi of photos he had seen of the last Apache warriors, those hardened desert fighters who had savagely refused surrender until they were finally, brutally conquered only by superior force.

The man's mouth was tight and slightly frowning, as if stoically indifferent to pain or pleasure. But it was the narrow eyes, seeming to shift from blue to gray, that struck Malachi as remarkable, and held him.

Predatory and purposeful, the eyes did not blink, did not move as Malachi staggered back. They remained locked on him, had been locked on him with hypnotic intensity since the professor had first recoiled. Unwavering in their focus, they were almost opaque with concentration, the stare of a panther crouching before a kill.

And then, with a breath, Malachi knew. *"You!"* he began, and stopped, uncertain, remembering the secret.

As if commanding the professor's submission to his will, the man suddenly rose; a fluid, strong movement of confidence that demonstrated his power to subdue, to control. But when the man moved slowly forward, the gray eyes somehow softened, and step by step became more and more open to reveal a pained and tormented soul trapped within. Malachi felt the first strange sense of safety.

With only the faintest trace of emotion, of remorse, the stranger spoke.

"Simon is dead."

Unable to stand, Professor Malachi Halder sat back heavily in the mahogany chair at his desk. The stranger was beside him, touching his shoulder, reassuring.

"Rest," he said.

With a trembling hand, Malachi wiped sweat from his brow, sweat sliding on sweat. Finding his breath, he inhaled and felt the room suddenly warm. But his flesh was chilled, and he unconsciously massaged a place below his sternum. Finally, forcing a calm, he looked up.

"I'm here to help you," the man said softly, then stepped away, moving cautiously to the window. Malachi saw that the curtains had been closed. The man edged back a corner of the curtain, staring into the street.

Malachi found his voice. "You're Gage," he whispered.

"I'm Gage."

Malachi felt something returning; an ability to reason, to measure the situation. He realized that the stranger could have killed him easily, armed or unarmed. And yet the man had done nothing.

"How did you . . . get in here?" Malachi asked, a deep breath following the words.

The stranger was expressionless. "I disabled your security system."

Amazed, Malachi wondered how the man had accomplished such a task.

"It's a simple thing, professor."

Malachi gazed evenly at him, said nothing. He had seen this man called Gage only once before, but the face was wrapped in bandages, burned by flame, sun, and sand. One arm was in a crude cast, the body mangled by wounds. Malachi was unable to identify that broken form with the strong figure standing before him.

Remembering the cunning of his enemies, the professor nodded and placed a hand on his chest, feigning continued pain. Head lowered, from beneath his gray brows, Malachi studied the man, struggling to conceal his suspicion.

Gage remained motionless, gloved hands open. "You'll know soon enough, professor," he said, simply. "When they come for you, you'll know."

"What has happened?" Malachi's eyes narrowed, and he was surprised to hear the emptiness in his own voice.

"Simon is dead," the man said, a bitter edge to his words. "And you're probably next. Or . . . Sarah. Or the translator. You've got to come with me if you want to live."

Malachi straightened, moved by the words. But even as he began to rise the stranger stepped to the side, cutting him off from the door. Malachi's analytical abilities had not deserted him, and he noted that the man had reacted even as he had *thought* of rising, not waiting for the initiation of the movement. The stranger's step toward the door had appeared slow only because it had begun so early in Malachi's decision to stand. But in truth the man had moved deceptively fast, simply without the appearance of haste. When Malachi had fully risen, the man was standing solidly between him and the exit. Malachi noticed he had taken a position that allowed him to view the hallway, or the room, with only the slightest shifting of his eyes.

"How do you know that Simon is dead?" Malachi said, his voice finding strength. "I went to see him yesterday, and I was informed by Archbishop McBain that he had fallen ill. I was told that they had flown him back to Rome. For treatment. Are you certain?"

"He's dead," said the man coldly. "He's dead in a house in Westchester. I was there." He hesitated. "He told me to help you, if I could."

Malachi looked around, sighed deeply. The room seemed strangely unfamiliar to him. "So, it begins."

The stranger nodded. "Yes. And we don't have any time. You're going to have to trust me. Where's Sarah?"

Malachi's eyes centered on the man, measuring. "How can I trust you? How can I know you are not here to kill me, and my daughter as well?"

The man took a step closer. "If I wanted to kill you, professor, you would be dead. And Sarah is easy to track down. But I don't have time. I knew I could find you quickly. And I know that you can find her. Now, take me to her and I'll put you both some place where you'll be safe, at least for a while." The man grew tense. "It's all I can do right now."

Malachi was silent, weighing the conviction. He was not so afraid as he had expected to be. Logic suggested that this man standing before him, this man he had seen only once and for a brief time, was, indeed, who he claimed to be. Still, Malachi hesitated, the caution of a half-century overruling all else.

The stranger stared out the bedroom door. Strangely, Malachi thought that he was gazing at the chandelier suspended above the main room and the staircase. The action confused the aging professor until he realized—the globe. The man was studying the golden, polished globe that decorated the chandelier, watching the reflected area of the first-floor entrance that could not be seen directly from the doorway.

And Malachi knew.

Whether it was reason or instinct or something entirely beyond himself, Malachi could not discern, but he was suddenly certain that this stranger was, in truth, the mortally wounded, dying American soldier that Simon had found beneath the desert moon of Israel over three years past.

The man turned back again. "Where's Sarah?"

Malachi moved toward the door. "She is just outside the city, at Saint Matthew's Seminary in Ridgefield. It is an hour's drive from here, but we can take the Lincoln Tunnel to save time. We must hurry!"

"Stay here," Gage commanded, cutting off the professor's movement. He pointed a finger at Malachi. His voice was a snarl. "Don't move until I return."

Malachi opened his mouth to object, but the man was gone, moving quickly down the hallway, toward the back stairwell. The steps descended into the kitchen, near the rear entrance.

Alone, his concern overriding all else, Malachi's pulse increased. He was frustrated and enraged to know that his daughter's life might be finally forfeit to those unseen enemies who had long threatened them all. But he felt helpless to combat his foes. As always, the situation remained beyond him. In the heat of the moment he found himself caring little for his own life. It was his child, who might now be lost, doomed by the cruelty of these...

A dark form moved towards him. Gage paused in the doorway, leaning close. "Do exactly what I say, professor. When I say. Don't ask questions. Do you understand?"

Malachi nodded, bracing. "I have no pride, young man," he intoned. "And I now find that I have very little fear. Do what you must do. I will do anything to save my child."

Gage leading, they moved quickly down the hallway. Gage passed the front staircase and Malachi, out of habit, angled towards the spiraling steps.

"No," Gage said shortly, looking back. "This way."

He descended the rear staircase towards the kitchen, not switching on the light. Malachi noted the gesture and was careful not to reach for the switch from reflex. But descending the steps in the dark caused him instant disorientation. He reached out to locate his position with the wall and crept hesitantly down the stairs. Distantly, he heard Gage moving in the darkness below him, descending smoothly and quickly before the faint sounds were completely gone.

"Gage?"

Silence.

Malachi descended another step. And another. In moments he was standing in the kitchen, surrounded by a darkened gloom that revealed only ponderous shapes of blackness beside him. Feeling a gathering panic, Malachi turned about, staring blindly into the darkness. He repressed an overpowering urge to call out.

A phantom came out of the gloom, moving in almost perfect silence. "Hurry!"

Gage spun him around, pushing him through the darkness as someone would usher a blind man through a panicked crowd. Malachi was astonished at the power that gripped his shoulders, the crushing strength that guided him through the shadows with reckless haste.

Gage stopped quickly, opened a door. Malachi was oriented enough to know that it was a closet in the lower hallway that connected the rear entranceway with the den. Two strong hands gripped Malachi's shoulders, pushing him into the closet, to a sitting position on the floor. The voice was a harsh rasp.

"Do exactly as I say! Don't move! Don't do anything! Stay here until I get back!"

Malachi felt Gage's rage. "What—"

"Do you understand?"

"Yes," the professor managed, nervously lifting his hands. "What—"

"Do as I say!" Gage hissed. "Don't make a sound! Don't move!" The closet door shut.

Malachi sat on his knees, his hands on the carpeted floor, using his flat palms for balance, he leaned slightly forward, his face inches from the wooden panel of the door before him. He stared, amazed at the situation and the darkness, feeling his racing pulse increase until his heart thudded painfully in his chest with each thin, high beat. The blood rush caused his breath to quicken and his senses to expand.

Now vivid with fear, Malachi waited, wide-eyed and still, listening. As time passed he heard only the disturbing loud sounds of his hands as they scraped lightly across the threads of carpet, his creaking joints and muscles cracking like thunder.

Disturbed by the impossible task of moving silently, Malachi tried not to move at all. He concentrated, listening for any sounds outside the door. Then, faintly, slowly, a subdued sound brushed past his face, a slight sound that was almost no sound at all. Was it his imagination?

A soft scrape on carpet. Something was out there.

Malachi did not breathe.

A silent moment passed, and another. Then a scraping so close that the hairs on Malachi's arms prickled.

Outside the door.

Steps were moving down the hallway, slow and cautious. Malachi strained to hear the faint scraping. Tilting his head, he leaned his ear closer to the wood panels. He counted, an automatic activity, numbering the force of attackers outside the door. Neck tight and jaw drawn in tension, he attempted desperately to discern one presence from another as the slight sounds moved past him, only a foot away. He lowered his eyes, trying to detect whether the almost indiscernible light beneath the door would reveal...

One shadowed movement...two...

Three.

Malachi swallowed painfully, and risked one tense, silent breath through a tightly drawn mouth. He shook his head, unable to encompass the surreal terror of it all, even as his mind conjured red images of Gage moving desperately through the dark; outnumbered and alone, predator and prey, playing the deadliest of games against the deadliest of foes.

Gage quickly ascended the back stairs and reached the second floor, his mind racing to analyze what he had seen through the glassed rear entrance.

...Three men...Civilian clothes...One down to pick the lock... No visible weaponry...Assume all armed and two more at front and rear entrances...But they weren't out there when I came in...They won't know I'm here...They'll move upstairs, where the light is...

He ran lightly down the hall to the bedroom, keeping to one side of the corridor to reduce sound. As he moved he freed his mind to devise a tactical response.

...Get them tight...Make them overconfident...Careless... Then ambush them...Worry about the ones outside later...

In seconds Gage was at the bedroom. Without hesitation, he ran into the adjoining lavatory. He turned on the shower and jerked the glass door closed, hoping they would hear the water downstairs, become confident of their target's location. Then he moved quickly into the bedroom, flipped on the radio, suddenly noticing he had broken a sweat.

No time left.

As quickly as he dared, Gage raced back down the hall, staying to the side nearest the rear wall. They would come up the rear staircase, he was certain. It was dark and isolated and unlikely to be as noticeable as ascending the front staircase at the balcony.

He reached the steps, risked a quick, panting glance down the darkened stairway, and ducked into a small room on the opposite side of the wall. Then he backed around the door frame so that he had a narrow view of the landing and reached around his waist, beneath his coat, to pull out his primary defense weapon.

Mind and body reacting on training alone, he silently notched the safety off and by feel, placed the selector switch into a fully automatic mode. Reflexively his mind recalled the specs of the weapon, reaffirming procedures for effective firing, clearing jams, clip changes. *It was an MP5 assault pistol, maximum cycling rate of*

45

900 rounds per minute, gas operated with the bolt staying open on the last round.

Mentally he rehearsed a clip change, reinforcing the necessary movement of rechambering. Then, without removing his attention from the darkened stairway, he lifted the heavy suppressor from his shoulder holster and screwed it carefully onto the short barrel. Although it had been three years since he had done it in combat, he had performed the maneuver so many times that it was done in seconds. No emotion. No thought. It was simply done.

. . . I've got three 50-round clips . . . If it ends with a firefight it'll be over with the first clip, one four-second burst . . . No second chance . . . Wait until they're near the top of the stairway . . . Then make your move . . .

A sudden thought shocked him, and Gage eased back quickly behind the wall, out of visual range of the staircase.

Stupid, he thought. *They'll have nightvision. They'll see me up here, in the dark, waiting for them.*

He reached into his coat pocket and took out the nightvisor. Then he put it on starlight and eased one eye carefully around the door frame.

They were on the stairway.

Out of combat for too long, the adrenaline surge almost made Gage leap out and begin firing. His hands tightened on the MP5, but he locked down on his control, waiting for them to reach the optimal range of contact. He breathed deeply, quietly, hoping his body would adjust to the stress.

It was the fever, the blood, and the hunt. It was burning through him, and he felt himself going to it, while beneath the fever he felt the cold, that strange deathly center within him, locking in, like radar, on the life essence of his foes. It would guide him, had always guided him, by telling him how much to release, and when, and when death was truly death.

For the moment, he gave himself to it. It was the only way to survive.

Gage concentrated, focusing.

His eyes, blinking sweat, centered on target, and his mind shifted into an evaluating combat mode. The men were not wearing nightvisors. The lead man was large, big-chested with a truck-tire gut, gigantic shoulders, and long, heavy arms. He was the handler, the man who would probably do the real work, finishing the professor with a fall down the stairs, a broken neck. An accident.

Behind the big man were two more, smaller in size and carrying, at port arms, what appeared to be CAR-15s. Gage blinked, focused intensely through the nightvisor, but couldn't be sure about the weapons. He scowled.

It wouldn't make any difference. They belonged to him, now.

They approached, a terrifying image of men who held no pity and no remorse, killers trained in the art of horror, silence, and death; merciless, intent on murdering an old man who had done them no harm.

Come on.

He had the advantage because stairways were always a tactical nightmare. There was no way to ascend them safely, ever. And they allowed no tactical defense, except that of returning superior firepower.

Gage had hoped that the water and radio would lull the group towards complacency, inspiring them to ascend the staircase quickly, eager to finish the job and be gone. It would be an amateur's mistake; professionals would never deviate from procedures of safe approach. But professionals were rare, and expensive. Most societies needing special services of clandestine force were content to hire second-rate mechanics, men good at the job, usually ex-military, but men who often made mistakes for the sake of expediency, mistakes made simply because they were unwilling to rigidly adhere, without any deviation, to a strict code of procedures that forbid tactical miscalculations.

They climbed the staircase, fast and close. Confident.

Gage waited, palms slick with sweat.

They reached the top of the stairs together and moved past the doorway. Gage saw the clear image of the large CAR-15 and made his move. He stepped out into the corridor behind them, the MP5 leveled.

"Far enough," he threatened.

With a quick start they turned.

Gage centered the MP5 on the man with the CAR. Instantly the man understood the dynamics of the situation. He didn't point his weapon at Gage. But he didn't drop it either, and the situation spiraled.

Silence, tension climbing.

The other heavily armed man, the one on the left, did nothing. But his eyes went solid and cold, his face twisted in anger. All three looked like they had been in this position before. But Gage knew they were afraid, just as any sane man would be afraid. And yet, as they had turned, they had repositioned. Gage saw instantly that the one on the left held a semiauto pistol. The third man, hulking in the semidarkness of the hall, stood to the right, his hands empty. Without words, almost casually, they made a movement to spread.

"Don't!" Gage felt his finger tighten on the trigger.

They held in place.

"I'm going to make this easy on you," Gage said. "Put down what you've got. We're going to take a little walk."

The middle man blinked, focused on him. Gage saw his hand shift on the rifle. "You won't get all of us," he said quietly, vague fear behind the words.

Gage pointed the MP5 center mass. "Yeah, but you won't be around to find out who lives."

No one moved.

"Now just do as I say." Gage hoped to carry the situation by his will, the determination of his tone. "Put it all down and turn around. This can go easy. None of you will be hurt if you just—"

The left man raised the semiauto and fired quick and smooth. Gage spun and dropped to the left, firing a long burst. Two of the men fell back wildly, and then something massive hit him in the chest, throwing him against the wall.

Stunning impact and the MP5 was lost. Gage realized that the big man had survived the lightning-fast, point-blank firefight to leap forward, colliding against him. Massively powerful, the man slammed Gage against the wall and then delivered one, two, three quick sledgehammer blows in succession, smashing his ribs and chest, pummeling.

Gasping, Gage reached for the Hi-Power semiautomatic pistol in his waist, but the big man grabbed his hand and smashed him against the wall.

Gage roared in pain, forgetting the Hi-Power while trying savagely to throw the hulking attacker back. But the big man hit him with a stunning punch to the face that tore off the nightvisor. Gage collapsed against the wall and saw the big man's hand sweep up, a long knife, and Gage came off the wall, grabbing the man's knife hand to...

In a volcanic effort behind a savage twist, Gage tripped them both. Locked together in the air, they rolled and smashed into the steps as they went down the stairs, the knife passing wildly over Gage, descending, stabbing again and again, and Gage was *there* as fire erupted between them, over them, Gage not knowing how or why and then they crashed to the first floor landing, and the big man came down on top of him, knife still in his hand, crushing Gage to the tiles.

A second passed and Gage gasped wildly for breath, struggling to reach out and trap the man's knife hand. Panting and enraged, he struggled for several moments before he realized he could not reach the blade. Before he realized that the man was not moving. Dead weight on top of him.

Not understanding what had happened or why, Gage twisted, squirming, to get out from beneath the man. He pushed the massive body off of him, and the man rolled limply to the side.

Blood. Shot through the chest.

Dead.

Gasping, Gage struggled up, looking down. He held the Hi-Power in his right hand.

He stared dumbly at the pistol, as if he had never seen one before. He did not remember drawing it in the chaotic battle down the stairs, did not remember aiming or firing the desperate shot. But he knew what had happened: In the terrifying descent down the stairs, in the frantic arena of kill or be killed, when he had been completely overpowered, his training had done for him what he could not do for himself—it had killed his enemy.

In a moment when his mind was totally overcome, when fear and rage had separated the mental from the physical, his body had done what it had done a hundred thousand times before, no, a *million* times before. It had finished the fight, adapting and adjusting and reflexively escalating force from level to level until it had found a way to destroy his enemy.

Exactly as it was trained to do. Exactly as *he* was trained to do.

A hundred million dollar's worth of military training had driven it into him, long ago replacing simple human instinct with lethal fighting skills. His reactions were more than instinct; he had not been born with the ability to kill so perfectly. Nor was it mere reflex; it was far too pure a reaction. Rather, it was as if his natural killer instinct had somehow melded to sophisticated fighting skills, creating an internal essence that was more than either would be alone. And they could never be separated again because the conditioning that had forged them had also altered them, changed them, so that they could never be what they were in the beginning, before the training had fused them into one.

Gasping, choking, Gage reeled and leaned back against a counter. He shook sweat from his head, recovering, gathering, breathing deep, slowing it all down until he could think again.

Unable yet to determine whether he was wounded, he leaned over and grimaced, trying not to think. But one thought could not be denied.

"Oh, God," he whispered, closing his eyes. "*Not again...*" With a moan he bowed his head.

The Hi-Power was heavy in his hand. Still breathing hard, he looked up the stairs, into the darkness. It had been too long, and his mind wasn't handling the stress adequately. He felt his emotions spiraling off, too fired, too hot with the blood. He tried to find balance, to focus. Felt only rage, and regret.

He needed a minute to figure this out, to find his place in it.
But he knew that he didn't have time. The dead men wore headsets
which transmitted automatically. The thudding sound of the MP5,
the screams, and even his chaotic descent on the stairs had certainly carried to the sentries outside.

Gage leaned over the dead man, staring. The man wore no
ballistic vest. Gage nodded, steadily slowing his breath. Good. The
ones outside probably wouldn't be wearing vests either.

Finally gathering himself, Gage checked for wounds, found
blood on his hand, forearm. In the darkness he felt his right arm
and located a jagged wound near his elbow. But there was no pain,
no feeling at all. It seemed to be a bullet graze, with a slight powder
burn.

He closed his eyes, concentrated. Had the man with the CAR-15
managed a burst in the frantic exchange? Gage couldn't recall
getting hit; only chaos, fire flaming towards him, returning fire,
ready to die, ready to kill.

Forget it. Finish wound assessment.

His knee was twisted, but not crippled, and his arm was bleeding, but not seriously. He could still move. The rest would come
later. It was always impossible to determine how bad wounds were
until hours afterward, when the adrenaline was exhausted and the
body protested the abuse. He might have fractured his arm or torn
cartilage in his knee. His body would temporarily deny the injuries, anesthetizing the pain, running on speed.

Quickly, ignoring the pain in his knee, Gage ascended the
stairs and found the MP5 and nightvisor where they had fallen. He
glanced down at the other two men, watching for a moment, and
knew that they were dead. Instinct told him, felt it for him, reaching out to find no life essence in his foes. By reflex he turned away,
shutting off his mind because it was too much.

He still had a job to do.

He went back down the stairs and angled left, towards the back
of the house. He put on the visor and switched to heat imaging as he
walked forward. When he reached the rear entrance, he peeked
carefully, slowly, around a corner of the kitchen. He selected a large
rear window and looked through it, to the back of the townhouse,
searching for the guard.

It took two full minutes of concentrated, sweating calm to
obtain a full field of observation. Gage only moved his head in
degrees, moment by moment exposing a quarter inch of his face for
a wider view. It was an action that went against the fever, the blood,
because his body demanded movement, was fired and on fire with
the scarlet heat that surged inside him. It was worse than he had

ever known it because he hadn't seen action in so long. But he ignored the biological demand, disciplining his body to do what it was trained to do. Obey.

It was the primary faculty, the highest qualifying criteria that had made him who he was: discipline. For his old world was one of speed, of blood drawn in heated conflict with his soul on fire. Yet at the same time he operated under a disciplined mind that allowed nothing, within or without, that would deviate from the unbending rules of engagement.

It required men who could unleash devastating carnage through almost incomprehensibly violent attack, but who could, in the next breath, shut it all down in order to initiate complex technical procedures that required a surgeon's emotional detachment.

It was never more difficult for Gage than it was in this moment. But he slowed his mind, focusing, doubling his efforts to ignore everything but the tactical action he had to perform.

So deliberate, so still was his slow lean that he could have, degree by degree, eventually stepped fully into the darkened room, exposing his entire profile, without ever appearing to have moved at all. But that wasn't necessary. Before Gage had exposed more than an inch of his face he found his man.

There. Across the alley, crouching and moving nervously in the shadows.

Clearly, the sounds from inside the townhouse had carried over his headset and alerted the man, but he hadn't yet decided what action to take. Gage eased back around the corner and closed his eyes, calculating.

...Forty yards...9mm won't drop at all...Contact at point of aim...Plate glass probably won't sprawl the round...First, get Malachi ready to move...The noise might bring backup from the front...Run across the alley on the shot, close on him...

Gage removed the visor, tried to loosen with a few deep breaths, and went back up the hall. Malachi uttered a brief, choked shout when he jerked open the door. He reached down to help the old man rise to his feet.

Malachi stood unsteadily, his aged legs stiff from kneeling in the closet. He grasped Gage's shoulders strangely with his hands, as if confirming that Gage was, indeed, alive.

"You alright, professor?" Gage whispered.

"Yes, yes," said Malachi, still obviously stunned by the momentum of events.

Gage leaned forward. "Listen carefully." The burning emotion of the last conflict made his voice harsh and coarse. "I have to take out a man guarding the back, then I'm going outside. Come running when I wave. But you'll have to move quick, understand?"

Malachi nodded. "Do what you must," he replied steadily. "We shall settle all this with the proper authorities at the appropriate hour. But now we have no time to waste."

Despite the tension of the moment, Gage was impressed by the solid balance of the old man's words. Without reply, he turned and moved back toward the kitchen. He put on the visor, extended the MP5 stock, and raised it to a shoulder position. Then, slowly, using the nightvisor to align the iron sights, he eased the tip of the barrel around the corner.

The man was still crouched across the street, still moving nervously. Trying not to think, Gage flipped the selector to single shot and lined up on the man center mass, just as he had done at the mansion earlier in the night when he had killed the guard to reach Simon. For a moment he held the sight-picture alignment, allowing his eyes to accommodate the lack of depth perception caused by the visor. Then he took a deep breath and pulled himself into his sniper mode, closing off his mind so that nothing would disturb his concentration. He held the sights steady, melding his mind and body to the weapon to release half the breath and hold again.

He gently squeezed the trigger.

The plate glass exploded at the impact of the silenced round, and the man screamed, falling backwards, clutching. Gage was out the back door and crossing the alley before the last shards of glass had landed.

Wheezing, the man was sprawled in the shadows, holding a hand over a shoulder wound. As soon as Gage stopped he knew that the wound wasn't serious. The round had splintered on the glass, sprawling, to hit the man in smaller pellets. Reflexively, Gage raised the MP5, centering, and his finger tightened on the trigger.

Wide-eyed, the sentry stared at him; a muscular, massive man dressed in black. Gage knew him for what he was—a shooter, a career criminal who was good at murder, hired to do a job on Malachi Halder. But the wounded man was an amateur at this game, and it was not a game for amateurs.

Gage felt the instinct, the heat; it was kill or be killed, leave nothing alive, finish it, finish it because only the strongest, the purest, the meanest would survive. It was his old world, the world he had dominated, ruled, and terrorized by the power that was his.

His hand trembled. *No! Not again!*

Gage shook his head, reached down, and snatched off the man's headset, kicked away the rifle. Then in a swift movement he took the man's automatic, a Colt .45, ejecting the chambered round and clip and tossing the gun into the darkness. Quickly he searched the man for a backup weapon; ankles, back, found none. Then he rose and stepped away.

Five seconds lost. Because of mercy.

And now the man would come for him again one day.

Something inside Gage told him he wasn't strong enough for this game anymore. Gage didn't listen.

He turned and waved to Malachi, who was out the door and down the steps with surprising agility. In seconds the old man was beside him. Leaving the wounded man on the pavement, Gage led Malachi across a maze of alleys and lots. Malachi followed without question and with remarkable stealth. Within minutes they were standing beside a dark blue LTD, parked on a street that had far more traffic than the one outside the townhouse.

"Get in," Gage ordered.

Without question Malachi got into the passenger side. Gage started the car on the first try and pulled slowly away from the curb, blending into traffic. After a minute he increased his speed. He automatically checked for following cars, watching the side streets. He made several turns, doubling back again to confirm that they were alone. Then he drove steadily south, eventually merging onto the noisy, glaring traffic that crossed the Hudson River through the Lincoln Tunnel.

As they descended into the darkness, Gage felt the rush: It was the game again. He knew the rules, had once accepted them. But he had changed. He was different now. And he knew he could no longer live by the rules.

It was only a shadow, a faintly darker shade that was there, and then it wasn't. Sarah's eyes locked on the open doorway, the brightly framed entrance to the basement of Saint Matthew's Hall of Ancient Languages. She didn't realize what she had seen, what had drawn her eyes to the entrance.

There was nothing.

Strangely disturbed, she continued to watch, a faintly alarming sensation awakening deep within her. But, vaguely as it had come, it was gone, leaving behind a ghostly awareness that caused her heart to beat more quickly.

Dimly she recognized the quickening as a warning, the instinctive arousal of some half-forgotten survival mechanism. Jade green eyes narrowed as she watched the door.

But, still, there was no sound. She had heard no one descending into the basement for several hours. She could assume she was alone.

But she continued to watch. Uncertain.

Stretching her long arms and legs, Sarah Halder leaned back in her chair, staring at the empty door. After a moment, she sighed, and something prompted her to rise and walk to the door, to look into the hallway. But even as she considered it, she realized how tired she was and resisted the impulse. Wearily, she shook her head, sweeping her long, dark hair, even darker now against the paleness of her skin, back from her forehead with an unsteady hand.

It occurred to her that she had spent most of her life in these halls. Much of what others had enjoyed most in life had slowly but steadily passed her by. But, she thought with a slight lift of spirit, she was still young, only 33. There was still time for what she had missed most of all.

She had tried several times at love, but relationships were always hampered by the life she had chosen. And she had spent a large part of the last 15 years in libraries or isolated archeological excavations, concealing her beauty in shadows or desert.

She knew she was still attractive. Tall, almost five-nine, she had the sleekly proportioned, panther-like body of an athlete. Years of walking over sun-baked hills, of digging in desert ruins, had burned her down, conditioning her with long and smooth muscles. Yet the scorching work and long hours of study had aged her, too.

She thought of the stray gray that thinly specked her raven-black hair, the white strands starkly noticeable against the natural midnight blue-black. And her skin was dryer now from the harsh conditions she had endured, and faintly wrinkled around her eyes. She wondered how much more of her life would pass before...

A memory came to her, soft and cherished, a memory of the man, and the one moment in time they had shared. She felt again the soft gray eyes that seemed to see her as she truly wanted to be seen, the quiet gaze that seemed to always understand, to know.

She remembered how he had listened to her every word, however simple, and how he had studied her every move as she nursed him back to life. She knew it was more than gratitude. His eyes had simply expressed what he was afraid to speak aloud. And though she had not understood his fear, the unexpected gentleness had touched her; unexpected because he was obviously such a hardened person, a soldier.

But from the very beginning she had found only tenderness in his voice, sensing something kind and beautiful and forgiving within him. Though some things were frightening, as well. For as she sat beside him as he healed, watching the fevers come and go through the desert nights, she listened to his dreams, heard him speak to the dead men, to those he had killed and to those who had died at his side. In the long nights she came to understand the pain in his voice, felt his guilt and regrets and remorse, wept beside him; he in his delirium, she in her sadness at such pain.

After they had smuggled him back into the country, and after his wounds were healed, he had risen one day to say a quiet good-bye.

She had never seen him again.

"Gage," she whispered. "Why couldn't you say anything..." A control rose up, and Sarah shut her eyes, tight. With a deep breath she brought herself back to her surroundings, glancing absently toward the door.

She blinked and rubbed her eyes, suddenly more aware of the burning and deep fatigue. She had stayed here too long, she realized, too long studying an ancient text that had, so far, revealed nothing significant.

Before her, photocopied sheets of the writings of Theophylact of Greece lay haphazardly on the table, and she tried to bring her mind back to the work.

For an entire week she had sat translating the half-readable text, finding that, in essence, it agreed with the testimony of Euthalius of Alexandria. But the poor condition of the parchment prevented definitive interpretation, and she was forced to recreate Theophylact's sequence of thought in passages where words were lost, continuing the logical process of the revered philosopher's reasoning and language despite the obscured lines, capturing his intent.

"I'm too tired for this," she whispered. Too tired for ghosts. Too tired for games.

She stared again at the page in front of her, leaned forward to focus on the almost unreadable line. *Just finish this*, she told herself. *Just finish this and go home.*

Even beneath the magnifying glass she could not discern Theophylact's Greek. He seemed to be discussing a Semitic letter written by Alria of Samaria which said that the biblical book of Hebrews was originally addressed to the...the...

"What...is he *saying?*" Sarah's whisper was loud in the silent hall.

Theophylact's lettering was all but obliterated at the point where he analyzed the intent of Hebrews' unknown author. Sarah leaned closer over the page, focusing intently on reading the mind of someone lost to the world for 1600 years.

Something was visible there, something she could faintly discern, a fragment of a single Greek letter that stood six spaces away from the last word of a shattered sentence.

She closed her eyes, reading the memorized text again in her mind, becoming one with the long dead philosopher who had penned the letter in 300 A.D. She began to write with him, appreciating the use of his language, understanding the direction of his thoughts and purpose of his words, even as she understood their brutality, withholding moral judgment in order to more accurately understand a former world.

Sarah opened her eyes and stared at the page. "Yes...of course," she said faintly, feeling the solid rush from her heart.

Quickly she scanned past the lost segment, reading further, finding letters, dots, and swirls, building the parchment in her mind. She continued the intricate thoughts of a man long lost to the Earth and saw the faint fragments of letters exactly where she had expected them to mark the page, and then it was there, as it was from the beginning before she had understood.

With her magnifying glass Sarah bent closely over the page, putting each Greek letter in place with her mind, watching them merge with the faint outline.

"Written to the inhabitants of Palestine, and then to the Jews who have fled..." she said softly, laughing. "I knew it..."

Instantly she was on her feet, moving to the phone beside the desk. She dialed and heard a singsong voice answer on the other end.

She laughed. "Barto, listen. Yes, it's Sarah. Listen, I've figured it out. Yes, I'm sure. Come on over. Uh-huh. I'm in the library. Alright, see you in a few minutes."

She set the receiver down and turned.

Shadows in the doorway moved.

Sarah dropped the phone, breath catching, staring straight at the doorway, vivid with fear.

Her gaze focused on the faint darkness on the tile floor in the entrance. It moved again. Except this time the shadow did not immediately recede but laid across the white floor for a long moment. When it moved backwards she moved with it, picking up the phone instantly.

A rasping sound behind her, feet shuffling.

Screaming, Sarah spun around, glaring frantically in the darkened library as she dialed. Something banged against a desk.

Inside the room. It was inside the room.

Sarah's scream shattered the silence as the horrifying, hulking man emerged from the shadows beside her. He moved forward, smiling, his black-gloved hands clenching, unclenching, in anticipation. She continued to scream and tried to frantically finish dialing. But then, looking blindly toward the doorway, she saw a second man. Bald and as large as the first, he watched as the smiling man moved toward her.

Sarah picked up the phone to hurl it at the dark form. But the man lifted a burly arm, batting it aside, and then he was on her. She raised her arms to ward off the blow that knocked her to the floor.

Sarah landed across the tile floor. Fighting, kicking frantically, she struggled to her feet, moving back, but the man grabbed her as she rose, slamming her against the bookrack. Shelves dug into her back. She opened her eyes, blood fast and hot.

The man's fetid breath touched her skin, cruel eyes studying her. His face had a deathly pallor, but the eyes were smart, cunning and calculating. Sarah clenched her teeth and moved her head as far back as possible against the bookrack. Hands locked on her arms with inescapable strength and held her in place. "It'll be quick," the man whispered.

Sarah felt something within spiraling out of control. Screaming, she tore violently away, but he tripped her as she moved. The hard floor struck her across the face as she fell, but still she tried to rise. He snatched her up again and slammed her against the bookcase, lifting until her feet were no longer on the floor.

"Finish it!" the man in the doorway shouted.

"You do your job and I'll do mine!" the big man shouted back. Sarah felt her upper arms being crushed in an iron grip.

Violently Sarah raised a knee into his groin and her nails raked the pallored face. For a brief second the grip lessened, and she fell to the side. She struggled to keep on her feet, but she crashed clumsily across the floor with the man wiping his face and coming towards her again and the doorway was empty...

What...where...?

Her attacker came at her and she kicked, screaming, but the man brushed her fighting aside, lifted and slammed her hard against the wall.

"Ah..." she gasped, her scream cut off by the numbing impact of the rack against her back.

"I'm gonna break your neck for that!" the bloody face whispered.

Enraged, he hurled her to the floor again, and Sarah seemed to lose balance within herself as her senses reached a pain-shock overload. She crashed against the floor. Numbed by the pain, she tried to crawl away, before collapsing. She shook her head and weakly raised a hand to plea.

Suddenly, a dark arm snaked around her attacker's neck from behind. The big man shouted wildly and reached for his throat, tearing at the arm.

Sarah scrambled back in a daze and registered that a third man, a stranger, had grabbed her assailant from behind, now holding him in some sort of headlock.

Bellowing, her attacker spun wildly then surged backward to smash the stranger into the bookcase. Shelves and plaster shattered at the thunderous impact, scattering books and wooden splinters chaotically along the wall. A falling shelf painfully struck her shoulder.

With a violent surge the stranger pushed off the wall with his feet, spinning her attacker back around. The big man screamed, cursed, arms flailing wildly in futile attempts to pull the stranger from his back.

Sarah watched, mesmerized, as they swayed above her. A high-pitched whine escaped her attacker's imprisoned throat. Gasping, the man's malevolent face twisted as the stranger's grip overcame, closed, and endured. Her attacker ceased pulling at the arm around his throat and fumbled frantically beneath his dark coat, tearing at an object, struggling to pull something free.

At the movement the stranger shouted, twisting to slam the big man into the wall. He spun him around again, and Sarah saw a dark object, a gun, clatter across the floor to her feet.

By reflex alone she screamed and scrambled back, avoiding the darkly polished steel. Then she looked up to see that the stranger had finally gained a distinctive advantage in the struggle; the hulking shape that had attacked her was weakening, staggering, while the strong arm encircling his neck tightened. After a long suspended moment, the library echoed with a startlingly loud crack.

Roaring, the stranger twisted the neck imprisoned within his grip, the blood force of some primordial rage shattering, breaking, driving death into death. He flung the body savagely to the side, smashing the dead man into the desk. Books and papers scattered as the hulking man's limp body slid heavily to the floor.

Sarah looked up, wide-eyed and breathless, as her rescuer swayed in the gloom, seemingly overcome by the power and rage that he himself had used to overcome.

Staggering and gasping hoarsely, the stranger lifted his face to the ceiling. Sarah thought for a moment that he might collapse. Then he seemed to find balance in the madness and turned toward her.

The voice that escaped her was a cry, a sob, as he leaned down and she rose, reaching out to the strong arms that reached out to her.

"Gage!"

His hands touched her face, her shoulders, seeming to search for injury. He leaned close to her, sweat glistening silvery on his face.

"Are you alright?" His voice was coarse with exhaustion.

"Yes," she said, hesitating. "What's happening?"

He shook his head. "There's no time. Your father's outside."

Sarah turned wildly to the door. "Where's the other—"

"He's gone," Gage whispered. "I've got to get you out of here."

Sarah stood on unsteady legs, feeling a faint trembling. She leaned against Gage, reached out and felt something wet on his arm. In the half-light of the library the dark stain on her hand was clearly visible.

"You're bleeding," she said.

Gage nodded, steadily holding her. "I'll take care of it. Is there another way out of here besides the stairs?"

She tried to think. "The elevator."

"No good. We'll have to take the stairs." He moved with her across the room. "Come on. We don't have much time."

One of Gage's hands held hers, and Sarah saw that he gripped a semiautomatic pistol in the other. He paused at the doorway, looked cautiously into the hall.

"We've got to move fast," he whispered.

Sarah looked into the lean face that was inches from hers, saw blood and sweat and fatigue and remembered the long nights, the days and weeks of recovery when she had watched over him, praying as he had hovered between life and death. Somehow, in the surreal terror of the moment, the nights seemed like yesterday, not lost to the desert over three years past.

She nodded, gripping his hand.

He led her into the hall, and she averted her eyes as they passed a massive figure. The second man, who had stood in the doorway moments before, now lay in the corridor. They reached the stairs and, Gage leading with the gun, they moved fast, up the steps to the first-floor landing where he hesitated, looking carefully out the door. He leaned back into the stairwell.

"Your father is in the trees east of the building, at the square. He's waiting for us. If I don't make it out, get to him and contact William Acklin in the Washington FBI office. Tell him everything. No lies. Tell him what I did, and he'll do what he can for you. Do you understand?"

Sarah felt a violent and uncontrollable surge of emotion that she had denied until this moment. She couldn't manage to speak. She simply nodded in response to Gage's instructions.

"Good," Gage whispered. And smiled.

Sarah remembered the smile, the warmth, and she longed to reach out to him. She wrapped both hands around the hand that gripped hers.

"Ready?" Gage asked softly.

She found strength. "Yes."

"Let's go."

He put his hand with the gun into the pocket of his waist-length coat as they left the stairwell and moved quickly across the lobby of the hall. His head turned left and right, scanning, and he led her down a corridor, away from the front entrance. At the end of the hall was the office of the Dean of Ancient Languages. Gage hesitated, looking back. Then he removed a small case from his coat and bent down, working on the lock.

"Is this alarmed?" He inserted a single black pick into the keyhole, and then another, working both picks together.

She placed a hand on his shoulder. "I don't know." Her voice sounded stronger than she felt. "I think so."

"No time to find out," he muttered. "Tell me if you see anybody coming."

Sarah looked back down the hall. The lobby, what she could see from her angle, was deserted. She heard Gage picking at the lock, seeming to have trouble. She sighed. Her father was safe, but she knew this would all lead back to whatever it was that was found, that discovery in the Negeb that had changed their lives forever. Increasingly nervous, she watched Gage. At least three minutes had passed.

"I was never any good at this," Gage whispered harshly, shaking his head. His hair was damp with sweat. He wiped a forearm across his eyes, concentrated on the lock.

Two more minutes.

The lock turned and Gage opened the door as an alarm instantly sounded outside the hall, blaring across the campus with a siren-like wail.

Gage moved quickly now, stealth forgotten. He hurried across the room, raised the window, and pulled a long, narrow double-edged knife from his belt. He jammed the knife into each side of the bracket that secured the storm window to the window frame and twisted, breaking the molding. The window clattered onto the grass, and he quickly lowered Sarah to the ground, then jumped down after her.

Outside, the campus seemed to sleep. A few students visible on the square continued to walk through the late night with easy calm, oblivious to the wailing alarm. Sarah remembered how many times she had heard and ignored the sound, but her hands still found Gage's arm.

He touched her face with his free hand.

"We're almost clear," he said. "Your father is over there." He nodded to a cluster of trees isolated from the rest of the campus.

Sarah's heart quickened with concern, and she followed Gage into the trees beside the building. Gage led her through the darkness, along a path she knew during the day but couldn't see now in the gloom. She held his hand for guidance, lost in the dark as he moved quickly forward. In moments they stood at the edge of the shadows, beside a sidewalk. She saw that they would have to follow the pavement for about fifty yards to reach the woods where her father waited.

Outside Saint Matthew's Hall of Ancient Languages a campus security guard pulled up in a patrol car. They watched, hidden, as the relaxed, burly form exited his vehicle and approached the building in a leisurely stroll.

Gage was motionless, scanning, studying an area about two hundred feet to their right—a forested section that seemed impenetrable to light. Trees, only dimly illuminated by streetlights and the building entranceway, left deep zones of darkness.

He scowled. No good way to do it.

Sarah's voice was close beside him. "What is it?"

"We've got to cross this street to reach your father," Gage looked at her, saw her green eyes catching the light, keen and distinct. Already, she had regained her balance. Remarkable . . . and beautiful.

Gage almost smiled, but then looked away, concentrating.

He studied the square. He didn't like the line of retreat, but it was the best he could come up with in the shortness of time. They would have to cross this street, exposing themselves to the light in order to escape.

The nightvisor's power was exhausted or he would have scanned the surrounding trees. As it was, he couldn't tell if anyone was hiding in the distant darkness, waiting. For once they left the safety of the trees, anyone with a rifle would have a clear shot. Time was running out. He still had to find the translator, the last one in the desert that night.

Unable to read anything in the shadows, he shook his head, frustrated. He looked back toward the Hall of Ancient Languages and saw the security guard round the nearby corner containing the broken window.

Time to move.

Gage leaned down slightly, looking once again into the intelligent green gaze. "If I go down, run. Your father is in those trees. Remember to contact Acklin in Washington."

Her almost indiscernible nod communicated far more than speech. Though fearful, it was steady and trusting. And strong. A strength created, demanded by something within her, a strength that was the servant of the intellect, not the master.

Gage gently took her hand. Together they walked into the street. They had taken only a dozen steps.

The bullet that ripped past their heads was so close, they felt the wind torn apart at its passage. Then the rifle shot thundered over them and Sarah was on the ground screaming. Gage fell to his knees beside her, firing as the ground exploded beside their heads once, twice, showering them in dirt and grass.

Gage rose, moving towards the direction of the shots, firing, screaming, *"Run! Run! Reach the woods!"*

And then Sarah was on her feet, staggering and then running, not looking back. She reached the woods in seconds as a tree exploded beside her with the impact of another rifle shot. Then she was in her father's arms, and the old man was shouting something as the trees around them were riddled by the assault of automatic rifle fire. Together they stumbled, reeled, and fell into the cluster of trees as the forest and the campus echoed with horror and chaos.

Sarah raised her head, saw Gage down, the gun lost from his hand. At the Hall of Ancient Languages she saw the security guard crouched behind a building, heard him screaming incoherently into a radio.

Gage jerked to one side. Was he wounded? Another rifle shot tore a chunk of wood from a tree near Malachi.

She saw the familiar white van and remembered her phone call at the same time sirens began closing on the campus. Screaming wildly, she ran to the edge of the woods, ignoring the rifle fire, signaling with her arms. Two more bullets struck beside her and she leaped desperately back, using the trees for cover, still screaming.

"Barto!"

The dilapidated van skidded to a halt outside the cluster of trees. From inside, a heavyset, balding language student with thick glasses and a bushy beard, mouth hanging agape, stared at her in shock.

A pause.

Then a rifle shot and the front windshield of the van exploded.

Barto bellowed and the van spun its wheels in a long, thin screech, hanging a tight turn that blasted it wildly over the sidewalk and grass to slide precariously into the cluster of trees beside Sarah. The right front fender smashed into an oak as it came to a stop. Two more shots ripped through the white panels, and then the door was jerked open from inside.

"Come on!" Barto screamed.

Sirens entered the outer perimeters of the campus.

Sarah and Malachi scrambled inside and Barto spun out, Sarah's fingernails digging into his shoulder. She pointed toward Gage, lying motionless on the sidewalk.

"Get him!"

A volley of rifle fire tore through the side of the van, and Sarah was thrown wildly as Barto, still in reverse, spun across the grass. He slammed on the brakes and the van stopped beside Gage. The body of the van separated Gage from the volley of incoming rifle fire.

Barto was shouting. "Get him! Get him! *Hurry it up!*"

Sarah leaped out and tried to lift Gage. But he only stirred at her touch, rolled over. His eyes fluttered open. In a daze he rose, staggering, and fell into the open side door that she quickly closed behind him.

The van howled as they roared up the street, but New York City police units, lights flashing and sirens hot, skidded to a stop, blocking the exit.

"Police!" Barto yelled. "They can—"

"No!" Sarah shouted above the protesting van and the screaming code equipment. "Not now! *Get us out of here!*"

The van skidded wildly as it caught a narrow alley and charged into the night. Gage was semiconscious, and she wrapped her arm around his neck, holding his head off the bumping panel floor. Behind them blared the code equipment of police in pursuit, and then Gage stirred, seeming to rise toward consciousness. His bloodied right hand reached up to grab the seat. Half-awake, he rolled his head.

"Hang on!" shouted Barto.

Sarah screamed as the van left the ground, pitching forward at the front before blasting its way through a wooden wall. The van crashed to the ground once more and beneath the floor panels she felt the tires spinning on loose gravel, fishtailing, and then climbing, rising on a steep incline. Behind them, the sirens fell back.

Barto killed the headlights, and the van spun chaotically through the darkness, trees scraping and limbs thumping off the side panels. Sarah knew that he had somehow gotten them off the campus, as well as any semblance of a road. Then the van hit a summit, left the ground and came down again, the windows shattering completely at the impact to shower the interior in a thousand flying shards of slicing white light.

The freezing night roared through the interior, and Sarah pulled Gage closer.

Barto hurled the van into a wild downhill run, twisting, sliding, spinning the wheel with the dexterity of a true virtuoso. Then the vehicle bottomed out, wheels rebounding forever between the van frame and ground, until the tires finally found purchase and entered another roaring, leaning climb.

Barto floored it, quickly ascending through the smashing, grinding gears. Sarah saw lights growing nearer, then the van swayed, hit smooth pavement, and they were in traffic again. Barto leaned forward, smiling, eyes bright with excitement.

Sarah turned her face from the icy rush of wind, skin already numb. But she felt Gage stir, awakened by the cold air. He struggled to raise himself, to watch.

Barto didn't seem disturbed by the wind in his face. He continued to lean forward, eyes narrow and peering, hands clutching the steering wheel. His round shoulders were bunched, aggressive, focused.

He didn't look back, didn't slow down.

For half an hour they raced through the night. In her arms Sarah felt Gage relaxing, even as he lay against her, her back against the door. Finally the lights along the highway seemed to grow thinner until they were driving through the darkness, away from the city.

Gage shifted, studying Barto. "You're the translator," he rasped.

Barto executed a smooth lane change, exiting the highway. Busy.

Malachi spoke loudly. "Yes, Bartholomew was our translator in the desert. He was the last of the three. Now we are together."

Gage said nothing, stared at Barto. "Where'd you learn to drive?" he managed.

Barto looked over his shoulder, smiling insanely, clearly enjoying his job. "Beirut," he yelled back, eyes gleaming.

Gage shook his head, leaned back against Sarah, sighed. "We've got to ditch this thing," he said.

"Good idea," Barto called back, nodding, squinting into the wind. "Where?"

Gage licked his lips, shifted, moaned in pain. "Go east...I've got an LTD in storage...at Patterson."

Barto looked back over his shoulder and nodded. Gage was struck by the excited eyes that glared down at him through the thick, tinted glasses.

Malachi bent over Gage, moved the coat aside, and studied his chest. A large patch was torn from his shirt, and Sarah saw that a white, fibrous cover, a ballistic vest, was also torn from the impact of the bullets. The old man helped lift him up, and Gage slowly removed the vest, rubbing his chest. Even in the darkness, Sarah saw the bloody patch of skin.

Reflexively Gage placed a hand on his chest, examining his wounds by feel in the shadows of the van. There was no penetration; the vest had held.

Remarkable.

Must have been using subsonic 9mm rounds. A high-velocity .223 would have cut through that thing like paper.

He rubbed his chest, looked at Sarah, nodded. She was close, and he felt Malachi's hand on his shoulder.

Barto called back. "Does, uh, anybody wanna tell me what's going on?"

"Not now, Barto," Sarah answered.

"Whatever." A moment more, and he called out again. "Do I need to take the interstate?"

"No," said Gage, drawing a deep breath, focusing. "Where are we now?"

"East Rutherford."

Gage nodded. "Alright. Go over the bridge. Take Central to Lakeview." He grimaced, coughing. "Keep it...slow."

"Got ya," replied Barto, bunching at the wheel, eyes scanning.

Leaning back against Sarah, *so soft,* Gage stared at the ceiling, trying to concentrate, to forget the strong, cherishing arms embracing him.

He shut down his emotions as best he could, organizing. Things were changing fast, and he couldn't go with his original plan. New York City was too hot. Automatically, he selected his second safe house. He heard Barto asking something.

"Where do we go from there?"

Gage looked at Sarah, soft green eyes touching him.

"North," he said weakly, feeling a slow shock settling beneath his fatigue. "To the Catskills. I've got a cabin...at Panther Mountain."

Barto sailed the van into the night, and they were alone and silent, with shadows passing over them. Gage shut his eyes, weary from his wounds as the cold dark rolled over them in an endless sea, smothering them, dominating them, stronger than all of them together.

White, fluorescent lights illuminated the massive oak table in the lower-level chamber situated beneath the visible complex at Langley, Virginia, but the light contrasted harshly with the mood that darkened the room.

Nathaniel Kertzman, deputy civilian investigator for the Department of Defense, leaned back in his chair, staring at the grim faces surrounding the oval desk. He listened intently, wondering at what cruel twist of fate had brought him into this deplorable and sorry situation.

"We are not *responsible!*" United States Army Brigadier General Sol Tessler shouted. Again.

"These were not our men! They were not on any special assignment! They were not on some rogue mission. Both of them had been out of Special Ops for over six months!" He pounded a fist on the desk, half-rose from his chair. "You will not put any of this on us! The Army will not be blamed for this fiasco!"

"Just settle down, General," said a severe, calm voice.

Kertzman shifted his eyes to Jeremiah Radford, briefer and special investigator for the Deputy Directorate of Operations for the National Security Council.

Radford's impeccable gray Seville-Row, chalk-stripe suit was impressively well-fitted, as always. A perfect complement to his wide, darkly understated tie, white, spread-collar shirt, and hand-made leather, lace-up Oxfords. Nothing but the best.

Kertzman suppressed a smile.

Radford's tanned face was smooth and void of scar or blemish; the face of a movie star, an actor. The perfect man for the job.

Radford leaned forward placidly, lifted a hand.

"We are not here to assign blame, General," he added, smiling faintly. "We are here to ask the necessary questions. Now, please, do not think we are going to point a finger at the Army for this ...fiasco. At the moment, we only want to know if there was any

American intelligence or military personnel involved in this situation at St. Matthew's or the professor's house."

Brigadier General Tessler shifted, calming, but he still punctuated his words with knifing gestures of his hand. "I can certainly understand why someone suspected the Army of involvement in this. But the rumors are unsubstantiated. Yes, Sims and Myrick were from Special Operations, six months out of Intelligence. But I want it in the minutes that I have personally completed my own investigation and confirmed that they were not working on any 'off the boards' assignment. They were discharged! Out! I want to make that perfectly clear." He lowered his hand, looked steadily around the table.

Radford nodded. "Thank you, General. You have, indeed, made that perfectly clear. Now, let's get on with the agenda."

Kertzman scanned the room, noting faces from Naval Intelligence, the Central Intelligence Agency, the Army, Federal Bureau of Investigations, and National Security Agency. Not surprisingly, everyone present was a heavyweight, a deputy director of respective special operations or holding a similar high command. All long-term career men, and Kertzman figured that they were all eager to handle the situation in ways favorable to their long-term careers.

"So," continued Radford, "has everyone read the reports?"

Nods all around, low murmurs.

"Gentlemen," he added, "we still have a few questions that need answers. We've all seen the ballistics reports, witness reports. We've read the cases made by police. I assume you've all read the homicide report of the men killed at the professor's home, the autopsy reports. All three of them are ex-military. I might add, *our* ex-military, with no significant clearance. The Agency doesn't know them, never worked with them. The only thing compromising our integrity is the presence of Sims and Myrick, who were killed in the basement of the college. Their security clearances were favored, at least red line. They had access to a lot of information, a lot of people. The DCI wants to know if they were really working in the private sector and just got themselves killed, or if this was some kind of renegade government operation."

Radford hesitated before continuing.

"You were all asked to investigate your departments for any possibility of an unsupervised operation." He tapped his pencil on the table. "Did anybody find anything?"

Kertzman watched as heads shook and a few empty hands raised to signify empty findings.

"I see." Radford gazed about the table. "Well, that's what preliminary inquiries through the NSA have deduced. They say that we had no active agents involved. But there is a final question we have to ask." Wearily, Radford leaned back. "There is some concern about the missing woman, her father, and another student. For the record, gentlemen, all foreign agencies have denied any official or unofficial involvement with any of them. Germans, Soviets, Chinese, whoever. But we all know that doesn't mean anything. They would deny it anyway. At least, if they had any brains, they'd deny it. But because Sims and Myrick died at the college, we have to check these things out. So I asked each of you to try and determine if this woman, her father, or the student have any involvement with any American or foreign intelligence service."

Radford scanned the faces at the table. "Well?" He tapped the pencil again.

Silence.

"I want you to all realize," he added after a moment, raising his eyebrows expressively, "that there are some very significant people who are extremely...interested...in this situation. As always, heads may be on the line. There are rumors circulating about some type of rogue military operation. But nothing provable. There's probably nothing there. It looks to me like some private interest wanted the professor dead, and another private interest wanted him alive. There's no evidence to indicate that it's any of our people, or that the government is even involved. It looks to me like this was a simple situation of deadly force which resulted in the deaths of three men at the townhouse. Then Sims and Myrick met their long overdue destiny at the seminary. Since they'd been discharged, I have to believe that they were freelancing. That's what the evidence indicates. They took a job, knew the risks. Their decision. Both of them lived on the edge. It was bound to happen sooner or later. And because they were freelancing, the NSA is not responsible, at least not directly. I can't speak for the DCI, but I'm going to recommend that he give the Bureau free rein to investigate this thing on a civilian level. That's where it started. That's where it should stay."

Radford leaned forward in his chair, elbows on the table. "So," he continued, "let me summarize. As far as I can determine from your findings, the three missing persons are not ours. None of our active people were involved in any sanctioned or non-sanctioned government operation. Whatever this is belongs to the private sector. And I can tell the DCI that the intelligence community has been cleared."

Everyone nodded. Radford shuffled the reports, preparing. "Good. Is there anything else we need to cover?"

No one in the room seemed eager to offer counsel.

"Mr. Kertzman?" Radford said quietly, acknowledging his presence for the first time. "I don't know how any of this falls under your jurisdiction in Defense. I don't even know why I was instructed to allow you to sit in on the committee. But, for the record, I'll give you the opportunity to contribute. Do you have anything to add?"

Radford seemed ready to leave.

Kertzman leaned forward, face impassive.

"Well," he began slowly, eyes scanning the faces of everyone present, "I think you've got a cluster and that somebody's lying."

Radford stared at him for a moment as if he wasn't sure, exactly, what Kertzman had actually said.

Kertzman understood the absurdity of his statement. Of course somebody was lying. Somebody was always lying. Lying was expected for senior supervisors of intelligence operations, even required, and no one would be present in the room if they were not both accomplished and silently dedicated to the unannounced necessity of the art. That was the nature of the business, and it was considered rude, asinine, and even somewhat bizarre to point it out. To do so broke ranks, in a manner, and injected an unsettling anticipation of honesty into a discussion that was both dangerous and vaguely insulting. But Kertzman didn't really care how they felt about him. They didn't have any authority over him; he didn't have to maintain relationships. He belonged to the Pentagon's Department of Civilian Investigation, and he could subpoena what he needed from them whether they liked him or not.

"Why do you say that?" Radford offered, finally.

Kertzman laughed gruffly, scornful. "Let's look at it. Number one, we've got three dead marines and two Army intelligence agents—"

"*Ex*-Army agents," General Tessler interrupted, pointing a directionless finger.

Kertzman stared a moment, nodded. "Alright," he continued, "we have two of the Army's *ex*-intelligence agents. Six months out. Dead at a seminary. We have three *ex*-marines, dead at the townhouse of a seventy-two-year-old archeology professor. Who also worked at the seminary."

Kertzman leafed through two autopsy reports in front of him. "Myrick," he added dryly, "the one police found in the hallway of the basement, was killed with a knife." He read from the page: "Respiratory function of subject was terminated by the vertical insertion of a double-edged tool between the first and second cervical vertebrae, severing the medulla from the involuntary respiratory section of spinal nerve clusters."

Kertzman folded the report, looked around the room. "*That,* boys, is not an easy thing to do. Not if it's done on someone like

Myrick, who weighed two-sixty." Kertzman leaned back, his considerable bulk obscuring the chair. Gazing about at the Chosen, the Beautiful, he felt seriously out of place.

Even in general appearance, no one else in the room would begin to compare to him. Six inches over six feet, Kertzman was imposingly massive with a thick gorilla chest and a truck-tire gut, a striking contrast to the trimmed, lean career men surrounding him who sported tailored suits. But Kertzman had never known success with clothes. His arms, for one thing, presented a problem with off-the-rack coats. They were heavy, muscular and long, with the overlarge forearms of a mechanic, forearms enormously developed and which left a viewer with the disturbing impression of primitive, brutal strength. His face, so unlike the handsome countenances surrounding him, was broad and intimidating, the unsightly mug of a Depression-era street fighter; the faintly scarred face had seen a fair number of bar fights and hard times in youth but had weathered the worst and reflected a deep, thick-skinned toughness from the abuse.

Beneath his low, broad brow, Kertzman's blue eyes studied the room with a lion's relaxed, confident awareness. Though the eyes could easily appear deadly in the wrong light, their ability to threaten was most often hidden behind a bland and sleepy demeanor, moving with a focus that shifted easily, quickly, from one man to the next, concealing an almost invisible keenness of thought, discerning. His brutish, bar-fighter face revealed none of the intellect that had led him through the bloodbath of Vietnam, police work, and the FBI to the secret corridors of the Pentagon and continually served to Kertzman's advantage. Never in a hurry to reveal his thoughts, he took advantage of the fact that his face often led people to perceive him as slow-witted, or easily misled.

Kertzman saw that everyone was staring at him. He decided to take them along. "Like I said, Myrick weighed two-sixty," he continued. "He was strong. Real strong. But somebody killed him in the blink of an eye with a fancy knife trick and then sent Sims into the Great Beyond with a broken neck. Now what's wrong with this picture?" Kertzman stared around him. "Anybody want to take a shot?"

No answer.

"Well then I'll tell you," Kertzman added. "In the real world you don't kill people like Sims and Myrick like that. You kill flunkey sentries like that. But Sims and Myrick were a lot better than that. They were hard to kill. Both of 'em were Special Forces. Paratroopers." He hesitated. "If you've been there, you'll know that means somethin'. They were cross-trained in intelligence and urban survival, covert operations, the works. Six months out and still fresh. They weren't fighters. They couldn't even *spell* fight. They were killers. They were two very capable, very dangerous men, but they were killed in a matter of seconds by someone who knew the game a whole lot better than they did."

Radford shifted, appearing disinterested. "So what's your point?"

Kertzman snorted, contemptuous. "What's my point? My point is that whoever did this was a professional, and a good one. This knife trick isn't even something we teach to Delta or SEALs. I've read about it, but I've never seen it. I thought it was real interesting, so I talked to a few people. It's a technique used by the Mossad."

"The Israeli Secret Service," added Radford.

"Yeah," Kertzman continued. "Israel. We don't use it because it's considered..." He thumbed through the pages of a cheap, weather-beaten pocket notebook. "'... too narrow a technique.' That means there's too much room for error. It's too chancy. Too easy to miss, have the knife deflected by bone. Then it doesn't kill quick and you've got a sentry screaming his head off and alerting everybody in the camp. We teach other things with the knife to our elite boys, but not this. As far as I can tell, it's strictly Israel. They like the knife, use a lot of techniques that no one else touches."

Kertzman waited, folded the notebook. Radford's face was concentrated.

"So," he added, "it looks like we got somebody using a fancy Israeli knife technique on one of our ex-Special Ops personnel." Kertzman studied the faces surrounding him. "Well, that certainly adds a new spin to things, doesn't it? And what about the three marines that were discharged from RECON, the ones found in the professor's home? Three men, all of 'em with specialized training in a marine fast-attack unit, all cut down with a high-tech weapon."

Radford tapped his pencil absently on the desk, stared at Kertzman. "So?"

"So?" Kertzman repeated. "*So?* So I'm saying that the same guy did 'em all. He did the guys at the professor's house and the two guys at the seminary. And this wasn't the work of some old geezer professor or a security guard, either. Or even a cop. It's the work of a professional. And not some idiot Mafia hitman or a terrorist. This was the work of a real heavyweight. Somebody who might have millions of dollars' worth of training. Somebody who knows how to play the game."

Radford slightly stared off, focusing slowly on Kertzman as he spoke.

"Alright," he submitted. "I'm not an idiot, Kertzman. None of us are. I agree that whoever did this is probably good at what he does. But we aren't here, exactly, to find out who, *specifically,* did it. That's the Bureau's job. Or the police department's. We're here to find out if this fiasco was part of some kind of governmental action gone awry. We're here to find out if anyone can verify an *active* federal agent's involvement."

Kertzman shifted, focused on Radford. "Whoever did this was active," he said quietly.

Radford paused in vague astonishment. "How can you say that, Kertzman?"

"Because," Kertzman continued, "whoever did this couldn't have gained this level of proficiency if he hadn't seen extensive, and I mean *extensive*, combat experience. I know. I've been there, and combat ain't easy. It's chaos. It's confusion and fear and everything else but efficiency. Almost nobody is really efficient at combat. Nobody. They're crazy if they are. A normal guy doesn't do very well in a situation where people are trying to blow his brains out. It ain't natural. The natural thing is to get out. That's the only thing I ever wanted to do."

"A lot of our inactive personnel have combat experience, Kertzman," said Radford. "They're all dangerous."

"Not like this," Kertzman continued, unfazed. "Whoever did this is beyond that. He's either the luckiest guy on earth, or he's trained to be something that's way beyond a normal field operative. And I'm puttin' my money on training. In the old days we called it brainwashing. Nowadays they call it conditioning. Training. We spend millions of dollars making people like this, and we just call it training. There ought 'a be a better word. But, whatever, this guy ain't no normal man because he obviously don't feel fear like a normal man. Somethin', maybe some kind of real intensive training, like we give to some Delta or SEAL guys, has made him cold. Stone cold. He might even be one of the best in the world at what he does. And that means he was in a unit that saw almost continual action. A unit that has cross-trained with some real heavy hitters, like Israel, the SAS, whoever. And that would put this man, our man, in a very narrow category. He might even be easy to find once we know where to look."

"You're getting all this from a knife technique?" Radford appeared irritated.

Kertzman was deadpan. "There's a few other things."

Radford shook his head. "Kertzman, even if this guy *is* real good, why does he have to be one of ours? He could be Russian. He could be Egyptian for all we know."

Shrugging, Kertzman replied, "Everybody else in this is American. We haven't seen anything to indicate any kind of foreign interest, no kind of power play. All the dead agents are ours. So I figure this is something internal." He paused, considering his own argument. "Yeah, that seems right, when you think about it. I'd say it's probably safe to assume this guy is ours."

Radford challenged him. "What about the student? Bartholomew O'Henry. You know, Kertzman, if you want to conjecture, we can do it all day long. What if he's not really a language student at all? What if he's part of some foreign support system? What if he's the one who's doing all this? That would make a lot of sense. The woman and the professor might have discovered him. And now he's attempting to eliminate them. The professor might have hired Sims and Myrick and the rest of them for protection."

Kertzman's stone-faced stare revealed nothing, but he pursed his lips as he considered the hypothesis. "No. I don't think so," he said after a moment. "I've studied that guy's file. I don't think he has the physical ability to pull this off."

"Why do you say that?"

"Because, like I said, real fighting ain't techniques and fancy moves. Real fighting is strength, speed, endurance, toughness. Who can last the longest? Hit the hardest? Who can take the most damage while putting the other guy through more than he can survive? That's combat. It's ugly. It's the meanest, ugliest thing on God's green Earth. And you've just got to be mad-dog strong, tough, able to take anything that comes to you while dishing out a whole lot more. It ain't pretty. And there ain't no rules. No, this student doesn't fit the profile. Not at all." He hesitated a moment. "It ain't him."

Radford was silent a long time. "You might be right, Kertzman," Radford said, and Kertzman was intrigued to sense a slight surrendering in the tone. "But you didn't answer my question. Why does this guy have to be active?"

"Because people this good never leave," said Kertzman in a flat tone, unyielding. "Sure, people like Sims and Myrick leave. That's no great loss. But we have too much invested in a guy like this. Too much money. Too many secrets."

Radford was probing the theory. "He still might not be active, Kertzman. He might be old. Retired."

"I don't think he's old," said Kertzman.

"Why?" The pencil tapped on the desk.

Kertzman shifted, leaning forward. "An old guy couldn't have done this," he said slowly. "No. This guy is too young to retire and too good to quit." Kertzman nodded, convinced. "He's active."

Radford stared distantly at scattered reports. The pencil had fallen silent. No comments were offered, no responsibility accepted. Nothing but an uncomfortable silence.

Finally, Radford met Kertzman's eyes. "We still have no real evidence, Kertzman. I can't write this report up the way you put it. You don't have anything but opinion. And that's not enough. There's really nothing but conjecture to indicate that this is the work of a professional, especially ours. If you were still a cop, Kertzman, you might have enough for something. But this is not enough for an intelligence finding. We're supposed to, at least, look like we can back up what we say."

Kertzman grunted. "Gentlemen," he said, his natural belligerence asserting itself. "This guy is active in some element of our government. He's an ex-SEAL or ex-Delta or maybe even Special Forces. But SF would make him old, because they haven't seen continuous combat since seventy-two. So he's probably not regular Army. I think he's cross-trained in covert civilian warfare with us and with foreign intelligence agencies like the Mossad. Of course, this guy could be foreign. Israeli, Russian, whatever. But I don't think he is. I think he's family. Maybe a CIA tactical guy out of Delta. Maybe a counterinsurgency guy out of SEALs. He might even be one of those guys we plant in foreign countries and wait to activate, the kind of guy trained to do it all, anything, whatever it takes to get the job done." He gazed around the table. "An artist. A psychopath."

Kertzman shook his head. "No, I don't have any proof. At least, not yet. This is all just a hunch. But it's based on evidence. And, like I said, if this guy isn't active, then he's not long gone, and he's on a rampage. And that, gentlemen, is a situation. He might be settling old debts or using what he's learned against us. Anything's possible."

Kertzman stared at everyone in turn. "You have to ask yourself, what is so important that one of our own operatives, if he is one of ours, would kill Sims and Myrick to protect? Or to hide?"

Kertzman let the question settle. "And what do all these people have in common? The college? What? What is the key that ties 'em all together? The Army? Special Forces? Rogue covert ops running some underground financial scam that's gotten out of hand? What kind of situation could be bad enough to cost five men their lives, two of which had security clearances to the highest levels of this government? What can be that bad? Or that big?" He paused. "When we find the answer to that, gentlemen, I can assure you that we'll find something that leads straight back to this room."

Radford folded his hands. "That's a little out of line, isn't it, Kertzman?"

Kertzman waited, allowing whatever influence he possessed to work its way into the nervous impatience of his listeners. He knew that they hated his words; and he knew that his determination to find the bottom-line truth was the only real power he had. If he allowed himself to be swept in with the rest of them, they would own him, giving him what they wanted, when they wanted. He would be a puppet, a yes-head nobody with no guts, no respect. He couldn't settle for that. Ten years as a city street cop, Vietnam, twenty years in the FBI, and four years as a Pentagon criminal investigator had given something to him, meant something. He knew that, now, if he ever sold out he would lose the soul-weight of every right decision, every back-against-the-wall gutsy move he had ever made, lose the center of what he had risked his life a thousand times to defend. It would have all been for nothing, meaning nothing. He couldn't do it, had decided long ago that he couldn't do it. So since his first days in the Pentagon with the stonewalling and the complexity concealing game-playing he had adopted one unbending code of conduct; anybody came at him hard, tried to crush him, he came back at them harder; pushed into a corner, he'd burn the house down laughing his guts out *and nobody gets out of here alive, boys!*

Kertzman smiled at the thought; better to be hated and feared than to live on his knees.

"Gentlemen," he began, with only the slightest trace of a Midwestern upbringing in his words, "regardless of what I can prove, if something looks like a bull, if something walks like a bull and smells like a bull, then it's probably a bull." He winked at Radford. "If you know what I mean."

He let that solidify, gazed around the table. Radford didn't move, stared at him. Then, allowing his anger to brace his boldness, Kertzman stood up, slowly walked down one side of the table.

"Do you know what we need to understand here, Mr. Radford?" he projected. "We need to understand a little bit about trackin'. About huntin'."

Confusion, or shock, blinked in Radford's eyes.

"Before I left South Dakota," Kertzman went on, "and came to this godforsaken part of the country, I did a lot of huntin'. Moose, elk, bear. Whatever. Any of you ever tracked a bear in the high country, brought it down with your own hands?"

Silence.

"Well, I have. They gave a lot to me, and I gave a lot to them. And I'd do it clean. No guides. No fancy machinery flying around chasing 'em into trees like the cowards do nowadays. It'd just be him and me, alone in the high ground. And sometimes when the rock would be so hard that I couldn't track, I'd begin to wonder if he might not 'a circled back around. Maybe he was tracking me."

Kertzman paused, eyebrows slightly raised. "Believe me, boys, that's a bad feeling. And I would always use a Casull .454 so I'd be close when the moment of truth came."

Radford gazed distantly at the wall. "Is this really important, Kertzman?"

"So there I'd be," Kertzman continued, smiling, "alone in the high country. And he'd be with me, huntin' me just like I was huntin' him. And do you know how I would realize it when he had finally come up in back of me?" Kertzman stopped at the far end of the table, looked around. "It was the silence," he said, a remembered fear steady and centered in his gaze. "One minute I'd be trackin', looking for sign, not finding anything. Bird and squirrel and every other kind of critter would be chirpin' and hollerin' and making a racket. Then, all of a sudden, this terrible silence."

Kertzman waited, allowing a quiet to settle on the room. "Then there'd be that ol' strong ammonia smell 'a bear. He'd be hunting me, right on me. The meanest thing you've ever seen on four legs was right beside me in the trees, and I couldn't even see him. But I'd know he was there. Because of the silence."

Kertzman walked along the table, stopped at the opposite end. He put both hands, fingers spread, on the smoothly polished wood. Radford appeared reluctantly impressed. Absently, he tapped his pencil on the table.

"So what are you saying, Kertzman?"

Kertzman leaned forward, meeting the NSA man's gaze.

"What am I saying?" he repeated, palms flat on the table. "I'm saying that it's awfully strange that I can't see no tracks in any 'a this. I'm saying that it smells like I'm real close to something I *should* see, but I can't." He nodded to Radford. "I'm saying it's awfully strange that everybody's so quiet in here."

Kertzman entered the spacious and lavishly furnished Pentagon office of Vice-Admiral Richard Talbot at 5:30 P.M. on Monday,
January 15, approximately seven days since the seminary incident
and three days since the Special Investigative Committee hearing.
A pair of glossy flags honoring the Navy and the United States
stood on either side of access into the Admiral's inner sanctum.
Kertzman glanced around without appearing to notice the surroundings. It wasn't the office of an Admiral; it was the throne room
of an emperor.

A secretary of advancing years, her stark white hair adding a
perfect complement to her impeccable lavender dress, turned her
studious attention to him as he approached the desk. Kertzman
saw her practiced gaze center only for a second on his identification
badge, but he suspected she had read every word.

"Nathaniel Kertzman," he said, knowing she already knew.
She probably knew everything. "I'm here to see Admiral Talbot."

"Yes, Mr. Kertzman," she replied with perfect, superior courtesy, gesturing toward the inner door. "The Admiral is expecting
you."

Kertzman moved past her. Surprisingly, since he had been
walking the most secretive corridors of this building for five years,
it took the full measure of his practiced control to appear calm and
relaxed.

Tall, thin, and authoritative, Admiral Talbot was a striking
model of military composure. Even at this late hour of the day, his
white duty uniform was flawless, dress shoes polished to a high
sheen, every carefully trimmed gray hair in place. Not muscular,
the Admiral still seemed exceedingly fit for a man in his sixth
decade, vaguely reminding Kertzman of a dedicated long-distance
runner. On his evenly tanned face a pair of clear prescription avia-
tor reading glasses glinted goldenly from the light of the restored
eighteenth-century ship lamps.

As Kertzman entered the office, the Admiral turned respectfully, regarding him with a sudden and friendly smile.

Kertzman instantly recognized the man speaking with the Admiral, Thomas Blake Carthwright, special assistant to the NSA's Director of Operations, formerly a special prosecutor in the Justice Department. Carthwright spent most of his time at the White House, but because of his seemingly vast responsibilities in overseeing American intelligence, Kertzman had often glimpsed him within the halls of the Pentagon.

Carthwright was dressed in an austere but impressively tailored gray suit that announced both his significant social station and his profoundly influential position. Though they had rarely talked, Kertzman had long ago measured Carthwright as both cultured and extremely comfortable with the rich and powerful, the product of Old Money. But, with a slight satisfaction, Kertzman had also perceived something more within the expensively dressed assistant, a sort of nebulous weakness concealed by his privileged status, an emptiness of soul hidden behind the carefully subdued arrogance. Kertzman didn't believe that Carthwright had worked his way up from the middle class. He was obviously smart, and powerful, but the brains came from an expensive education, and the power was inherited. Kertzman didn't respect either of them.

The Admiral's voice. "Do you know Mr. Carthwright?"

Kertzman extended his hand. Carthwright's grip was solid, confident.

"It's a pleasure to meet you, Mr. Kertzman," he said, seeming to select the words carefully. "I've heard a great deal about you. I hope you don't mind me sitting in on this."

Kertzman looked at Admiral Talbot, who nodded.

"It's alright, Nathaniel. Mr. Carthwright is here to contribute to the situation. Have a seat."

Admiral Talbot gestured with the thin manila file that he held in his hand and sat behind his desk, focusing on Kertzman down a long, thin nose.

Massive in the dim light of the office, Kertzman sat into a large, plush, black leather chair situated directly in front of the desk, leaning slightly forward, an elbow on one knee, hand on the other knee. Brutal face hardening in concentration, Kertzman cut a quick, narrow glance toward Carthwright as the NSA man eased casually and comfortably into a red, gold-studded leather chair beside him.

Kertzman possessed an intimate understanding of the tactics of intimidation. All of them had been used on him at one time or another, and he had used a few himself. But he was slightly unnerved by the sudden and profound intensity of the Admiral's centered gaze. The old man's voice was low.

"So how did the meeting go on Friday?"

Kertzman met the Admiral's gaze, thought of Carthwright. "I just told it like I see it," he replied. "A lot of it, I've already told you."

The Admiral waited. "And?"

Kertzman frowned, vaguely confused.

"Admiral, just what is it that you want to know? I already told you what I think. I can't prove anything. They thought I was just shootin' my mouth off. They'll do the investigation their way. They'll go by statements, paper trails, work the system, try to find computer records that lead somewhere. In this case I don't think they're going to find any." Kertzman shrugged. "I don't agree with them. They don't agree with me. It's their show."

Admiral Talbot leaned back in his leather swivel chair, rocked silently for a moment. The hawklike gaze continued to search. "But what do you suggest we do?" he asked quietly.

Kertzman felt a game begin. The impression, as always, made him angry. He knew that Carthwright had a hand to play, but he couldn't put it together.

"Look, Admiral, I don't have any authority in this situation. Two days ago, when you asked me for my opinion, I told you that there might be active military elements involved in this. But then, Sims and Myrick might 'a just been a couple 'a yahoos on a personal vendetta. For all I know, they might 'a been killed by the janitor. The truth is, I got no idea. But there are a lot of unanswered questions."

The Admiral continued to stare at him. Kertzman wondered how far to go.

"It's that situation at the seminary that doesn't fit into anything," Kertzman continued, hesitant. "Whoever sent Sims and Myrick across the river is a real mystery. It keeps bothering me, sort of like when I feel a high cold blowing in over heat. There's a pressure in the air. And it just feels bad, like a cyclone's brewin'." He paused. "You might not see it, but you can feel it. Smell it. It's like . . . a feelin' of danger that just don't leave, no matter what you do. And then there's that shootin' in the professor's house. Archeology. Theology. This Hall of Ancient Languages. None of it makes any sense. Guys like Sims and Myrick don't die at seminaries. They die trying to steal industrial secrets or they get shot down flying dope out of Central America. Despite the way I feel about 'em, I have to admit they were good at what they did. And in the open market they'd make a lot of money doing wetwork. But not over anything to do with religion. Sims and Myrick had probably never even seen a church or a seminary. And whoever it was that put them down don't belong there, either. I don't know what kind of intelligence network, working out of a place like that, could be so important that men could get killed over it. I mean, I would anticipate that we would have something, like recruitment or language training. But nothin' big enough to end in a tactical fiasco like this." He waited, face hardening in thought. "The thing is, we've got killers running around in a place where they shouldn't be. Instead of trying to find out who, exactly, killed 'em, which might be impossible, I suggest you find out what Sims and Myrick were doing at the college." He nodded. "You find out why they were there and you'll probably get a line on whoever it was that did 'em in. I think that's the best way to go."

The Admiral leaned forward. "Indulge me, Nathaniel," he said. "Hypothesize. What does your investigative instinct suggest about this alleged operation? Why do you believe they were there?"

Kertzman organized his logic, tried not to repeat himself. "My best guess is that Sims and Myrick wanted to steal somethin', or hurt someone. I don't know what, or who. Maybe they wanted to hurt this woman who's missing. Retribution. Something like that. Not directly related to the seminary. It's people that were the target, not the school. And then this mystery man got involved for some reason. I don't know what. Maybe he was squared off against Sims and Myrick in some sort of weird covert operation. Maybe they're all runnin' drugs or working a private sanctioning agency, and now they're in a feud over profits." He hesitated, shook his head again, a dismal gesture. "God only knows."

Talbot's interest seemed to sharpen. Kertzman allowed a glance at Carthwright, saw only astute and polite attentiveness, dignified and patient.

The Admiral shifted. Behind the polished glasses and hawkish nose Kertzman sensed a keen intellect turning in tightening circles. Carthwright moved forward, debating some turn of thought.

It was the Admiral who spoke. "Do you know why the NSA asked for your opinion on this, Nathaniel?"

Kertzman shook his head. "No."

"Because," he continued, rising, "we believe there is a situation that has gotten . . . out of hand."

Carefully, Admiral Talbot moved around the desk, an approach of purposeful and measured authority. He sat down on the edge at the front, the imposing image of an elite military commander, leaning over Kertzman.

"What I am about to tell you must not leave this room," Talbot said, in a conspiratorial tone. "It is, as you already suspect, a sensitive matter. No doubt I do not need to remind you of your contractual agreement."

Kertzman weighed everything, wondering where the game would lead. "Alright," he said, "I'm reminded. But I don't play games, Admiral. And I'm not military. Not anymore. I don't even know why the NSA asked me to sit in on the—"

Talbot silenced him with a gravely raised hand.

"I'll explain it to you, Nathaniel," he added slowly. "You were selected by the NSA to sit in on the meeting because the White House has authorized a Special Inquiry into a rather unusual military situation. And Justice has been selected to run the investigation, with the cooperation of the Joint Chiefs."

A long silence.

"What kind of military situation?" Kertzman's voice penetrated the heaviness.

Without hesitation the Admiral answered, "An investigation to determine whether there are rogue military personnel of this government engaging in nonsanctioned covert operations against the American civilian sector."

Unblinking, Kertzman said nothing, wondered how much of the drama was for theater.

"These activities, if they do indeed exist, are highly illegal military affairs," continued the Admiral, his voice solemn and heavy. Then he shook his head, as if answering an unspoken question. "The nature of these operations are officially unknown to us, but members of the NSA suspect that they are extensive. Possibly, they only involve members of our military engaging in nonsanctioned surveillance and intelligence gathering. But there is also the possibility that far more serious crimes have occurred. It is even possible that crimes of a violent nature are involved. And there are allegations that some of these military operations have involved the use of deadly force against American civilian authorities." He paused. "So, as you can see, I am not misstating to say that the situation may be out of hand."

Kertzman said nothing. Didn't move. He was suddenly and sharply aware of Carthwright's poised presence.

"Mr. Carthwright and I have brought you here because we want you to lead the investigation," the Admiral continued. "Needless to say, it must be done quietly and with exceptional circumspection. You will be dealing with professionals, men trained in the craft of intelligence. If they suspect that someone is attempting to uncover their network, they will immediately close ranks and cease operations. Then we'll never locate them and the military will be compromised for decades to come. That would be intolerable. We cannot allow an elite society, even a society from within our own ranks, to misuse either our authority or our resources."

Carthwright finally spoke. "I want you to know, Mr. Kertzman, that this operation has been approved at the highest level." He allowed the thought to settle into Kertzman. "It is very serious."

Kertzman released a dismal sigh, felt things spiraling away from him. Admiral Talbot handed him a file.

"This is one of the primary suspects in this rogue operation," said the Admiral.

Kertzman looked at the thin file and felt something strange, something he couldn't identify. He hesitated as long as he could justify before opening the folder.

An eight-by-ten glossy photograph of a man, a soldier apparently in his late twenties, greeted him. Kertzman's eyes narrowed as he studied the photo. It was a stern face, apparently taken at some point of intensive military training, possibly in the desert. Sand and blackened grime caked the man's face and neck above the filthy, brown desert fatigues. Curious, Kertzman focused on the face, noted the few thin scars, the deep tan, and he perceived a weathered toughness of the skin that made the man seem older than his years. He looked closer and saw that the man's eyes were coldly focused, sharp and disciplined.

Strangely, Kertzman was reminded of three army specialists he had seen in 1967 when he was stationed in Saigon. It was some mysterious kind of reconnaissance group that had come out of the bush after three months of in-country fighting. He remembered how they had walked past him and how one had mechanically turned his head, meeting Kertzman's astonished gaze. Kertzman had never forgotten what he had felt in that moment, never thought he would feel it again; it was the chilling gaze of Death walking. Hungry. Prepared. Still in the jungle on city streets.

Kertzman sighed, shifted. "And why is he a primary suspect?" he mumbled. "What makes you think this guy is in on any of this?"

Admiral Talbot didn't falter. "Upon your hypothesis during the committee hearing, and after Mr. Radford's subsequent report, the NSA initiated a file search of personnel who met a criteria of cross-training in special warfare." He gestured to the file Kertzman held. "This man, Staff Sergeant Jonathan M. Gage, formerly of the United States Army, is one of our most, ah, highly skilled operatives in that regard. He was a former member of Delta Force, has all of the elite commando training. After being discharged from Delta he became part of a subunit out of Central Intelligence Covert Operations where he acquired even more specialized training in counterinsurgency, particularly in the area of preemptive sanctions against terrorists. Most importantly, he is suspected of treason."

Kertzman raised his eyes at that.

"Gage vanished in August of 1990," added the Admiral in a serious tone. "Vanished under peculiar circumstances and without a trace during a regrettable and highly classified CIA covert operation in the Negeb Desert. Israel. The bodies of ten other team members who were with him were ultimately recovered and identified. But Gage's body was never found. It is suspected, but not confirmed, that he betrayed his country and possibly even set up his own team to die. We have received scattered but unconfirmed reports over the last three years that he may still be active in the intelligence community. So, we do have sufficient cause to suspect that he may be alive and may also be working somehow with other members of our military to influence the high ground of this government."

The Admiral seemed impressed by his own speech. Kertzman was impassive. Figuring it for himself.

"Mr. Carthwright," the Admiral continued, "is special assistant to the NSA's Director of Operations. However, because he is an ex-Justice Department prosecutor he is temporarily on leave from the Agency and has reassumed his authority to oversee an investigation on American soil, in accordance with standard legal procedure and policy." He hesitated, searching. "Now, if this man, Jonathan Gage, and his cohorts are found, the Attorney General will issue federal warrants of arrest. Indictments will be sought, court martials performed with strictest adherence to policy against all enlisted personnel. But since Gage is now a civilian, we will prosecute him on a civilian level. Then we will institute full procedures for rectifying any misconduct or misuse of military personnel or equipment, as well as compensation to victims as it is allowed by civil law."

Kertzman tried to reason the situation through more completely. "And why is Gage, if it *is* Gage, doin' all this?" he asked abruptly. "What are these people workin' to get?"

Talbot shook his head. "We do not know. That is one cause for the investigation."

Kertzman pondered that.

"To summarize, Nathaniel," the Admiral continued, "we want you to discover if this man is somehow involved in this plot. And if he is, we want you to apprehend him. Bring him to justice. Bring an ending to this network of traitors."

He ominously accented "traitors," and Kertzman was suddenly aware of what it was like to command true power. He felt strangely uncomfortable, out of place.

"Why me?" he asked, acutely searching the lean face, glancing towards Carthwright. "There are probably a lot of men who are more qualified. Certainly easier to work with." He waited on that, then, "I don't see why you would pick my name out of the hat."

Talbot almost laughed, then leaned forward, clasping his hands, as if he were momentarily impressed with his own thoughts before focusing on Kertzman again. "Because I've watched you, and studied you. You are the most hated and feared man in the Pentagon. Your name can darken any room in this building, which is the largest building in the world. Few men can enjoy such a boast. There are others, yes, but not many who are as determined, or as obstinate. You're only fifty-four. That's old enough to know how to do this discreetly, but not so old that it's too tough an assignment physically. You're only four years out of the Bureau, so you can resume your FBI authority without having to go back through Quantico for federal recertification. You're smarter than the rest, and you possess something that very few of the other investigators have."

Kertzman couldn't help himself. "And what's that?"

"You're a natural hunter, Nathaniel! You've had combat experience in Asia. Then you spent years as a police officer and twenty years with the FBI before you finally came to the Pentagon. You know how to deal with men like this. You know how to find clues, investigate, track ghosts in a fog." The Admiral waited for the soft sell to sink in. "And your integrity is completely unquestioned. There will always be disputing interests, but for the most part your reports are unchallenged for their honesty, accuracy, and investigative thoroughness. Believe me, my friend, you're the best man for the job."

Carthwright spoke up again: "And we know that you can get the job done, Mr. Kertzman."

Kertzman turned, purposely slow, to gaze into the confident face. "How do you know that?"

"Because you'll have a trump card up your sleeve," Carthwright added.

Kertzman blinked at the allusion of speech. It seemed slightly incongruous coming from someone so stately as Carthwright. Kertzman wondered if Carthwright was attempting to un-refine his language in order to meet what he presumed would register most effectively in Kertzman's un-refined intellect. The thought annoyed Kertzman, but his face revealed nothing as he stared at the NSA man.

Carthwright clasped his hands together, calm, concerned. "You will be working with a man who trained Gage. A man who knew him in Central Intelligence. His name is Robert Milburn, and he's been through every course, every school that Gage ever graduated from. He knows the specifics of every battle Gage ever fought. With any luck, Milburn might even be able to second-guess him. And Radford will also be working with you. He can get you anything you need. With Milburn and Radford working under you, you should have a good chance of success."

Kertzman grunted, noncommittal.

"Gage must be stopped, Mr. Kertzman," Carthwright continued. "That is absolutely essential. But, of course, you must stay within the law. According to domestic policy you yourself are not authorized to initiate any tactical situations. If you see a combat situation developing, you'll be required to notify appropriate special agencies. You know the procedure. But," he raised his hands vaguely with the words, "whatever occurs, we trust that you will handle the situation discreetly. You have our full support. This entire meeting has been taped and documented. You can call the Office of Security to confirm. We are not trying to pull something over on you, Mr. Kertzman. This is a legitimate investigation, and we would like for you to do the fieldwork. Find this rogue operative, bring him to justice so that he can be prosecuted."

Kertzman studied Carthwright's even gaze, saw the petition to join in the crusade. He searched the face, but there was nothing else to find. "Who's the top man in this?"

"Me," Carthwright answered calmly. "Just me. There is no other chain of command, above or below. If necessary, you'll use the Digital Information Relay Center in the basement for communications. Then, neither the CIA, the NSA, or the FBI can monitor your messages. Everything is arranged to maintain strictest secrecy." He seemed to ponder the thought, stressed, "Needless to say, it is absolutely essential that we keep all American intelligence networks out of this initial investigative phase."

Kertzman waited, vaguely annoyed. Then he turned toward the window, staring into the grayness with a concentrated intensity.

Outside, a gathering wind tore dead leaves from trees, and his thoughts were just as cold, chaotic, and he felt a disturbing sensation. It was as if a faint track, obvious and revealing, were missing; some half-glimpsed trace in the dust that he couldn't quite read. Kertzman concentrated, trying to find, to discern, the faint sign. He knew it was there, felt it was there, but couldn't see it.

Everything was verifiable.

Call the Office of Security. Confirm it.

But there was something else. He could sense it, smell it. Hiding in plain sight. The thought was maddening.

Beyond the glass, a silent wind bent the trees, sending leaves into clouds and a darkening sky. Kertzman watched, distantly thoughtful.

There was a storm coming in.

Kertzman saw the thunderclouds in the grayness, a cold winter long overdue. And it came to him, a bad feeling, a real bad feeling. He hesitated, remembering that he was six months out. And he knew he could walk away from it, let them hunt it down themselves with lawyers and depositions and computers, leaving him to walk into an easy retirement.

Or he could walk into it, hunt a cold trail.

A man's got to live with himself.

Kertzman felt a new awareness when he spoke. The Admiral seemed a much less imposing figure when he looked at him again.

"Alright, Admiral Talbot," he said quietly. "I'll try and find out what's going on. But I want full documentation on everything I do. 'Cause if I'm gonna do this, I'm gonna do it right. I'll follow this thing wherever it leads, no matter where it leads. Right up to the Pentagon, if I have to. Right up to the Joint Chiefs." He nodded curtly. "Right up to you."

Admiral Talbot's lean hand settled on Kertzman's shoulder.

"I knew we could count on you, Nathaniel."

Testing the pain that lanced his forearm where he'd been shot, Gage clenched his fist, found strength. After two weeks, the pain was finally fading, the wound almost healed.

Good enough.

He closed his eyes, leaning his head back against the cedar, where he rested in the glowing, early morning. He felt the cool breeze, appreciating the solitude. A thought rose up, but he turned his mind from it. Because he knew he couldn't stay.

Not now.

Simon was dead, and he was thrown back, hard, into his old world. And he sensed that it would get a lot worse before it ended. Tired, he released a focused breath and bowed his head, trying to find balance. He had never wanted to return to that life.

Not ever.

He scowled and felt the substance of what he was, now. Felt it, solid and filling. It was strength to him. He wondered if he would be able to keep it.

Soft sounds.

Gage half-turned his head, listened without opening his eyes. Caught the faint scent in the breeze.

Sarah.

He knew she was there, followed her quiet footsteps but waited to open his eyes. When he finally looked up she was beside him. Graceful and easy and natural in blue jeans, a denim shirt, and brown boots with her hair dark and thick, framing her oval face. But it was the smile, always the smile, that reached him first; comfortable and understanding.

"You want to be alone?" she asked quietly.

He knew that if he said yes, the smile wouldn't fade. She didn't play games, understood so much that he could not tell her.

"No."

"Good," she said and settled onto the grass beside him. And didn't say anything more.

It was one of the things he enjoyed most about Sarah. She didn't have to say anything, be anything. She could always find the right place, an almost ethereal balance between words and silence. He had come to regard her calm composure with profound respect.

A wintry sun rose slowly, casting a brighter glare over the once-golden glade. Gage felt the wind increase in strength and by reflex his mind switched to an analysis of sniper fire, to angles and elevation, power and bullet weight and maximum impact and a thousand thoughts that shattered peace of mind. Before he could stop himself he had shook his head, muttering something indiscernible, trying to remain in the moment.

Sarah turned her head at the sound, her narrow and careful green eyes regarding him with a measured look. But she said nothing, and after a moment resumed watching the wind gently tugging leaves.

"It's a nice place to stay, don't you think?" she said.

"Yeah," Gage answered. "A nice place."

"It reminds me of a place I grew up in, way out in the Northwest," she added carefully. "We had a little glade, or clearing, like this. I liked it."

Gage listened, smiling faintly, watching her eyes as she talked. They were the only eyes he had never tried to read anything behind.

"Father was back teaching again in Seattle," she continued. "I was in my third year of critical care nursing, but I'd decided to drop out. It wasn't how I wanted to spend my life. So I had a lot of free time. I'd go into this field every day, take some books, study. I enjoyed reading outside. It always seemed more...alive to me. Sometimes I miss it. Sometimes I miss a lot of things that were simple." She paused. "Is this where you came after you healed up in New York? After we smuggled you into the country from Israel?"

Gage caught the slight hesitation in her voice at the final question, and he had already nodded, more than willing to answer, grateful she had asked.

"Yes. I set this place up a long time ago as a safe house, just in case I ever needed it. Turns out I did. In the end it was the only place that was truly safe for me or anyone else. That's why I came back."

She nodded slightly and turned away, gazing at the two heavily wooded slopes that flanked the cabin. The enclosing hillsides were high, steep and overgrown with thick brush and an almost impenetrable stand of trees that made the forest seem dark even in the day. Only the cabin was clearly visible, standing alone in the small clearing that was utterly barren of thorns and brush, resting solidly between the slopes. It was a strangely level arena of shattered stone, crushed into the mountain long ago with glacial strength and which now claimed its own measure of peaceful sovereignty from a brutal and surrounding world.

"This place really is beautiful, in a way," she said. "It's hard, and it's cold, sometimes." She looked at him. "But it's peaceful. And honest."

"Yes," he nodded, holding her gaze. "It is."

A brighter smile, and she said, "And what do you do now? With your time, I mean. Do you just hang around here?"

He shrugged. "Yeah. Pretty much. I stay here. I built the cabin myself. Took me about a year. Lived in a tent while I worked. But there's still some finishing work that needs to be done. I've kind of gotten out of it lately, though. Haven't driven a nail in a while. Nowadays I read a lot, I go into town for supplies." He laughed. "I know it sounds boring. But it's a good life for me. Sometimes I've gone into the city to visit Simon. Not often. But a couple of times."

"He really loved you."

"I know."

Sarah tossed a lock of hair back from her forehead. "I think he thought of you as the son he never had, as the saying goes. After he found you in the desert, he felt that it was all ordained."

Silence joined them for a time, and she spoke again. "Is your arm alright?"

Stretching his right arm, Gage made a fist, testing. "Yeah. I think it's alright. I'm ready to go back into the city. Maybe find some answers. I'll try and get Simon's letter from the church, then we can find the next step in all of this."

"I think my father has some answers," she said. "So do I, I guess. At least a few. And Barto."

Gage nodded. "We're gonna talk tonight. We'll cover some more ground. I already know a few things. I know this manuscript is valuable to these people. Valuable enough for them to kill for. But I don't know what's in it."

"Father knows what's in it."

"I know. But I think we'll all know a lot more when I get Simon's letter from the church."

Her voice was low. "Will it be dangerous? To get the letter, I mean? Do you think they'll be expecting you?"

"Probably." He felt instant regret for saying it, but he knew he couldn't keep any secrets from her. Not really. Not about anything that mattered. She was too sharp, her intuition too keen, too discerning. He knew that there was nothing he could say that she could not sound out almost instantly by her uncanny ability to somehow always feel the truth in him.

Silent, he waited, looking away.

"I'm sorry for what you had to do," she said finally. "I know it was hard for you. I know you don't want to return to that life. We never talked about it, really, you and I. You never said you didn't want to go back to being a soldier. But I could tell."

He looked down, sniffed indifferently. His hands were clasped. "Yeah. It's hard, I guess. But it was always hard. I'd just forgotten, is all."

"Are you alright? I'm not a psychiatrist or anything, but I know that sort of thing can have a hard impact on a person's state of mind."

He shrugged, frowning. "I try not to think about it. I...did what I had to do. If I could have found another way, I would have gone with it. But everything happened so fast. It was just split-second decisions, training. There was just no..." His voice trailed off.

Motionless, Sarah waited, a calming and perceptive gleam in her green eyes.

"Thank you for saving my life," she said, finally.

Casually, she brought her knees up, laying her forearms across them, staring out over the forest, the glade. Neither of them spoke for a long time.

"It's difficult," she said, "finding right and wrong in all of this."

Releasing a hard breath, Gage shifted. "There was only one right and wrong to it, really. And that was the decision to get involved in the first place. From then on there was just surviving. Just a dangerous game. Because, really, none of this is different from police work or standing on a wall in the military. I'm putting myself between you and some very bad people." He shook his head, looking away. "I'm rusty, is all. I'm having a hard time getting back into the mindset. It's almost got me killed already. I can't seem to get back into it. My heart...isn't in it."

"Was it easier when you were a soldier?"

He shook his head slightly. "It was never easy. But I had a different attitude then. I was a lot colder. More efficient. I didn't make mistakes like I've made so far. Back then, when I was in combat, I didn't look at people like they were...people."

She blinked. "What were they?"

"Targets," he said, simply, turning to her. "That's all. Just targets. Back then, like I said, I was efficient. Surgical. I didn't hesitate, or let men live when I knew that tomorrow I might walk into a rifle sight and they would be behind it. It was kill or be killed. Everybody, on all sides, understood it. That's just how it worked in the field. If you lost in the situation, you died. No questions. But now I'm hesitating. I'm letting people walk away, or trying to give them a chance to back down." His jaw tightened, his face harder. "I need to get the scent back in all of this or I'm going to make another mistake, get myself killed. And if I'm dead I'm no good to anybody. I've got to stop thinking so much. Just do the job."

She watched him, unblinking. "Not everyone could do that kind of thing."

"No," he said somberly, "not everyone could, or should. But I'm different. I'm trained to operate like that. I'm just having a hard time getting it back together. I've got to get my head straight and put all of that right and wrong stuff in its place. I mean, there's always going to be right and wrong. But not in combat. In combat there's just good moves and bad moves. Good moves kill the enemy. Bad moves get me killed."

Leaning forward, she touched his arm with her hand, eyes narrow. She didn't seem shaken by his words.

"I know it's hard for you. Because you're not what you were, Gage."

"No," he said, blinking once, steady. "I'm not what I was. I don't take orders anymore. Not from no man. Now I only fight for what I think is right."

• • •

A sea breeze broke over the white, walled balcony of the granite bastille that rose like a fortress from the thundering cliff, far above the sandy air, torn and slashed with foam from the crashing tide.

The conquering darkness of dusk was settling against the ocean-stained walls of the majestic edifice that dominated the Italian coast with an authority that was both sentient and commanding; an oppressive force that stood unchallenged on ancient stones.

Cloaked in an elegant but simply designed purple robe, the man, crowned by a mane of shoulder-length white hair, stood on the mist-torn balcony of the structure, staring into the darkening sea. The pale sun's dying glow failed to penetrate the ocean's expanse, but danced faintly in flaming waves. And yet, still, he watched, as if reading something beyond the somber hue.

For a long time he stood, imperious and alone, until a thin, formally attired man approached him.

"All is in order, sir."

Silent, the white-haired man turned at the words, revealing a face of lean aristocratic beauty, concentrated and calm, placid to its depths, evenly tanned and aged far less than his fifth decade. The blue eyes seemed to glint deeply with immeasurable intelligence and benevolence, even challenging the obvious measure of experienced strength that graced his muscular form with masculine poise.

Without words he nodded politely and walked across the balcony into the structure. Then, once inside the palatial fortress, he moved to a glistening black obsidian table, lightly placing a hand on the open folder, ignoring those who waited.

In the dusk, standing alone at the end of the ageless volcanic slab, the white-haired man was outlined against the sun. In the solemnity of the moment, cloaked in the purple glow of his Romeo Giglia waist-length robe, its silver clasps shining in the faint light, he seemed regal. His cotton twill shirt was open at the collar, and his heavy-soled laceless boots blended perfectly but casually against his black cotton pants.

Neither of the other two men in the room moved or spoke while he gazed upon the file. After a moment the man's Atlantean face was raised, patiently searching the eyes of the others present at the table. His gaze settled upon a priest.

"And shall you illuminate this for me, old friend?" he asked quietly in a pacific, calming voice of solitude. "Will you be the one to unravel this mystery?"

Father Stanford Aquanine D'Oncetta only shook his head, respectful, but demurring. The white-haired man nodded, equally respectful, but commanding, and gracefully turned his attention away.

A tall man, the only other occupant in the room, stepped forward. "We have encountered grave problems, Augustus," he said with a faint British accent.

Augustus smiled at the remark. "It does not require sensitive ears to hear thunder, Charles." He laughed lightly. "But there is no need for fear. Our forces are invisible, and our defenses complex. We are not vulnerable to attack."

Charles Stern removed his tweed jacket and laid it across a black, lacquered rattan chair. "The situation is slightly more complicated than that, Augustus. You know about this man, Gage. He will be dealt with shortly. But there is something else." He hesitated. "We still do not know where the priest hid the manuscript. And now, unfortunately, Santacroce is dead."

D'Oncetta raised his eyes. "Dead?"

"Yes," Stern said, a faint trace of dejection in the tone. "After we finally located the priest we took him to secure quarters and began the interrogation. Some time after the medication wore off, the priest attempted to grab a weapon..." He made a vague, fatal wave of his hand. "Sato..."

D'Oncetta smiled serenely, leaning back. "A most masterful interrogation, Stern. Sato is a most useful operative. Does he, by chance, have access to a nuclear device? I should like to know." He motioned majestically toward the glass wall, sweeping along the expanse of ocean. "There are many, distant lands of the world that I have not visited yet."

Stern stepped closer to the priest, tall and imposing.

"You're a fool, D'Oncetta!" he said. "Don't attempt to blame me for this failure. Yes, Santacroce is dead. Sato is too easily capable of that! But I warned you of this man Gage. I warned you that he would cause complications. But you refused to recognize the threat that he posed. And now, not only have you allowed him into the Westchester mansion, but you allowed him to reach, to *rescue*, Halder and his daughter."

D'Oncetta laughed. "I did not *allow* anything, my friend. As you say, Gage is a most capable man. And, in all honesty, we took every possible security measure."

"Your people are amateurs, priest." Stern shook his head. "Gage would go through them like chaff."

"He did." D'Oncetta surrendered the argument. "Perhaps you would pleasure an opportunity to meet with this man?"

Stern was unfazed. "Yes, D'Oncetta, I would pleasure that opportunity. And I would eliminate him because I would not underestimate him. I would respect him as he must be respected. As wisdom demands that he be respected. I would not allow arrogance to blind me, as it does you."

Augustus raised a hand for silence, focused on D'Oncetta, who had ceased smiling at Stern.

"And the containment plan has been initiated?" he asked the priest.

"Yes," replied D'Oncetta carefully. "Extensive arrangements are underway to insure that investigations are directed and controlled. Our resources are comprehensive. I do not foresee any impediments that might circumvent the prearranged decisions."

Augustus nodded, looked at Stern. "Charles, what did you receive from the priest before his unavoidable death?"

Stern's control appeared complete. "We know that he has buried it somewhere. He telephoned Father Simon the day after he removed it from the Archives and told the old man where he had rehidden it. We obtained that much during the interrogation. Apparently Santacroce was asking for absolution, a confession. Before he died he told us that Simon requested permission to put the information in a letter, in case something untoward happened to him. If Gage reached the old man, and we have every reason to believe he did ..." He cast D'Oncetta a sullen glance. "... then Simon surely told him of the letter."

Stern took a casual, relaxed step towards Augustus. "Simon was under surveillance from the beginning, Augustus, so we are certain that he never left the Cathedral of Saint Thomas until we removed him ourselves. Especially not after Santacroce was taken. Therefore we are certain that if Simon did, indeed, leave Gage a letter, it is hidden somewhere in the cathedral. And that is where Gage must come to retrieve it." He paused. "As of this point, our staff, who have penetrated the basilica, have informed me that Gage has not entered the grounds. Of that they are certain. They are watching for him."

Augustus's glacier-blue eyes glinted. "And can we locate this letter, discover where it is hidden within Saint Thomas, before the American arrives?"

Stern continued, "Saint Thomas is exceedingly large, Augustus. It would take months, perhaps even years of random searching to uncover it. Such an action would immediately attract the attention of Rome. And, as you know, that is something we must avoid. Clement is already angry."

"So what do you suggest?"

Stern walked closer to speak face-to-face with the elegantly robed figure. "Gage will come for the letter, Augustus. He would come for the letter if hell itself stood in his path. My plan is to allow him inside the church. Allow him to retrieve the letter for us. Then we capture him to obtain the letter and interrogate him to discover the location of Halder, his daughter, and the translator."

D'Oncetta interrupted, smiling. "A wild plan, Stern. A method of the truly desperate. It seems that you have gained nothing but desperation from all your exacting labor and toil."

"We have deception and confusion serving us." Augustus descended upon D'Oncetta. "And those are always our greatest weapons. Together they have sustained us since the beginning, and they are sufficient to protect our purpose until its consummation."

A gigantic ocean wave smashed into the cliff, reaching halfway up the wall to slash the air with a foaming, thunderous roar.

"Only one step remains between sea and land, my friends." Augustus glanced solemnly upon each of them before centering his gaze into the distant darkness. "And to hasten that end we must find the manuscript. It will consolidate our forces, revealing the master plan hidden from us for these many years. It will illuminate the secrets of our ancestors, teach us the methods of their power." His voice fell lower, quieter. "Then Israel will fall, and the world will be purified."

Reaching, Augustus slowly removed a large, glossy photograph from the file on the table. It was a photograph of a man, aged into his late twenties, taken at some point of heavy training in the desert. Eyes cold and focused stared off the page.

"No one can prevent our victory," he continued. "We have gained too much ground. But you are correct, Charles. This man, this Jonathan Gage, has already complicated matters. And if old Father Simon sensed that his life was finally forfeit, he might well have left something for his 'adopted son.' We know, by our unknown communion with Simon in his private prayers, that he believes Gage is destined to serve some divine purpose in all this. The old priest has prayed for Gage often enough to annoy even me with his ceaseless requests for grace. But Simon's mystical vision for Gage will be their undoing. Because Gage will indeed come for the letter, even as Simon asked. He will feel compelled to fulfill his loyalty to the old man. And then we shall have Gage, the letter, and the location of the manuscript."

Augustus turned with superior benevolence to D'Oncetta.

"Return to Rome, my friend. Smooth over our peculiar activities with those at the Palace. Do what you can to placate Clement's wrath. Simon was his friend. If he wishes to speak with me, advise him that I shall be pleased to obey his desire. Then rest. You have done well. Charles and The Order will deal with Gage."

D'Oncetta rose, bowing respectfully, and with only a slight, condescending glance at Stern, turned away.

Kertzman frowned. He was in a foul mood. An Army 201, the standard military record of training, assignment, commendation, and distinctive service was open on his desk ... the file of Jonathan M. Gage.

Kertzman's ugly, gray concrete office in the Pentagon's E Wing was spartan and, after seven years, still largely unfurnished; a working man's office.

Two photographs decorated the room. One was a Vietnam-era picture of him carrying a badly wounded soldier to a medical chopper. The other, displayed prominently on his regulation-issue green metal desk, was an actual posed photograph of him and his wife. Taken three years back, it revealed a smiling Kertzman embracing his wife with the relaxed happiness of their thirty-third wedding anniversary. Kertzman stared at the photo a moment, remembering.

He glanced at his watch. Ten minutes.

Ten minutes before Radford and this new guy, Milburn, would arrive. He didn't have much time. But he was almost a bona fide expert at reading, writing, and even, when the rare occasion had compelled him, falsifying files.

Kertzman's conscience had never been troubled by the rare and successful deceptions he had committed since he became a law enforcement officer over 34 years ago. He reasoned that when you're dealing with snakes you sometimes have to think like a fox. And he had never *really* crossed the line of what he thought was right. Oh, he had come close a few times, had maybe even danced across it for a second to snatch someone who really needed snatching. But these were isolated instances, not a way of life.

Kertzman remembered "Wild Jack" Stormcloud, the full-blooded Navaho who ran heavy crack traffic through the Dakotas from Texas for five years. As a South Dakota trooper, Kertzman worked for two years to build a case against Wild Jack, and had constantly failed. Not enough evidence. The Indian was crafty. But it had all come down in flames when Kertzman planted enough cocaine in Stormcloud's vehicle to justify an arrest, and then a search of his property. After that, enough legitimate evidence was eventually uncovered to buy Wild Jack a long prison term. Good enough. Kertzman had never regretted the act. He wasn't above stooping down to pick anyone up. But, he told himself, he had never hurt someone who was truly innocent.

Kertzman grunted; there weren't too many of the truly innocent left.

Frowning, Kertzman concentrated on the information before him. He skipped the preliminaries, initial assignments, inprocessing, and immediate basic courses. His sleepy, lionlike gaze swept down the page to find something more interesting, searching...

Jonathan M. Gage

- Graduated Northern Warfare School in January, 1979, Fort G, Greely, Alaska.
- Received Master Parachutist Badge in February, 1979.
- Graduated Special Forces, Pathfinder, in March, 1979. Earned Master Parachutist Badge.

Kertzman shifted, unimpressed. He hadn't found anything yet that would make this guy so special, but he knew there was a lot more to come. He flipped the page, scanned past stations and basic language schools until he found a more interesting section.

- July, 1979, trained in Special Warfare Tactics with British SAS, earned British SAS Badge.

Uh-huh, said Kertzman softly to himself, here we go.

- Graduated from three-week Sniper course at classified site in Nevada, September, 1979.
- Entered Advanced Demolition School at Fort Devons, Massachusetts, in January, 1980. Graduated top of class.
- Completed HALO (High Altitude Low Opening) School in April, 1981, at Fort Benning.

The HALO listing reminded Kertzman of the startling and mesmerizing moment he had watched a Navy SEAL practicing a low altitude opening after falling 11,500 feet from a 12,000 foot jump. The poor guy's main chute had flagged and there was no time to deploy the backup—a primary danger with high altitude low opening jumps. Kertzman could mentally replay the ten-year-old moment like it was yesterday, the body striking the ground at over 100 miles an hour, rebounding limply from the impact to soar over 30 feet into the air, falling again. A sickening and hypnotic sight.

Kertzman grunted sympathetically with the memory, went on.

- Entered Basic Special Forces Scuba School, January, 1982. Graduated top of class.
- Entered Covert Warfare School, February, 1982, under joint U.S.-Israeli Command Center. Course taught by agents of Israeli Secret Service, United States Army Delta Force. Graduated third in class.

There it was. Kertzman's gaze centered on the listing. That explained the seminary.

- Entered Advanced Tactical Warfare School, March, 1982, at the National War College. Graduated second in class.
- Entered Underwater Demolitions at Norfolk, May, 1982. Eight-week course taught by Department of Navy Special Warfare Unit designated as SEALs.
- Recruited for Delta Force in August, 1982, and began eight-week qualification course. Graduated top of class and assigned to Delta Command, Fort Bragg, North Carolina, in October, 1982.

Grimly, Kertzman turned the page, read over a list of combat missions. Finally, he scanned the list of badges, service awards: Master Parachutist, British Parachutist, Ranger TAB, Pathfinder, Sniper, Jungle Expert, Demolition Expert, Special Warfare Expert, Scuba, Air Assault, Silver Star, two Purple Hearts, a Bronze Star...

- Resigned at rank of staff sergeant in July of 1986.

Sighing, feeling a vague depression, Kertzman read the list of commendations over and over again, puzzled. Then, tiredly, he laid down the file. For a long time he stared at nothing, wondering. Then he leaned back, gorilla arms hanging limp at his sides, and gazed sullenly at the steaming coffeepot across from the desk.

A still small voice told him, this is as wrong as it gets. This guy wouldn't betray his country. Sure, Sims and Myrick would. Even high-ups like Kim Philby of Britain or Edward Lee Howell of the CIA would. But Sims and Myrick were just underqualified spooks playing high-tech spy. And Philby and Howell were only soft-gut rich boys who liked easy lives and overcomplicated beliefs, who had never had to bloody their hands for what they believed, guys who never had to put it all in the wind, hoping against hope they would survive the storm.

This guy, Gage, he was different. He'd *been* there, and then some. Twenty combat missions, 36 confirmed kills in Delta, eight from Sniper, and the rest on fast-entry assaults in classified missions. Kertzman knew that the actual number of non-confirmed kills was probably three times that much.

A soft whistle escaped Kertzman's lips. Gage had *paid* for what he believed. It didn't make sense that he would turn.

Still, if anyone could be the man, Gage could. But it didn't feel right. Didn't even look right by the statistics. Gage would have passed psychological tests out the kazoo. So he was wrapped tight. Had to be. Kertzman didn't know what Delta Force was using now, but they had begun using nightvision, laser-optic surveillance, and satellite location of individual troops long before any other branch of the military had even heard of the technology. And that was 15 years ago. No telling what they possessed today. It was all classified, top secret or above. There were discreet rumors of cyborg-type armor that enhanced strength and endurance, lightweight clothing made of ballistic materials that changed colors automatically to match surroundings, like a chameleon, and other rumors of Star Wars-type weapons. But, whatever, Gage was part of it, and that meant he had received the highest clearance, the highest trust.

An old jungle instinct, 20 years gone but strangely alive of late, alerted Kertzman to the approach at his door. He was on his feet before the two men entered without knocking.

Radford entered first, his charcoal gray, wide-lapeled Seville-Row suit announcing him. And Kertzman took a second to size up Milburn; just under six feet, light-medium build with a military haircut gone long and shaggy. Kertzman shifted to the face, saw the bland, ubiquitous, carefully cultivated expression of a professional federal agent. He saw the customary, slight smile, wide-open eyes, and knew there was a whole world of lies behind those eyes. Milburn extended a hand.

He shook the hand. "Mr. Milburn."

"Call me Bob." A beaming smile.

"OK," said Kertzman curtly. "Have a seat. Let's get on with it."

Radford appeared comfortable in the green, plastic-covered metal chair. Milburn settled in, shifting his coat, loosening his tie with a slight twist of his head.

Nervous?

Kertzman logged it, like he logged everything. Just another incidental nothing he would keep *back there* in case he might need it later.

"So," Radford began, "I guess you know, Kertzman, after our little meeting the other day I did some checking." He gestured to the file. "I would never have thought of it if you hadn't led me to it. But there it is: Plain as day."

Kertzman muttered an indescribable sound, not a grunt, but more of half-word grunt *something* that intimated what his brutish decorum prevented him from actually saying.

"Maybe," Kertzman added slowly.

"If anybody could cause problems, it'd be him. Bob, here, knows Gage better than anybody in the world." Radford placed a hand on Milburn's shoulder. "I think we can use him, Kertzman. He was in Gage's unit in Delta, all of them fast-entry types. Cowboys. He knows how Gage thinks, how he moves, what he's trained to do. He knows what Gage prefers, his weaknesses, his friends. And with any luck, he might even be able to second-guess him."

Kertzman stared at Milburn. "Fast entry, huh?"

Kertzman had never reserved any profound respect for these elite, specialized units. In Vietnam he learned that most of the time they parachuted themselves into white-hot zones they couldn't EVAC out of and were forced to radio for the regular grunts, like he'd been, to rescue their specialized little teams from annihilation.

"Is there any other way?" Milburn replied, a truculent gesture of his chin.

Kertzman almost smiled, resisted the impulse. "I don't know. Tell me about it."

Milburn had obvious pride in what he had been. "Fast entry means no warning, Kertzman. Delta doesn't believe in warnings. We never have. That stuff is for the FBI or ATF. When we move on an objective, we do it without warning and it's explosive. It's maximum force from the first step, finished in thirty seconds. That's the only way to stay alive. That's the only way to keep the objective alive. All of that 'throw down your gun' stuff is for the movies. Warnings defeat your entire purpose, just like hesitation. If we go in, we hit everything, armed or unarmed. No hesitation. No prisoners. No mercy. It's maximum force from the first step. No exceptions. We neutralize everyone, and then we secure the objective."

"Like Gage did, if it was Gage, in the professor's house," said Kertzman. "Or at the seminary."

Milburn nodded. "That's what he's trained to do. And I can promise you that he'll react like he's trained to react. He can't stop himself." He leaned forward, gesturing. "Would you like for me to explain to you specifically what Gage did in Delta?"

"I'd like to know why you two are so certain that it's Gage," said Kertzman. "From the way I see it, it could be anybody with this kind of training."

Radford was quick. "We've done some additional investigation, Kertzman. We have some ... people ... who have informed us that Gage is somehow involved in this. And the physical description that police and bystanders provided at the campus fits him." Radford lifted his hands expressively. "We have some depositions. I haven't had a chance to show them to you."

Kertzman fixed him with a dead gaze, a wisp of anger faintly visible. "Well I need to see those depositions," he said flatly, adding a slight growling end to the sentence.

Radford had already removed them from his briefcase. "They don't say much," he said, apologetic. "But it's enough. I think it would be prudent to pursue the investigation."

Kertzman was aware that his gaze had settled, unfocused, on the depositions, realized his mind was trying to put together what he had heard with what he had learned from Gage's file. No need to read them now. He could get to them later. He looked at Milburn and leaned back, studying the CIA man.

"Alright, Mr. Milburn," Kertzman said slowly, folding massive arms over a bull-of-the-field chest, "why don't you tell me what you know."

• • •

Concealed in somber light, Augustus gazed upon the open military file of Jonathan Gage. A single lamp, subdued and soft, illuminated the room while Stern, arms folded, waited patiently to the side.

"How many men did Gage dispatch, Charles?" Augustus asked.

"Six," replied Stern rigidly. "He wounded a seventh."

Augustus looked up sharply from the file, his face concentrated. "Wounded, you say?"

"Yes."

"And why did Gage allow this man to live?"

Stern shook his head. "I don't know."

An ice-blue stare fixed on him. "Was it an error, Charles? A mistake?"

Stern took his time to reply. "Gage is not the kind of man who makes mistakes," he said slowly. "I believe he made a conscious decision not to kill the operative. I don't know why. It goes against his training, against the actions of his past. But it is the only explanation that aligns with facts."

Augustus's face reflected deepening thought. He looked down again, his fingers resting lightly on the face in the photograph as if to somehow capture thoughts of the mind contained within.

"Members of The Order are already in New York," Stern continued. "Within hours they will be waiting for Gage at Simon's cathedral. And then they will wait for him to come retrieve the letter that reveals where Santacroce hid the manuscript. At that point we will capture him, as I said, and obtain the letter. Then we interrogate him to find the location of the rest. And after that we eliminate them all, according to the containment plan."

Augustus continued to focus on the face in the photograph. He asked softly, "And why do you believe Gage takes a stand against us, Charles?"

The voice was so quiet Stern strained to hear it against the waves roaring beneath the cliff.

"Vengeance," Stern replied. "He wants to avenge the old priest. Or, perhaps, Halder has convinced Gage that destroying the manuscript will also destroy our plans. It is difficult to know, for certain. But, for the most part, I believe it is vengeance. That's why Gage never worried about us monitoring his meetings with the old priest. He knew that Simon was involved in something and wanted us to know that Simon was under his protection. The old man only met with Gage to talk with him about spiritual matters, to encourage him not to return to his old life. I am convinced that Simon did not even know we were monitoring their meetings. But I believe Gage knew. He would have seen the surveillance team. He sees everything. And he met with the old man, anyway. To send us a message."

"Yes," said Augustus meditatively. "He was telling us that Simon was family. And that is why you believe Gage comes against us? For vengeance?"

"Yes," replied Stern, considering. "But vengeance is an uneven motivation. Gage's emotions will make him less effective. Although he is still proficient enough to neutralize D'Oncetta's toy soldiers, The Order will eliminate him."

"Perhaps, old friend," Augustus said quietly, still not looking up from the file. "But I do not believe it is vengeance which motivates Gage." Augustus stared at the photograph even longer, finally breaking his silence in a cryptic voice. "No, not for vengeance does Gage come against us. It is...absolution that he seeks."

Stern stared at the robed form. "Absolution, Augustus?"

"Yes, Charles. Absolution. Freedom. His own redemption is the treasure Gage seeks. Not vengeance." His aristocratic face hardened in concentration. "Yes...old Simon taught him well. It is for his own salvation that Gage takes a stand against us. And he will not stop until he finds it. Not for fear, or pain, or however much suffering he must endure. His love for Simon was great, but his love for his newfound God is something more. Something more...altogether."

Augustus gazed into the cold gray eyes.

"Yes...a very dangerous man."

"A grand conspiracy, professor?"

Gage tossed another stick of wood into the fireplace with the skeptical question, sending a shower of sparks upwards into the chimney.

Malachi laughed softly, amused. "There *are* no grand conspiracies, Gage. Only small ones, as you might say. And even the servants and emissaries, who perform their tasks so readily, do not themselves truly understand what dark forces have mastered their fate. The truth is an apparition within a fog, a spectre hidden behind a haze of ancient and modern legend."

Gage settled onto the floor, leaning against the couch where Sarah casually reclined, nursing a cool glass of wine. Hours earlier they had gathered in the rustic cabin's front room, watching the somber night settle beyond the windows with oppressive cold.

Barto, a pacific calm gracing his wildly bearded face, munched meditatively on a marshmallow that he had roasted in the fire with a straightened coat hanger. A half-bag of marshmallows rested on the floor beside his chair.

Malachi leaned against the mantel, staring into the flames. In the glow of the fire the old man seemed younger than his seventh decade. But Gage knew that the strain of their ordeal had extracted a sure measure of strength from the tall, thin frame.

"That's really not much to go on, professor," Gage muttered, not looking up. "I sort of need a name."

Malachi shook his head, apologetic. "I have none, Gage. There is a priest. Father Stanford Aquanine D'Oncetta. He is the emissary of a small, unknown consistory of cardinals. But the cardinals are only the servants of someone else, and D'Oncetta is, in truth, the lackey of whoever that may be. He is the only one I can identify. Simon could never persuade Pope Clement to tell us any more."

"So you don't know any of these people?"

Malachi sighed. "No. I do not. I have tried. But I do not know. Neither Simon nor I has ever been able to discover even a single name besides D'Oncetta. It might be an entire council of people, or it might be only a single man. No one knows."

"Someone knows," Gage said.

Malachi looked at him. "Who?"

"Clement," replied Gage coldly.

"Yes." Malachi raised an eyebrow, regarded the muscular form reclining against the couch. "Yes, Clement knows." He stared at Gage a moment, as if divining the intention behind the quiet words.

Gage shifted, staring into the flames. "Tell me why this group wants this manuscript so badly."

A soft, bitter laugh echoed from Malachi. "That is not easy to say."

"Why?"

"Because you must first understand what they believe, Gage. Then you will understand more clearly why it is that they want the manuscript."

Gage was indifferent. "Alright. Tell me what they believe. We can start from there."

Malachi was silent, considering. "It seems clear to me sometimes," he began, "and then sometimes it becomes obscured by its complexity." He stared at the crackling, hissing fire, his old face bright with flame. Looked up again. "Did you know, Gage, that the ancient Egyptians considered the Pharaoh to be God?"

Gage nodded.

"How easy it has been for men, even from primitive times, to seek immortality in themselves," Malachi continued. "Immortality. Power. Freedom. Strength to accomplish whatever man's will would desire."

Outside, an owl's booming howl echoed in the night.

"We have traveled so short a distance in so many years," he said. "Today men stand on the shoulders of formulaic logic that leads them, without alternatives, they say, to the ultimate decision that man alone, within himself, contains the power and the secrets of Godhood. And they lean heavily upon their complicated reasoning to explain why such a decision is the only true destination of high and critical thought. But if that is true, then why have profoundly primitive cultures, inhabiting vanished civilizations long lost to the Earth, forever held this same conviction? Why? I will tell you why. Because fearful man is forever destined to approach the void, to move towards that verge which separates the now from the unknown. It is *the* human tendency, as Kant explained. Yet man, because he is inherently selfish and self-serving above all things, will travel no road without the full measure of what he might possess. In his self-centered dominion, man will surrender nothing that must not absolutely be surrendered. So he is faced with the dilemma of entering the next world without losing what he has gained in this one." Without humor, Malachi laughed curtly, a sound of contempt. "A difficult thing, to be sure.

"So in ancient times men studied the Cosmos to find the bridge across the ocean of death. And he saw that the sun, in all its life-creating power, was what gave the Earth continual sustenance. Therefore, to him, the Cosmos became the source that he might use to escape death, creating within himself the power to claim eternal life while at the same time possessing all that he loved, surrendering nothing."

Malachi glanced at them.

"A powerful temptation, if primitive. The Pharaoh was considered to be God because of his soul's divine union to the sun. He was considered more than mere man, and more than Nature. He was the ultimate Sun-Man, or Man-God, in the most natural sense. He was one with the Cosmos, holding the keys of life by the power of his will and by the power of the sun. For his very will was his life, both for the here and the hereafter. Seemingly, it was the ultimate escape from death and from moral limitations.

"You see, evil did not exist, at least not for the Man-God who found his freedom in the vast and infinite universe. For Nature itself was neutral to good and evil. The only moral limitations that might be imposed on the Man-God were the limitations of his own, divine will. And evil could be defined as that power that prevented him from exercising that free moral will. The end purpose of his existence became, therefore, the power to create that thing that was the object of his desire.

"But at the emergence of the Hebrew God, the Man-God was confronted by his ultimate nemesis. An enemy that perfectly defied his deific claim. So Yahweh, the Ancient of Days, became the scorned and rejected scourge of the world, despised as an enemy of the ultimate free man. The ageless collision of forces. Man and God. And men who would not kneel accused the God of Israel of being the waste product of a condemning moral code propagated by foolish men who must *create* an imaginary God that is beyond themselves. And Yahweh was condemned in the old world as the foolish false creation of weak men who were simply unable to survive or rule by the power of the Cosmos and by their own hand. A conflict of decision, of decided faith or non-faith. And it was on this ground of the unknowable that the battle first began."

Malachi cast Gage a frowning glance.

"I call it unknowable because this ground is ultimately the dominion of faith, Gage, where nothing can be completely understood empirically, and a man must decide, for himself alone, to believe as he would believe," he continued, solemn. "I am old, now, and I have forgotten much of what I knew. But I still understand the limitations of empirical thought. I recall all the questions of fundamental certainty that evaded the critical reason of Descartes, Augustine, Hegel, Pascal, and Kant. So I do not claim to completely understand ultimate truth, nor do I stand alone in my ignorance of it. I know that I can defend my faith as far as reason may ascend, in any discipline of thought, be it philosophy or theology or science or archeology. And I am certain that I hold a perfectly and ultimately reasonable faith. But, in the final plain of human reason, faith is faith, and knowledge is knowledge. God always has been, and always shall remain, the ultimate mystery. Always there will be fundamental questions of uncertainty that only faith may bridge. And it is because of what I know of these fundamental questions, and faith itself, that I say with confidence that reason will never fully close the void between the known and the unknowable. Faith, alone, is forever the final step." He paused. "It's true, you know, that the secret things belong to God. And yet those who worship the Man-God, or this Sun-Man of the Cosmos, have, since time immemorial, fought with swords of red hate to destroy the restricting moral influence of men who would live by the words of Yahweh. And this is because the Man-God, from the very beginning, has regarded Yahweh's very existence as a hated and mortal threat to his moral autonomy. And for certain, the very idea of an omnipotent and holy God is an attack upon the ground of what he holds most dear: Himself.

"It is nothing unique to the history of man," Malachi sighed, continuing. "One side elects to believe that the Cosmos, or Nature, or the Superior Man himself, holds the keys of eternal life. They believe that man himself should be the ultimate measure of Good and Evil. While *we* believe that a holy and righteous God has given man the commandment that we must worship Him with all our heart, mind, soul, and spirit, abide by this Law, and claim no moral sovereignty for ourselves. One side claims that they themselves are God *as* Man, the ultimate expression of what is good and right and true. The other side simply chooses to worship and serve the God of Abraham, Isaac, and Moses, who proclaimed that we must worship no other God before Him."

Malachi paused, frowning.

Silence hung like a heavy cloak over the room.

"The dream of the God-Man is to decide his own moral dominion, and by the freedom that he claims, extend that moral dominion over the Earth," the old man said, distant eyes on flame. "It is a perversion of a solemn truth, for man was, indeed, created to have dominion over the Earth. But not by the might of his own hand. No, and not by the power of the sword, nor the strength of flames." He shook his head. "No, it was by the mercy of God that man was born to subdue the Earth, remaining within the justice that God ordained.

"And it was against this dark dream of mortal *cosmic* dominion that Simon died resisting. Because he knew what the end of that dream would be. He remembered what oppression was wrought in the holocaust of ancient empires who held the God-Man as a supreme being. He remembered the dynasties of Mesopotamia which worshipped the gods of the Earth; evil monarchies that forced the predatory will of the strongest upon the weak. For always the strongest rule where there is no dominion higher than man himself.

"We should learn from history; it reveals former things. In ancient worlds there were many religions that held man himself to be the all-embracing Absolute of good and evil, the decider of his own destiny by the strength of his arm. They rejected the concept of an invisible, omnipotent God who created man and then revealed Himself to man, a God who established codes of conduct that could not be altered in the fleshly domain. And, even as it is now, it was a time of decision. A time to decide by an act of will to serve the God-Man or serve the Hebrew God that, alone, breathed life into dust to make flesh, and still retained the right to decide life or death *for* that flesh."

Malachi shifted, released a long breath.

"Measure a god by the sacrifice he seeks. Measure a man by the prey he selects. Is it revealing that the ancient empires who worshipped the free moral mind of a master race always selected their sacrifices among the weak, the defenseless, or the poor? Is it a coincidence that all the past dynasties ruled by the God-Man, or Sun-Man, mortared their altars with the same blood? And it's true, you know.

"From the Druids to the Massalians to the keepers of demonic Baal to Dagon to the priests of the Aztec's Xipe Topec, the Sun-God, it was always children and the weakest who were selected for death. Always the weakest. Never the strong, no. And why is that?" Malachi turned towards them, vivid and bright. "I'll tell you why. It's because man without an omnipotent God to restrict his actions will forever serve the *beast* that lives so strongly within, becoming a predator over a fallen world. And, as nature demands, the strongest men become the strongest predators. And as any predator, men will select easy prey before strong. And children are always among the weakest, the most defenseless."

Stillness in the room was unnatural, the poise of listeners afraid to move within the dark content of the words.

"Yes, Gage, predation is the final plateau of the God-Man concept. Not love, and not mercy. For a jungle does not recognize mercy; it only recognizes strength. The strong rule, and the strongest rule completely. And it is this cruel fate that has always been the end of those who find their god in Nature, or in themselves, or in the Cosmos or the Sun. Man as God. Nature as God. The Sun-Man. They cunningly devise whatever idealogy that will allow them to justify their moral autonomy and their predatory lusts. A thousand faces for the same being. A thousand names to personify a god who is exactly what they want him to be. And they violently reject the unyielding moral code imposed upon man by Yahweh, a God who has always enforced a code of justice that would defend the weak, and punish the cruel."

Gage noticed that Malachi's face seemed tired. But he still needed some answers.

"And how does the manuscript work into this?"

"Our enemy believes that the manuscript reveals the names, the family lineage, and the place of birth of the ultimate God-Man, or Sun-Man," Malachi answered steadily, evenly. "And *he* is the one they have waited for during the long centuries. They believe that this God-Man, this superior being, will bring into reality the perfect kingdom, their kingdom, on the Earth. They believe that this ultimate being will conquer the world by the strength of his arm, and the universe by the superiority of his mind. They believe that he will drive the archaic concept of Yahweh from the entire world, rebuilding the Earth in the image of himself. We shall all be one, they say." He shook his head. "Yes, we shall all be servants of the God-Man, which is much better than simply being servants of God. Though it seems to me a petty jealousy. The God-Man would simply have us worship *him*, instead of the God of Abraham, Isaac, and Jacob.

"And this, they call enlightenment..."

He paused. "In any case, Simon and I did indeed read the manuscript, though Simon alone read the section of text that contained the Name. And now, obviously, the manuscript has been stolen from the Archives in Rome, where Clement had suppressed it. And our enemies, these servants of the prophetic God-Man, have chosen to silence any of those who might know enough to protest the crime. But something has gone wrong. Their plans have not succeeded. Did you not say that Simon told you of a priest, Santacroce, who repented of stealing the manuscript and buried it again instead of delivering it to the conspirators?"

Gage nodded.

"Yes, so it seems," Malachi intoned. "And now we are faced with the dilemma of finding and destroying the manuscript before these unknown predators can again obtain it."

Gage seemed confused. "Why does it have to be destroyed?"

"Because we must not allow them to discover the name of this Man-God, Gage. Or the place or the year of his birth."

"Why?"

Malachi turned to him. "Because if our enemy could discover his name, they could nurture him, bring him up. They could have the foundations of his kingdom in place far before the time he is ready to assume the mantle of power."

"And then what?"

"They would turn over the world to him."

Outside, an owl's booming cry carried through the night. Gage stared steadily at Malachi, trying to figure it through.

"So if they don't have the name, then they'll have to wait for him to emerge," Gage reasoned. "They won't be able to protect him, to nurture him. They won't be able to set his kingdom in place. He'll have to do it for himself."

Malachi nodded curtly, stared again into the fireplace.

"Exactly, Gage. And that will be an expenditure of his power. An expenditure that this God-Man does not wish to make. He would like to reserve all of his strength to attack his enemies, to unite the vassal countries that will serve him. Then he would be able to destroy many more of those who stand against him. You see, to build this empire himself, he will have to divide his efforts, his attention. He does not want to spend his time and energy building what could already be in place."

Gage stared down. "And Simon was willing to die for this."

"Simon believed it was worth his life, yes," the professor answered. He stared into the flames, suddenly morose. "The God-Man will come, Gage. It is foretold. It is prophecy, and not prophecy contained in this cursed manuscript. No, it is part of God's plan that the beast will come. He will be defeated in the end of time by the Messiah, in the last great battle on the Earth in the plain of Meggido, not far from where we found you dying in the night. But Simon also believed that anything he could do to weaken the evil one would greatly serve Christ, and save many lives in the future. So, yes, Simon was willing to die for this."

With a gathering intensity Gage focused on the old man. "Beast?"

Malachi did not look up. "It will be a man," he said gravely. "And it will be a beast."

For a long moment Gage's storm-gray eyes remained locked on the professor, the room utterly still. Even the flames seemed subdued. The long silence lengthened, even longer, until finally Gage broke the tension. When he spoke his words were startlingly clear and unhesitating, like a man who speaks louder than necessary to compensate for something else.

"This manuscript...it wouldn't have anything to do with the Antichrist, would it, professor?"

Malachi turned from the fireplace, his face bright with flame. "As a matter of fact, Gage, it does."

"Yeah, yeah, I got it already," Kertzman said, brutal forearms on the desk. A mug of black coffee, topped with thin circles of an unknown, sinister-looking residue, rested beside him, steaming. "I understand what he did in Delta. He was a fast-entry man. The first in, quick decisions, resourceful, all that. But he left Delta in 1986." Kertzman studied the file. "It says he joined Central Intelligence. Why don't I have anything on that?"

Radford spoke up. "Uh...there's a little trouble with clearances."

"Oh?" Kertzman growled, raising his eyebrows ominously. "How'z'bout I get on the horn and talk to a congressman on the Oversight Committee and get all the clearances I need in two minutes?"

"Well, I—" Radford began.

A sledgehammer fist struck the desk. Kertzman was on his feet, brutal, dangerous. He leaned massively forward, huge squared fists pressing into the desk. "Don't mess with me, boy!" he growled, shook his head. "I'm the cowboy who's running this show! Come up against me again and we'll see who's got war experience!"

"Kertzman, look, I'll get it for you," said Radford quickly, rattled but managing, remarkably, to hold steady.

Kertzman noticed that Milburn, unlike the almost perpetually pacific Radford, had actually started at the outburst, and badly. Curiously, Kertzman notched that one for reference. Bad form for a former Delta guy.

An awkward silence followed the moment while Kertzman studied both of them. He had not really lost his temper. He never lost his temper. That was something he had learned in police work almost 20 years ago and remembered it with an old adage: Never let your temper get your head shot off. But he had grown tired of the posturing, the arrogance, had chosen to react with a little fire in order to establish domain, settle these two in their place. Kertzman

117

felt the temptation to continue with the belligerence; it was generally the best approach when dealing with obnoxious cretins. But it was enough. Control was established, territory recognized and accepted by all.

"OK," he muttered after a moment, sitting. "So what did Gage do in CIA?"

"TAC," said Radford quickly, nodding to Milburn. "Bob, here, will explain."

Milburn caught the ball without hesitation. "I suppose you know the problem with counterintelligence operations, Mr. Kertzman?" he asked cautiously.

"No," Kertzman responded flatly. "Educate me."

Milburn twisted awkwardly, a quick gesture.

Another one, thought Kertzman.

"Basically," Milburn said, "counterintelligence differs from normal intelligence work in that counterintelligence attempts to penetrate the security of a foreign network while at the same time preventing any security violations of our own. As you know, our security is often compromised in this field. That's why all of our internal reports are so closely monitored and analyzed. It's a constantly evolving environment. Almost everyone, at one time or another, is in bed with somebody else so it's difficult to maintain integrity. Sometimes we plant a double agent on the Russians only to find out later that he was feigning defection, and feigning alliance with us, too. Instead he'll turn out to be working for someone like East Germany." Milburn made a fatigued gesture, waved his hand. "Double agents. Triple agents. Betrayals. Secret alliances. Games beyond comprehension. It gets complicated."

"I'll bet," said Kertzman.

"In any case," Milburn continued, "over thirty percent of our counterintelligence activities are compromised by some type of security leak. But the percentage is a lot higher in tactical operations where some contractor in the field can turn a lot of money from the other side for a small bit of well-placed information. The stakes are high in that stuff, and a lucrative reward is considered well-spent if it buys information about an opponent's upcoming tactical move, like the sanction of a defector or a preemptive terrorist hit. So in order to shortcircuit this long-term security problem we came up with the concept of a small, self-directed tactical assault unit that would have little connection to formal intelligence channels and would, therefore, be relatively secure."

"Like Israel did in 1972 after the Munich Olympics," said Kertzman, anticipating. "They took six men, gave them money and a list of names, and told them not to come back until they'd killed all of their targets."

"Yes, it was like that." Milburn sighed. "Only not so badly designed. We didn't want it to end up in another Iran-Contra scandal or Watergate fiasco."

"And how did you prevent that?"

"First of all, by selecting the best. Most of the field operatives in Iran or Watergate were supposed to be professionals, but they did sloppy work. Everyone except Liddy, that is. He was good but he used a bad crew. They were incompetent. Just look at the way they tried to pull off the burglary. They had the wrong tools for gaining entrance into the building. Carried incriminating information on them. Taped the locks shut so that anybody could discover entry. And half of them cracked up completely under interrogation." He shook his head. "*Amateurs.* It was stupid. Reckless. Those guys don't even exist compared to the people we selected for Black Light."

"Black Light?" Kertzman grunted.

"That was the designation for the unit," Milburn replied. "Gage was codenamed 'Dragon.'" He paused, leaned back slightly, settling in. "Black Light was a unique unit. It designed its own plans, its own timetables with no idiot supervisors who didn't understand the complexities of tactical assault messing around with things. The Pentagon has known for decades that military tactical teams should be able to design their own plans without civilian interference. Civilians aren't trained to plan or run a tactical operation. It takes millions to even train someone in the military to make decisions like that. You know that much, Kertzman. This arrogant, stupid interference by civilian White House officials, including some presidents, in America's military operations is the primary cause of our catastrophic failures. Commanding men in battle is not a civilian skill. I don't care what you've been elected to. Commanding men in the chaos of battle is a difficult military skill acquired from a lifetime of study and training."

Kertzman nodded. "Yeah, I know. I've seen it. Saw it in Asia. Saw it in police work." He concentrated, probing. "And Black Light was created to go around civilian interference?"

"Right," Milburn said. "The Pentagon couldn't command a team like that because of too much civilian supervision, especially from the White House. So the CIA developed the team, ran them."

"And these guys were America's best commandos?"

"Black Light recruited exclusively from Delta and SEALs," Radford said, a touch of pride. "And Gage was the best fighter Black Light ever saw. He might have even been the best fighter that *any* unit ever saw. That's why he was coded 'Dragon.' Every intelligence agency in the world was afraid of him. They said he was unkillable."

A long silence. Kertzman took a slow, relaxed sip of coffee, sniffed. "So how come Gage was so good?" he asked, flat. "All of you guys had that fancy warfare training."

Milburn shook his head. "Gage was different, Kertzman."

"How so?"

Concentration was evident on the CIA man's face. Kertzman knew he was having trouble finding the words.

"Gage had all the training, yeah, just like the rest of us," Milburn continued. "But he had something different. He had this...strange ability to somehow instantly read a chaotic situation. He was, like, a genius at selecting the perfect tactical response to almost anything. I mean, a real genius. In the jungle, where he could really move around and utilize the terrain, he was a nightmare."

"All you guys go to tactical schools," muttered Kertzman. "I read the file. Covert warfare. Urban warfare. All kinds of warfare. That's part of standard training."

"You don't understand, Kertzman," Milburn answered. "Gage was beyond all that. Way beyond it. He had some kind of...gift ...for unconsciously memorizing terrain, positions, angles of fire, distance. In the most intense firefight you could ever imagine Gage could somehow anticipate the movements of fifty soldiers before they knew what they were going to do themselves. It was like a giant chess game in his head, and he was way ahead of everybody else. It was like he could capture this...tremendous oversight of things. Not just the small picture. A lot of guys can do that. He would have the big picture. It would just *be* there, in his head, the perfect thing to do in order to defeat the enemy. He was at his best in a chaotic situation." He shook his head again. "You're either born with that kind of ability, Kertzman, or you're not. All the training in the world can't give it to you. I knew lots of guys with millions of dollars worth of tactical training. But they could only get the small stuff covered in a combat situation, like a single room, or one side of a building, an alley or ravine. Gage could see it all in his mind, every side of the building, every entrance, every stairway or doorway with distances, approaches, angles of attack, and the best places for ambush. He had the ability to make a split-second analysis and select the perfect tactical response. And let me tell you something, Kertzman, not one man in a million can do that. Not one in ten million. It takes unreal mind speed. Computer speed. That's one reason he was so unbeatable. He was a pure tactical genius."

The room seemed uncomfortable. Kertzman cleared his throat. "So, uh, Gage drew up the plans?"

"He made it a team effort," Milburn said. "He ultimately approved or disapproved ideas, because he was the best at it. But everyone worked on the plan, came up with something everybody could live with. Team integrity, team responsibility. Everyone depending on everyone else in a plan that everybody designed. A lot of close guys. Trusting. It was the only way the unit would work. Like I said, the idea was brilliant. The execution was brilliant, carried out to perfection. No mistakes. And since there was little channel of clearance, there was little threat of leaks. Nobody could call and say, 'you'll be hit at so-and-so time,' because nobody knew. It was an almost perfect idea. Self-controlled and self-financed."

"Self-financed?" Kertzman's implacable eyes opened slightly. "You mean like George Doole was self-financed with Pacific Corporation?"

Milburn nodded slowly, lowered his eyes. The name required little reference: George Doole, Jr., longtime CIA clandestine agent who ran three air proprietaries in Indochina from the early sixties to 1974 and cleared a tax-free, unaudited, legal fortune in the process.

The Central Intelligence Act of 1949 specifically stated that all profits accumulated by clandestine proprietaries could be utilized "without regard to the provisions of law and regulations relating to the expenditure for government funds." As a consequence, dozens of CIA personnel accumulated substantial financial profits through front companies designed to cloak clandestine services. The profits were exempted from government audit and largely ignored by the CIA because of fears that monitoring finances would compromise the secrecy of covert operations.

And, usually, when the CIA decided that a front company no longer merited continued operation, career intelligence personnel would often demand to purchase the company in bargain deals and take early retirement, preferring the huge financial gain that they were accumulating to paltry government service. Consequently fearing that some of the personnel would purposefully reveal the existence of the front company if their demands were unheeded, the CIA, as policy, would complacently agree to sell the company's assets.

Kertzman knew it was the CIA's obsession for secrecy that allowed the financial indiscretions. And he had learned a long time ago that every man had a price.

"Totally self-financed," Milburn continued. "Gage's unit, Black Light, owned a small international transport airline, several arms dealerships, auto dealerships in various countries, including the United States, the works."

"Did the Intelligence Oversight Committee know about this?" Kertzman asked, sensing the size of it all.

Milburn nodded. "They approved it."

"You gotta be kidding me!"

"Calm down, Kertzman," Radford broke in. He raised a hand defensively, and it looked like the NSA man might fall over backwards if Kertzman made a sudden move. "It was an approved CIA operation," he added quickly.

"It *sounds* like a CIA operation! This is just like Task Force 157!"

"Kertzman, Kertzman," Radford said placidly, quickly recovering his ramrod comportment. "It was all legitimate. Approved. It's not a scandal."

But Kertzman knew that it was probably cracked to the core with deceit and lies. Enough money could do that, could turn a good man into a greedy man, a soldier into a broken hero running on fear. The only reason the government didn't see more of it was because few people ever had the opportunity to walk away with enough to keep them hidden for the rest of their lives.

Kertzman scowled moodily, stared between them. It was a moment before he recognized his own thoughts. *Old,* the faint voice told him, *I'm getting too old for this.*

Retirement was beginning to look more and more tempting. Absently, Kertzman reached out and picked up the mug, deliberately took a large swallow of scalding hot coffee. Then he set the cup down, slowly, with a brutal calm. Looked flat dead at Milburn.

"Go on," he said gloomily. "Tell me, exactly, what Black Light did."

"Protected assets," continued Milburn calmly. "It sanctioned defectors that were too far gone to turn back around, neutralized terrorist threats, snatched people we needed to interrogate. Basically it executed any orders that Gage received from his supervisor. Gage was only a staff sergeant, but he was in charge. There was no civilian field personnel. In the beginning Black Light had twenty-one carefully handpicked men, and they rotated on missions to keep everybody fresh. No inefficiency in combat. They were artists. The real thing. Mechanics. And they did it all. Everywhere. They designed and completed snatches, thefts, sanctions, surveillance, whatever it took. Towards the end there were only eleven men remaining. Because of the high-risk missions, attrition was high. And because of security problems we had trouble with replacements. But those eleven were still working assignments, handling the front companies well enough."

Kertzman waited a moment. When nothing else followed, he said, "Gage must be pretty smart. Handling a half-dozen companies and a hit team, too."

"Well, he had a lot of people who didn't know any better running the companies," said Milburn. "Few of the support people ever knew that the companies were CIA-owned. They might have suspected, but that could be handled. The most difficult aspect of the entire operation was orchestrating the integrations of civilian support services for Black Light without attracting attention from civilian employees. It was always complicated, but Gage managed it."

Milburn looked away, slightly twisted his head. "It's strange. As smart as he was, Gage had one truly unbreakable rule: Keep it simple. I heard him say it a thousand times. He figured, the simpler it was, the less he'd have to worry about. 'Always keep it simple,' he'd say. 'Then there's not much that can go wrong.'"

"But something did go wrong," Kertzman said gruffly.

Milburn stared at him, face suddenly impassive. Kertzman waited a minute, got tired of it. "So what went wrong, Milburn?"

"I don't know."

"Sure you do."

Milburn stretched his arms, sat back. "Something went wrong, Kertzman. That's all we know. We found out later that Gage was liquefying assets of corporations, stashing the money somewhere. We never tracked it down. We think he set himself up to slide out one day without a trace. Don't know why, exactly. He's probably got some safe houses, some farms somewhere. But they're impossible to find. You know how it's done. Always remove yourself three layers from the signature. Establish flags in the first two identities to alert you if someone's checking. We know he spread the money around on the team, told people to prepare for that great day because this gravy train wasn't going to run forever. He gave away a lot, but we know he kept enough for himself to live comfortably for the rest of his life. Then the entire unit was wiped out in Israel."

"Israel?"

Milburn nodded. "They were only there for surveillance. But they were wiped out in a firefight. No survivors, but Gage's body was never identified. It's possible that he was in a building when it went down and was simply burned up. Lost. But we suspect he's alive. We suspect he might have even set the entire ambush up to cover his tracks, to vanish with the money."

Kertzman was silent, troubled by something he had heard, but he couldn't place it. Despite the fact that he didn't like Milburn or Radford, he had to admit that the idea was plausible. "How much money are we talking about? Millions?"

"More."

Kertzman's eyebrows raised. "Ten million?"

Milburn appeared uncomfortable.

"More?" asked Kertzman loudly.

"Listen, Kertzman," he said, gesturing with empty hands. "There's no way to really tell. But it's a lot more than a million. It might even be a lot more than ten million."

Kertzman leaned back, frowning. The uneasiness that he had already felt was suddenly and deeply underrun by another, stronger current of doubt. This was deception beneath covert operations beneath mystery men on unknown and probably illegal missions with an untraceable fortune. He was surrounded with betrayals and secrets and no one he could trust to tell him the truth.

Without thinking Kertzman reached into his left shirt pocket, absently searching for a cigarette, remembered he had quit.

He shook his head. Might be time to start back.

Sarah sat, arms around her knees, watching silently as Gage cleaned and oiled the semiautomatic pistol. Before him on the kitchen table lay equipment he would take to New York: a night-visor with two fully-charged battery packs, a Browning Hi-Power, four extra clips, a long thin wire, pocket-sized maglight, a tightly taped cellophane bag of assorted pills for pain, all of them high-impact barbiturates, and a small black daypack that contained three stun grenades, a fragmentation grenade, and an alarm by-pass circuit device.

Gage glanced at her, smiled, as he went through the routine of oiling the Hi-Power. She smiled back, but her eyes were separated from the effort.

Barrel cleaned, Gage inserted it into the slide with the guiding rod and spring. Then the slide went into the receiver, and the holding pin was inserted. Instantly, like a machine, Gage cracked the slide a half dozen times, checking and rechecking the motion, a rhythmic series of clicks that repeated themselves again and again, human hands moving with reflexive familiarity over the weapon.

"That's a ritual," Sarah said suddenly.

Gage looked at her, laughed. "Yeah, it is."

"You're superstitious."

Gage shook his head, appearing shocked. "No, not super-stitious. Not really. I've done things differently in the past, broken from my routine before a mission. But then it would prey on my mind." He shrugged. "I can't explain it. I do the same thing every time out because..."

"You're superstitious." She laughed

Gage shook his head, smiling. "Yeah, OK. I'm—careful. So I don't get distracted worrying about whether I forgot something. It gets me into a mindset."

From a black bag beside the table, Gage lifted a matte black submachine gun, another MP5, a replica of the one he had lost in the firefight on the campus, only larger, without the cutdown barrel. He had already cleaned and oiled the weapon and six extra clips. Methodically, he began loading the clips with 30 rounds of armor-piercing 9mm.

Sarah stared silently at the weapon.

"Why do you carry so many bullets?" she asked.

Gage calculated that it wasn't a voice of fear, or even of moral judgment. Simply a question.

"It's the rule," he replied, frowning. "I've learned that if you're going to walk into a hot situation you need to have as many rounds as you can carry. In a firefight you'll use a lot of them real quick." He shrugged. "Everybody does. It's the heat, the panic. And I've been out of it for a while. I don't know how I'm going to react. I used to be good at this. But it's been a long time."

"Three years too long?"

He nodded quickly, wearily. "Yeah."

She waited so long to speak that Gage began to worry.

"I know you don't want to do this," she said quietly. "Are you going to be able to handle it?"

Gage continued methodically loading clips for the MP5. He sniffed, frowning. Didn't reply.

Sarah didn't repeat the question, let it rest. Just like he had known she would let it rest if he didn't reply. When he did finally look up he met her unblinking gaze, patiently centered, steady and intent, on his face. And he remembered that her concern was simple and genuine, a heartfelt announcement.

Theirs was a strange relationship, nothing promised, nothing demanded. Yet they shared a silent affection, expected a supreme level of trust. Sometimes, when their eyes met, she would make an almost invisible gesture or nod, and he knew that it was his to understand. He often looked to her, waiting for such an expression, knowing that she would not hesitate if there was something she needed to say without words. He had come to regard the subtlety of her actions with deep respect, knowing that she was wiser than he. But the relationship had changed him, even in the past days, because with every moment they spent together, he seemed to become more; using superior judgment, understanding more clearly and speaking more clearly what he felt in his heart, holding himself to a higher standard. He knew that she expected no less from him, demanded, in fact, but not from selfish self-interest. Instead, she expected so much from him precisely because she held him in such high regard. And he would not disappoint her.

He took a deep breath, looked back down at the clip. "Yeah, I think I can handle it," he said wearily. "I'm just tired of doing the things I used to do." He paused. "There's a certain kind of emotional baggage you pick up from this stuff. A fatigue, I guess. I didn't want to go back into it. Violence can take over your soul. I'd gotten out of it. There was a time when it didn't mean anything to me. I did it for my country. Now it's different. It's . . . just tiring."

Sarah was silent. Gage continued to methodically click rounds into the second clip.

"Can't we handle this another way?" she asked.

"Not that I know of. We could notify the FBI but that would only open us up. We'd be targeted again. Then, even if we lived, we'd never find out who's really behind all this. I know how the system works. I have to get my hands on that letter, and then the manuscript. But I'm sure they'll be waiting for me at the church." He hesitated. "But then there's nothing I can do about it. I have to go in."

"And if they trap you?"

Gage stared at the clip, clicked in another round. "I'll deal with it."

The silence was communal, and Gage knew the subject needed to change. It had become too much.

She asked, "Did you ever talk to Simon about your old life?"

"Yeah," Gage said, a sudden smile. "I couldn't see joining the Catholic Church, but he was my patient and devoted confessor." He waited on the sensation that floated across his mind. "He was a good man."

"Yes, Simon was a very good man," she agreed. "He would sometimes talk about you, you know how he was, in a whisper. I think you made him very happy in the last few years. You gave him a lot of joy. His son."

Gage laid the second clip aside, picked up a third. "I hope so."

She leaned forward slightly. "Gage, can you tell me what you did when you were a soldier? I know you were in the Army. And I know that some people shot you up and left you for dead in the Negeb. Before Simon found you in the desert. But I don't know what you were doing there. I don't know what any American soldier would be doing in a desert of Israel in August of 1990. I've always respected you on it, even in the beginning. I've never asked. Just like I've never asked why you have to stay in hiding. Just like I never asked why you left us." She paused. "I thought that one day, when you were ready, you would tell me."

Gage looked up as she crossed a line into his past that she had never crossed. And he realized that nothing can remain constant. They would have to move ahead, or go back. He began loading the third clip, slowly, talking with the mechanical movements.

"I was a soldier," he said somberly, nodding. "I was part of a CIA tactical team."

"Tactical?"

"Covert Assault Team," he answered, no hesitation. "I left a special assault unit of the Army in July of '86 for the CIA. I thought it would be a higher service, do things so far out that they might actually make a difference." He shook his head. "But I was wrong. Dead wrong. I mean, we did a few good things. But so much of it was just lies. Lies on lies as far as the eye could see. It seemed like all the good got lost in the sauce. I should have stayed in the Army."

Sarah watched him closely, no judgment readable in her gaze. "And what kinds of things did you do?"

With a steady tension Gage looked into her eyes. "I did whatever it took."

Waiting, he watched her face. Sarah's mouth tightened slightly in what was neither a frown nor a smile, but an almost hidden grimace of compassion.

"I'm not making excuses for you, Gage," she said softly, calming. "But you were a soldier. For our government. Most people, especially people in the church, who sometimes live in a fantasyland, never realize how hard combat truly is. Or what kind of man you have to be to survive. I know you were hard because you had to be hard. You were a little lost in it, I think."

He said nothing, frowned as he loaded rounds.

"And what did you do?" she prodded. It needed to be in the open or it would be between them forever. "Exactly, I mean."

Gage felt a slight astonishment that she could be so calm, searching him out, discovering him. It was because he did not want to lose her affection and respect that he had never told her before. But, somehow, he sensed that she had known all along, had guessed it long ago. After a slight pause he continued, looking at the clip.

"I did whatever the CIA ordered me to do. Whatever it took. I was always in the air, at sea, whatever. Designing attacks, executing attacks. We hit terrorist cells, sanctioned defectors. That was good, I think. But then we did some things that were wrong, too. Real wrong. Had to be. But I was in it, then. Up to my neck. And I didn't have the guts to get out. It was all I knew, this world of lies and violence and deception." Hesitation, a grimace. "It was a hard life. I just found my way through it as best I could. That's just the way I was, then. Day after day. Mission after mission. Some of the assignments I could understand. They were good hits. But too many of them were just stupid. Incomprehensible. The targets weren't verifiable threats, or even intelligence operatives. It didn't make any sense but I . . . followed orders. Did whatever I was told.

Part of me didn't care. Part of me did. But I didn't care enough to stop myself from doing it. I told myself it was for my country. But, really, I knew better. I . . . hurt a lot of people." A strained pause. "It's hard to live with."

Sarah wanted to reach out, but she held back. "I didn't think that the CIA assassinated people."

Gage made an awkward, quick gesture with his head. "They don't assassinate foreign leaders in times of peace. But they'll eliminate defectors, terrorists, or foreign assassins who are planning to hit someone in our government. Sometimes they even sanction foreign doctors in the Middle East who interrogate our people with drugs and surgical torture. I've done four of them who worked for the PLO." He paused, raised his eyebrows to nod slowly. "Now those were solid hits. Something that needed to be done. They won't be torturing anybody else, that's for sure."

She nodded. "Is all that stuff documented?"

"My missions were reported. But not all of them were fully documented. But then I wasn't supposed to fully document them. That was understood from the beginning. Usually, there would be a phony mission to cover the real mission. It's one method of concealment. A real mission concealed within a phony mission concealed within something else. Lies on top of lies. Confusion beneath confusion. Make it so complicated nobody can really ever figure it out. Strategy for deception."

"And how long did you do that?"

Gage shrugged, laid down the clip, picked up a fourth. "Four years."

"Until that night Simon found you in the desert. On the site of the tunnel."

"Yeah," Gage answered, lighter. "Until that night."

Sarah leaned forward. Gage glanced up and saw the focused, intelligent understanding, easy and relaxed, on her face.

"What happened that night, Gage?"

Gage looked out the kitchen window, hesitating between rounds. "I was assigned to sanction two investment bankers of a Geneva firm who were in Beirut meeting with OPEC." He waited, concentrating. "But . . . it didn't feel right. I couldn't figure it. I'd already sanctioned a Geneva banker six months earlier. And I couldn't figure that one, either. I had taken my orders, followed them. Didn't ask any questions. But I was getting tired of taking orders that didn't feel right. So I called them on this one. I confronted my supervisor, told him I wanted to know why we had orders to sanction investment bankers who had no known ties to any foreign intelligence network. I told him that the target wasn't a player, didn't call any shots. I wanted some answers. Then I told him that something strange was happening with the unit. We were making too many hits against people that had no relationships to national security."

He notched another round.

"It was a bad scene," he continued. "But I knew that I was right. We'd done too many hits that couldn't be explained away by security interests. Too many hits in South Africa. Too many in South America." His eyes locked on the wall. "It was strange. We'd hit a lot of very rich, very powerful targets. It didn't make sense. They were heavyweights, but not in the field of intelligence. I didn't tell him that I was calling it off. But I was. I was slipping out. I'd built a back door so that I could go under if things went bad. And they were. Fast. But before we could get out of Israel, it ended for everybody."

She nodded slowly.

"I'd half-expected something to happen," he added. "But not so soon. I wanted to get back to the States and slide out before a confrontation." He released a deep breath. "Anyway, a few hours after my confrontation with him, somebody's army cut me and the team down in the building where we were staying, got us in a crossfire." He took a breath, continued quietly, "I don't know how long it lasted. It felt like a long time. We gave them a fight, but we were outnumbered. Outgunned. Everybody was hit. I got it pretty bad and I knew we were all going to die, so as a last chance, I fired up a satchel of C-4 and ignited thirty bags of potassium nitrate to blow the entire building, to either kill everybody on both sides or to cause so much confusion that some of us might escape and evade."

Gage looked at her, saw her unspoken question. "Fertilizer," he said.

She nodded.

"Anyway, the building went up. Smoke, fire, the whole nine yards. It was our only chance to escape. But I don't think anybody did. Somehow, I survived the explosion, crawled into the desert."

"Why the desert?"

Gage was silent. He had finished with the clip. He seemed reluctant to pick up the fifth.

"I knew we'd been betrayed. Like I said, I'd half-anticipated something like that after I went to my supervisor. If the unit was actually dirty, I knew I would be considered a security risk, along with the rest of the guys. So I'd set up precautions against it, but they got to us anyway. When it happened I was certain that it was ordered from our side. I didn't know who to trust. I couldn't go to the embassy or a safe house. Didn't have enough contacts of my own to go under. My only real chance was to put some distance on them. Get some room to maneuver. Somehow, I made it into the desert. I had to start walking anyway because of the pain. Burns make you move. Burns like I had make you move a lot. You can't stay still. And I was dying from thirst. I never remember being that thirsty. It got to me after a while. Pain and thirst. I lost it. Somewhere I stumbled off the road and ended up in the sand."

Gage lifted his face as if staring at the sky. "I'll never forget that moon," he said distantly, softly. "Big. Bigger than I'd ever seen it. And white. Pure white. And I knew I was dead." He paused. "They train us to overcome anything. Any kind of pain. Hunger. Cold. They teach us to sew our wounds shut with hair, if that's all we've got. Single focus, they call it. Knowledge and single focus. Don't think about anything but what you have to do, and do it. Ignore the pain, or sever a nerve to endure it. Whatever it takes. I've done it all. But everybody has a limit. And I'd reached mine.

"I remember looking up at the sky, everything numb. Gone. And I knew that it had all been a lie." He smiled bitterly. "My whole life had been a lie, just denying the truth. But I was about to die. No more time for lies. No more reason to lie. I was already dead, as far as I knew. And it was on me, this judgment. I felt it, knew it. And I knew that I'd best make peace with God because I was about to meet him. And my debt was pretty heavy, for sure."

It was long before Gage spoke again. Everything on the table lay forgotten.

"I guess it was the first time in my entire life that I ever prayed for forgiveness. For anything. But I did." He hesitated. "I don't really remember anything else."

Gage's tired eyes gazed upon Sarah again. "When I woke up I was in your tent. Simon was there. And Malachi. When I healed up I knew it would be cowardly, and wrong, to deny a truth that I had admitted beside that tomb. I had believed in God, had recognized God for who He was. I held to it after I recovered. And it changed me, little by little. I never went back."

Somberly, looking away to nothing, Gage waited a moment, face troubled.

"Until now."

• • •

"That's enough," said Kertzman, rising. "I'll be in touch with one of you in a few days. I'm going to do some checking around on my own. If you need me, you've got my beeper."

"Good enough," said Radford, standing with Kertzman's movement. "I'll start working the system, checking on whoever Gage knew in the field that is still out there, find out if he's made any contacts. I'll put out the word on a little compensation for anyone who knows anything."

Milburn rose without a word, walked towards the door.

"Hey, Milburn," said Kertzman.

Milburn turned, regarded Kertzman calmly.

"How is it you know so much about everything Gage did in Black Light? You said that Gage only answered to the DCI."

"No, I didn't," replied Milburn, a slow blink. "I said he answered to his supervisor and the DCI."

Kertzman saw it coming.

"I was his supervisor."

. . .

Midnight.

Robert Milburn watched stoically as the five mysterious and somber men checked the equipment he had collected: a wide and expensive arrangement of high-tech, fully-automatic weapons, infrared nightvisors, adjustable laser scopes, listening and tracking devices, a case of HCI high explosive with microwave detonators, and several thousand rounds of teflon-coated, armor-piercing ammunition.

In an attempt to appear uninterested, Milburn stood on the far side of the mansion's library, arms casually folded, watching as the men cleaned the weapons, loaded clips, working the compact, easily concealable assault rifles with obviously superior reflexes and knowledge.

Milburn attempted to discern which armies the men had trained with, watching who would select which weapon, how they would clear and load. He knew that, as a general rule, each of the world's elite armed assault units specialized in a different weapon. And each man present had obviously received very specialized military training. Even when a soldier left his initial unit and went freelance he would, by training, gravitate towards the weapon he had spent the most time with. But Milburn couldn't discern any origins from the men surrounding him. Each one seemed perfectly comfortable, perfectly knowledgeable with every device assembled in the room. It was as if they had no mechanical preference, no weakness.

Absolutely perfect.

A blond-haired man, large and muscular, probably in his late twenties, approached Milburn.

"Let me introduce you to our team, Mr. Milburn, in case you need to address one of us specifically," the blond man said with a thick German accent.

Milburn said nothing, shifted his eyes to the room. The most imposing of the five, the Japanese, had removed his shirt and was wrapping a long, wide white elastic bandage around his ribs and torso. Milburn knew the process.

It was a pre-battle preparation dating back to feudal Japan. Ancient samurai often wrapped their torso in bandages before war, insuring that any chest or rib injury would be quickly stanched. The bandages would almost immediately close an upper body wound, minimizing fluid loss, stalling shock and maintaining blood pressure long after a life-threatening injury normally rendered a man unconscious.

Milburn watched closely.

The Japanese, large and muscular for an Oriental, continued the wrapping with a practiced, polished ritual. It was something he had done many times.

Milburn heard the German speaking.

"I am Carl." He gestured toward the room. "And that is Samuel, Sergei, and Ali."

Milburn glanced at the other three. Samuel and Sergei appeared almost identical with their vague, bland features and short-cut brown hair. But the one called Ali projected a distinctly menacing presence. Possibly Nigerian, he had coal black skin with utterly black eyes. By far the largest and strongest man in the room, he was imposingly massive, intimidating. And Milburn thought that he moved with the easy confidence of irresistible strength, an appearance reinforced by his deep, overly muscular chest, shoulders, and massive arms.

Milburn reckoned that Ali stood six-ten, would probably go three-fifty or more. And he recognized that the Nigerian claimed an unnatural muscularity, a physique developed from decades of dedicated weight training, enhanced by steroids and a multitude of artificial stimulants that dramatically exaggerated physical development. Milburn wouldn't have been surprised if the Nigerian could have bench-pressed a thousand pounds. Half a ton. Even without drugs, he would have been in the upper one percent of what a person could ultimately achieve through heavy conditioning.

As one, they ignored Milburn's presence, but continued to prepare clips, each loading his own, occasionally exchanging a low word with each other. Ali was loading a heavy, full metal Street-sweeper—an automatic shotgun—holding the awkward weapon as lightly as a toy in his large hands, expertly placing the twelve-gauge rounds into the cylinder that could rotate the devastating blasts at a thunderous rate of one shot per second. Only the Japanese remained alone and silent, methodically completing the wrapping.

Keenly interested, Milburn watched the Japanese open a black-lacquered case. Then solemnly, from within the lifted lid that revealed black velvet within, he reverently removed a single, sheathed blade. Milburn was entranced by the profound respect evident in the man's motion, felt spellbound as he slowly removed the blade from its leather sheath.

"That's Sato," said Carl quietly.

Forged with the familiar curve of a Japanese *tanto*, the fighting knife was fully 18 inches long, with at least 12 of the inches in blade. The edged section ended with a plain, oval brass handguard and an intricately wrapped six-inch leather hilt topped by a solid-looking black metal pommel. Even with a casual glance, it was obvious to Milburn that the blade had been specially designed and carefully handmade by a master craftsman. But though Milburn was familiar with all the best knife makers, he couldn't identify the work.

On closer inspection, Milburn estimated that the blade was well over an inch in width, and almost a full quarter-inch thick for the entire length. It ended in a thick, high point. Overall, the blade lent an atmosphere of supreme indestructibility, even as the Japanese himself.

Milburn had never known a professional soldier who had held any reverence for a knife because most military conflicts were settled, quite simply, by superior firepower. A knife was, as a rule, meant to function as a tool, an instrument for digging, for prying, rarely ever playing a decisive role in combat.

The only exception to the rule was when a knife was wielded by a true master, a highly trained knifefighter. Someone who could stalk silently, swiftly, and patiently, closing with cold skill and cold concentration on a target to terminate with a single, painless killing move. In that dimension of war a knife could be the most effective of weapons, an edged deliverance to violent death that commanded a scarlet respect even in the world of professional terrorists. An instrument of horror. An assassin's weapon.

And yet the most difficult aspect of knifefighting was not the profoundly complex skills of mind and hand necessary to wield the weapon, but the content of soul that allowed a man to look his quarry in the eyes, time and again, at the moment of death, at the moment when the edged steel severed life from a victim's body by drawing a deep, momentarily bloodless line.

Eyes remaining bland, Milburn shifted slightly, awkwardly, at a sudden coldness, attempting to shake a strange stiffness from his shoulders and arms.

After checking the blade with religious solemnity, the Japanese lifted the sheath again and carefully slid the steel into the concealing black leather. Milburn shifted his gaze from the sheathed blade to Sato's face, registering the almost sensual pleasure evident in the black eyes.

Absently Sato nodded, seemingly oblivious to the others who had ceased their preparations and were watching him in silent tension, and, Milburn thought, respect. Then the Japanese turned to regard Milburn with implacable composure.

Milburn held the gaze a moment, rigidly refusing to reveal any of the respect summoned from within. Attempting to appear uninterested, he looked tiredly away. Milburn felt his jaw tighten with the effort of control. But inside his flesh, where there could be no lies, he could not deny the quickened, heightened heartbeat. Milburn had felt the fear before, but only in moments of combat. Yet now the vivid lightness, the speed, and the thrill were alive in him and it initiated a deeper fear, a fear of his own weakness in comparison to the Japanese.

Stiffly, Milburn shrugged, resolutely attempting to ignore the sensation.

The German, Carl, had sat down, relaxed and strangely jovial, on a nearby desk. A Steyr AUG assault rifle, a suppressed, 14-inch barrel inserted for silenced, close combat, was laid on the desk beside him. Five fully loaded clips of the 4.85mm rounds were also on the desk.

Milburn noticed that Carl had selected the clear plastic clips that allowed the shooter to visually monitor how many rounds remained in the weapon. It was unlike the usual black matte magazines that the others had chosen, and which did not allow a quick visual inspection of remaining rounds, a potentially lifesaving move in heated combat.

"Tell us about Gage," said Carl through his German accent. "We have all studied his file. We know he is out of your revered Delta Force. We are familiar with their methods. But you worked with him. What else can you tell us that is not in the file? We would like to know his preferred methods for penetrating a security screen."

Milburn looked blandly at Carl, wondered when it was that he had sold out his country, his beliefs, his life. And for what? For money? All the money in the world wasn't worth this. Nothing could be worth this.

"He's a hard man," Milburn said quietly. "He's the best there is."

Carl laughed loudly, genuinely amused, joined by the others. Only Sato looked up, solemnly staring at Milburn, steady and searching, open. Then Milburn felt a sudden surge of adrenaline as the Japanese stepped forward, moving closer, the blade hanging beneath his left shoulder in a specially designed rig that allowed easy access from under a coat.

Laughter from the others faded as Sato stopped quietly at the desk, gazing down at Milburn. Milburn blinked. He had not realized how tall Sato was, a visual trick caused by the Oriental's unusually massive, intimidating muscularity.

"Tell *me* about Gage," Sato said in a low tone.

Milburn stared into Sato's face, opened his mouth to speak, but respect for Gage faded into nothing in comparison to what stood in front of him now. Milburn shook his head, searching for words, lost track of his thoughts.

Sato waited patiently, coal black eyes intently, steadily focused on Milburn's face.

Milburn realized dimly that he was waiting for something, some confidence that wasn't going to come. He steadied himself, decided to just say it. He looked directly into Sato's black eyes.

"Like I said," Milburn repeated. "He's the best there is."

Sato seemed to laugh, but it was more of a faint, lessening shade of his aspect than a genuine human tone of humor. Then the massive form leaned closer, and Milburn felt the heat, the depth, the savage power of something that wrapped itself chillingly around his bones.

"This Gage, he is different than before?" Sato asked quietly.

Milburn didn't know how to reply.

"He serves a god, now?" Sato whispered. "Is this not true?"

Milburn shifted uncomfortably, resisting the impulse to move away. "He's religious, I guess." He hesitated. "Or something."

Milburn stared into the dead black eyes. He had never talked about anything like this before, didn't believe himself.

Sato laughed aloud this time, but the coldness in his eyes was untouched by the savage smile. In a smooth, almost invisible effort he moved and the broad steel *tanto* was magically held within the brown, strong hand, poised at an angle only inches from Milburn's face.

Edged light danced before Milburn's eyes.

"This is *my* god," Sato whispered. "I have known many like Gage. He hopes that his god will save him. He hopes that his god will intercede for him. But Gage will die, like the rest have died. And when I am through with Gage I will show no mercy to his merciful god."

"Tonight," Gage said, leaning on the mantel of the smoldering fireplace. "I'm going after it tonight."

"When are you leaving?" Sarah asked.

"An hour," Gage answered. "I'll be in New York by midnight. That's a good time to make a run for it. If they're watching for me, they'll be tired. Maybe careless. If I try to get to it in the daytime it won't be as easy. I'd have the advantage of a lot of people moving around, and they wouldn't be able to identify me as easily. But I wouldn't be able to mark them as easily, either. I think it's best to try it tonight, when I can find them. There won't be that many people on the streets. If something goes wrong, it's unlikely that anybody will get hit but me."

Barto looked up from the flames, stared at him intently. And Malachi rose from the straight-backed wooden chair beside the window, walked forward. He stared at Gage a moment, fists clenched in a nervous silence.

Then Barto spoke up, with his musical, singsong voice. "Maybe they've already found the letter, Gage. Maybe there's no reason to go in."

"No, they haven't found it," Gage responded. "Simon was smart. They could search forever in that cathedral and they'd never find it. But I know where to look. He's left messages for me before."

Barto considered. "Are you sure they'll be waiting for you?"

Malachi continued to stand in the middle of the room.

"They'll be waiting," he answered grimly. "It's what I'd do."

Sarah closed her eyes with a concentrated intensity and laid her head back against the couch. Her brow was hard with thought, or emotion. And in the tense stillness that followed, Barto rose and walked across the room to stare up at Gage through the thick, opaque lenses of his glasses.

"I know you're a tough-guy soldier and all that," Barto said cautiously. "But you can't do it by yourself. You're gonna need a driver."

Gage stared at the big man, felt a warm sense of affection. Barto might be overweight, nearsighted, uncoordinated, and the last person you would ever overestimate. But he had heart. And heart deserved respect.

"I might," Gage said, smiling slightly, debating the question. "I haven't come up with a plan, yet. But it's not going to be pretty. It might be a two-man job."

"What will they do?" Malachi asked, stepping closer.

"They'll let me come in," Gage said, putting his hands in his jean pockets, gaze wandering along the room with his thoughts as he constructed the probable sequence. "Some will hide outside to alert the others by radio that I'm arriving. I probably won't be able to locate the sentries. They'll be in the upper floors of surrounding buildings, watching the church through the windows. Difficult to detect. After I enter the church, the ones outside will shut off the exits, windows. Then when I get my hands on the letter they'll close the trap from inside the church. The guys outside will be for insurance, in case I make it past the ones inside." Gage shrugged, weary. "That's generally the way it's done."

Malachi walked forward, face troubled. "I will go with you," he said. "Perhaps I can be of assistance. I know the interior of Saint Thomas well."

"No, professor," Gage said. "You need to stay here. Watch over Sarah."

The old man received the comment carefully, then turned away, gazing at Sarah. "As you request," he said, with a touch of sadness. "You know this world far better than I."

"I know these people are obsessed enough to do anything. So we can't put ourselves into a position where they can get to us too easily." He leaned against the fireplace, grimaced angrily.

"I want you all to know," he began, "that this is going to get a lot worse. These things always do. People are going to die. A lot of them. And it might be us. There's no guarantee that I can deal with this. These people are good. I might not even make it to New York. They might have a federal warrant of arrest out on me."

"Do you think that is the case?" Malachi offered.

"No," said Gage grimly. "I don't think they want me stopped before I get to the church. They sure don't want me in the hands of somebody they don't own. And, despite how powerful they are, they don't own everybody. No, they want me to reach the letter. I think I can get it first and, if things work right, even get out with it."

"And when you get the letter?" asked Barto.

"Then I'll get the manuscript."

Malachi nodded, catching the direction. "Yes," he said gravely. "And they will harm none of us because we will use the manuscript for barter."

"If we can," said Gage. "Maybe we can negotiate some kind of dead man's switch."

Sarah looked up. "Dead man's switch?"

Malachi glanced towards her. "It is a term coined from the early American railroad engineers," he said, smiling slightly. "In the early train engines, the engineer would hold a certain switch closed with his hand. As long as the switch was closed, the train ran at speed. But if he released the switch for any reason, the brakes would be applied and the train would stop. It was a safety mechanism. As long as the engineer was alive the switch would remain closed and the train would run safely. But if anything happened to the engineer, you see, the engine would cease to operate."

"They can also be used in bombs," Barto piped up.

Malachi gazed down at the translator, a bit astonished. Gage also turned his head, a curious glare. Barto looked cautiously at one, the other.

"I learned it from a newspaper," he said.

"Of course," said Malachi, after a moment. "In any case, it is powerful influence for barter. We shall destroy the manuscript, anyway. But they will not know it. They will never be sure. And it might buy several years for our lives."

"First I have to get the letter," said Gage. "I wouldn't doubt that everyone appointed to work at the cathedral is involved in this. These people have resources. It will be tough. Maybe impossible. But I really don't have much choice." He smiled somberly. "If it gets bad, I'll try and keep the violence away from all of you."

With solemnity, Malachi focused on him. "Violence is an ugly thing. I deplore it." His gaze was steady. "But not as you might believe."

Gage shifted his eyes to the old man. Something in the tone attracted his attention.

Malachi smiled. "Does an old man surprise you?"

"I guess," Gage said, smiling slightly, wondering where it would go.

"Then I will say it again," Malachi repeated resolutely, raising an eyebrow. "Yes, I believe that violence is a terrible thing, a tragic thing. But not like you might expect. You see, I have lived a long time, Gage, and I have seen the evil done by men, and I have learned that not all violence is unjust." He hesitated a moment, glancing around, smiling obscurely. "I only speak from what I know, and hope that it is sufficient to communicate what I believe, and assure you of my confidence in your actions. Did you know, Gage, that the Greek word, *diakonoi,* used to designate ministers who teach God's Scriptures in church is the same Greek word used in the Bible to designate those who wield the sword to establish justice on the Earth?"

Gage's face was impassive, mouth grim.

"Strange, is it not," said Malachi, "that the Bible would use the same word, *diakonoi,* to designate those who teach the Word of God and those of a government who wield the sword, establishing by physical force God's code for moral justice? And for this, among other reasons, is why I believe we must confront these people, even to the point of using physical force, if necessary, to defend both ourselves and others."

Gage gazed into the professor's face, saw the dancing light of the flames illuminating the aged and august countenance. It seemed that the professor was fully at home with his beliefs. His words did not seem manufactured to suit the occasion, but had been considered, pondered, and calculated through a long period of study and critical reasoning.

"Many Christians feel that any type of violence is wrong," Gage offered.

"That is foolishness." Malachi shook his head as he spoke, seemingly unable to contain his feeling to words alone. "It is God who established man's moral code of conduct to be a reflection of His own holy character." His old voice became edged with impatience. "In truth, Gage, it is a simple thing. But there is an aversion to responsibility in the world, and men may conjure reasons to the horizon to explain away their laziness and lack of courage. But in essence I will say that God has given man a moral code, and that moral code requires man to enforce justice, to deliver punishment, and to protect the needy. So in order to accomplish these tasks, God long ago bestowed upon man the solemn right to use force, even physical violence. You see, God values justice on the Earth very highly, Gage. Even the death penalty was ordained by God as just punishment for certain crimes committed by man. So this argument that all violence is wrong is not only unbiblical, it is immoral."

"What about, 'Vengeance is mine, sayeth the Lord'?" asked Barto.

"True," Malachi said turning to him. "And there will surely be vengeance in the world to come. And God *does* forbid vengeance for personal satisfaction. But that does not mean God is reserving all dispensation of justice for the hereafter. That manner of logic is foolishness. God intended that just and moral men would reflect His holy nature by inflicting justice upon those who would oppress the Earth. Anything less than this would lead to monstrous cruelty, anarchy, and unbridled chaos. As Christian men we should not stand to the side, arms folded, praying and watching passively while cruel beings stride arrogantly and mercilessly past, grinding the broken bodies of the weak, of children and those who cannot defend themselves into the dust! No! We must reach out with strong hands." Malachi's hands clutched the air, grappling. "And with strong minds to lay hold of these murderers, yes, even shed their blood if necessary, to bring an end to their cruelty. It was God Himself who placed such an inestimable value on human life, Gage. And we must also place such a value. We cannot allow men to terrorize with death and violence and oppression. And if it is necessary to use force to stop them, then we must use whatever force is required. All men have a moral obligation to defend the weak, to protect the poor. Anything less than this is cowardice. To say we must not use violence because violence is immoral is only a cowardly excuse for escaping the responsibility that man has been so solemnly granted by an omnipotent God, a god who, since the beginning, has used His servants to strike down those who would so oppressively shed the blood of man."

Malachi's voice rose in volume, his face flushed.

"If this argument for pacifism were taken to the logical conclusion, Gage, no one would be able to serve as president, as a mayor, senator, police officer, or in the military. Because all of those offices endorse the use of force, even physical violence to the point of terminating human life." He hesitated, regret and duty striking a conflict within his tone. "Force is sometimes necessary to protect us from evil men. It is, sadly and often, a necessity of life, and I have not been a stranger to it. I have not flinched in my years to raise my hand against man when I saw it as my moral duty to protect myself, or the weak. It is a solemn responsibility that I have sorrowfully accepted, and I will not use my own cowardice or any complacent, isolationist perversity to separate myself from the hard truth that man must sometimes shed blood to serve and honor God."

"As I've done in the last week, professor?" Gage asked quietly, without looking up.

"Yes, son," Malachi intoned, turning fully to Gage. "And as you might well do again." He waited. "As we might all do before this darkness has passed."

Gage stared at Malachi a moment, looked to Sarah, who seemed to begin to rise without moving at all. Her gaze was centered on him. Barto, also, was looking at him.

"All of you need to have a plan, in case I don't make it back," Gage said. "I'm not trying to be dramatic. I might make it, I might not. But I'm going to leave you access to all the money you'll need, just in case. None of you can count on me. You can't count on anyone. These people are serious. Those guys at the seminary were amateurs compared to the talent that real money can buy. If this organization operates like the rest, and I'm betting that it does, it's probably brought in some heavy hitters to try and stop me quietly."

Barto looked up, "Why do you say that?"

"Standard operating procedure for these covert affairs," Gage said, shaking his head dismally. "Escalation of force, but in a different way. Not like the army does it. They don't just get there first with the most men. This kind of escalation in force is usually done with quality, not quantity. If the people they've been using aren't good enough, they'll find themselves better fighters, better firepower. People who can do the job without attracting any attention. Attention is always bad."

"Why won't they just get more men like the ones they had?" Barto pressed.

Gage grunted, face grim. "Too many people. Too many mouths that can talk. They like secrecy. Everyone in this work is obsessed with it." He waited, scheming. "Contrary to what a lot of people think, these covert societies don't use big armies. They use very small, very capable teams who can be absolutely trusted. They want to keep things quiet, real quiet, letting in as few people as possible. That's essential for them. Too many heads, too much talk, no matter how much you pay people. But they'll want the job done right next time. My best guess is that they'll bring in some kind of very elite squad. A group of high-priced, very skilled fighters. The kind of guys I used to work with."

"What are you going to do?" Sarah spoke up.

Gage turned, looked at her openly. "I don't know, yet. But I won't do anything stupid. After I identify how bad the threat is, I'll probably use some kind of diversion. A fire, maybe. Something to cause enough confusion for me to get in and out unnoticed. That's all I can think of right now. I'm not going to try one of those weird, across-the-roof deals. That's usually just a good way to get killed."

"I'm going with you." Barto walked up to Gage. Determined.

Gage studied him a moment. "Alright. Be glad to have you."

"Is there anything that I can do?" Malachi asked. "I will bear any burden to assist you."

"You're doing enough," Gage said with a respectful nod. "Sarah will need you to help her figure a way out of this if we don't come back. And it's way too dangerous for everyone to go."

Malachi held the gaze a moment, unafraid. Then nodded.

"When do we leave?" Barto asked.

"In an hour," Gage answered. "As soon as I get the gear packed. We'll be in New York by midnight."

A vampiric darkness spread webbed wings over the silent, deserted Cathedral of St. Thomas, crouching upon the gray stone gargoyles like a monstrous, brooding thing to cloak the ancient edifice with a warning atmosphere of evil, pale possession.

Gage stared at the haunting, spired towers and watched the overcast sky that moved tenebrous clouds immensely behind it all with unearthly dominion. He felt the wind that caressed the nightmarish gargoyles with night, caught the scent of a city in decay.

Cold air from the East River moved over him with the stench of dead things, and in the distance he heard the heavy traffic of Whitestone Bridge, the sounds coming toward him, into Queens. Around him, beyond the shadows, people walked silently and peacefully through the darkened night, oblivious to the deadly game playing out before them.

Gage raised his head, scanning.

Nothing moved upon the basilica, not above, not within. Even with the nightvisor on thermal imaging Gage read no heat at the towers, the walls, or crouched within the doorway of the thick-walled bastion. Still, he knew that the greater threat awaiting him was concealed deep inside, far from any possible detection.

Moving with a practiced, cryptic steadiness, he turned, gazing again at surrounding buildings. He detected several thermal signatures but had not determined which ones were a threat. He had targeted two possibilities, signatures that remained too constant, too unmoving, too steadily near the windows of their small rooms.

In the back of the building he had found two more possibilities, using the same method of study; whatever did not move was unnatural. And he knew that what seemed unnatural would probably be unnatural. He calculated that, with the combined angle of sight, the four locations held every direction of approach under observation.

Face hidden in shadow, Gage scowled, focused again on the cathedral.

145

No easy way to do it.

He glanced at his watch.

Soon.

Then, in the distance, he heard the approach of fire engines. He raised his head, listening.

Closer.

Blood fast, the beginning.

Gage felt the adrenaline, tried to calm down. He concentrated, breathing steadily, relaxed. With a slight movement, he waved his hands at his side, drying sweat on the palms. His breath picked up its pace and he inhaled deeply, again, released.

Concentrate. Focus. Channel everything into the movement.

Imperceptibly, he shifted his weight from one foot to the next, almost appearing to not move at all. It was a risk, but some forces could not be denied.

Almost time.

He waited, breath steady, pulse holding. *Better than before. Not so wild. Under control.*

Gage raised his line of sight to encompass both forward infrared signatures by using unfocused, peripheral vision. He watched the targeted rooms intently as the sirens screamed towards the block. No movement. Both of the thermal images were absolutely stationary.

Closer now. Sirens converged on the church.

Gage watched a moment longer. He smiled.

The heat signatures didn't move. Didn't move at all. But Gage knew that any normal person would move, even just a little. Most people would be curious, or at least concerned that it might be their building on fire. But these two didn't move. Because they were trained not to move. Because they knew there was no fire, knew it was a diversion.

Never leave your post. Never allow yourself to be distracted. Always remember your primary objective.

Two in front, for sure. He decided to trust his judgment, included the two he had selected inside separate buildings at the rear. At least four. But no team works in four. It was always at least six, or eight.

He nodded, concentrating. He could anticipate as many as four more men inside, but probably not more than two. Whoever these guys were, he was certain that they used the smallest team possible, for security reasons, just like everyone else. And six was the standard for every elite combat team in the world.

Chaos pulled up in front of the church.

Gage waited a moment more. Inhaled once. Expelled the breath in a slow, forceful effort, mind speeding with tactics, approaches, and maneuvers that blended, shifted, tumbled in varying combinations, adjusting his approach to what was happening in front of the church. It came to him, the angle, the movement to break the perimeter, simple, simple, keep it simple.

Into it now, everything considered, calculated.

He removed the nightvisor. Slid into the night.

• • •

St. Thomas swarmed with yellow asbestos coats. Six primary response units had unloaded the swarming but efficiently coordinated firefighters into the street. Busily hooking up, surrounding the building, the moving figures turned helmeted heads toward every possible crevice, searching for escaping smoke.

Nothing.

No smoke. No fire.

St. Thomas's priest, a tall, imperial man, approached the elder firefighter who also approached him, walking quickly down the center aisle of the cathedral.

Obviously in command, the fireman held a large black maglight in one hand and a radio in the other. His coat was buttoned to the neck, the top flaps overlapping to prevent incendiary debris from spilling down his chest.

"Where is it, Father?" An old and experienced voice of calm concern.

"There is no fire, Captain," the priest replied, a tone of utter calm with a faint British accent. "Gentlemen, I believe that some irresponsible person has called in a—" The priest turned his head, distracted by the firemen who brushed past him, axes in hand, disappearing into the depths of the church. "...false alarm. It has happened a great deal lately. I apologize to you."

"You haven't called in a fire?" The captain's face grew angry, more serious.

"No, I—" the priest began.

The captain raised a radio. "Unit 23 to Dispatch," he said and received a static reply. "Cancel any additional trucks. We've got a false—"

Frantic yelling erupted from a corridor. "We've got smoke! A lot of it!"

"Excuse me, Father," the captain muttered, moving without hesitation toward the corridor that echoed with frantic shouts. He spoke hurriedly into the radio: "Unit 23, disregard last traffic. Have units respond."

Another utterance of frantic shouting came from corridors located on the other side of the cathedral.

"Got it! I got it in here!"

The captain turned, an expression of brutal concentration, glaring at a dozen yellow coats and helmets rushing down the second corridor. The building echoed with scattered shouts and commands. He turned towards the priest.

"Is anyone else in here, Father?"

"No," the priest replied quickly.

"Good. Now I'm going to have to ask you to leave." He didn't wait for any agreement. Turning, he shouted, "Lay me two three-inch lines back here!"

Smoke billowed out of the corridors, spiraling towards the shadowed recesses of the cathedral ceiling.

The captain turned again to shout, saw that the priest still stood in the same place, staring at him, mouth open, face troubled. The captain only focused on him a second, turned to another man.

"Escort the Father outside, Jake. Now!"

"Come on now, Father," said Jake, a 50-year-old fireman with a Wyatt Earp mustache, white hair visible beneath the yellow helmet. "We'll take care of it for you. You know you can't stay in here. It's too dangerous."

"But—" said the priest.

"Now, don't argue with me, Father." Jake was good at his job. Was experienced with those who could not bear to see their beloved cathedrals ravaged by flames. "There's nothing you can do," he added consolingly. "We'll take care of it."

Then the tall, dignified priest was led hurriedly down the center aisle by a kind and compassionate hand, rushed to the door even as more firefighters, all of them wearing air packs and full face shields beneath their helmets, swept in with hoses.

• • •

Outside the church the stately priest stood calmly to the side, hands clasped in solid composure behind his back, speaking quietly and quickly.

He seemed to pray, and his words were lost in the colliding shouts and instructions, completely ignored by the sturdy professionals moving so frantically around him. Then, as if prompted by an invisible listener, the priest shifted, cautiously increasing the volume of his words.

Still discreet, his voice drifted into the bustle of the street: "... Samuel will remain hidden within the church. All others abandon listening posts. Initiate target acquisition by assigned zones. I repeat, abandon listening posts and deploy to surrounding streets.

Initiate target acquisition by assigned zones. Maintain frequency silence unless target is sighted. Converge on designated street with sighting..."

• • •

An ax shattered a locked door deep inside a corridor in the rear of the building, strangely separated from the cathedral itself and the center focus of other firefighters who swarmed up and down the smoke-filled hallways, searching for the heart of the blaze.

The fireman entered the room, approached a wooden shelf on the far side, near the open window. He raised the ax to strike the shelf when he turned suddenly, saw someone pass the doorway, moving quickly.

Immediately the fireman moved away from the shelf, kicked over a wastebasket, pulled open a closet door, shouting something indiscernible into the hall.

A man stepped into the doorway, a man of medium height, one hand held beneath his coat. For a tense moment the man glared at the fireman, peering through the facemask.

"Hey, buddy!" said the fireman. "You can't be in here! You're going to have to move outside!" The firefighter took a step closer to the man.

An angry movement and the man directed a highly compact assault pistol at the fireman.

"This was so predictable, Gage," the man said in a British accent, laughing. "Standard civilian interference. We knew you'd try it. We planned for it. I just waited to see where the fire broke out and retreated to the other side of the church, watching to see who would break away from the rest of the pack. When you came in here, I knew. Just like I knew there wasn't any fire. Only smoke. What? Markers?" He laughed. "The color's right for it."

The man lifted a compact radio to his face. The firefighter tensed, tightened the grip on the ax. Reacting reflexively but calmly, the man adjusted the pistol, aiming center mass, and finished speaking into the radio.

He gestured at the ax. "Drop it, Gage. I'm no fool. It's not a gun. But I know what someone can do with it."

Staring at the gun, the firefighter held the ax a moment more. Then the man raised the assault pistol, arm straight, sight-picture alignment on the firefighter's chest.

"No more warnings, Gage," the man said placidly.

Frantic scurrying outside the corridor. Yellow helmets appeared behind the man.

Gage dropped the ax, hands moving low.

"Hey!" a firefighter shouted.

The man holding the assault pistol half-turned as they approached, pulling identification from his pocket.

Gage quick-stepped to the side, hand coming up from where it had dropped the ax, passing his waist and unbuttoned asbestos coat, pulling the Hi-Power.

Instantly the man whirled, firing one-handed. Murderous thudding of the assault weapon shredded the closet, the stream of rounds following Gage to the side, a half-step behind. Then the unsilenced Hi-Power roared, hitting sternum-high on the man, knocking him off balance.

Shouting maniacally, the firefighters behind the man leaped to the sides, bellowing.

But as they moved and the man recovered from the shock of the impact, Gage gripped the Hi-Power with a modified Weaver Stance. Instantly he fired ten more times. Ten deafening recoils bringing him off-target ten times in a blinding white strobe-fire, Gage aligning again each split-second and firing, shells flying past him in the roar of blue smoke and the man falling back in the static white-black bursts of light and then it was over; a man down, shells clattering on the floor with the overpowering, choking thickness of lung-burning powder clouding the smoky air.

Tactical reload.

A clip was dropped. Another slammed in. Gage released the slide, locking the hammer back with the safety for a quick, single-action first shot. Then he was at the bookcase, using his elbow to shatter a shelf that he could have removed silently if he had taken an extra second. But it didn't matter now.

Screams and angry shouts echoed down the hall.

He reached behind the shelf, pulled out a cellophane-wrapped letter from the wall.

Shouts retreated into the cathedral.

... Nobody is going to come down the hall ... That was too much gunfire ... Cops will be outside ... Don't allow them to isolate you ... Shock everybody into an instinctive reaction so they won't have any time to think ... Then move with them ... Get outside!

Gage moved into the hallway, no one in sight, the distant sounds of frantic warnings, boots, and shouts merging in the cathedral. He heard shouting outside. Things were heating up quick. In thirty seconds he'd be the only one in the church. Then they'd just close it off and he'd be trapped. Not even Houdini could get outside after every exit was closed. He had to get back to Barto waiting four blocks away. To Sarah.

As fast as he could, he ran towards the cathedral, pulling two concussion grenades from his pocket. He pulled the pins, holding the levers in place with each hand.

Voluminous and weighty, the coat wrapped itself around him like a waterlogged blanket, heavy and stiff. Still, he hurled himself down the corridor, rubber boots smacking the stones, echoing in his ears above the painful ringing caused by the Hi-Power.

Breath hot, blasting. Tired. Sweating.

He reached the cathedral at full stride, saw that it was almost empty with a disorganized collection of frantic figures running toward the doublewide doors. A group of about ten firefighters, confused, glaring, knowing something had happened but uncertain what, emerged quickly from a darkened hallway to the left of the pulpit.

Gage dropped both concussion grenades behind him, kept running towards them.

"*Run!*" he screamed. "*He's killed him, he kil—*"

Twin explosions thundered, striking lightning across the smoke-filled cathedral in a deafening sound wave, booming off the shadowed recesses of the ceiling and crashing down across them like the wrath of God.

Shouting explosively, the firefighters turned as one, charging back into the corridor.

Gage smiled savagely and then he was with them as they threw themselves recklessly down the dimly lit hallway. Frantic and contradictory instructions were shouted by everyone in unison, each man convinced he knew the surest means of escape and Gage was screaming, "Go straight! Hurry! It's the only way out! Hurry! He'll kill us all!"

In a wild, swirling tide of yellow coats and hats they crashed into the wooden double doors at the end of the corridor. Not even for a second did the lock and chain resist the combined mass that struck it, and they spilled out together into an eastern courtyard, turning without hesitation to charge chaotically towards the street.

Gage followed them, shouting and cursing like the rest. In seconds he was at the front of the church. He glanced around, measuring the state of confusion on the street. Several firefighters, crouching behind vehicles like war veterans, had already pulled illegally concealed firearms from boots and pockets and were glaring angrily towards the cathedral. An elderly fireman was shouting into a microphone. Sirens were hurtling towards the cathedral from surrounding streets. A lot of them. In seconds this place would be shut down like a vault.

Time to move.

A large number of firefighters retreated into the surrounding streets, seeking more positive cover behind walls and brick stairways, still yelling in confusion. Gage joined them, running heavily beneath the weight of the fire-resistant clothing, pushing his way through until he passed the alley that ran north off Paulette Avenue, one block north of the cathedral, fading into the darkness.

He eased down the alley, saw a large blue garbage disposal tank, and stashed the firefighter garb in the cylindrical container. Then he put the silencer on the Hi-Power and placed it in a black daypack that he carried inside the asbestos coat. The nightvisor, one remaining concussion grenade, and a phosphorous grenade also went into a pack. Finally, he pulled the blue T-shirt out of his pants, concealing the double-edge fighting knife in a sheath at the small of his back.

Sirens everywhere.

People were shouting and running frantically down the street through the suddenly hot night. Gage watched them pass the narrow opening in the alley, illuminated by the harsh white light of the street lamp.

Sweat dripped into his eyes. Breathing heavily, he wearily wiped a forearm across his brow and leaned over, hands on his knees, resting. He waited a minute, using the seconds to focus, to concentrate. Then he raised up.

No time to waste. Have to put some distance on this place.

He checked his pants pocket, made sure the letter was securely present. Then he shook his hands to loosen and moved north out of the alley, emerging onto the street again.

Discreetly, he unzipped the pack about six inches to place his hand inside it, finding the familiar grip of the Hi-Power. And, still concealing his hand and pistol inside the canvas, he walked slowly forward. Casual.

The mood was calmer but still chaotic on this block, two hundred feet removed from the scene of the chaos. People moved quickly, away from the sirens and shouting echoing down the street. Though some ran toward the scene with the light-footed street readiness of inner-city war veterans, eager to see what had caused the commotion.

Gage gazed about for a second, scanning, and moved left, keeping to the pedestrian pace of those around him. Not too slow, not too fast.

Calm, calm, keep calm.

He rounded the corner off Fairbanks and turned north again, passing the black iron grating that protected the front of Strong's

Liquor Market. Thirty more feet and something began nagging at him, some half-remembered rule that he had forgotten.

No time to ponder it. Keep moving.

Ninety more feet and he was near the end of the block, doing his best to appear nondescript in his hiking boots, blue T-shirt, and blue jeans. He crossed the street to approach the dark-colored LTD on the passenger's side.

A dim, incipient warning flashed across Gage's mind; mistake, mistake! It was an alarm he couldn't identify, and he neared the car to see Barto alert, both hands clutching the steering wheel, waiting for him to return.

Gage realized what it was when he was 15 feet from the vehicle, saw Barto's wide-eyed readiness, the tight hands waiting eagerly to ferret them away from the scene.

So obvious ... so easy to see ...

It was an all but forgotten remark made at Pathfinder School held at Fort Benning early in that hard, cold winter of 1979 after Gage had twice failed to track down a grizzled old sergeant on the frozen slate of a lower Appalachian mountain.

A trapper and former professional poacher, the sergeant had confessed to Gage after the exercise that the only man who had ever tracked him down in the mountains was an old Georgia Ranger who had foregone the hunt through the forest. Instead, he found where the trapper had parked his pickup truck, then waited for him to return with his fresh kill.

"*Yes sir.*" Gage remembered the old sergeant's words with a bright white flash of alarm. "*He was smart, that 'un. He never went into the woods. He just found my truck, waited for me ...*"

An adrenaline surge electrified him, but Gage kept walking slowly, eyes vivid, absorbing everything; the crowd congregating at the distant corner, the man and woman walking parallel with him on the opposite side of the street, the big Japanese strolling casually towards him, ten steps away, hands hanging empty at his sides.

Rules of engagement.

First, neutralize the man with the most dangerous weapon. Second, if there are no major weapons, sweep left to right. Third, if no weapons are visible, neutralize the man who holds the closest point of contact.

No weapons in sight. The Japanese had the closest point of contact. Don't worry about the rest.

Eight steps away. Eight seconds.

Gage estimated that he would pass the Japanese side by side directly beside the parked LTD.

Seven steps.

Large for a Japanese, eyes slightly down, hands empty, strolling, moving casually but that doesn't tell anything and there's no time for this...

Five steps.

Closest point of contact.

Four steps.

Four seconds.

...Do something!...Force him to react!...Push him!...Find out what he is!...NOW!...

Instantly Gage angled away, stepping off the sidewalk to walk towards the driver's side of the vehicle while thumbing the safety of the Hi-Power down, grip loosening on the bag.

Gage knew that if the Japanese was a threat he would have to move now or...a blur...

...MOVE!...

The Hi-Power came out and Gage fired two frantic shots at point-blank range that he knew had gone wide. The Japanese was on him. A blinding movement with an arm lashing out. Gage twisted to avoid the silver flicker that passed dangerously close to him to...*hit!*

Gage turned a half-step to the left, leaped back toward the sidewalk, and he knew the blade had not missed his arm. There was no pain, no sensation, and no time to consider. But he knew it had not missed.

Recovering instantly the Japanese turned and Gage raised the Hi-Power again. The Japanese, white flicker of the knife still held in one hand, pulled a large black pistol with his other hand, an automatic. They whirled face to face, distance of four feet.

Two point-blank thuds from Gage's Hi-Power and the Japanese's massive handgun erupted between them.

An invisible baseball bat struck Gage in the chest, slamming him backward to the ground. A moment passed before he could think or pull a savage breath. Then he roared at the pain and rolled, stunned...

Oh...God!

Gage reached for the Hi-Power, couldn't find it. Coughing, he rolled to his side, forgetting the pistol, trying to initiate escape and evade procedures. He ignored his chest, the vest. If he was hit, he would probably die. But if he didn't escape he would assuredly die.

Breath gone, gone.

Get it back, pull, you don't have much time! Get it together!

Gage made it to his knees to see that the Japanese was down also, the magnum lost in the shadows. But the man had retained hold of his knife, the footlong blade protruding from the top of the fist.

Blurring movement down the street.

Blood hot and without blinking Gage reflexively shifted his eyes, identifying instantly: men. He focused: two men. Running towards him, automatic weapons in their hands. Not cops. Cops in civilian clothes wouldn't have automatic weapons.

Threat!

Forty seconds. Forty seconds before they arrived. An estimated two minutes before police. Barto was screaming, out on the street, running around the front of the vehicle. Gage groaned, brought one foot under him, began to rise.

Cursing angrily, the Japanese also staggered up.

Gage moved towards Barto, the car.

A short burst of rounds from the men running towards them hit the LTD and Gage leaped back, away from the vehicle to avoid the pattern of fire. He hit the ground, sprawling, awkward, sliding to cut his palms on the concrete. Gage rolled up again to one knee, full rage rising, trying to control the chaos to assess what he was facing.

The two men were thirty seconds away. Then suddenly the Japanese advanced towards him.

Gage struggled up. Breath gone. Pain.

Fight! Ignore the pain!

Gage heard the LTD take more automatic fire from the oncoming men. Then Barto was shouting something, then diving into the car. In a second the engine of the LTD fired up. A portion of the windshield blew out and the car tore, screeching, away from the curb. Barto hung a hard left, crossing the street to roar away down an alley.

Gage turned as the Japanese advanced, obviously hurt from the Hi-Power's round. But the fact that he had gotten up told Gage that the man was wearing a ballistic vest, just as he was. Blade low, the Japanese walked forward, face twisted in pain, the purest purpose of vengeful death in the directness of his approach. Grimacing from wounds as he gained his feet, Gage roared a primal challenge and pulled the stiletto from the sheath at his back. Sweat, blood in his eyes, he moved toward the Japanese.

Nothing else now. Just this.

They quickened their steps, leaping forward as they met.

A blinding exchange of light that flashed in, caught, swept back out, and empty hands followed the opponent's blade for a trap but the blades were too fast, the opponent too experienced, and the steel of each man passed in again, a bizarre clang of steel and then out, separating, missing a second time as each man leaped outside the other's reach.

With a bellowing scream the Japanese whirled. Gage roared, knife flashing a feint, then blocked a savage blow to catch the Japanese in the leg with a kick. The Japanese countered, slipping outside the blow. Cold steel tore a passage through Gage's ribs. Sensing the injury but not feeling, Gage reacted instantly, smashing a fist into the man's face to knock him back. And Gage retreated, knowing the trauma of a quickening blood loss.

Face confident, smiling savagely, the Japanese recovered and advanced, feinting, testing, and then suddenly bridged the gap to sweep his blade in a murderous backhanded slash. Gage had reacted to the feint but saw the blow and frantically jerked his head back as the blade ripped a path through the air in front of his throat. Then, before the Japanese could stop the momentum of his arm, Gage lashed out, his strength and the entire weight of his body behind the velocity of his blade, driving a straight knife-strike toward his opponent's chest.

Reflex training alone drove his arm, powering a blow backed by countless days of brutal conditioning. Gage had learned that, in war, pure physical strength was often the simple, true divider between the living and dead. So he had made conditioning a foundation of his training, spending hours running, then lifting weights only to pound the heavy bag afterwards with punches and kicks for fierce, endless rounds. And, finally, when he had continued for as long as he thought he could continue, he would fall into a sort of mystical rhythm, pounding the bag, lifting weights until he couldn't move his arms, pounding and lifting more, and then moving back to the bag. And he had trained as he would fight, knowing that was where true perfection of movement would be found, at full speed with full power, never letting up, never pacing. Throwing everything, punch and weight, as if his life depended on each blow until unendurable fatigue separated his mind from the movement and the movement itself was all there was. And in achieving the absence of self Gage knew that he was training his body to fight for him without his conscious mind, forging a deep muscle memory that would execute a necessary move with killing efficiency even in a moment when he was too injured to think.

Blasting beneath the Japanese's outstretched arm, Gage slammed the blade into his side, penetrating the ballistic vest with a slicing impact that a bullet could never match. Gage felt the blade strike bone, glance along the ribs.

A savage grunt exploded from the Japanese and Gage grabbed the man's right forearm, the most easily controlled section of his opponent's knife-wielding right hand. But, reacting to the wound in his chest, the Japanese also grabbed Gage's knife hand. Gage tried to tear his wrist loose, managed to pull the blade clear of the man's ribs and vest, and twisted with a Herculean effort to stab downwards, trying for a femoral artery.

The grip was unbreakable.

Gage surged again, trying to tear his wrist loose.

What...strength!

Eyes blazing inches from the other's face, they staggered in a tight circle, each trying to tear his knife hand free of the other's relentless grip.

Gage pulled futilely, failed.

It's over! Get it free or die!

A screaming, superhuman effort and Gage frantically twisted his wrist against the man's thumb, inside and up, felt thin shreds of his skin tear off in the grip.

Free!

A split second. Gage shouted, hot and livid with the instinct and slashed inward to—

A brutal front kick slammed into Gage's chest, knocking him back. Dazed, he crashed to the sidewalk before he groaned at the pain and rolled over, staggering numbly to his feet. He rose, right-side forward with the right knife hand waist-high, eyesight centered by reaction training on his opponent's chest.

In his shaken higher mind Gage realized that the kick had been inhumanly powerful, explosive, a sledgehammer blow that had numbed much of his upper body even beneath the throbbing pains of the magnum and the blade. But he couldn't assess the damage. His chest didn't feel right, but there was no time. Staggering, he circled to the left, feeling the wounds now, so many of them, trying to concentrate.

The Japanese leaped forward, moving to Gage's left to cut off his movements, immediately eliminating three of Gage's best angles of attack. And Gage realized that he was facing a highly trained knifefighter, a man who by unconscious reflex automatically reacted with the perfect tactical movement.

A master.

The knife flashed in and out, and Gage felt the edge rip through his upper arm. Then the blade razored across his forearm, drawing another deep wound, and Gage lashed out with the stiletto, missed, kicked, and swept the Japanese off balance.

Ignoring his numb, bleeding left arm, Gage circled to the left, cutting off three angles of attack that the Japanese might use.

A master knifefighter's mind reacts in combat much like a computer, instantly factoring complicated circles and angles of movement, immediately altering a counter with each tactic of the opponent to formulate another complex series of movements, setting the mind for an attack that remains five to six strokes in advance of where the bodies are poised at that moment to constantly prepare a counterattack to match the most minute shift or change of his opponent's status.

Mind speed is essential because once an opponent initiates a movement it is mentally impossible to devise a reaction if the general pattern of counterattack has not already been preselected.

Change is constant, the lower mind instinctively designing responsive reactions while high reason searches for angles that will penetrate an opponent's defensive shield. Both opponents attempt to test speed, probe defensive skills, design attacks and counters, and psychologically intimidate the enemy while simultaneously dancing back and forth at a distance outside their opponent's arm reach—the killzone.

Unless a dramatic decision is made to bridge the gap, both men attempt to stay outside the killzone but close enough to close the distance with a quick leap, slipping their opponent's guard to strike a blow. The greatest danger comes in closing the gap, and the danger stays high for every second fighters remain within the killzone because physical, responsive reflex is always slower than the initiation of an opponent's movement.

It is commonly accepted that anyone, no matter how skilled or quick, can be hit at close range. And if an opponent is holding a knife, even one blow is sufficient for defeat. So the ability to bridge the gap, strike and separate successfully without suffering severe damage, is a highly valued area of expertise with knifefighters.

In the end, an opponent need not even strike an enemy's vital organs to finish the conflict. More often, an encounter between master knifefighters ends with one opponent going into shock from moderate blood loss sustained through venous cuts—a result most easily accomplished by striking a deep wound upon an enemy's arm, just deep enough to reach major veins. Once the bleeding begins, shock is no more than six minutes away and will itself terminate the encounter. Then for opponents satisfied only to end the combat in death, shock will incapacitate so that an easily executed killing blow to the neck or chest can be delivered.

Forearms are frequent targets, easier than the chest or neck, and are focused upon. Also, arms and wrists are much more easily reached without entering the killzone or exposing a vital body part to attack. And once an opponent's wrist is deeply cut he can no longer hold a knife, becoming virtually helpless. In knifefighting this tactic is called "defanging the snake."

Without fangs, a snake is easy prey.

A wash of fatigue came over Gage, a quickening blood loss, thinning the adrenaline rush that was only barely keeping him above shock. He felt the pain, exhausted breath blasting hot from his chest, and struggled to hold it together. His peripheral vision was gone, tunnel vision all that remained. Over the Japanese's shoulder he glimpsed the two men running towards him, faces panicked, weapons visible.

Ten seconds out.

Move!

...He's too close to escape...Injure him and then break...Take a bullet in the back but don't—

Screaming, the Japanese leaped.

No time!

Sweeping the blade inside, the Japanese closed and Gage quick-stepped to the left, reached across with his left hand to try a trap of the man's right forearm and swept his dagger, still held in his right hand, across the Japanese's wrist. But the Japanese saw, changed the movement, pulling back the direction of his forearm.

An incredible explosive twist and the Japanese whirled, spinning his body to sweep the blade in a tight half-circle with all his weight behind it.

A wild turn down and away saved Gage's throat, the blade seeming to slice across his back.

Then Gage threw himself wildly back, off balance, trying to gain distance, but the Japanese was lightning, leaping on top of him, bearing Gage to the ground, roaring, laughing, an unstoppable force conquering him, and Gage saw white fear because this was it and saw Sarah because he had failed...

"Sato!" a tall man screamed, collided against them, throwing the Japanese to the side.

Gage crashed awkwardly to the sidewalk, blade still in his hand. But he couldn't rise, blood loss increasing fast, pale shock descending hard. Blackness fading in from the edges.

Shouting above him, a chorus of shouts with the Japanese advancing and one of the men standing over Gage, shouting back at...Sato...with an authoritative, British accent.

"*Schnell!*" Gage heard a voice above him.

A foot pinned Gage's wrist, twisted the knife from his grip. Gage's eyes flickered open, focused, saw the one who had spoken—a German, blond, the muscular kind that the Polizei preferred for riot control; strong, fast, a manhandler.

"Let's get out of here!" the German shouted, panting, face in sweat. "Get the backpack!"

Gage heard a car slide to the curb beside him.

Something cold was being wrapped around his wrists. With an effort Gage lifted his head, glared down. Standard handcuffs, police issue. His hands were cuffed in front of his body. Dazed, he rolled his head to the side, saw a beige Cavalier. Then he was lifted, carried quickly, and thrown haphazardly into the backseat. Through a thick overlaying of fatigue and shadowy, glossy blankets of abysmal pain Gage heard a quick debate, a somehow familiar man in the passenger's seat arguing fiercely for more restraints, the driver shouting: "*No need, he's hurt too badly.*"

Then the car roared away from the curb, driving quickly through the night.

Orienting slowly, Gage identified a sound, a siren, and in a minute saw flashing red and blue lights pass the car, headed in the other direction, the direction they had just left. He remembered the chaos, the confusion.

Ten minutes, the car driving steadily. Gage felt the blood loss taking him. He fought it, concentrated, slowing his breath, attempting to reduce the level of oxygen in his system, still the shock as best he could. He closed his eyes, tried to rest, saw black holes zooming away from his vision, the sides spinning in spotted pale-black circles. The car rocked back and forth on the uneven road.

Vomit erupted into his mouth, hot with bile. Grimacing, Gage clenched his teeth, refusing to release, held it, concentrating. He swallowed. It returned, hot and hating. Grimly he held his mouth closed, lips tight, swallowed again.

Breathe hard. Tired.

Not yet.

How badly do you want to live?

Barto had left him, but there was Sarah ... Malachi ...

Discreetly, Gage tried to slide his wrists out of the cuffs, tried to pull steadily, drawing the steel over the hands. He would peel off his flesh if necessary, anything, just to get free. The steel bit into his hands, sharp, pain, too much pain. Gage pulled harder, the pain too much, sharp shooting pain breaking his concentration, his strength, his will.

He let go.

This is too much. Too much. Can't take it.

Gage relaxed, breathless, faint.

There's got to be a better way.

Seatbelts. Yes!

He had learned the technique somewhere, he couldn't remember where. It didn't matter.

Gage felt for the metal tongue of the seatbelt beneath him. Choosing not to reach, he attempted to identify it by body pressure. If he could just get his hands on the chrome metal locking plate, with its square hole cut into the quarter-inch steel, he could snap one of the tiny steel pins that attached the handcuff chain to the wristlocks. It would snap at the wrist with only 20 pounds of vertical pressure.

Then Gage felt it, directly beneath him, the cold steel plate of the seatbelt lock pressed against his T-shirt. He rested a moment, calculating.

Once he got his hands on it, it would take at least ten seconds of twisting at the pin before it snapped, provided he had that much strength remaining. But if the guy in the passenger seat saw him move, identified what he was doing, he was dead. A bullet in his head.

Exhausted, not knowing what to do, Gage closed his eyes and rested.

After a minute he felt unconsciousness claiming him. He shook his head, opening his eyes to fight it off. He focused on the man in the passenger seat. The tanned face looked left, stared down at him. Gage wondered what kind of pathetic sight he was lying there, bloodied and beaten, waiting for death. The man appeared worried, and Gage recognized the face, a face from his past. Someone he had known.

But the name wouldn't come to him. Only pain, the cold of shock settling in.

Gage counted the seconds, breathing steadily, still staring at the man's head. He rested, allowing his physical conditioning to assert itself, letting his body adjust to the overwhelming pain, the wounds, the rapidly increasing blood loss that would soon throw him into unconsciousness. In a few minutes, he knew from experience, he would be out. But before that, if he rested, he could gain one last surge of energy, even if it was from will alone.

Then he would make his move. As soon as the car merged onto the interstate, speed at fifty, sixty. He would strike the passenger, hard, and throw the handcuffs around the neck of the driver, crash them all. A high speed accident. More than likely, they would all die. Especially him, as wounded as he was. But there was a thin chance that an accident would provide an opportunity for escape. Even if it didn't, he would rather die fighting than to surrender to this.

Frantic screams.

A rending storm of fire and sparks collided against the driver's side of the Cavalier, and Gage's head smashed with numbing force against the door. Then in a deafening concussion the car was lifted off two wheels, settled down, crashing.

Gage rolled wildly, concealing his movement within the chaos, and the seatbelt lock was in his hand.

Collision.

Grinding metal and a strained engine roar. The Cavalier was locked side to side with another vehicle speeding recklessly along a ramp and then, earsplitting machine gun fire as the driver cut loose with a weapon, the vehicles separating.

Rolling with the explosive rocking of the vehicle, Gage slammed the steel plate of the seatbelt over the handcuff pin and twisted, pushing violently against the steel pin with all his waning strength.

Thunder collided against the Cavalier again, driving them in a tangled, screaming, grinding mass off the highway. Gage braced himself against the seat in white flashing gunfire as glass exploded across the interior.

Shadows.

White light.

Darkness, light, floating.

Crossing, rolling over him, beneath him.

Nothing else.

Gage rolled his head, opened his eyes, watching, separated from himself. A bearded man, hands clutching the steering wheel.

Lights.

You're alive! Think!

Gage focused, blinking. He was in the backseat of the car. He looked around. No, not that car. Another car. Head aching, he moved, tried to lift himself. Ah, pain! So sharp, so much of it. Sharp, slicing pain.

Fight it! Don't give up! Overcome!

Groaning, tearing open thinly clotted wounds with the effort, Gage rose to an elbow, focusing with a dead gaze at the man, the driver.

Barto.

Barto turned at Gage's movement, looked over his shoulder.

"I got ya, pal," he said, focusing again on the highway. "It was close, but I got ya." He seemed nervous, exhausted. "The cabin or a hospital?"

Gage took a deep breath. "The cabin."

Slowly, face twisted with the effort, Gage slid painfully into an upright position, leaning against the door. He looked at his wrists. Blackened in blood. Stickish.

The handcuff pin had been snapped. Too exhausted to feel any relief, he leaned his head back. He had done it. In the chaos and the confusion and the pain, he had done it.

Barto shook his head.

"I thought you'd say that. But you need a doctor, Gage. One of the other two guys didn't even make it. Head on into an embankment. The guy in the passenger seat must have jumped. I didn't see

167

him. You wouldn't have lived either if you hadn't been in the back-seat. I'm sorry, but I had to try something. I figured we could all die together if it didn't work. I pulled out of it at the last second. The car's busted up but it'll get us back. I've got the map. We're taking the back roads. We've got two more hours left to go."

Gage nodded. "Where's my bag?" he mumbled. Dry blood was caked on his lips. Then Gage realized that he couldn't see out of his left eye, felt softly with his fingers to find crusted blood, a contusion, the eye swollen shut.

"Here," Barto lifted the bag over the seat.

Gage took the bag, blood everywhere. He had trouble holding it, his grip weak, unfeeling.

Tired, now. The worst part over. Time to relax, tend to wounds. He foraged blindly, removed the cellophane pack, took out two solid blue pills, both of them high-strength, prescription painkillers, swallowed them.

"You really need a hospital, man," said Barto, his voice strained.

Gage laughed brutally, leaned his head back against the seat again. "Keep the speed slow," he mumbled. "Be careful . . . We can't risk getting stopped. Just . . . get me home. Sarah knows how . . . to fix me."

Barto made an indefinite sound, twisted his head nervously. Gage closed his eyes, sensing blood and death, such cold, timeless death, holding him, clutching him with white grinning fingers. Gage struggled, roused his will to resist, but its claim could not be denied.

It whispered to him. *"I will be cheated no more . . ."*

Fighting it, sensing his heart tiring, slowing, Gage reached for the adrenaline injection in the medical kit, anything to fight off unconsciousness. But even as his hand touched the canvas backpack he felt the blackness. Pitching forward, he fell timelessly into dreams of infinite darkness.

• • •

"How badly do you want to live?"

Sitting on the ground, sweating under the scorching, oppressive North Carolina sun, Gage said nothing. Around him, smothering and also drenched in sweat that rolled over their faces and arms, soaking their green T-shirts to their dirt-grimed bodies, no other member of the Delta Force qualifying team said a word, either. They were awed into silence by the frighteningly formidable, weathered image that stood before them.

Clad in dirty jungle fatigues, the man repeated the question. "How badly do you want to live?"

He sounded as if his throat were toughened leather, as toughened and leathery as his face. He was barely over 40 years old.

Well under six feet and lean, but deeply muscular like an anaconda, Sergeant Mac Haynes stood before them. Waiting. He was quiet, revealing nothing. His eyes were dark and narrow, black slits in his face. His hair was shaved on the sides, high and tight, a disciplined military sheen.

Trying to be inconspicuous, Gage lowered his head, grimacing in the heat.

It was the fifth day of intensive training in advanced Delta Force hand-to-hand combat. They were learning methods of silent sentry removal and covert entry, acquiring the skills needed to penetrate any security shield or leave a trail of dead soldiers across any nation or jungle in the world. It was a series of hard 20-hour days, of ceaseless fighting and more fighting, endless techniques, termination zones, methods for sanctioning human life. And beyond the dangers of practicing the training techniques without actually killing anyone, the ferocious Delta instructors made it even more hazardous by standing freely and relaxed one moment and in the next hurling a surprise attack that could render a man unconscious. The perpetual attacks created a dramatically heightened atmosphere of danger where everyone walked, even to the mess hall, in a ceaseless status of Condition Red, prepared at any moment to evade a fist or kick. Eventually, after he had narrowly anticipated and deflected a dozen brutal attacks that came out of nowhere, Gage began to catch himself reading even the shadows or rustling leaves, the wind, constantly aware of all the movement or non-movement in his immediate surroundings, his body always poised to evade, to attack or counterattack. After a while, once he became comfortable with it, when it became so natural that it required little thought, he couldn't imagine what life was like before. It seemed all there was, all there had ever been, this world of combat.

The five-day course included a session ominously tagged "The Will to Survive." It was scheduled for the last day of the week-long course so that if anyone got seriously injured they could be rolled forward for the rest of Delta Qualifications after being released from the hospital.

Again, it came.

"How badly do you want to live?" Sergeant Mac muttered softly, with a thin smile, eyes twinkling in an evil glint. "We're going to find out, ladies. We're going to find out if you'll live or die when you get out there in that ol' mean jungle." He laughed. "We're going to find out about pain, ladies. We're going to eat it. We're going to drink it. We're going to love it." He leaned over them, hands hard as oak hanging at his sides.

"Do you love pain, ladies?"

A chorused "yes, sir," boomed out.

Sergeant Mac smiled, an aspect infinitely more frightening than a man who screamed. Anyone could scream. Only the truly diabolical ones could smile at you as they pushed the mind and body past the point of human endurance, into madness.

"Yes, you do," he continued. "'Cause you're all good boys. You love pain because you know the more you love it, the less it can hurt you. You know that if you love pain, then you won't be afraid of it. You can just keep goin'. On and on. 'Cause it's in the mind, boys. In the mind. You don't need no soft bed. You don't need no soft clothes. You don't need no food. Or water. Or friends. You don't need nuthin'. You can live naked in a swamp. You can live in a gator den. Like I do. You can eat rats and sleep in a snakepit. But you don't need sleep. Sleep is for them other people, them ones that don't love pain. Like we do. You ain't like them. 'Cause you love pain. So today you're going to take it." He seemed to grow happy, smiling. "You're going to take it, and take it, and take it until you fall out on me. Until you know what you truly are, ladies. Until you're lying there in the dirt. Dirt up your nose and in your ears and in your mouth. Until pain is all you know, all you remember and all you want. Until pain is what your mamas fed ya. Until pain is what you was born for. Just pain, ladies, pain."

Silence.

Gage shifted slightly, casting a narrow glance at Sandman.

Wide-eyed, the big black man caught the look, his dark chiseled face frozen, his gaze wide and fixed.

As two of the 40 members attempting to qualify for Delta, they had volunteered for the course. Friends since they were together in the 10th Special Forces, they had long known about and dreaded this day, along with everyone else. But they also knew that it was a sacred rite of passage into the United States Army's most elite special warfare unit; an ordeal by fire where only the strongest survived for selection into Delta Force, permanently attached to Delta Command, Fort Bragg.

But first they had to survive. They had to survive Sergeant Mac.

Sergeant Mac stepped forward, smiling. He glanced to the tree-line; the sun barely over the horizon was crimson, hazy. "Now this is what you're going to do, boys," he said. "You're going to put on these nasty ol' packs, here."

He reached down to what Gage knew was a 50-pound pack. His fingers knotted around the material like talons, closing and holding effortlessly as he stood. As he continued to talk, Gage used the moment to also reach down, quickly retying his boots, adjusting them for the long, torturous run over North Carolina hills.

"Yes sir, you're going to put on these little ol' packs, and you're going to run to that hill way out yonder." He pointed down the road. "No, you can't see it. It's twenty-five miles away. But it was there yesterday. And it's there today. So we're going to run over there. And then we're going to run back. That's fifty miles. With a fifty-pound pack. And then, when we get back, I'm going to watch you do some PT. Until you die." He winked. "'Cause we ain't gonna burn all the daylight on this, boys. No sir. We'll still have too much to do. When we get back."

Gage took a deep breath, preparing. He was already sore and beaten from endless miles of running, training on the obstacle course, the constant punches and kicks. His body was a mass of contusions, the skin mottled from shallow internal bleeding where muscles had torn and blood vessels had burst beneath the brutal impact of fists, shins, or boots. But, though the contusions were frighteningly colorful, black and yellow and red, they were rarely crippling. Only painful, as the instructors would repeat. For those who had sustained massive bruising, like Gage suffered when he failed to anticipate a devastating punch by Sergeant Mac, painkillers were issued.

Gage had taken three codeine capsules before the day's exercise, and for the moment they allowed him to move his tender, torn muscles without agony. Yet at this stage, with the pain he was in, it was tempting to quit, especially with what he was about to face. But he knew he would never quit. It wasn't in him. He tried not to think about how the codeine would wear off somewhere in the run, leaving him alone with the pain. And he knew they wouldn't be issuing any more. Today, they wanted to find out what he was made of.

Frowning, he finished tying his boots.

"On your feet!"

Instantly, 40 men in dirty green fatigues were on their feet.

Gage quickly hoisted his pack, tightening the belt strap to bear the greatest weight. He clicked the shoulder connecter last, allowing as little weight as possible on the shoulder straps, providing some relief for his chest. Then he picked up the M-16, holding port arms.

"Doubletime!" Sergeant Mac yelled out.

Two columns of heavily packed soldiers moved down the road, Gage and Sandman setting the quick pace, leading each line. Gage knew that the run would cross a large, deforested section of the military reservation, acreage that swirled continuously with chalky red dust, each drifty gust of wind lifting a small cyclone of dirt that would eventually coat their faces with sunbaked clay, clogging their noses, mouths, and eyes.

A long dirt road, scorching under the summer sun, stretched out before them.

They ran.

Gage ignored the grimy sweat that dripped from his forehead, his chin, nose.

Sweat, sun, smothering heat. Miles and miles and miles. Ten miles, fifteen...

Perspiration soaked Gage's fatigues to black, then red with the dust of each plodding step. But Gage wasn't thinking about it, about anything. Somewhere he began, as usual, to pass into the zone, somewhere in himself, forgetting everything else, just running. He moved mechanically with the spell of mindless effort, of endurance. Nothing else there, thought gone, just running, the distance, road and dust. One step after another. His eyes became fixed and his hands went rigid, melded to the stock of the M-16 with the saplike resin he had sprayed on each palm. His numb feet shuffled, one step after another, another and another; dust swirling, step after step.

Miles and miles, heat and sun.

In the zone, mindless, a machine.

Then Sandman, laboring. "This is... *insane*," the big black man whispered, leaning forward against the heat. "People *die* doin' this..."

Silent, Gage nodded, awakened from his stupor, careful not to catch the wrathful attention of Sergeant Mac. But inside, where it mattered, he was only running. He felt nothing, knew nothing, because he knew that's how he would survive. He wouldn't be here. His body would do it for him. He would run until his body quit, his legs went out, or heat took him. But he wouldn't be thinking about it. Until the real pain came when everything would change. It would make him mean, pushing his soul back to his mind, where he would have to embrace the pain and the death or quit, quit everything. Because pain wrapped around death would do that; it could scare you, break you. The only way to beat it was to love it, to embrace it, to not be afraid of it. He wondered how much he could love it, how much he could take before it broke him. He had come close, before, to truly embracing it, but he had never pushed his body to the point of death. The fear had always defeated him. He had not wanted to embrace the pain when it was wrapped around death. But today, he knew, he would face death. He would know if he could embrace the pain.

Five miles more, Gage no longer aware of the sweat on his brow, no longer blinking at the stinging droplets that pricked his eyes. He stared straight ahead, moving, always moving, one step after another. No, don't think about how far. There's only one step, here, and another. That's all. Never think about how far.

Behind them, on the road, an ambulance moved slowly along, ready to catch the first to surrender to heat exhaustion, the first who could not bear the pain. Then a cadence broke out, and Gage joined it, singing out, keeping step to the words until it was gone. And then another began and he joined that, too, as they neared the halfway point, seeing the hill in the near distance.

Sergeant Mac was running beside him.

"We're almost there, ladies!" he boomed out, hearty. "Keep it up! We've got a long way to go before we get home! Gage! Give me a cadence!"

Gage led the call, keeping the pace regular, rhythmic, his mind coming back with the words. He watched the crest of the hill, felt the weight increase on his legs as they climbed the slope.

Sandman groaned beside him, breaking count, falling back.

Losing a face of sweat Gage looked to the side to gain the big man's attention, to yell out the count. Then Sandman groaned and lurched forward, hands tightening on his rifle, keeping the cadence.

They climbed the hill, to the top.

"Ten minutes, boys!" Sergeant Mac called out, leading. He turned at the crest, hands on his hips, watching as the two columns parted, separating down each side of him, red-baked soldiers collapsing in the dust, hastily pulling canteens, pouring water over face, chest, into upturned mouths. The jeep, filled with fresh, cool canteens, was waiting. But instead of going to it for water they fell like dead men over the red hillside, scattered soldiers with open mouths heaving breath in the airless heat.

Sandman fell prone to the dust and rolled to his side, gasping, mud-colored chalk swirling over him in unfelt wind. It was Gage, alone, who moved on floating legs to the jeep, his mind passing something, moving to something else inside himself, something that had begun feeding on the pain, enlarged by it, angered by it.

Yes, today he would know. He would know all there was to know about pain.

Moving directly and without stopping to the jeep, Gage picked two fresh canteens, traded his empty ones. Then, feeling the anger that gave him the strength to embrace the real pain, the main center of all that he had feared, he turned steadily and walked back to the crest of the hill.

He stood 20 feet from Sergeant Mac, waiting, rifle in hand.

Leathery face reddened by the dust and the sweat, Sergeant Mac turned and walked two steps through a sea of sweating, collapsed bodies before he noticed Gage standing on the crest, staring at him. He stopped in stride, eyes narrowing like gun sights.

Gage turned his sweat-soaked head, indifferent, to meet the gaze.

Sergeant Mac waited a moment, and then he nodded. He laughed. He clapped his hands, once. And then he went to the jeep, happily trading his canteens. He seemed to move back with a lightness, a joy in his step.

"On your feet, ladies!" he called out, smiling quickly at Gage. "We ain't got all day!"

As before, they went down the hill, running.

They passed what they passed before. But it was different to Gage; everything was less, and less important. The only thing that mattered to him now was how far he could go within himself, how deep he could go within the pain.

Red clay dust in the humid air as they plodded forward. It was only five miles from the hill that the first ones began to surrender to the smothering heat.

A cry went up, the column breaking as a man collapsed.

"Keep it up, girls!" cried Sergeant Mac. "Medics'll get 'im!"

Above his mind, in the heat, Gage heard the cry and knew what had happened. He knew the ambulance would attend to the wounded. But he wasn't there. He heard the cry and he knew. But he wasn't there. He was here, inside, beneath the heat, in his mind.

Sergeant Mac moved up the column, was a pace to the side and slightly behind Gage, where he held steady. Gage knew why Sergeant Mac had moved close, felt the eyes watching him.

Don't show...any weakness...

Not thinking, Gage felt the truth, the true reason why he would not be broken, not by anything. Part of it was simple; a desire to be the best, the toughest. Part of it was a determination to stay alive, to ultimately be the strongest survivor in a savage world. But deep inside, because he was truly a soldier, he knew that he would also endure because he simply wanted the respect of the feared Sergeant Mac. For that, Gage knew he would embrace the pain.

The day wore on, breaking stones with its heat, and men began to fall; ten, fifteen, and then twenty sprawling onto their faces in the burning roadway, moaning, crying out and struggling up only to stagger blindly to the side to fall away, lost in delirium, red heat, exhaustion.

Medics took them away. To somewhere else, where they could be like the rest.

Gage never remembered the final few miles. He only remembered his gaze wandering across the horizon, losing focus, his mind zoning so deeply he forgot where he was. He forgot Sandman beside him, forgot it all until there was only the running. He remembered only the running, his mind coming back to it again and again, red dust, step and step, rifle and sweat, pain.

Running, pain, running and pain.

His shoulders were burned deep by the straps, his chest numb. His hands frozen to the rifle like claws, stiff and swollen. But long ago, somewhere in the dusty steps, Gage had found comfort and strength in his wounds, in his battered and blistered feet that soaked his socks in blood. Somehow, it made him happy. Even as he knew he would feel different, somehow, and somehow less, if his wounds were taken from him, if the pain were taken away from him.

Leading, Sergeant Mac angled at the end of the roadway, where tall brown posts decked with rope marked the beginning of the obstacle course. They finished the run, 15 soldiers staggering across the line, fleeing the dust, the road, to the shade of the evergreens and pines.

"Take a break!" Sergeant Mac called out, winded, as the last of the line came across. He turned to them all as they staggered in fatigue. "You've done well, boys! Only the men who make it to this line are considered for Delta! And now that you're all warmed up, we'll see what you are really made of! You got five minutes to rest up! Drop your packs!"

Fourteen soldiers fell to the ground.

Sandman collapsed like a tree, his pack on his back, too tired to shift it off. His face was contorted as he heaved in humid gulps of air, red air that burned the lungs and nostrils with each ragged breath.

Floating in fatigue, Gage stayed on his feet and turned. Eyes vacuous, he shed the pack, dropping it hard to the ground and instantly felt as if he would ascend into the air, so light. But he knew it was false, would fail in moments when stiffening legs began protesting the abuse.

Standing, he stared at Sergeant Mac.

Expecting it now, the old sergeant stood, waiting. He smiled wildly as Gage stared at him. Smiled like a man who loved it.

"You still alive, Gage?"

Gage laughed shortly, breathing hard. He shook his head. "You can't break me."

"Can't break you, huh? And why's that?"

Gage thought for a moment, didn't know how to answer. He just knew that it was something inside him, a lot of things inside him.

He knew that the more he hurt, the harder he became, living and dying at once; the perfect world.

"What's that you say?" Sergeant Mac grinned, sweating, turning an ear forward. "You say you want to run the obstacle course?"

Gage grunted, uncaring. "Till you get tired of callin' it," he rasped.

Sergeant Mac leaned forward in a booming yell. "On your feet, ladies! On your feet! We got daylight! Lots of it! We're gonna run us an obstacle course! Over and over, girls! Over and over! Gage says he can't be broke, but we're gonna find out! We're gonna find out what it takes to break the boy! Let's go! Let's go-go-go!"

Sandman staggered up, aghast. He stared at Gage. "I knew you was gonna do something like that," he gasped, eyes wide. "I knew it..."

Gage gestured to the course, breathless. "They ain't gonna break me. I'll run this thing from now on. Ain't nuthin' gonna break me."

"I knew it," said Sandman, face stiff in shock, shaking his head. "I knew it..."

On the third run through the course they lost the first man. And with every trip after that, they lost another. Hours passed, with dangerous leaps from log to log, the tower, climbing and descending the ropes, long black splinters digging into their hands, slicing fingers, pain ignored in the speed of movement. Then Sergeant Mac gave them a break with pushups and situps, hundreds and hundreds of them, and then the obstacle course again, and again, until they were nothing but movement, movement and pain, pain, pain.

In the end there was only Sandman and Gage, side by side as the glowing, golden sun fell to the trees on North Carolina's dark green horizon. Finally even Sandman could go no more, falling to his face as his arms failed, unable to press one more pushup while he laid, breathing heavily, moaning, speaking to someone that was not there as Sergeant Mac, screaming now, gave him a direct order to stand.

Gage was stretched out beside him holding a pushup position, eyes closed in trembling pain, arms shaking, quivering. He heard Sandman's legs churning as Sergeant Mac continued to scream, scrambling blindly before they fell still. The big man was out cold. Unconscious. Escaping the pain.

Sweating, eyes unmerciful, Sergeant Mac turned to Gage. "On your *feet*, boy," he whispered.

Unsteady, swaying, Gage stood. He blinked through the mind-numbing exhaustion, the pale clouds, trying to focus. Sergeant Mac stood in front of him, his hands, flat and hard like boards, at his side, raised to his waist. His eyes smiled, gleaming with joy. And Gage understood. But he didn't know if he could pull it off with strength leaving him fast, empty and pale.

"Come at me, Gage," whispered Sergeant Mac. "Show me what you learned this week in all of that kung fu hand-to-hand. Hurt me. Show me what you can dish out. Show me what you can take."

Wearily, fluid and slow in fatigue, Gage had already moved, not waiting for anything. Even though his arms were dead, his legs gone, he closed the distance with a shuffling movement.

A flat hand like a plank hit him in the chest, his wound, laying him back. Gage screamed at the scarlet pain.

He hit the ground hard, screaming still and then he moaned, crying aloud, and rolled, palms pressing flat against the ground, struggling to rise, to stand. He gained his feet, turning to see Sergeant Mac smiling, holding the ground. Gage shouted and rushed, leaping forward as quickly as he could and thinking more but surprised to shock as Sergeant Mac's boot lashed out to smash into his thigh, a fist coming in that...

A stunning blow and Gage was down again, rolling, holding his head with a hand and finding himself in his fatigue again rising to his feet, only movement, beyond it, even, where there was nothing but him and death, and the pain. Then he reached his feet and was slammed back again, not knowing where the blow came from, where it went.

Who was he fighting?

And somehow, again, he was up on stiffening legs before he felt that he had been struck down, again, gazing at a sky not totally night, above him. And then he was rising yet again, numb everywhere, fighting to gain his feet, to fight...

Struck down, again.

Rising, rising...

To be struck down, beyond exhaustion now, beneath it. Gage tried to stand, to find the earth in the whiteness and somehow he knew he was *there*, inside death. There were no more secrets hidden from him inside the pain, no mysteries, nothing. He knew it all. And the pain could not defeat him, not as long as there was still blood inside him, not as long as he could still stand, fight, endure.

Get on your feet!

He stood.

To be struck down.

A dim physical impulse told Gage he was hurt again, lying on his back on pine needles beneath a cobalt blue space of sky; stars through a patch of broken trees and the face of a man, dark in the dusk, smiling now, with a friendly hand on Gage's chest, gently holding him down, and Gage heard the words.

"You're the one, son," the voice said, hand gentle on his chest. "You're the one..."

$$\bullet \quad \bullet \quad \bullet$$

Light.

An old man's shout...A woman's voice; stern, impatient, commanding...Hands lifting him, moving him...carrying him... lights passing over...

Gage weakly opened his eyes; fog, mist.

A woman...Sarah...yes...doing something...white...speaking to him...encouraging...hands wrapping him in something warm.

Gage focused on the woman before she shoved the needle into his arm, warmth and oblivion.

He closed his eyes.

I won't fail you...God help me...Not any of you.

"Well it don't get no worse than this."

Radford dropped three file folders on Kertzman's desk, then collapsed heavily in the green metal chair. Kertzman thought that the NSA damage control man looked remarkably disheveled for this hour in the morning.

"I've read 'em," Kertzman mumbled, leaning back in his chair, blacksmith arms stretched out so his massive hands could cup a steaming mug of coffee.

Radford almost allowed a glimmer of surprise to shine through. "Read them? How? I just got them five minutes ago. First shift faxed them in."

Kertzman grunted. "I got sources. A couple of old-timers. Everything has happened in New York, so I told some buddies of mine to keep a lookout. Told 'em to call me if there were any big-time ex-military guys killed. There were a couple. An ex-SEAL was killed in a domestic. His wife shotgunned him while he was asleep—"

"That'll do it," Radford interjected, a short shake of his head.

"Then an old Army Ranger was shot in a liquor store holdup. Lower East Side. Police got the offender. Just a thug. But when I saw the incident at St. Thomas, and the rest of it, I knew we had probably found our man."

"But how did you get the reports? The FBI guys in New York put a hold on them. Ordered no copies except for NSA. The bureau confiscated the evidence, everything. I didn't think anybody knew about this."

Kertzman laughed. "You gotta be kiddin' me. You think that anybody below the rank of captain in NYPD gives a hoot what the FBI thinks? Everybody knows about this. There's probably a hundred copies floating around. Inside *and* outside the department. First-year rookies in the transit police probably got copies. The FBI putting a hold on it only made it more popular. A guy I know faxed them to me at my home last night."

"Over a private line?" Radford asked, too accustomed to intrigue to be genuinely surprised, but appearing somewhat interested at the interworkings of Kertzman's life. "That's illegal, isn't it?"

"Yeah," Kertzman mumbled, and then hesitated to release a long, rumbling belch. "He called me last night, told me about a real weird gunfight on the interstate between a Cavalier and an LTD. Everybody's talking about it. Even the State Patrol's mad. And they don't get mad at anything. Takes too much energy. Turns out the driver of the Cavalier is a no-name. His ID, Sergei whatever, doesn't check. NCIC doesn't know him. Nothing. So FBI does a print check, matched him against a KGB operative named Arkady Torkarev. No record of passing customs. Not supposed to be here. I got all that this morning. That's what really got my attention. Anyway, Torkarev was killed deader 'a wedge after kissing a concrete embankment in the Cavalier, so we can't ask him any questions. Then a former member of the British SAS was . . ." Kertzman hesitated, "and this is the real clincher, this SAS guy was shot by a *fireman* in St. Thomas Cathedral. And that's only ten miles away from the accident." Kertzman stared at Radford. "That's a Catholic church."

"Yes," Radford replied quickly. "Yes, thank you. I know."

"Yeah," Kertzman continued, "so this SAS guy is cut down in a church by a fireman, who can't really be a fireman, so it's gotta be our man. And then there was a real mean knifefight, or gunfight, or both, on Paxton, three blocks from the church only minutes after the SAS guy went down. A big Japanese and a white guy. It's all related. I'll bet everything I've got on it. So we got a dead SAS guy and a dead KGB guy. Both of them killed in strange situations with no offender in custody for anything. So I ordered a print check on it and it all comes back to Gage. Nine millimeter casings. A knife. An ax at the church. It was him, alright. He was in a major headbashin' contest with somebody." He shook his head for a moment, felt strangely agreeable. "You're right, though. It don't get no worse than this."

Radford sighed. "Have you heard from Carthwright?"

"Yes." Kertzman didn't appear to want to communicate the message.

Radford ignored it. "So what did he say?"

"He was Carthwright," Kertzman replied, shrugging.

Kertzman was finished, but Radford kept staring at him.

"He isn't happy," he added finally. "He didn't sound good. He wants us to find a location for Gage, run him to ground. He doesn't seem to care if it ends in a tactical situation or not. He just wants it to end."

Radford nodded, agreeing. "Good. So what are we going to do?"

"Did the police get anything on the LTD that left the scene of the accident?"

"No," Radford replied. "No sightings. The black guy, or Japanese or Indian or whatever he is, is gone, too. Vanished without a trace, as they say in police work."

"With no direction of travel," Kertzman added.

"Whatever. He hasn't showed up at any hospitals. We have nothing. Just the Cavalier. It was registered to a warehouse that operates out of Manhattan. A legitimate operation. No connections that I can find. Owners say the car was stolen some time last night. They didn't notice it was missing until today." Radford shrugged. "It could have happened. They've got a lot of cars. There was forced entry into the garage. Looks real. Discovered this morning. There's nothing to indicate otherwise."

"Who owns the garage?"

"Unlimited Storage."

"And who owns that?"

"AmTech Incorporated."

"And who owns AmTech?"

"A holding company."

"And who controls the holding company?"

Radford sighed. "I don't know. Probably a bigger company."

"Trace it back."

"OK," Radford nodded. "I'll find something."

Kertzman thought for a minute. "Where's Milburn?" he asked, indifferent.

"You're asking me?" Radford seemed taken back. "I don't know. I'm working my end. That's all I know about." He looked closely at Kertzman. "I would like to bring this all to an ending, Kertzman, if you know what I mean. This is really starting to stink, and some of that is going to rub off. I didn't ask for this assignment. I was volunteered for it. I know that a lot of those guys in the Pentagon had suspicions, but you're the one who really nailed down something serious going on, figured this wildman was one of ours. You're the great white hunter. Killing bears in the mountains, no helicopters and all that jive. So maybe you should figure out a way to track this guy down."

Radford's tone was pushing.

Kertzman didn't seem to notice, continued to stare at the mug. His voice was distant, thoughtful. "Have you studied Gage's 201?"

"Yeah," replied Radford. "I know everything there is to know."

"The Black Light file?"

"That, too."

"Is anyone still alive that was in the unit?"

Radford considered that. "I checked on that, like I told you I would. There's nobody still active in the field that he worked with. I put out the word on a little reward for anyone who hears from him."

"I didn't say 'active,'" Kertzman replied moodily.

Radford gazed at him. A long silence passed.

"Kertzman, surely you don't expect me to just randomly contact people Gage knew in the unit." Radford's voice was indulgent. "That's a lot of footwork, isn't it? I mean, some of these guys are drunks. They don't have phones. They've fallen to the wayside. When these guys go back to civilian life they sometimes lose it."

Kertzman was impassive. "Yeah," he said, "contact them. Find them all. There can't be more than a half-dozen. Find out where they're working. Find out who owns the companies they work for. Run the companies against this Cavalier. Cross-check everything. Look hard for somebody working for a transport company that rents aircraft. Anybody who owns a gun store or has a Class Three Firearms License, or even a Class Two. The Bureau will have it. Find out if any of them have purchased nightvisors, APGs, fully automatic weapons, anything that Gage might have used in Black Light. Find out if any of them have access to NCIC. Run a tag search through the Information Center and see if anyone ran the tag on the Cavalier at any time within the past forty-eight hours. Find out where the ammo used at the church was purchased, see if it can be traced back to a town within one hundred miles of where any of his old buddies live. Find a connection. Get everything on everybody, everyone who's still alive, that is. There's going to be something, somewhere. I'll take care of the SAS and KGB guys."

Radford seemed to be figuring a better way to do things. "What makes you think Gage is still in contact with anybody in his old Army unit?"

Kertzman scowled, shook his head. His gaze wandered the room for a minute, face concentrated. "Gage ain't perfect," he said slowly. "He needs help. He's like everybody else. Somewhere, he's made a mistake. You can count on it. Just find it. Then we'll find him."

"That's a lot of work, Kertzman."

"Use some of the NSA staff," Kertzman said. "They don't have anything better to do. And they don't have to know anything about what they're doing, anyway. Tell 'em to crunch numbers. They're good at it. It's probably all they're good at."

Radford opened his mouth to show offense.

"Save it," Kertzman growled, a tone of granite. "Just tell them to find some number that can link one of Gage's old teammates, somebody who went out before the big showdown in the desert, with some company associated with the Cavalier or the bullets or the Hi-Power or anything else."

Radford was quiet, reluctant.

"Alright," he said, after a moment. "I'll get some people on it." He waited. "What are you going to do?"

"I'm going to New York. The British are sending over somebody to claim the body of their guy. They seem a little peeved. He'll be in today. Leaving tonight. I want to talk to him."

Radford looked at him a moment, thinking. "Yeah, that's probably a good idea. Maybe you can find something. You want me to tell Carthwright?"

Kertzman rose to his feet. "I'll tell him. He's still in Washington. I've got to meet him this morning, give him a status report."

Radford also rose. "You want me to tell Milburn anything if I see him?"

Kertzman shook his head, reached for his keys. "No."

Radford nodded, started for the door.

"Hey, Radford."

"Yeah?" He stared back at Kertzman, ready to please.

Kertzman's impassive face was stone. Dead flat eyes focused on Radford. The voice was abrupt.

"How come you got volunteered for this operation?"

Empty hands were raised in the air.

"No reason, Kertzman. It sure ain't because I like looking at your pretty face, I'll tell you that."

. . .

Sarah changed the white cotton shirt that had become stiff with blood, made certain Gage was sleeping soundly, and left him in his small bedroom. She took a shower, put on a clean pair of jeans and one of Gage's T-shirts, walked through the house to find Barto and Malachi.

The cabin, not large, was silent. The three additional bedrooms were tiny and used mainly for storage, particularly the one in the back of the house that was crammed with crates, a desk with a small computer that was hooked into a telephone modem, and a small Army cot. She knew that most of Gage's more dangerous high-tech combat equipment was stored in the garage under lock and key. The battered LTD and Jeep were also in the adjoining building, which was almost as large as the house itself.

She entered the front room, the only room of any real size in the entire cabin, to find Barto and Malachi sitting quietly at the kitchen table. She smiled faintly at them as she entered the room, poured herself a cup of coffee. Her pale face revealed dark circles under the jade green eyes. Her hands trembled.

Malachi stood as she entered, walked to her for a solid, comforting embrace. She held him for a moment, then separated to walk towards the table, sitting down. Malachi followed and sat down beside her, wordless.

Barto said nothing, stared out the window. She reached out and took his hand.

"You did what was right," she said tiredly.

Barto made a sudden movement of his head. "I didn't know what else to do. He wouldn't go to a hospital."

"Well, I think he might still live," Sarah said, removing her hand, leaning back. "You did all you could. We all did."

"What about his injuries?" Barto's voice was edged.

"I used up all the silk," she replied wearily, sweeping a trembling hand through her hair. "He had a lot of cuts. But the only really serious one was on his forearm. It missed his radial artery by a half-inch. Probably missed his major nerves too because they run along the inside of the arm, not the outside, where the cut was. But I can't tell for sure. There was a lot of venous bleeding. That's his main trouble right now. He needs a transfusion. Closing the wounds took a lot of stitches. I cleaned out the incisions as best I could with the time I had but . . ." She paused, sighing. "I think he might have a couple of broken ribs. I can't tell. There's some swelling, some tenderness. But they might just be bruised. Even a doctor couldn't tell without an x-ray."

Barto seemed shaken again. "You really think he might make it?" His eyes were widened behind the glasses.

"He might," Sarah answered. "He's been hurt like this before. Worse. It's a way of life for him. Surviving, no matter what. Or it used to be. He's strong. He's trained to deal with this kind of physical trauma. I've given him something to help him sleep. That's all I can do right now. But I think he's got an infection. And I don't have anything to treat it with."

She paused, face pained, and took a slow sip of coffee.

Tense silence reigned.

Slowly, Barto bent over the letter laid on the table, scanning the page, eyes moving with a minutely focused, discerning concentration.

Dully, Sarah looked at the page. "Can you read it?"

"No." Barto shook his head. "Only Gage can read it. It's some kind of code. A mixture of numbers, some Latin. From the Silver Period. It doesn't make any sense. The letters and numbers are just symbols for other letters, or entire words." He studied the page a moment more. "It must be something Gage and Simon came up with together."

Malachi agreed. "Yes. Simon would have taken every precaution. He did not underestimate our enemies. But, as you said, Sarah," he nodded gently to her, "Gage will live. That is the most important thing."

Sarah said nothing, nodded. She took a deep breath, then rose, walking toward the bedroom. "Excuse me, I need to check on him."

"Will you be staying beside him?" her father called after her. "I will prepare something to eat."

Sarah glanced back, continued forward. "Yes, I'll be beside him."

Her last words were so faint Malachi couldn't be sure of what he heard, but he thought he understood.

"... I'm always beside him ..."

• • •

Rose-colored wine rested on the table, and Stern reached out to receive it. Augustus gazed down at him, ice-blue eyes understanding and patient, and set the decanter aside with a cultured appreciation for both wine and the intricately molded flagon.

"Misfortune merely delays victory, Charles," the white-haired man said encouragingly. "Our hands shall write the denouement, the final page."

Stern took a sip of the wine, swirled the liqueur in the crystal. "Mine was the error, Augustus. I should have used more men. The Order are consummate soldiers, and we anticipated his moves. But Gage has great courage. And courage alone can sometimes decide a situation."

"Even the bravest men know fear," Augustus responded, smiling. "Even the wisest men become confused by the chaos of war. That is certain."

Stern nodded. "Yes."

"Arkady and Samuel will be replaced when this situation has passed," Augustus added. "Tell me of Milburn. He has been useful to me for many years."

Stern stirred, as if fighting off fatigue, his voice remaining calm.

"He survived the accident. He was sitting in the passenger's seat, in the vehicle that contained Gage. He managed to jump clear before the car collided with the embankment. He was injured, sustaining a few cracked ribs, some contusions. But he is still capable of functioning in his purpose. I am certain that it was the language student who forced them into the wall. He obviously followed Arkady and Milburn after they put Gage in the car. Then he somehow managed to free Gage and escape."

Augustus nodded, respectful. "Gage is a formidable foe," he said. "His allies demonstrate considerable loyalty."

"Yes," Stern said. "Gage understands offense and defense as one. He does not consider stages. It is all a mosaic, a unity. For him tactics are not a science, but an art, an almost mystical blend of knowledge, intuition, and imagination. An extension of his personality. He can virtually create a situation, simply by the power of his will and his knowledge, combined with his courage. Sato is unstable and sometimes difficult to control. But if he had not located the car, Gage might well have escaped us completely."

"Yes, Sato is a valuable man." Augustus nodded with the words, took a sip of wine. "How are his wounds?"

Stern released a short laugh. "I never thought that I would see the man who could injure Sato. But he is healing. In a week he will be well. He suffered a loss of blood. But he had prepared for it beforehand. He is always prepared."

Augustus seemed relaxed, stood before the windowed wall, gazing out at the ocean growing steadily deeper with the dusk. A reddish glow stretched across the horizon, spreading scarlet threads over the dancing, waving sea; dark waters bloodied with a crimson tide.

"Is Milburn continuing to search for Gage's stronghold?" he asked slowly.

"Yes. They will locate him soon enough. This man in the Pentagon is quite skilled. A hunter, they call him. That is why he was selected. Then, when Gage's safe house is located, they will all be eliminated. Everything is arranged. Containment will be complete. The investigation shall begin and end with the American, and with the Pentagon. None of our forces will be exposed."

"Then all is well," Augustus remarked, bearing teeth in a strangely savage smile. He turned, walking to the obsidian table, glistening in the scarlet glow. "And you are certain that Gage is badly wounded?"

"Yes," Stern replied. "He must retreat to recover."

"It is to our advantage."

"His wounds will heal, Augustus."

"Yes, Charles, his wounds shall heal," the robed figure replied. "But wounds change the will. And that shall change the man. War is more than casualty, old friend. It is defeating the spirit of your foe. Gage will heal, but the healing will wound him, also. And then we shall wear him down even more. We will make him exhaust so much of his strength that he will begin to show the strain of the conflict in his decisions, in his actions. And that will be the beginning of his defeat. Piece by piece, we shall claim what is his. We will see his defeat approaching because we will watch him deteriorating before our eyes, ravaged by the wear and tear of resisting our superior strength. That is what will ultimately finish him; a long, relentless strain on his will and strength until he is unable, finally, to meet us any longer in combat. Then he will be ours."

Stern stared at the white-haired man, the wine goblet ignored in his hand. "Yes, I see." He hesitated a long moment, then spoke with a bitter edge. "Yes, you are right, Augustus. It will probably be the wear and tear of combat that truly defeats him, not a sudden, strategic move. But, sudden defeat or not, when we find Gage's location we will attack with every confidence of finishing him there."

Augustus nodded, frowning, then he turned to the window, suddenly moody, staring at the sea.

"Remember, Charles, Gage is the purest of his kind. We have already lost two valuable men. Men who were of the highest order, the sixth ascendancy. They, too, were the best at what they did. But it is written that the sword devours one side as well as the other. So there is no reason for dismay. And yet we must admit that the price we have paid for the manuscript is great. Clement remains enraged and has banished D'Oncetta from the Vatican. And our Middle Eastern allies have begun to question the wisdom of our actions. It is clear that Gage must be stopped. But it must be done quietly. No more attention must be drawn to our affairs. You must use wisdom. We can attract no more attention."

Augustus's icy gaze centered on Stern.

"Gage is wounded and in retreat. But beware, Charles. It is the retreat of a wounded lion."

TWENTY-THREE

Alone in a howling cold, standing morosely between two faintly tarnished marble lions, Thomas Blake Carthwright waited patiently on the sidewalk, centered at the entrance of the Smithsonian Institute's Museum of Natural History.

Carthwright turned as Kertzman approached, shoving his hands deeply into the pockets of his black, cashmere Armani overcoat. Its broad, heavy collar was turned up against the freezing wind. Kertzman continued to walk forward, moving with the crowd until he stood in front of the CIA man.

"I'm here," he said, adding brusquely, "looks a little different than our last meeting."

Carthwright smiled. "There are a few complications."

Kertzman waited, expressionless.

Carthwright motioned to the street. "Walk with me, Mr. Kertzman. I understand that the Lincoln Memorial is almost deserted this time of day."

"It is," Kertzman said gruffly and followed slowly as Carthwright crossed the wide metal grating, over Pennsylvania Avenue and onto the sidewalk of the park, walking south into the cold wind that tore leaves from the trees and the ground with equal indifference. In the distance, Kertzman saw the Memorial, white marble glowing massively in the early morning.

An icy, invisible wave swept across the park, blasting through the pores of Kertzman's coat into his bones. He found it brutal and comforting; nature separating the weak from the strong. It was his place.

"Does it get this cold in Dakota?" Carthwright asked casually.

Kertzman nodded. "Colder. A lot colder."

"Your people must be hardy."

"We do what we gotta do," Kertzman replied. "Ain't no sense in complaining."

"Yes." Carthwright pulled his coat more completely around him and glanced over, seeming to take notice that Kertzman wore only a thin, cheaply-cut sportscoat for protection against the howling cold front. "As I said, there are complications."

"I figure," Kertzman replied with a short, humorless laugh.

"Some people are concerned about the progress of the investigation."

Kertzman glanced at him, saw only professional concern. "So what?"

"That's not the type of concern I'm talking about. This concern is . . . unofficial."

Slowing his stride, Kertzman focused on the words. "And who might these people be?"

Carthwright shook his head. "I am not certain. But it seems that it is someone who has considerable influence. Perhaps a number of people."

Kertzman stopped walking. Carthwright took two steps and then also stopped, turning to look back. His thin blond hair was tossed by the wind.

"You know, this is getting uglier and uglier," Kertzman said after a moment. "Did you know what Gage did for the Agency?"

"In a manner," Carthwright replied, a nervous sigh. Kertzman thought he saw a trembling.

"Why didn't you tell me?"

"I knew that Gage was one of the animals out of Covert Operations. I didn't know, exactly, what Black Light did. It didn't matter to me. And, honestly, Black Light was never a very well-respected unit in the intelligence community. Just soldiers. Not players. Not people who understood the craft. They were just people who knew how to blow things up, steal things, kill people. All that cowboy stuff. But anybody can do that. It takes a different breed to be a spy. Someone who can work the game. Someone who can sacrifice." Carthwright hesitated, bunching against the wind. "Besides, I knew you had access to the files."

A sudden gust of wind almost moved Carthwright up a step. He swayed. Kertzman felt his face going numb, fingers tingling, hurting from cold. He felt tempted to put his hands into his coat, decided to let it go. Part of it was because he didn't like giving in to the cold, part of it was Carthwright. Kertzman had already decided he wouldn't show any weakness around the NSA man, not to anything. Not ever.

Kertzman glanced at the Memorial, still a long way off. He looked back at Carthwright.

"You lied to me," he muttered, hard and unforgiving. "You could have told me more when I walked into this thing. So I could have gone in with my eyes open. You could have. But you didn't. That's the same as lying."

Carthwright seemed to consider that. "Yes," he said after a minute. "I suppose I could have. Secrets and a culture of secrecy can sometimes cloud judgment. It was my mistake. I apologize."

The wind was cold, the silence colder.

Kertzman laughed without humor, shook his head. "You know," he said slowly, "I've just about had it with secrets."

"Yes, I understand. It can become tiring."

Kertzman waited a moment, trying to figure it out. "So is that why you called me here?" he asked. "To tell me that some people you don't know are concerned about this thing, but you don't know why they're concerned?"

For a while Kertzman wasn't sure Carthwright was going to respond.

"Yes," the NSA man said finally. "It sounds ridiculous, doesn't it?"

"It sounds like a lie," Kertzman rumbled. "And I've just about had it with lies, too."

"Please, Kertzman, I want you to listen to me," Carthwright said, seeming to take it personally. He stepped forward until they stood face to face. Kertzman calculated that Carthwright was only six inches shorter than he was, but outweighed by about 150 pounds. Kertzman stared into the face, saw the skin pale with cold.

"Alright, talk."

"This place is not secure," Carthwright began, voice lowered. "But, with these people, no place is secure. So I'll just tell you."

"Tell me what?"

"You just do whatever you have to do to find Gage," Carthwright mumbled through the cold. "Concentrate on Gage. Don't start rolling over stones on this conspiracy theory. It might become . . . unsafe. I can't tell you more." He waited. "I'm going to have to ask you to trust me on this, Kertzman. I don't want these people to . . . do something."

Kertzman scowled. "*Do* something!"

A nod.

"You gotta be kiddin' me!"

Carthwright shook his head, a quick movement.

Kertzman stared at him. "Is Talbot in on this?"

Carthwright shrugged. "I don't know." He hesitated. "I really don't have any idea. All I know for sure is that somebody with weight is behind it. Maybe a lot of them. Gage was into something that was way, way off the books."

"But Black Light wasn't off the books," Kertzman said. "The Director of Central Intelligence or his designee sanctioned every mission. Every mission was documented."

"Was it, Kertzman?" Carthwright leaned close. "If Black Light was legitimate, then why does someone want Gage dead so badly? And what is a document, anyway? Documents are just documents. They can say whatever we want them to say. They don't mean anything. They never have. Falsifying documents is how we survive in this business. I'm telling you right now, Kertzman, this investigation goes back to Black Light and whoever *really* controlled it in the Reagan years. It might be somebody high in the State. It could be somebody on the Hill. There's no way to know. But I think that whoever it was wants Gage dead. And we're both in danger. Just stay away from the high-ups in this, Kertzman. That's what I'm telling you. Just go after Gage. Find him." He hesitated, nodding. "Bring him in."

Kertzman was silent. And after a moment Carthwright began speaking again, slower.

"You have to ask yourself some questions, Kertzman. Who did Black Light really work for? Who passed the orders to the DCI? What was the true purpose of the unit? Think about it. Because it doesn't add up. The CIA hasn't had any real serious tactical work to do since Vietnam. After '72 almost all of the mercenary types were terminated, released. This is a *spy* business now, Kertzman. With satellites. With pictures taken from orbit that can tell us what kind of magazine a person is reading in his backyard. It's a game of computers, of analysts in white lab coats or doctors with degrees in psychiatry. The CIA doesn't need a bunch of deadeye gunslingers executing people all over the globe." He gathered his intensity. "And this is the crux. Covert military actions like that always work with our foreign political policy. It's not a military decision to use a unit like Black Light. It's a political decision. It's an Executive Office decision. And that's because a unit as powerful as Black Light can, almost overnight, change the political structure of any country on Earth." Carthwright paused. "Including ours."

He glanced around, continued. "Think about this, Kertzman. What if a person, or persons, decided that they were going to go around the White House and the president during the Reagan and Bush years to determine America's foreign affairs? And what if they used an ultra-secret unit like Black Light to do it? Don't you think that those people would be willing to kill Gage to protect that secret? Or even kill you and me if they needed to?"

Carthwright turned away for a moment, shook his head, looked back. "Kertzman, what government in the *world* would need a unit like Black Light for just an occasional sanction? I mean, we do preemptive hits against terrorist cells, an odd sanction of a dangerous defector. But that's small stuff. And Navy SEALs handle most of it. We don't just go around killing foreign agents, military officials, or national leaders. They can just kill one of ours! It's counterproductive." He paused, took a deep breath. "Unless," he added, "Black Light was so off the books that no foreign country was ever able to trace responsibility back to us. Unless the White House was so ignorant of its activities that there could never be a leak. And if that was the case, Kertzman, then Black Light could have been into *anything*." He looked helpless, shook his head. "Anything at all. They could have decided the course of any nation on Earth in a thousand different ways. They could have set the internal course for this country a long time ago and nobody would have a clue." He paused. "Now, for argument, let's assume that Black Light was a very secret, and very powerful, foreign policy instrument of some unknown controllers in the CIA or NSA. Then the unit got wiped out in Israel. Everyone but Gage. And let's assume that, for some reason, Gage has become a security problem. Let's say he's gotten involved in some sort of private war in the civilian sector, and now his old bosses are running scared. Now they're afraid Gage might be caught doing something in the private world, that he'll start talking and things will eventually unwind all the way back to Black Light and how it decided a lot of our foreign policy issues behind the president's back. Behind Congress's back. Then this country will have an entirely new scandal and new heads will roll."

Kertzman's face was stone, his silence massive.

Nervously, Carthwright waited a moment, eyes scanning the distant sidewalks. He spoke without looking back at Kertzman. "In the late eighties, Black Light was classified beyond me. I never really knew what the unit did. Everyone heard rumors about it, suspected that it was a paramilitary group out of Covert Ops. But when I got deeper into this investigation I *knew* something was wrong. I didn't say anything at first because I didn't know what to make of it. But now I do. These cowboys, no matter how good they are, have no place in the spy business anymore, Kertzman. They haven't for a long time. They're a liability."

Carthwright turned back. "Look at the obvious," he continued, "because it doesn't add up. Black Light was launching constant covert military strikes and most of the documented missions don't even make sense. The documents claim that a mission was for surveillance or a theft or something else equally meaningless. But you know and I know that we wouldn't use a group like Black Light for something so frivolous as surveillance or thefts. Or even kidnappings. Every man in the unit would have fifty million dollars' worth of training. That's a valuable person. We couldn't risk losing one of them on some ridiculous stunt that a freelancer could do. And yet Black Light launched a mission every four or five weeks. So what were they really doing?" Carthwright shook his head again. "Who knows? They weren't doing what the documents say they were doing, I'll tell you that. Which means that we have no idea, really, what the unit was up to or who they were receiving orders from."

The NSA man waited, his face confused. "Kertzman, we're lost in this." He shook his head again. "These people are masters at secrets, at concealing things. Gage did what he did and now somebody wants him dead to protect that secret."

Kertzman felt reluctantly impressed, but he tried to hide it behind a visage of stone.

"I'm talking about *forces*," Carthwright said, his voice firmer, more confidential. "I'm talking about people who can make things *happen*. And I'm telling you to watch your back, for all of us. In all honesty, Kertzman, I don't know you. It wouldn't mean a whole lot to me if you got killed. No offense. But—"

"None taken," Kertzman said.

"But you're in a game that could cost us all our lives," Carthwright continued, trembling now. "Somebody is using me and you to find this guy, Gage. We have to follow through or we're going to lose a lot more than a few inches around here. But somebody else in the family wants him worse than we do. And I don't mean prison. They want him dead."

"So what do you suggest I do?" Kertzman growled.

Carthwright's answer was quick. "Find him. Forget who's running this show. Just find the guy and let the rest go. Because if you threaten these people we're all dead. All of us."

"How do you know all this?" Kertzman's voice was disbelieving.

Carthwright nodded. "I know. Believe me, I know."

Kertzman almost laughed, focused on the NSA man. "That ain't enough, tough guy. You're gonna have to do better or I'm walking. Let you have it. Find him yourself. I couldn't care less if I lose a few inches around here. I'm a short-timer, and I don't have to put up with them too much longer. And I sure ain't no hitter. I'm not going to find this guy just so somebody can bushwhack him. If I can't find out who wants him, then I'm not going after him."

Carthwright shifted. "That's not a good idea, Kertzman. You're in this now. If you don't find him, they'll just take care of you because they'll be afraid of you. They'll think you're going to run a game on them instead of finding Gage like you're supposed to. Finding Gage is the only thing that is going to end this and keep us all alive. That's all we got."

"And if I don't?" Kertzman growled, ignoring the numbness in his face, hands, and feet.

"I know the game better than you do," Carthwright said, his voice solid, confident.

Cold and a long silence.

"No deal," Kertzman said, turning. "I'm staying in. But I'm going to play it my way. I'm gonna push it to the wall. I'm going to document this meeting, just like everything else. I'm going to fix it so that if I get killed a lot of people are going to burn. Even you. It will be the biggest stink this city has seen since Water-Iran-Gate and whatever else has come down the pike in the last twenty years. The family jewels will be exposed, buddy, wide open, for all the world to see. You can count on it, and you can pass it on. I might go down, but I'll take a lot of people with me when I do."

"You'll never touch them, Kertzman," Carthwright replied steadily, fixing him with an almost disappointing gaze. "This is the real world. And these are the people who run it. You and me, we don't even count. And we've actually got some power. But these people are way beyond us, Kertzman. Way beyond."

"Maybe," Kertzman replied, nodding. "We'll see."

Sensing vaguely that he had just committed suicide, Kertzman started away, leaving Carthwright in the cold. Then a sudden thought made him turn.

"Just tell me one thing," Kertzman said.

Carthwright responded, weary. "What?"

"Who assigned Radford and Milburn to this?"

Clearly, Carthwright was reluctant to answer.

"I'm going to find out anyway," Kertzman said.

Carthwright's stare wandered away for a moment, eyes roaming, a sudden concentration evident in the face.

Gazed back at Kertzman.

"I did," he said.

TWENTY-FOUR

As a dead man rising, Gage stood at mid-afternoon. Sarah heard the movement, turned and saw him standing, swaying, one bandaged hand clutching the ribs that had been so badly bruised.

His glazed eyes were flat, unseeing, and there was a pale, bloodless mask on his face. Beneath the paleness Sarah glimpsed an effort of will that struggled to command the body, but the body would not obey, began to wither as he stood on dead legs. Suddenly he took a step, stumbled.

"Gage!" she shouted, but he was already collapsing as she ran. She caught him as he fell heavily forward, strained to direct his body to fall onto the bed. Then he crashed back, unconscious, as if struck, catching a single deep breath and then no movement at all, eyes closed.

Sarah stared at him a moment, felt a vague fear, reached suddenly for his neck. For a minute she let her fingers rest on the carotid artery, searching, before she found it. Then she waited, measuring the almost invisible respirations against the pulse. After a moment she calculated the ratio.

Pulse was weak at 44 beats a minute, respirations were too low. She knew from experience that anywhere in the mid-forties to low-fifties was normal for him. But the beat was thin, too thin. And the respirations were shallow, weak.

She felt for fever. He was hot, beginning to sweat. She bit her lip, moved back away.

Movement behind her. She turned, saw Barto, her father.

"We heard you shout," Barto said hesitantly. "Is he . . ."

"No." Sarah shook her head, storm in her eyes, mouth tight. "Not yet."

A sound.

Startled, Sarah turned back to the bed.

Gage's lips moved, the faint sound of delirium. A word.

Sarah bent low, watching the face. She felt Malachi and Barto pressing up behind her. Her father's hand was on her shoulder.

Gage whispered something indiscernible.

Silence.

Barto's voice was almost nothing. "What's he saying?"

"I don't know if I heard him," Sarah said quietly, still watching. "Just a couple of words. But I don't understand what he wants."

"What do you *think* he wants?" Barto asked.

Sarah sighed, shook her head. "Sandman," she whispered, brow hard with concentration. "He said . . . Sandman."

• • •

Antique white but blackened by the traffic exhaust of the surrounding streets, the Department of Forensic Science building for the Federal Bureau of Investigation in New York City was almost empty when Kertzman arrived.

Using one of the reserved spaces, he parked the LTD in the rear of the building and placed a placard on his dash that notified any well-doers who might want to remove the vehicle that it was the property of the Federal Government. Then he started for the building.

Sunlight was gone, and as Kertzman completed the four-hour drive from Washington he had used every minute to work the facts, figuring the angles of everything. But he kept coming back to the same thing: Carthwright.

It all came back to Carthwright.

From Carthwright's position in the NSA he could have easily run Black Light, from beginning to end. Either for himself or for somebody else. And now it appeared that he was covering it all up, trying to find Gage, running the investigation himself.

The walk across the lot was full of memories, words, and phrases that Kertzman had collected. And he matched everything that occurred to him against a single rule: Who would benefit from this?

Kertzman knew from all his years as a street cop and ten years in the FBI that almost nobody did anything without motivation. Few people ever even assisted a law enforcement officer simply for the good of humanity. Usually they helped only because they wanted the Law to do something for them that they couldn't do for themselves. They wanted revenge, or they wanted to legally eliminate their competition. Nothing was for free. Everybody had a motivation.

So what was Carthwright's motivation in directing this investigation? To save himself? To protect someone else? To see justice? And why did Carthwright deliver the warning? Was it really from unknown *forces*? Or was it from Carthwright himself?

A bad feeling settled on Kertzman. No, he thought, it can't be that easy. It could never be that easy, or that obvious.

And other things didn't fit: Carthwright had gone to great pains to make this manhunt a highly visible, thoroughly documented government operation.

"...*Call the Office of Security and confirm...This meeting has been taped...Document everything...*"

But if Carthwright was guilty of having run Black Light, the last thing the NSA man would want to do is make the investigation highly visible. No, Kertzman thought, if Carthwright wanted to silence Gage, he would have done it from a distance, without bringing himself into the picture.

That single aberration was the only clue that made Kertzman suspect that Carthwright might not be guilty. But the rest didn't make sense. No sense at all.

Kertzman shook his head as he continued forward, turned his thoughts to something else: Milburn.

That was a lot easier to figure. If Milburn was Gage's supervisor, then he would know a lot more about Black Light than he had shared. He would know what secret purpose Black Light had really served. But Milburn didn't have enough weight to have run the unit by himself, so he was obviously taking orders, then and now. Which meant that Milburn was probably hunting Gage for the singular purpose of killing him. But for whom? Who was running Milburn?

There it was again: Carthwright.

Kertzman frowned. He made a mental note to look Milburn up when he returned to the capital.

Then something else came back to him.

No reason.

The words whispered to Kertzman as he neared the doorway of the building.

"Hey, Radford. How come you got volunteered in this mission?"

No reason.

But nothing happens without a reason. Not in a city where destroying people was a recreational activity. Not in a city honeycombed with tunnels that led to secrets that could destroy political dynasties and where Congress was bought and sold in deals that weren't even discreet enough to be called back room. And certainly not in an investigation that could bring down the highest-ranking members of America's intelligence community.

As Kertzman reached the building he only knew one thing for certain.

He couldn't trust anyone.

• • •

He was strong, even with age.

He was 83 years old. And his legs felt strong with the strength of youth as he walked slowly, resolutely, up the highest slope above Urbino. Hands empty, he moved with easy grace, maintaining a dignity that did not lessen because of his somber clothing or the mistiness of night settling over the tiny Italian settlement below him.

Reaching the ridge with steady steps, he paused, turning to gaze down on the hamlet. His breaths came deep, steady, the healthy breaths of a man who regularly found his way into the hills and mountains of his beloved country. Behind him, maintaining a respectful distance, his three servants followed, awaiting, guarding.

Alone on the ridge he cast an austere shadow over the township. Tall and large, he still retained the stolid, roundly proportioned physique that had borne him with imposing presence through youth and middle age. It was a farmer's body, hinting of well-used, hardened strength, with long arms and large, capable hands. He moved easily on stout legs that could walk for hours, even days, through the hills, legs that had held their stride across eight decades though they were now slightly withered by time.

His face was long and full, but unrevealing of any personal quality. It was the face of a scholar, a philosopher; the patient face of a man accustomed to long days and nights of concentrated thought. He was completely bald, beardless, with an almost severe lack of any pleasing aspect. It was the countenance of a man who embodied something to the point that he had completely submerged himself within it; the face of a man who had cast his presence into the void so that he might signify some greater purpose.

Melancholic, he gazed across the dusk. Strangely, he was still able to discern the finest details at a distance. His keen dark eyes scanned the city, wandering along the tiny cobblestone streets, streets that remained twisted and convoluted, forever resistant to the oppressive demands of modern society. He took a deep breath, nodding.

Not in five centuries had the city changed. Far from the traveled path, it rested in the very shadow of the Alps, to his back. Isolated and difficult to approach, it had long been a refuge, a return to an earlier time when men could understand where battle-lines were drawn, to a time when wars were fought with clarity, and purpose.

Unlike today.

A sadness rose within him. He mourned the loss of Simon, his dearest friend, even as he profoundly regretted the mistakes that he had made, mistakes committed by the old fool that he had slowly become. He cursed himself for praying for peace where there could be no peace, for risking lives to placate the lusts of a tyrant.

For a moment his mind returned to the years when he was a simple man, when he had truly enjoyed the quiet act of communion, and prayer, before prayer became unimportant. He remembered the time when he simply believed, before he ascended to the Throne.

Solemnly he watched the distant sun burn orange through the grayish clouds that masked a deeper darkness on the edge of the approaching night. His deeply concentrated eyes strayed along the horizon, wondering at the man who resided there, the man he had once called a student, a brother, a friend. And, once again, a mourning controlled the steady heartbeat within his chest. His life was before him, a life of compromise and intrigue, of plots to deceive and plots to conquer those who would deceive even more gravely than he.

It was a battle of gray light, with neither side wrong, and neither right, each as diabolical and desperate as the other. It was a war over ideals, where ideals were the first sacrifice, a make-believe battle for a make-believe dream. But, though it was born in madness, it was, in the end, a ferocious and unmerciful battle that he had won; becoming the most cunning and powerful of his kind, forging the strongest alliance of fools.

No, he thought sadly, it was not mere foolishness that had motivated him. Cowardice, too, must have its share of the glory, the cowardice of a man who had long ago forgotten what it meant to truly serve God. But it was too late to undo what was already done. His fears had become flesh. And what he had despised most of all had become his closest companion.

The guilt-weight of his sins felt heavy upon him, and he regretted what he had created, regretted the deceptions, the ruthless exercise of power that would astonish kings and presidents. He regretted his cowardice and, finally, regretted that his efforts to forge peace with a monster had caused the death of so many.

Silently, watching the horizon, he nodded softly. For he had decided that the hour of regret was almost passed.

Yes, he thought, soon there would come an ending to this. By the power that was his, by the all but incalculable power of the first and last great Throne of the Earth, he would force a hard ending to this.

After a moment he turned, gazing down the path at the three who so sacredly served him, honored him, and motioned for them to approach.

With old authority he spoke quietly to the first servant, a young man, steady and alert, who listened to his voice as he would listen to the words of an ancient prophet.

"Summon D'Oncetta," the old man said. "Tell him that Clement would see him."

A yellow crime scene ribbon warned against entrance into St. Thomas Cathedral. Kertzman flashed his federal identification to a bored and unimpressed uniform cop in the doorway and entered the building.

It had only taken Kertzman fifteen minutes at the Forensic Science building to discover what he needed to know. The SAS guy had worn a ballistic vest, but two of the rounds had penetrated, hitting center mass, and two more had scored as head shots.

Kertzman would have to go to the Bureau office to examine the guy's possessions, including whatever identification and weapons he was carrying. But he'd do that later. For the moment he had something far more important to attend to.

Sir Henry Stephenson of England's Department of Foreign Affairs had already departed from the morgue when Kertzman arrived, leaving instructions for delivery of the former SAS member to Kennedy Airport, and a flight to England. Stephenson's note to Kertzman had suggested a meeting at the Cathedral of St. Thomas, providing the rendezvous could be concluded before his ten o'clock flight out of Kennedy.

Kertzman entered the building, saw the elderly form of Sir Stephenson immediately. Standing with stately composure at the front of the church, the Englishman was staring at the deeply recessed ceiling, as if discerning what damage, if any, had been done by the smoke. Kertzman had taken ten steps when Stephenson turned, smiling pleasantly. The liaison for England's Foreign Office extended his hand and Kertzman took it, aware of a steady pressure, soft on the surface, but distinctly solid beneath the measured and careful contact.

"It is my pleasure, Mr. Kertzman," said Sir Stephenson with a supremely cultivated courtesy. Kertzman saw that Stephenson was a man of a pleasant, though bland appearance.

Silver-haired, of moderate build and in his late fifties, the Englishman carried himself with the easy, powerful dignity of a privileged governmental official. He wore a gray pin-striped suit of unknown make but with a decidedly English cut and patent leather Oxfords.

"Same here," Kertzman replied, nodding curtly. "I hope I'm not interrupting your plans."

"Oh, no," Stephenson replied, a smile of warmth, agreeable and unwavering. "I hope I am not inconveniencing you. I merely wanted to examine the scene of the crime before my flight departed tonight."

Kertzman nodded. "So did I." He looked past Stephenson, down the hallway to the right. He pointed. "I believe a lot of it happened down that hallway. There's a room down there where the shootout took place."

Stephenson turned, nodded. "Yes, I am familiar with the excellent reports of your police. Shall we look over the scene?"

Kertzman thought about what he really wanted to ask, decided to wait. "Sure," he said. "We'll talk as we go. I know you don't have much time."

Together they found the room where it had all happened. Red tiles marked the space where the SAS man had gone down, and a lot of white chalk circles marked the floor where spent brass had been collected.

Kertzman entered the room, eyes scanning, seeing everything. Stephenson remained in the doorway, an austere man studying the dimly lit room with expressionless concentration.

Kertzman spent a few minutes reading the layout, finding an explanation for damage, recreating the action in his head. He looked at the closet, studying the pattern of torn wood that reached across the floor, into the desk towards the spot where Gage must have stood.

Kertzman's voice was quiet. "Your SAS man, this Sergeant Samuel Maitland, must have went down there." He pointed to the bloodstained tiles.

Sir Stephenson studied the site, nodded silently.

Kertzman looked again at the shredded wood. "Looks like Maitland just held his finger on the trigger of that Uzi he was carrying and moved the weapon from right to left, firing all the time. Is that how the British Air Service trains 'em?"

"Yes," Stephenson replied, almost absently. "That's how the SAS are trained. Never waste short bursts with an automatic weapon. Hold the weapon behind the target, squeeze the trigger, and move the barrel forward, sweeping the pattern of fire over the location of the target. The only difficulty is in not moving the barrel so quickly that one leaves man-sized holes in the pattern of fire. It is supposed to be a certain formula for contacting the enemy."

Kertzman looked up from the floor. "Not this time."

"No," Stephenson agreed, and looked at the distant wall.

Kertzman didn't turn. He had already noticed that the wooden shelves of the wall were strangely damaged, a piece lifted from the bookcase with no evidence of fire damage, no bullet holes disfiguring the wood panels. Someone had purposely lifted the panel, removing it.

Sir Henry Stephenson studied the shelf. Kertzman studied Sir Henry. After a moment, Stephenson felt the concentration, looked down to meet Kertzman's gaze. The Englishman's smile was so faint it was almost unnoticeable.

"You want to check it, Sir Stephenson?" Kertzman asked blandly.

The Englishman's voice was faintly amused. "I should like for you to have the honor, Mr. Kertzman."

Kertzman moved carefully to the shelf, pulled a small flashlight from his coat, shone it into the crack. A flicker passed over a thin shred of cellophane clinging to a jagged wooden splinter of the wall. Frowning, Kertzman lifted the cellophane carefully, examined it in the light.

Sir Stephenson revealed no surprise, no emotion, no overly acute interest, and studied the shred without touching it. Then he focused on Kertzman, nodding courteously. Kertzman removed a white paper envelope from his pocket, placed the cellophane inside, and together they returned to the sanctuary.

Kertzman was the first to speak. "Makes you wonder, doesn't it?"

Sir Stephenson nodded, gazing casually towards the ceiling. "Yes, Mr. Kertzman, it does make one wonder."

For a minute Kertzman stood beside the quietly dignified Englishman. Then he walked a short space, gazing about, knowing he had already found something revealing but not understanding what it was. He stopped beside a pew, turned back.

Calm and composed, the Englishman was unreadable, the perfect public servant. Kertzman centered on him as he spoke.

"The fire department located two smoke markers," he said quietly. "I guess you've already recognized what color it was."

Stephenson laughed mildly. "I know little of military affairs, Mr. Kertzman. Only the most limited things. I understand some of the tactics, their training. But I have no expertise, as you do. I am only a civilian liaison for the Foreign Office."

Kertzman was getting tired. The long day had started badly, and he wasn't in the mood for dancing.

"So tell me," he began gruffly, "why does England send over a man of obvious position to retrieve the dead body of an SAS boy gone bad? Seems like a lot of work."

Stephenson's gaze was placid, innocent. "Oh, no, Mr. Kertzman, it is really a trivial thing. Simply a technicality. I am here to arrange for the transfer of the remains. And I am here to make assurances from the Foreign Office that her Majesty's Service had no sinister activities afoot on American soil. That sort of thing. I shall depart tonight, leaving this investigation in the proper hands of highly skilled American authorities like yourself."

Kertzman half-laughed, looked towards the altar. "Yeah, I figure. And what do you make of that piece of cellophane I found behind the bookcase?"

Sir Stephenson raised his eyebrows, considering. He glanced back towards the hall, waited a moment. "It might have been there for a considerable time. Possibly, it means nothing. Perhaps one of the firemen accidentally damaged the shelving in the chaos."

"Could be," said Kertzman. "But, then again, it might be something else."

Sir Stephenson gazed back at him, eyes open, waiting.

Kertzman felt tempted to provoke the Englishman. "It might be that something was hidden behind that shelf. Might be, your boy wanted it. And died for it."

"Make no mistake, Mr. Kertzman," Stephenson said slowly. "I know nothing of the true nature of this affair. But I can assure you that the British government has authorized no undertakings on your continent. Sergeant Samuel Maitland was discharged from SAS over three years ago. He has not been our responsibility for quite some time."

Kertzman nodded wearily, ran a broad, calloused hand over his flattop, smoothing the short black-gray bristling haircut. Then, tiredly, he rubbed his eyes, and abruptly focused on Sir Stephenson with renewed concentration. When he spoke Kertzman's words contained a fresh speed, a new effort at logic, aggressive and vaguely hostile.

"Let me tell you something, Stephenson," he growled, and the Englishman seemed to instantly lock onto the tone. "I'm tired of dancin' with mystery men. What are you?"

Sir Stephenson said nothing, held a demeanor of professional calm. "I am a public servant," he replied plainly. "Much like yourself, I suppose."

"Well," Kertzman added, "I know a little about how you yahoos work. You don't say anything. You come in and look and slide out, reportin' to your boss what you saw. And all those White House pansies accommodate you, kiss up to you because they want to maintain relations. Everybody's real happy, cozy. But I ain't lookin' to maintain relations. I couldn't care less if you like me or what you think about me. I'm here to find the truth, if there is any. And I want to try and keep anybody else from gettin' killed. That's my responsibility. And since your boy was involved in this, that makes it your responsibility, too."

"I repeat, Samuel Maitland has not been our responsibility for some time," Stephenson remarked coolly.

"You trained him," Kertzman responded. "You taught him how to use that fancy machine gun where you move the barrel and keep firing and all that crap. Never miss the target. Only, I think he went up against somebody just a little better."

"It's impossible to become too much better," Stephenson interjected casually.

Kertzman was secretly pleased that he had somehow goaded the Englishman into responding, but he didn't expect much more.

"Maybe not," he added. "But it don't really make any difference to me. He was still your responsibility. And now he's on my soil and I've got to deal with him. That means you owe me."

Stephenson's eyes glimmered.

"Maitland was part of a group that was working with a KGB officer," Kertzman said.

"I am aware of that."

"Are you?" Kertzman's voice was openly hostile. "Are you also aware that we've got five dead American soldiers who were probably also working with Maitland and this KGB guy?"

Stephenson waited a moment before responding quietly. "Yes."

Kertzman pressed. "You seem to be taking it real well, Sir Henry! If I were you I'd be a little upset that a hotshot SAS man was working with the KGB. Unless I knew why. Then I'd probably be real calm. 'Bout like you." He hesitated. "So why don't you tell me something about this situation? What do a bunch of heavy hitters, men trained to do nothing but kill each other, have in common? Can you tell me that?"

"I should think that would be obvious, Mr. Kertzman," the Englishman responded casually. "Skills."

Kertzman absorbed that. "What did Maitland do in the SAS?" he asked suddenly. "You said that a person couldn't get too much better."

Stephenson replied without admiration or respect. "He was a legend."

"A legend at what?"

A pause.

"We have secrecy acts, Mr. Kertzman. I, too, am subject to them."

Nodding, Kertzman continued, "Yeah, I know. But that don't mean you can't give me an idea why 'her majesty' wasn't happy with him."

"You presume."

"I know he ain't in SAS no more," said Kertzman. "I learned that the KGB guy ain't in the KGB anymore. I know that Sims and Myrick aren't Army Intelligence anymore. But all these guys are still working, so they're working for somebody. I just can't figure out who. But I will." Kertzman stepped closer with the words, throwing decorum to the wind. "Believe me, Stephenson. You can help me or not, but I *will* find out the truth. I'm going to find out what is happening. I've got a wheelbarrow load of dead soldiers who were once capable of terrorizing any nation on Earth. But they keep getting wiped out. So there's a war going on over something, and it's a miracle the players haven't destroyed a city, yet. But they might if this keeps up, so I intend to put an end to it. We're responsible for the men we've trained, Stephenson. You're responsible for the man you've trained. Maitland couldn't have done any damage at all if you people hadn't taught him how. So you need to tell me what you know. If you don't, the blood's going to be on you. You might not care about that. But I'll take it personal. And if it's in my power to blow this thing wide open for the world to see, I will. I'm tired of dancing. Tired of it. So if you want these secrets to *stay* secret, you'd better talk about something."

Stephenson remained impassive. "And do you want the Russians to also participate in this investigation?"

"Forget 'em," said Kertzman. "I don't have time to deal with the Russians. I got too many people in this now that I don't trust. Including you. But I need somebody to tell me somethin', and it might just as well be you. I'll figure it out if you're lying. But if you're honest, and you actually tell me somethin', I might even be able to finish it for you."

Sir Stephenson's silence was balanced on a cliff's edge. Kertzman's stone gaze and resolute posture never relaxed as the moments passed.

Finally the Englishman spoke. "Did you discover yet the name of the Russian?"

Kertzman nodded. "Yeah. Arkady Torkarev. But the State Department hasn't released anything on him, yet. They just told me he doesn't work for the KGB anymore. At least, officially."

Stephenson spoke quietly, calmly, perfectly at home with secrets, and with sharing secrets in strange places. "Correct, Mr.

Kertzman. His name was, indeed, Arkady Torkarev. In 1971 he graduated from the Advanced Intelligence School in Moscow and was subsequently assigned to Covert Operations of the KGB, where, in time, he distinguished himself."

"What did he do for the KGB?"

Stephenson's tone was so casual that he might have been discussing trade relations, but Kertzman was chilled by what he heard.

"He supposedly masterminded the assassination of Pope John Paul I, and the Warsaw killing of Yuri Demonivich in 1982, of the West German Intelligence Service. And, also, in 1981, he sanctioned Ludmila Zhivkova of Bulgaria with a traffic accident."

Kertzman scowled. "Why did he kill a woman?"

Stephenson continued steadily, "Ludmila Zhivkova was the daughter of Bulgarian leader Todor Zhivkova. She was also a *summa cum laude* graduate of political science from Oxford University. When she returned to her country in 1981 she petitioned for Bulgaria's independence from Moscow. The Soviet Union demanded her silence. She would not comply. Torkarev was sent to dispatch her. We believe she actually died by poisoning. That was Torkarev's most familiar method of sanctioning. However, her body was mangled by the accident and was never autopsied, so the exact cause of death was never determined. Then Torkarev orchestrated the unfortunate death of Georgi Markov by heart attack at Waterloo Station in London on December 21, 1988. And he was without question responsible for the sanctioning of Vladimir Simeonov, who perished in London in 1989 under mysterious circumstances."

Kertzman gazed into the distant shadows of the cathedral, trying to put it all together. "So Torkarev was an assassin," he said, almost to himself.

"No," said Stephenson, lifting his chin slightly. "Not an assassin, Mr. Kertzman. Men who point guns and pull triggers are assassins. Men like Oswald are assassins. They are also fools." He paused. "You see, Mr. Kertzman, guns and rifles and bombs are the tools of idiots, of incompetents. Torkarev was more than that. Much more. He was not an assassin. He was an artist, a magician. He was the man who came and went, and someone died while he was there. But there was no unusual cause of death. No violence. No crime. No reason for international protests or retributions. Someone merely died. Strangely and sadly."

"Meaning what?" growled Kertzman.

"Meaning that Torkarev stood at the highest level of the food chain, Mr. Kertzman. A superior breed of soldier, and a genius at what he did. He was one of the best soldiers in the world. The rest were fools by comparison."

Kertzman stepped closer. "And Maitland?"

Stephenson removed a cigarette from a silver case. Slowly, he lit it with a polished gold lighter. Then he exhaled a long steady stream of smoke.

Kertzman thought that he looked eerily composed.

"That is something else, altogether," he said quietly. "The information about Torkarev is available to you in your country's files, if your government chooses to release them to you. So I have, in reality, told you nothing that you did not already know. But I am reluctant to tell you specifically about Maitland's activities for my government."

Kertzman said nothing. He didn't know what he'd do if Stephenson stopped talking.

"I can say, however, that any presumptions you might have would probably be correct," Stephenson continued carefully. "As I said, Sergeant Maitland was a legend in the Special Air Service. He was quite exceptional."

Kertzman focused. "So why did the SAS terminate a topgun?"

Stephenson blew out a long stream of smoke. "I don't know."

"Sure you do."

Stephenson's short laugh echoed in the church. "No, Mr. Kertzman, I do not know."

Kertzman weighed what he had heard. "There's something you might want to consider, Stephenson. You said Torkarev was the best. Real quiet. And Maitland was the same."

"Yes."

"But they made a mess of this. Guns. Attention. A car crash on the interstate. They're supposed to be slick. Clever. Quiet. The kind of people who don't leave tracks."

Stephenson nodded. "That is their preferred method."

"Which means," Kertzman added, "that they must have wanted something from this church real bad. Something that just might have been behind that wall. Something important enough to even make a scene over, if they had to."

For a moment Stephenson said nothing, then a thought seemed to settle on him. "Yes," he added with a purposeful solemnity. "I have considered that. And these five men who died earlier, before Sergeant Maitland and Comrade Torkarev, were they also, as you say, topguns?"

"No," Kertzman responded. "Sims and Myrick were good. But they weren't in the same league as these guys."

"And they were the first to meet this man who apparently dispatched Sergeant Maitland?"

"Jonathan Gage."

"Yes, this Jonathan Gage. And he is yours? Is that not correct?"

"Yeah. Delta. Then CIA."

"He is quite capable."

"Looks like it."

Stephenson took a minute, staring into the shadows. Kertzman saw the hesitation, also saw that the Englishman was about to say something that might actually make a difference.

"There is no harm in a simple discussion," Stephenson began. "Especially between two dedicated and honest public servants." He exhaled a long thin ribbon of white smoke. "I would like to offer a conjecture."

"Go ahead."

Stephenson moved his leg absently, shuffling a step, drew again on the cigarette. "These first five men who were finished by Gage. Obviously, they failed in their mission. Then Torkarev and Maitland arrived, and they also were failures. But, as you said, they are men who operated in quite a different league."

Kertzman had already seen it. "Yeah," he said slowly.

"So," Stephenson remarked, "I wonder, do you perceive that it might be considered an escalation of force?" He paused, smiling slightly, but openly. "Mobilize the regular infantry. But if that is insufficient, then use a specialized, very elite squad?"

"Maybe," Kertzman said. "But why? What are they fighting over? Who are they working for?" A thought came to him. "Do you think this might have anything to do with American foreign policy? Maybe a renegade military unit out of the CIA? Something like that?"

Stephenson seemed to consider smiling again. He didn't. His voice was serious. "Oh, no, Mr. Kertzman," he said, respectful. "But I would anticipate that someone would suggest that to you. Yes, that is exactly what I would anticipate." He paused. "A red herring, so to speak."

"You seem to know an awful lot, Sir Henry," Kertzman growled. "Do you know who Maitland and Torkarev worked for?"

Stephenson shook his head. "No. I wish I could, but I cannot. Nor can I tell you what these men are fighting for. But, for the purposes of discussion, let us ask this question: What do Sergeant Maitland and Torkarev have in common?"

"They were the best at what they did."

"Yes."

"And these other men, Sims and Myrick?"

"Were good. But regular troops."

"Yes, regular troops," said the Englishman, fixing a subtle but strange gaze upon Kertzman. "Not superior beings."

An odd phrase.

"No," Kertzman said slowly, noting the strangeness of the language. "No...not superior beings."

"And, surely," Stephenson said carefully, continuing without hesitation, "if Sergeant Maitland and Torkarev were the vassals of someone who wanted to create a private army of these 'superior beings,' it would be suitable to conjecture that he had properly begun."

The cathedral was deathly silent.

After a moment, Stephenson laughed lightly. "Strange that I should be reminded, Mr. Kertzman, but it occurs to me, oddly, that Hitler was obsessed with very elite squads of his own, so-called superior beings. In fact, the Third Reich was founded on the principle of a generation of supermen who could execute seemingly impossible missions. It was the heart of Hitler's concept of a ruling elite. The perfect soldier, born to rule and to decide the fate of all those less perfect than the blond, blue-eyed master race. And the truth was, with their fantastic dedication to duty and their absolute devotion to skills, Hitler's elite squads were, indeed, quite superior. And dangerous."

Kertzman listened steadily. He knew it wasn't a history lesson.

"In fact, Operation Iron Eagle, the secret SS plot to assassinate Churchill, would have succeeded brilliantly but for a single, seemingly innocuous radio transmission intercepted in Enigma coding and deciphered by Ultra. Even today it must be admitted that the plan was fiendishly well-designed; a small team of six elite SS men, all in British uniforms speaking perfect English who had already penetrated the security of Whitehall and Parliament before they were discovered. They had waited patiently for an opportunity to sanction the Prime Minister when we luckily closed the net on them. A devilish close thing, I tell you, and a cunning operation. Almost changed the course of the war."

Stephenson exuded the air of a man prone to rambling.

Kertzman waited for what was important.

"You have to admit, Mr. Kertzman, Hitler was a genius, and quite committed to the superiority of a master race. Even if he was, also, quite mad. But that was a plague of the Third Reich. Genius and madness. By genius they conquered all of Europe." He paused. "Except England, of course. And by madness, and the combined military might of the New and Old Worlds, they lost it. But that doesn't diminish their genius, their brilliant accomplishment at building the mightiest war machine that man had ever seen."

Stephenson shoved a hand into the pocket of his tweed overcoat, bunching against the cold settling over the church. Kertzman felt strangely cold, too. But it wasn't the church. It was the eerie, purposeful direction of the Englishman's words. Stephenson was hesitating but seemed to be homing in on a certain and unalterable course. Kertzman was certain that Stephenson was confiding things he shouldn't. And he knew that he should feel a sense of gratitude towards Stephenson, but the tone of the Englishman's words had darkened his soul.

"How often these brilliant military monarchies are ruled by madness, Mr. Kertzman," Stephenson pondered quietly, gazing away. Then he turned suddenly, fixed Kertzman with an innocent stare. "Did you know that Hitler was zealously religious? It seems appropriate that we should mention it in a cathedral, doesn't it? But not religious in the sense of the Christian faith, or Judaism." He released a faint sigh. "No, on the contrary, it was black magic that Hitler cherished so dearly. Astrology. *Archeology.* He believed that certain archeological treasures long lost to the world held secrets of power. He believed, in his dementia, that certain archeological treasures could reveal sources of ancient power. He believed that these sources of lost power might help to establish a new kingdom on earth, a kingdom ruled by his Aryan Supermen." He smiled. "Madness, wasn't it? All that devotion to black magic and Satanic rites with the dream of a ruling race of superior beings?"

Kertzman was suddenly aware of how dark and isolated it felt to be standing in the open cathedral.

"In fact," Stephenson continued casually, "before he was assassinated by Czech resistance fighters, Field March Reinhard Heydrich, the Butcher of Prague, was infamous for his obsession with occult rituals. He believed that the Third Reich was the incarnate kingdom of dark spiritual forces long banished from the Earth by the hated Christian God." Stephenson laughed. "Quite extraordinary. A type of madness rare in war, or even in the intelligence field. Although many of us in ... public service ... do have strong beliefs in God." He focused on Kertzman, smiling slightly. "Do you believe in God, Mr. Kertzman?"

Kertzman frowned. His voice was cautious. "I ain't never met a real man who didn't," he said.

"Yes," Stephenson nodded. "Quite true. But few are so unbalanced as to believe in the nonsense of ancient powers, sorcery, that sort of thing. Don't you agree?"

Kertzman said nothing, and the Englishman continued. "Yes," he added, "most people are far too well-balanced for such nonsense. But, as history demonstrates, it does happen. After the war it was discovered that Hitler must have launched a hundred of his elite teams on bizarre missions to discover lost artifacts or to assassinate his enemies. In retrospect, we can see that he was constantly obsessed with using small, elite squads of his master race. Strange, isn't it, how so many of history's madmen have fallen foolishly victim to this idea of small armies of supermen who will force reality from the fires of their nonsensical dreams. Mind you, these madmen do not value the pedestrian concept of a simple, highly skilled soldier. No, history demonstrates that they are more often obsessed with the concept of armies of superior beings, beings born to conquer, to rule, to decide fate for the rest of us."

Stephenson tossed his cigarette to the floor, ground it out. "In any case, Hitler failed in his dreams. But it was a fiendishly close thing, I believe. Yes, what with his fanatical squads on their bizarre missions. And they were feared because they were, in truth, so fanatical. Even the mere appearance of an SS company in World War II signified that our enemy had launched a severe escalation of force."

Stephenson sighed, moved to step away, and then hesitated, turning to look at Kertzman. "Of course, you realize, we are just discussing history. But sometimes, I do believe, there is a place for such talk, don't you agree?"

Kertzman said nothing.

Sir Stephenson smiled. "Yes, Mr. Kertzman, I do believe there is. By the way, have you ever read *The Will to Power* by Nietzsche?"

Kertzman managed to shake his head. "No."

"An interesting book," the Englishman said steadily. "In fact, a dangerous book for those who hold to the dream of a super race." Then Stephenson fell into a pedantic recitation, as if quoting.

"A dark and ruler race is building itself up. A race born to conquer, to destroy, to crush down the weak of the earth. The aim should be to prepare a transvaluation of values for a particularly strong kind of man, a being of superior strength and superior ability, a man most highly gifted in intellect and will. This man and the ruling elite with him will become Lords of the Earth—the ultimate beast of prey."

• • •

An almost unheard sound, a faint computer beeping from the cabin's back room, caused Sarah to turn her head, and instantly she knew, somehow, that it was important. She stood, unmoving, in the kitchen, holding a cup of coffee that she had made to fight off sleep, but her mind was ignited by the sound, fast and calculating.

Beep, beep.

Instantly she moved. "Barto!" she yelled, not knowing why but sensing that she would have no time for a mistake if she was right.

She stopped in the open doorway of the cabin's third bedroom and saw that the computer, positioned carefully on a desk in the corner, had come on. The screen was lit with a message.

It beeped again.

She ran forward as Barto followed her into the room, alert, electric with energy. His wide eyes centered on the computer. Sarah sat down in the chair at the desk, stared at the screen to read the message:

> SANDMAN/DRAGON
> ACK: COND

Breath quickening, understanding instantly that Jonathan Gage was not truly, completely isolated in his life, Sarah typed a quick message into the computer.

> GAGE IS INJURED

She began to hit Enter.

"No!" shouted Barto, grabbing her hand.

She turned towards him. "Why? This is what he was talking about! He needs whoever is at the end of this line!"

Barto's breath was quick, his words quicker. It was as if they both knew they had a narrow window of time to respond to the message.

"Move aside. They're going to want a code," he whispered, sliding into the seat. "They're as careful as Gage. If we type something that's wrong, they might think it's some kind of trap. They won't come."

The computer screen beeped three more times. The message disappeared for a second, with a skip of Sarah's heart, and then flashed back.

"It's a code," Barto whispered, staring at the screen, the keyboard. "Sandman is sending, so Gage must be Dragon." He waited, said slowly, "But what is ACK? It must mean... acknowledge! It must mean to acknowledge... something."

"His condition!" Sarah yelled. "He wants to know Gage's condition, his status! He's trying to find out if Gage is alright. The answer is probably going to be a number or something he used in the Army!"

Barto was speaking fast. "But I don't know anything about the Army. What do we use? If we scare them off we won't hear from them again. We have to—"

Beep, beep, beep.

The message appeared once more.

Sarah closed her eyes, concentrating furiously, sensing that, if the sender waited any longer, the message would not come back again. Her mind was spinning. What was the international color for assistance? Orange. Unless... no, wait.

"Type in yellow," she shouted.

"But—"

"*Do it!*"

Barto typed in "Yellow" and hit Enter.

The word Yellow was indexed below the initial message. A long pause. Then the computer screen beeped again.

J-O-QSL.

"Oh, no," whispered Barto. "What is *that*?"

"Here!" Sarah pushed her hands onto the keyboard.

"Wait a second, Sarah—"

"*Be quiet!*" She fired the words into Barto's face.

His hands jumped off the keyboard.

"We'll never figure these games out!"

Then, deciding to take a chance, she concentrated on the keyboard and began to type. Quickly she hit Enter, and the message was sent, flashing across the screen:

GAGE IS INJURED. HE IS DYING. THIS IS SARAH.
HE IS ASKING FOR SANDMAN. COME QUICKLY.

For a second the message remained on the screen, then the communication was broken. No response. An automatic program evaluation, not a message sent from the other end of the line, was displayed:

END OF TRANSMISSION

Barto released a deep breath, placed weary hands over his face. Sarah bowed her head. "Jesus," she whispered.

● ● ●

The shadowed room was cheap.

It even felt cheap, with a cheap bed, a dusty, battered desk, an old television, and nothing else. Kertzman felt it was right for him. It was a coward's room. A room built for a coward.

He sat on the edge of the bed, staring at the locked door, watching the night through the sheer, curtained window. It was a moonless dark, a deep, silent, expansive blackness that scorned streetlights and neon, smothering everything in a thick cloud of night.

It was the kind of infinite, breathing night that he knew in '68 when he could *feel* the jungle, the surrounding darkness, knew that something was out there, moving towards him, somewhere close. He could almost see the shape, a man, part of the blackness itself, not a real thing, too silent to be real, coming closer, always at an angle, through the forest.

Kertzman shook his head. *Yeah,* he thought, *I can remember.*

He knew that he needed time to think, to figure this out, but he had been too tired for the haul back to Washington, too disturbed to take a flight. So he had driven north on Palisades Parkway until he turned, without any real reason, on to Convent. In a moment he had passed the imposing Rockland Psychiatric Center on his left, with its ten-foot high, fenced perimeter and guarded entrances. And a half-hour later he located this small hotel at the intersection of Gilbert and Middletown.

Taking his briefcase, he used an emergency backup identification and cash, checking into a corner room. Then he sat for an hour on the edge of the bed, staring at the locked door, absently clutching an old, World War II-era Colt 1911 in his sweaty right hand.

Fifty-four years old.

I'm too old for this, he told himself. *Seen too much, from 'Nam to Dakota to the Pentagon. Too much of this. I ain't got the nerve no more.*

Something told him he had used it all up. Somewhere down the line, in some hellish battle he couldn't even remember, he had used up that best part of himself that, in the old days, would have given him the edge, would have helped him bull his way through this.

The gun wasn't comforting in his hand. It was a toy; a coward's answer to a fear that was way beyond.

Still, he gripped the checkered walnut handle, absently feeling the thin sheen of gun oil on the blue steel.

Seven shots. That's all he had. Seven shots.

Use six of 'em on the bad guys, he thought. *Save the last one for myself.*

Kertzman laughed brutally, shook his head. He never thought it would come to this, never believed that he would crack. Not until Stephenson told him what he was truly facing.

Forces, Carthwright had said. People who make things happen.

Kertzman felt the sweat on his back and chest getting colder.

It would be easy to do. Just play the game and finish it. Find this guy, Gage, and step aside to let these people do what they have to do. Walk away.

Superior beings. The best in the world at what they do. The strongest, the smartest. A master race.

He had denied the fear with Carthwright. Had denied it all the way down to New York, but then, listening to the Englishman in the church, something inside him, brittle and cold with a denied fear, had snapped; something he didn't understand.

The thoughts stayed with him, disturbing him, eating away at that unknown fiber of his soul that had always sustained him. He knew that, somewhere out there, Gage was fighting these people. He would always be fighting. That's all he knew. He was a warrior, a soldier, a survivor. Gage would never lay it down, never give up. He would fight them until they took him down hard, then he'd make them pay for every inch. He'd force these so-called supermen to the very edge of what they could endure, make them curse the day they heard of Jonathan Gage, Black Light, the U.S. Army, or anything else.

Somehow Kertzman knew this wasn't really about national security or foreign policy. From the beginning it had been something worse. A lot worse. Kertzman had felt it when he was standing in the church, had seen too many of the mysteries coming together.

Something about it was vaguely nightmarish and unnatural; the seminary, the church, the old professor. Too many things that could never be connected to national interest. Even if someone, maybe Carthwright, wanted Gage dead because of Black Light, there was someone else going down here. Something worse.

Kertzman's hand shifted on the .45.

A master race; the ultimate beast of prey.

Kertzman knew that what was on the line here was about a lot more than just surviving, living for another day. No, there wouldn't be any running away from these people. Because if he ran they would always have a hold over him. There would be no freedom, no peace, no way to live with himself. Not if he bowed his head, tucked his tail between his legs, and hunkered down like an ol' beat dog.

Kertzman absently licked his dry lips.

Something told him: That ain't no life. Ain't no life 'cause every day you'll feel the eyes, watching, and you'll know they're watching a coward. You'll spend the rest of your life hiding what you really are.

Kertzman shook his head, the .45 hanging forgotten in his hand.

No, he thought, *I won't live like this. Not like this. Dead would be better than this. Dead ain't half so bad as this. At least I could live my last days in peace, and respect, and die with just myself instead 'a ghosts.*

Kertzman sniffed, moving his head, loosening, and looked down at his hand, at the .45. He thumbed the hammer back on a chambered round, studying the Colt's blue-black gleam.

Just a gun. Nothing in it. Nothing that he didn't put himself. And the surest way out of this wasn't going to be by a gun. He would have to outsmart them.

Then, slowly, with steady, gathering certainty, a game came to him; a game where he might find the truth and even get himself out alive at the same time.

Just work the evidence, he thought. Work it hard, and make a good show. But don't put it all together, not really. They'll think you're doing your best, running this guy to ground. Only don't finish it. Don't look where he should really be. Mess up just enough so they'll never figure out that you're holding back. They'll know that you're not getting the job done, but they won't suspect that it's from a lack of trying. In the meantime, track this guy down on your own and find out what's really happening, take the real bad guys down.

A long time passed as Kertzman worked the details of the plot. But he wasn't sure if he could carry it off. He concentrated, replaying all the moments that meant something, trying to find where they had made a mistake. A lot of it was easy.

Milburn was a mistake. An obvious one. He was on the other side, probably since Black Light was active in the late eighties. And Radford couldn't be trusted. He didn't get volunteered for this because of "no reason." He was in it for a purpose—somebody else's purpose.

Carthwright was a maybe. But Kertzman knew that would make it too easy.

The trick would be stalling everybody without arousing suspicions, while he ran Gage to ground. If the investigation even came close to pinpointing Gage's safe house he would have to do some subtle misdirection. But not enough to arouse attention. And that wouldn't be easy. He could probably slide something past Milburn, and even Radford. But Carthwright would be sharper. Dangerous.

Kertzman shifted, his mind playing out a dozen different scenarios of how it could work. But immediately he knew it would be a close thing.

Too close.

Wiping a cold, sweaty brow with a hairy forearm, Kertzman glanced down again at the Colt.

Frowning, he flicked the safety, locking the hammer back. Now if he thumbed down the lever of the .45 he would have one good, fast shot.

He released a deep breath.

It'd have to do.

A white, distant shade shone through the cold. The softest rustle of noise; faint, invisible.

Sarah opened her eyes, saw everything at once. The glow in the distance behind the windows, a large dark form, a...black man ...moving carefully around Gage's bed.

Instantly she was on her feet, her hands searching for something, a weapon. But even as she stood she realized, in the space it took for her to move, that the big man was not an enemy. She knew, she understood it all, so well, with the necessary speed of thought forced upon her by the situation, who the black man was.

Moving carefully, gingerly, the big man lowered Gage's arm. And as she reached her feet he turned his head towards her—a smooth, dark, ebony face, masculine and dignified, quietly strong and instantly reassuring by its complete lack of any threatening intent. And for a split-second as he looked towards her, he smiled. Then he turned back to Gage.

With expert deftness he checked bandages on the wounds. Sarah moved closer with quiet, careful steps. She knew they had locked all the doors and windows. Everything was, as Gage would call it, secure. But the black man had found his way into the cabin in the dark, past Malachi and Barto sleeping soundly in the other rooms, all the way to Gage's bed where she slept in the chair.

Silently, as if he did not want to stir Gage, the big black man removed something from a small black bag. Sarah recognized it instantly. It was an IV from an Army-issue trauma kit.

The big man attached the IV to the wall beside the bed and expertly inserted the needle into Gage's arm, causing him to stir slightly. A subsequent series of injections were forced into the IV, the drip released at what Sarah thought was nearly full-flow, and Gage was immediately sleeping soundly again. Then the man moved to the table, with Sarah, dazed and still somewhat afraid, only steps behind him.

At the table, the big man removed rows of encapsulated medi-
cines, syringes. Then quickly, with a completely casual and, even,
comforting manner, he turned towards her, silently holding up one
of the medicine capsules. Gingerly she reached out and took it,
somehow certain of who he was.

"Sandman?" she whispered, searching the wide, sensitive eyes.
The black man smiled, nodding.

Sarah closed her eyes for only the most fleeting, glancing second, surrendering to the hazy, comforting sensation that fell over
her. Then she looked at the capsule—a strong, very expensive all-
purpose antibiotic designed to fight a wide array of infections from
blood disorders to pneumonia. In a glance she noticed the other
capsules, identifying them by color coding: cephalexin, chloram-
phenical, dicioxacillin, and gentamicin.

It was everything Gage would need. It was even more than she
had in the desert. The worst was over. He would recover with this.

Sandman looked down on her. He was extremely tall, well over
six feet, taller than Gage and much, much heavier. Yet his enor-
mous size did not seem imposing, but rather reassuring. The close-
cut black hair was unimaginative, unannouncing; a practical cut
for a practical and simple person. It was the face that captured
Sarah's attention; muscular, strong, promoting the impression of
granite, but somehow benign and serene, with calm, comforting
eyes that seemed to constantly smile.

He moved with a limp, as if his left leg were deadened at the
knee. In her initial shock, Sarah hadn't thought of it, but now she
understood. He was crippled, handicapped, and wore a prosthesis
from at least the knee, possibly higher.

Silently, he motioned for them to sit down in the two chairs.
Sarah obeyed, moving silently with him. Sandman sat down heavily beside her, reaching down with both massive hands to bend his
knee, positioning the leg. Apparently, the prosthesis began in an
area higher than the knee, possibly mid-thigh or even at the hip.

Sandman nodded his head, winked at her. "He'll be alright," he
said in a warm voice.

Against her will, Sarah felt the tears begin, moved her hands
to her face. She would no longer have to rely upon her judgment
alone. But she didn't want to cry, refused to truly release her fatigue or her fears. She wiped the silent tears away with the heel of
her hand as they crept from her eyes.

Sandman's comforting hand was on her shoulder, and then his
deep voice, "Everything's gonna be alright...It's gonna be alright...Ol' Sandman is here..."

• • •

It was their soft conversation that awoke Malachi and Barto, who entered the room in the late dawn to find them together. Barto made a bizarrely heroic move to do something, but Sandman's unassuming presence instantly defused any adverse reactions. Malachi seemed to take the arrival, even at first glance, with utter calm, and gazed upon the big black man with the attitude of some-one experienced at dramatic surprises.

Over coffee at the kitchen table, Barto and Malachi seemed as relieved as Sarah at Sandman's arrival. In low tones they discussed Gage's condition, and Sandman assured them that he would be on his feet in a few days.

"Yeah, he'll be alright," he said easily as he walked, with pain-ful slowness, towards his coat. "I've seen him get out of a lot worse. I was the medic for our old unit. Navy trained me. Gage was trained, too. But he wasn't a regular medic. He never really liked it that much." He looked at Sarah. "Those are some good sutures. Regular ol' square knots. They work as good as anythin'. You got any more silk left?"

Sarah shook her head.

"That's alright. I got plenty." Sandman nodded. "I'll fix up Gage's infirmary. It looks like he might need it." He paused. "Yeah," he added, after a moment, "it looks like you did alright. Good decisions. But you didn't have any antibiotics to fight the infection. You didn't have enough to work with. You do now, though, and I'm here, so everythin's gonna be alright."

Sandman reached quickly into his coat, and Sarah's heart reflexively skipped a beat. Then his hand came out of the coat clutching a large metallic radio. Hardly breaking the rhythm of his words, he spoke into the device. A small red light blinked on as he pressed a lever on the side.

"Sandman to Snake. It's clear. Come on in." He set the radio on the table. "Yeah," he continued casually, "it was a real shocker when that big ol' message came across my computer screen last night.

"Gage and me touch base on the tenth and the twentieth of every month. Nine o'clock at night. Just a little ol' status check kind 'a thing. Sometimes there's somebody in a little trouble. But not for a long time. It's been pretty quiet for a year or so."

Sandman shook his head, smiled easily at Sarah. "Then that big ol' message comes across my computer last night and I think, 'Oh no! My boy done somethin' big! And it looks like he got himself shot to pieces doin' it!' I was so shocked I didn't know what to do. I wasn't sure if it was a trap, or what. So I came in real quiet, checked things out real good before I waltzed in here."

Malachi spoke warmly, "You are a good friend for him."

Sandman nodded, almost pensive for the first time. "I should be. He set me up, helped me a lot. And he'd do anythin' for me. There ain't too many like him, no more. He don't care about money, and he's got all the money in the world. He don't care about nuthin' except his friends. There ain't much more, he says. He wasn't always like that. He used to be hard." He paused. "But he ain't like that no more. He's changed a lot. But even in the old days he wouldn't 'a let ya down."

He nodded again, as if agreeing with his own words, and tapped his knuckles on his leg. A hollow plastic echo sounded in the kitchen.

"My leg is still in Colombia, but the rest of me is here." He laughed heartily, easily. "It was Gage who carried me to the bird. Not everybody would 'a done it, I can tell you that. Not in a firefight that was lightin' up Maicao like a Christmas tree. It was mean, boy, let me tell you. It was like the sky was on fire." He motioned with his hands, a sliding motion. "We had gone in to hit an airfield flyin' dope up from the coast, up through Mississippi. Green light on everythin'. Orders to just go wide open, do whatever it took. Don't leave nuthin' standing. But they were ready for us, a hundred of them crackhead gunboys. We thought it might be a tough hit, and it was, boy, it was."

Sandman shook his head, stared for a minute. Sarah was still wondering about the radio transmission.

"Anyway," he continued, shrugging, "we was in the meanest firefight you ever seen. I got hit by so many rounds I lost count. I just saw my leg layin' over there." He pointed vaguely with his hand. "And I thought, 'Well, I'm gone.' And I guess I would 'a been." He pressed his thumb and forefinger of one hand together, an image of pressure. "But sometimes that ol' femoral artery will clamp itself off when you get hit in the leg like that. It'll just do it by itself. Stop the bleeding. That's what happened. That ol' femoral artery just collapsed, shut down, stopped the bleeding all by itself, or, least ways, enough of it. Gage finally got to me, called a bird, hauled me to the bay. Then he went back, takin' it to them. He was mean, boy, I'm tellin' ya. I ain't never seen nuthin' like that. Never. He was everywhere, killin' people left and right. Stackin' 'em up. There was some judgment done that day, son, some separatin' the sheep from the goats. And I don't think it went too good for a lot of them drug-runnin', bushwackin', murderin' scumbags." He shook his head emphatically. "No sir, I don't think it did. Now, if you ask me—"

A shuffling noise in the door made everyone turn. As soon as Sandman saw the form standing in the cold light of midday, he returned to his amiable discourse, but Sarah's eyes remained on the second man.

Alone, mean-looking and obviously freezing, a lean, wiry Mexican was poised in the open frame, carefully holding a short black rifle. Though overall small in size, the man had powerfully sloped shoulders with long, simian arms that carried the large weapon easily. Another rifle, much longer and with a scope attached to it, was slung over his back. He was dressed in dark, dirt-caked civilian clothes, but carried a canteen and an array of military weapons. Sarah saw a radio, an exact duplicate of the one that Sandman had laid on the table, attached to his left hip. A wire extended from the radio to a listening device he wore in his left ear.

Beneath his long, thin black hair, the Mexican's face was disfigured and unsightly. Obviously pockmarked from youth, it had been hideously scarred by fire, leaving a ragged, reddish mass of burned tissue on the right side of his face and forehead. A traditional black patch concealed his right eye. The other eye focused on Sarah for a moment with the indifferent, calculating gaze of a snake, before sweeping the interior of the room, eventually settling on Sandman.

Sandman looked blandly at the Mexican, then nodded towards the room where Gage was lying before resuming the momentum of his story, which Sarah could no longer follow. Slowly lowering his weapon, the Mexican moved towards the bedroom. Barto glanced quickly at her, wide-eyed, wondering. But her nervousness vanished when she looked at her father. Serene and steady, surprised at nothing, the old man calmly watched the events unfold.

Malachi couldn't wait for Sandman to finish his speech on what seemed to have transcended into the current geopolitical crises of the world.

"Who's *that?*" Barto interrupted.

"Oh," said Sandman, waving a hand, "that's Chavez. He don't talk much. You'll get used to him." He paused a moment, focused on Barto. "We came in together. Chavez was in the woods, watching. If something had gone down he would 'a taken care of it, best he could."

Barto seemed transfixed. "What would he have done?"

Sandman made an indifferent face, shrugged. "I don't know, for sure. He's got that M-79, that big ol' grenade launcher. And on top of that, he's just mad-dog mean. I guess he would 'a just shot a couple of APGs in here and blown us all to kingdom come, then killed everybody else with that 40x sniper rifle before slidin' into the woods. If it was a trap, he couldn't have got me out. We already knew that. But he would 'a caused some real serious misery while he was here. He knows that both me and Gage would rather die 'cause 'a him than 'cause of some scumbag out for revenge."

Malachi spoke again. "Does Gage have need to fear revenge?"

"Oh, yeah, for sure," said Sandman. "Somebody out there would like to do him in, no doubt. He's lucky he ever made it out of the desert to begin with." He hesitated, looking around the table. "Do ya'll know what any of us used to do?"

"I do," said Sarah.

"Yeah, I figure you do," Sandman replied, with a short laugh. "I know about you. He's told me. I know he would a' told you, even if he never told nobody else."

Sarah smiled slightly, leaning back.

Sandman gestured with his hand. "You guys know?"

Malachi nodded, "I know a great deal."

"I'm catching on quick," offered Barto eagerly.

Sandman seemed to contemplate, silent for almost the first time. "Where's the priest?" he asked suddenly. "That old man who saved Gage in the desert?"

Sarah and Barto said nothing. Malachi's face tightened for a quiet moment before he replied, "He is dead. He was murdered by the same people who are hunting us now."

Sandman leaned back in his chair, face slightly shocked, and curious. His large black hands rested on the table, and he gazed about, wondering for a moment. "So ya'll are holed up here," he said. He glanced toward the room where Gage lay. "Boy, I'll bet you somebody pays for *that!*"

A moment passed, and Sandman nodded. "OK," he said slowly, studying the tabletop. "I got it. There's a whole lot more to come." He nodded again, looked up. "Well, one of ya'll are goin' have to catch me up to speed. Then I'll brief Chavez. We've probably got a few minutes before he comes out."

Sarah rose. "I'll check on them."

Sandman's hand instantly gripped her hand, lightly but affirmingly. "Please, ma'am, don't do that. Chavez, when he's a mind to, he can be meaner 'an 'a snake an' all, but Gage has done a whole lot for him and his family, and he loves Gage more 'an his own brother. It's best to leave 'em alone for a minute."

Sandman leaned closer to her, lowering his voice to a whisper. "Chavez, you see, he's real religious an' all. An' he's probably sayin' some kind 'a prayer over Gage or somethin'. One of them Mexican Catholic things. He might even be sheddin' a tear an' he sure don't want you to see him doin' that. Just give him a second. Then he'll be comin' on out like nuthin's happened."

Sarah sat down, nodding compassionately, understanding.

"Now ya'll tell ol' Sandman what's been goin' on!" Sandman said expansively, leaning back, nodding.

Malachi said, "It is not pleasant. Many people have died. And there is the danger that even more will die before this is through."

Sandman nodded again, solemnly serious though still smiling. "That's alright, professor. Ain't nobody gonna live forever."

Immense and opulent and lonely, the Throne Room of the Vatican was quietly lit by subdued golden lamps, creating a distinctly somber atmosphere, a darkened atmosphere to match the darkened mood of the regal figure who sat silently, clothed formally in white, on the Papal Throne itself.

By order, the cavernous chamber was deserted, leaving only the throned figure, Pope Clement XV, and the black-robed priest who approached him with steady, faithful strides. A thoughtful frown deepened the lines in Clement's aged face as the younger priest, 30 years younger but still in his fifth decade, knelt before the throne.

"Forgive me, Holiness." Father Stanford Aquanine D'Oncetta, bent to kiss the Fisherman's Ring worn habitually upon the Pontiff's right hand. "I realize that it has been three days. But I was overseeing affairs in America."

Clement nodded. "Yes, the responsibilities of an internuncio are vast, are they not, Father?" he replied slowly.

"Yes, Holiness, vast and complex," D'Oncetta replied with only the faintest, suppressed tone of suspicion in his words. Then he bowed, stepping back. "An ambassador of the Throne must be ceaselessly at work."

Clement leaned forward, resting his elbows on the gold-colored wooden arms of the throne. For a long moment he said nothing but studied the dignified and cultured man before him.

"I live to serve, Holiness," Father D'Oncetta said finally. "How may I assist you?"

Clement's gaze was unpleasant. "I would be your confessor, Father," he intoned. "I would hear your sins."

D'Oncetta's eyes narrowed. "That would be a lengthy ordeal, Holiness," he replied without hesitation, glancing casually about the chamber.

"There is no need," observed the old man. "We are quite alone. It is only you and I, as it should be. Only one aged priest discussing the sins of his life with another. Except that you are not so old as I, though your sins may be far greater."

D'Oncetta held the Archbishop's concentrated aspect. "Sin is a matter of perspective, Holiness," he replied, an edged chill to the subtle tone. "There are not two within the Palace who will agree upon a single thought or action, regardless of how good or evil it may be."

"I have not come for semantics, Father," said Clement suddenly. "I am here to advise you of what you must do to serve me."

D'Oncetta's face brightened. "And what shall I do for you, Holiness?"

"Return the manuscript."

D'Oncetta stood in silence. "What you ask ... is difficult," he replied. "The manuscript is not mine to return."

Clement laughed without humor; a bitter, mocking tone. "It was not yours to remove, Father. So surely it is not yours to return. But return it you must. Or you will understand, for perhaps the first time in your life, the true meaning of power."

"To be more clear, Holiness," replied D'Oncetta, unfazed, "I cannot return the manuscript because it is not in my possession, as you presume. Nor is it in the possession of Augustus, who you once taught and loved, and who sends most sincere condolences for Simon's unfortunate death."

In solemn concentration the Pontiff's lips drew together in a grim line, the dark eyes hardening as the head bent slightly forward.

"It would go well with you not to mention the name of Augustus again within these walls, Father," Clement said slowly. "Long ago your master chose a different path. And it shall consume him, in the end, though the end may be long in coming. God knows. We can only pray that his terror will soon be finished."

Silence was tense between them.

"Despite the bitterness you feel in your heart, Augustus holds only the warmest regard for you," replied D'Oncetta after a moment. "He regrets that Father Simon has died ..."

"Simon did not die," said Clement. "He was murdered by ... *mercenaries.*"

"No," D'Oncetta disagreed, shaking his head solemnly. "That is not true, Holiness. It was not the hand of man, but the excitation of events that precipitated Simon's collapse. The autopsy reports will confirm that his death was wholly natural. It is regrettable, but blame cannot be placed on any but age."

Clement sighed, shook his head. "Do you take me for a fool, Father?"

"No, Holiness."

"Then you are wise. Yes, wise indeed. Remember, D'Oncetta, that I still hold the Keys of this Blood. Even Augustus is not outside my reach. And my sins are not so great that I will not add one more."

D'Oncetta seemed unsettled. "And what, specifically, shall I tell him, Holiness?"

"Advise him to return the manuscript," replied Clement. "Then tell him that he must remove his residence from the coast of my country. He may reside no longer on my shores. That is something I should have ordained long ago. Tell him that those Cardinals who are in allegiance with his evil designs will have no further communication with him. And if I discover a violation of my commands they will be harshly treated." He stared at the priest a moment, as if debating within himself. "Finally, advise him to remove his hand from the lives of Malachi Halder, his daughter, and the translator. If any of the Americans are injured, Augustus will feel the full power of my wrath."

D'Oncetta seemed to ponder the implications of the words. "And if Augustus does not comply?"

"All of his hidden gold will be seized," said Clement sternly. "His concealed ownerships of banking empires will come under investigation. Communications with his multitude of intelligence and military officials will be exposed as counterintelligence activities that supposedly threaten the welfare of their respective nations. And the coalitions which he is building will be laid bare to the canyons of their bones for all the world to see. There will be no more secrets, D'Oncetta. Deliver that message to your master. Tell him that if he does not submit to all that I have said, and if he does not withdraw his hand from the lives of the Americans, there will be no more secrets."

D'Oncetta was steady. "Such an action would also expose the Church of Rome to scorn, Holiness. In the state of things, with the challenge to infallibility, the challenge, even, of authority on government affairs of the church, moral decay within and without, and other, more embarrassing moral dilemmas that we need not mention, such an action as this might well be the final blow to—"

"All things have a price, Father," said Clement wearily. "Your veiled threats do not frighten me. The Church will endure. It has endured far worse, and is beyond even our foolishness to destroy."

D'Oncetta nodded. "Perhaps, Holiness. But perhaps, also, you might grant consideration to the wisdom of others of eminence who live beneath the Dome of Michelangelo. Perhaps you might learn from the errors of those who have come before you."

Clement laughed. "How so, Father?"

"What I mean, Holiness, is that you might consider whether Augustus and many of those within your Palace might be wise and right in what they say. Perhaps what Augustus says might indeed be best, even for yourself. As you know, he only wishes to forge an alliance between the Church and the emerging powers. In the opinion of many, such an alliance would not be an evil thing. It might even allow the Church to accomplish more good than it could, otherwise, without such a unity of forces."

"You speak as a priest, Father."

"I am a priest," said D'Oncetta, undisturbed by the veiled sarcasm. "And I ask that you hear me out completely before you exercise your wrath. Give me some of your time, Holiness. I ask that you base your final judgment upon what you hear."

Nothing could be discerned from Clement's lowered gaze. But he nodded, solemn. "Then speak, Father, and I will listen. Persuade me, if you can. Convince me that your views are correct and that mine are wrong. Demonstrate that I am only an old and foolish man. I have always said that every man has something he might teach me." The Archbishop of Rome smiled beneath narrowed eyes. "Yes, speak with me."

Father Stanford Aquanine D'Oncetta moved closer. "Let me begin, Holiness, by saying that those who are well-suited for the task, including many of your own Bishops, those who have aligned themselves with Augustus, are convinced beyond doubt that their sage views are correct. They are confident that their actions will be for the benefit of all."

"A snake may be right in action and in what he believes, but that does not make it right for his prey," replied Clement. "And we are not created to be predators. Not even those who claim to be . . . well-suited for the task."

D'Oncetta hesitated. "Yes, but with all respect, Holiness, your words do not change the opinion of many within your own fold. The events that are unfolding are beyond that logic. We have entered a new age, seen new forces . . ."

"There is no such thing," broke in Clement simply, frowning.

D'Oncetta waited a moment, concentrating, before continuing. "There are . . . forces . . . among us which are at work, forces destined to claim dominion on the Earth. This kingdom is already here, Holiness. Even if I were to agree with you and submit humbly to your designs, I could not stop the coalition of powers outside this Palace that are already melded together, concentrating wealth and dominion in the hands of those who are, by natural selection, destined to rule."

Pope Clement XV was silent a moment. "And who might these men be, Father?" he asked abruptly. "Who are these men who are born to rule?"

"Some men are born to serve, Holiness," said D'Oncetta, lifting his hands emptily, shrugging. "And some are born to rule. A man's nature is as unchanging as his flesh. He cannot make one hair black or white, cannot raise himself an inch in stature, as the Scriptures say. And neither can a slave make himself a king, Holiness. It is an abomination.

"Some are born to power, and are endowed with the intelligence, the wisdom, culture, and superiority of mind and being to wield that power. The rest are simply there, to tend and keep, to insure that those things which must be done, are done. They fulfill their stations in life. And, as cruel as it may sound, Holiness, ninety-nine percent of those who are living exist to serve the other one percent. Even now, the minions, if I may use that word without offending your sensibilities, have no idea how empty and hopeless are their lives. They live to work, endlessly, like dogs, and to desperately support their families however they can. They do not understand the secrets of power. They have no superiority of intellect or birth that would qualify them for a ruling status. They survive. They work and insure that things are completed. And, in this, their position is important. But they are not capable of true decisions, decisions of power. They do not understand international finance, or the future, the Cosmos, or even their own state of being. They do not understand sacrifice, or tolerance, or unity. They understand only what they need for their day-to-day lives. For how often have their lives hovered one inch from annihilation while they have slept blissfully on? They slept, while men such as you and I, or Augustus, bore the burden of decisions that would set the course for their lives and their children's lives. Even now, upon every hour of every day, decisions are made by men of wealth and position that decide the most private aspects of their existence. And yet they are rarely aware of it, or, even, at times, complaining about it."

D'Oncetta stepped forward.

"I know what you are thinking, Holiness. You are thinking that all men are dust and must return to dust. And that there is no man innately greater than the rest. You are pondering the thought that it must be the greatest and cruelest arrogance that the few would presume to decide the fate of the many. But in this, Holy Father, you are wrong."

Clement's face was unreadable, the lowered eyes hidden in shadow.

"I will not burden you by sharing knowledge that you already possess," continued D'Oncetta, raising a hand solemnly for indulgence. "Nor would I be so ambitious as to presume that I might persuade you of my philosophical views. I only say this to humbly prove a single premise. And that is, that this union between the gathering powers and the Church would be a good thing. A fruitful thing. Many who hold power within the Church itself are convinced that it is the only wise course of action."

D'Oncetta stepped forward as he spoke again. "Clearly, Holy Father, you simply cannot expect those who are born to a superior status to leave their fate in the hands of those who have little. That would be unwise in the extreme, and would lead to the disintegration of society. Why should the Church of Rome not join hands with the elect in hopes that we might also be in league with forces of power and affect the world for good?" He paused, stressed, "This is wisdom, Holiness. If we stand against these forces we may be stagnated in our efforts, or even crushed. But if we work *with* them, we will share in the power. We will be able to continue our measure of influence in the world. Sleeping with the devil is not as evil as it may sound, if the end purposes are our own.

"And it is no true loss, Holiness. For society itself will never allow the poor to control the reins of power. There is nothing that you or I can do to alter it. So why not use the situation for good? Why not join hands with the rich so that we might do whatever good we can for the poor and the downtrodden?"

Clement raised his face slightly. "And what do these...poor ...do for the world, Father?"

D'Oncetta motioned dismissively with his hand. "They labor in their employment. They live, they sleep. They make decisions that affect the smaller aspects of their lives. They are public servants, teachers..."

"Carpenters?" Clement asked in a curious tone.

D'Oncetta gazed narrowly upon the old man. "Yes, even carpenters." D'Oncetta leaned closer, speaking clearly. "Please hear me, Holiness. It is something that not even you can change. The poor and the ignorant will always be with us. Christ himself said this. So it is both necessary and altruistic that we take care of them. But the best manner of taking care of them is not to let them make their own decisions. We will help them by managing their lives. And if we are truly benevolent, then both the rich and the poor will enter a new kingdom of earthly prosperity."

Clement slowly nodded. "Yes, I see, Father. So these are inferior beings that Augustus assists? These are men of a lesser birthright?"

Cautious, D'Oncetta spoke. "Holiness, I know better than to match words with you. You are far, far too wise." He bent slightly forward, bowing. "Destroy my argument, Holiness, if you wish. But this is what I see, and what I believe."

"So," intoned Clement, as if he had not heard, "then poor Simon, born to an illiterate sheep farmer and raised without the benefit of classical education was, by recognition of his downtrodden beginning, also an inferior being?"

D'Oncetta steeled himself before he spoke. "There are some who would profess this, yes."

Clement nodded, seemingly distracted. Then, absently, he raised an old and wrinkled hand, as if hearing a faint and ghostly voice, or as if...remembering. He waited a long time with the curious tension of listening, staring vacantly into the black space beside D'Oncetta.

"Strange," Clement began in awe, "how, with age, one's mind can turn suddenly and morosely maudlin with memories." He paused. "*Strange*...how the soul can quickly leave the place it inhabits, as my mind does now, to dwell again in distant days."

Clement focused again upon D'Oncetta. "Tell me, Father D'Oncetta, would you mind quoting me some of *De laudibus Dei*, written by Darcontius of Carthage? Any of the poem's two thousand hexameter verses will suffice for my pleasure."

D'Oncetta's face was confused, and he opened his mouth, as if to apologize, before he realized. Then his distinguished features froze, hardening, his eyes glinting like polished obsidian orbs.

Clement laughed distantly, shook his head, as if reminiscing. "Yes, I remember how Father Simon would sometimes sit for hours and quote the beatific Latin of that great epic. Or how he would sometimes, for my sheer amusement, orally translate Milton's *Paradise Lost* into Latin, rewriting the text in his mind, improving as he saw fit upon the dull English." Clement laughed again. "Yes. The memory warms an aging heart."

His gaze grew serious once more. "And, while we are on the subject of superior knowledge and wisdom, Father D'Oncetta, I have often had difficulty understanding the true meaning of the Copernican turning point in the theory of knowledge and faith as it was captured by the philosopher from Konigsburg. Do you think that you might be able to illumine my mind in this, as Simon would so often do while we walked through the hills near Umberto? I'm sure it would be a simple task for someone so superior as you."

Grim, D'Oncetta looked vaguely away.

And as if absorbed by his thoughts, Clement shook his head.

"If I remember correctly," Clement continued, laughing as a man laughs at happy memories, "Kant's critique of pure Reason was the beginning of the end for the Enlightenment, setting cruel philosophical limitations to the proudly claimed omnipotence of Reason." He smiled. "Yes, I recall how Simon could discuss the hidden implications of the death of Reason for hours, always bringing the spiraling tendrils of lofty logic down again to that central, Copernican theory. Yes," the old man nodded, "I was hoping that you might also be able to explore its depths."

D'Oncetta said nothing, maintained a steady and elect bearing.

"Yes," Clement continued, "I understand. It is difficult, is it not? Please, forgive me for reminiscing, Father. But sometimes, in the strangest hours, I wish to hear my old friend's words again. It is impossible for me to duplicate the context of his august learning. But I can remember how he would explain how subjectivity always colors true reason, therefore coloring judgment and *a priori* thought. He found it humorous that men would use pure reason to establish moral standards, or even, to establish the meaning of reason itself. He likened it to measuring one fish by another fish."

Clement laughed again. "I can remember how he would often joke merrily at those who proclaimed so proudly that reason and superior thought would deliver them or lead them to moral enlightenment. Yes, he would speak for hours on how truly synthetic judgments which decide ultimate issues and genuinely increase our knowledge are possible only in mathematics, and not metaphysics. And when he had intimately explored virtually all the dimensions of *a priori* knowledge that fail to achieve true knowledge and which can never build a tower to God, he would categorize all of the pomposity where it truly belonged, as suprasensible thought that offers only the illusion of logic, but was not truly logical at all. Merely the proud reasoning of proud men. And he would explain how, if one demands certainty in thought, then he will surely meet with failure. He would talk about how, in knowledge, *enough* is always merely 'something,' and not 'everything.' Because everything cannot be understood through language or thought. Ambiguity is everywhere. But I am sure that these are simple thoughts for one such as you, Father D'Oncetta. Perhaps they are even insulting for one who stands among the master race, and who has, by association, humbly donned the mantle of a superior being. But then neither Simon, nor I, ever made claims to superiority. We merely continued our poor search for truth with hope, with study and discipline and tolerance. And with a dedication to what we believed was right. Surely, our actions were unworthy of a master race of the intellectually enlightened."

D'Oncetta was silent, face expressionless.

Clement leaned back against the throne, his farmer's hands clutching each of the solid golden globes decorating the armrests.

A defiant silence reigned between them.

Finally Clement spoke, all mockery gone. "You might have learned much from poor Father Simon if you had taken the time to speak with him, D'Oncetta, instead of eliminating him."

Slowly, D'Oncetta took in a deep breath, released it suddenly. "I see that there can be no agreement between us, Clement."

"No." Clement shook his head. "There can be no agreement. But I will take no official action against you, Father. I shall not make you a martyr. You deserve to be called a criminal, yes, but not a martyr. And you deserve to be called a murderer, for that is what you are. But I know that your crimes can never be proven. Even so, do not be deceived. The Judge of all the Earth has sealed your fate. And I do not speak of the nebulous Cosmos which Augustus so zealously worships. It will not be the neutral God of Light that supposedly melds Augustus's spirit-soul with Eternity, allowing him to speak with men who are long dead and men who have never lived. No, it shall be a different God, a holy God who sacrificed Himself on Golgotha."

Clement's voice contained the drum, drum of doom. "Until that day, however, until you ascend from this fleshly tomb and stand before the judgment seat of Christ, you must deal with me. And I tell you this, D'Oncetta, you are never to set foot in Città del Vaticano again. Not while I live. You may continue your intrigues with the cursed Cardinals who have aligned themselves with Augustus, but not on holy ground. And you may tell Augustus that Clement stands against him."

D'Oncetta shifted, his gaze unfaltering. "This is your final word?"

"It is my final word," Clement said grimly. "Because the time for words has passed. I assure you that when you see me again, Father, you will curse my name."

The black-robed priest raised his hand, pleading indulgence. "Allow me, first, Holiness, the opportunity of delivering this message to Augustus. I believe he may well heed your warning. But, of course, he will need time to consider means of forging that peace. Many lives are at stake, and events have occurred for which there will be consequences. We will need time to study the situation, to placate our allies and create a suitable ending. By your own great love for mercy and grace, I ask that you give us time to deal with these potentially dangerous issues."

An ominous silence cloaked the throne room, and Clement's eyes glinted flintlike in the gloom. He recognized that Augustus, his old and cunning enemy, would never surrender his dreams of a global empire of the ruling elite. But he also knew that mercy must have its say, even for monsters.

Slowly, he nodded. "As you request, Father D'Oncetta. Tell Augustus that he has one month to consider his error and make amends. But he must take no action against the Americans, or peace will be severed. Advise him that if he does not return the manuscript within that month, we shall both discover whose forces are truly superior."

D'Oncetta bowed. "A wise decision, Holiness. I am sure that Augustus will wish to speak with you personally. Where shall the meeting be held?"

Clement lowered his head, resting for a moment before raising it again.

"In the graveyard by the sea," he said. "It will be on the ground that Augustus cherishes most that I will begin this battle."

Booted feet resting on his desk, Kertzman began to read the heavy stack of reports recently out of the NSA office.

Since the disturbing night with Sir Stephenson in the church, Kertzman had reverted to wearing an old pair of sturdy, brown corduroy pants, a heavy cotton, western blue workshirt, and boots. It was rugged footwear and dresswear, the kind of clothes he would want to be wearing if he were going to either run or fight for his life.

By reflex, at Stephenson's tone of danger, he had also reverted to the oldest golden rule of hunting: Always bring enough gun for the job. A new Colt .45, a slightly modified 1911 with an oversized safety and beveled magazine port for fast reloads, had never left his side, and even now rested on his belt in an easily concealable cut-down Velcro holster.

Six extra clips loaded with 230-grain, full-metal jacketed hydroshock hollow points were shoved into his cowboy-style boots, seven rounds to a clip, three clips on each ankle, for a total of 49 shots. Now, no matter what happened, he wouldn't go down without a very memorable fight.

He reached for a cup of coffee. Then, casually, with a discriminating eye, he scanned the reports, spending less than five seconds on each fully written page before knowing whether there was anything of merit, then turning to the next. It was boring. Tedious. His concentration wandered. A cardboard box filled with the personal papers and effects of Father Simon, the old priest who had worked at St. Thomas and who had died a few weeks before the infamous shootout at the seminary, rested on a corner of Kertzman's desk.

Absently, Kertzman glanced at it.

He had confiscated the papers without bothering NYPD with a federal evidence request before he had left the church, and he knew it was a long shot that he would find anything of interest. It was a shotgun approach, checking everything, anything, just to find a lead. A desperate move for a desperate man.

A quick perusal uncovered private devotional letters, treasured notes, travel logs, archeological diaries, and a passport. Kertzman had no reason to suspect that the deceased Father Simon had anything to do with this, but he felt a brief impulse of pride to know that he had, in any case, covered everything. At least he had retained *that* much emotional control after Stephenson had shaken him up with the superman speech. But as he continued to stare at the box, Kertzman became slowly curious, and his mind geared down into a surprisingly concentrated mode.

After a moment, with a gaze of slowly intensifying suspicion, Kertzman laid down the report he was reading. Then he reached out to pull the box closer, tilting it to stare down into the haphazard contents; a blend of letters and notebooks. He fished out a handful, opening a black archeological diary dated to 1976.

Thumbing slowly, he glanced through it, found places and dates, personal observations of finds, locations of discoveries, things Kertzman couldn't understand. He dropped it back into the box, moved to the next book, and the next, studying one after the other, scanning, absorbing, getting a basic understanding of the old man.

Then a thought, faint and thin, came from the distance but closed hard and gathered fast as it neared, concentrating and sharpening in clarity until Kertzman suddenly reached out with a quick movement and stood, staring down into the box. In seconds, rummaging roughly, he found it, lifted a small blue passport from the pile.

Mouth slack, eyes widening slightly in excitement, he immediately had it open, scanning, studying the stamps and markings, turning the pages quickly and not knowing exactly what it would look like. Then there it was.

Entered: *Israel. June 19, 1990.*

His soul confirmed the rest before he saw it.

Departed: *Israel. August, 1990.*

Kertzman's teeth came together hard, lips drawing back savagely. Eyes gleaming, he smiled. *I found you!*

A sign, a track, something leading out of this desert. Kertzman saw it all: Gage, lost in the Negeb in August, 1990. Father Simon, also in Israel in August, 1990. And deep inside, where he had begun tracking a cold wind trail to the lay of the land, Kertzman suddenly knew where Malachi Halder would also be found in August of 1990.

Israel.

Kertzman read the faint imprints in the dust, felt it; a dim gathering of an almost invisible sign, long worn by time, almost gone. But it was there.

He was certain.

That's the key, he thought. Something had happened in the desert that tied them all together.

Taking another sip of coffee, Kertzman sat back down, heavily, the scenario revolving in his head for long moments, again and again, solidifying. He knew he had found *the* clue, something important. It made sense.

He leaned back again in the chair, picking up another report. No longer bored, fired with fresh excitement, he allowed his eyes to scan the pages with new speed: no sightings of Gage's car, no traces of him, nothing. Nothing.

Kertzman laughed, snorting contemptuously. He was still committed to covering Gage's bloody tracks, but now he saw that it would be a lot easier than he had feared.

Two weeks since the incident in St. Thomas and the NSA, the largest intelligence agency in America, had turned up exactly nothing. The FBI had matched the ammo to a store in Phoenix, Arizona. No connection to anybody who worked in any agency associated with the Cavalier. No connection to anybody who had ever worked with Gage or Black Light or even, as a long, *long* shot, the United States Army. The Hi-Power was British military issue, and it had been released to a colonel of the Special Air Service in 1974. Kertzman had traced the colonel back to the Puerto Rico Special Warfare School in July of 1979, where Gage had cross-trained with the SAS. That was the only good connection.

The colonel had died in 1984, and no trace was possible on ownership of the weapon. The British said that, as far as they knew, it was supposed to be in his estate. Kertzman laughed again at that. It wasn't.

There were absolutely no sightings of the LTD. And that, for Kertzman, was the truly amazing part. No sightings of a shot-to-pieces late-model dark LTD with a smashed-to-smithereens right side and two seatfulls of shattered windows. Yes, it was possible, with the car traveling on back roads, away from city lights. The damaged right side would have been away from traffic, the glass not so noticeable at night. He had seen it happen before. And there was no real coordination of information between law enforcement agencies. It was slightly possible that no one had even looked for it at all.

In fact, it was amazing how small an amount of truly accurate information did, indeed, circulate in the national police community. Somewhere between the despised uniform officer on the scene, through the sergeant, to the lieutenant, and finally through dispatcher and back again through the same chain of command in a hundred other departments, anything could happen with the simplest wanted bulletin. And often did.

Probably only two or three cities had even transmitted the bulletin for the LTD. It wasn't required that they did; it was professional courtesy. And on a hot Friday night, courtesy was at a minimum, as was excess radio traffic. So unless the departments had specific reason to believe that the LTD was in their neighborhoods, dispatchers would probably have kept the bulletin off the air entirely. Kertzman thought it likely that virtually no one had broadcast it. It wasn't a verifiable homicide at the time, just a felony hit and run, an important event to civilians but just a slightly interesting call for veteran officers. And Kertzman knew from experience that tired third-shift cops, working the late half of a late night, sleepy and not really caring about anything except an early breakfast and some coffee to stay awake, wouldn't have gone to any real pains to look for it, even if they *had* received the bolo. Still, though, with a car as noticeable as that, it was probably close.

"You got lucky on that one, partner," Kertzman said softly, and put the report down. Then he picked up a thick, triple-ringed book from the clutter.

And saw it.

In another shotgun approach the Bureau had run a registration check through the National Crime Information Center and had come up with a full listing of all post-1980 LTDs still recorded under any tag for the greater northeastern area of the nation. The list was 275 pages long, single-spaced with four narrowly divided columns for each page. Kertzman estimated over 20,000 listings.

Frowning, he skipped over 200 pages of original owners and transfers. Gage wouldn't be that stupid. Then he began reading the names of corporations listing possession of an LTD for business purposes.

A long, painful tension and 30 minutes later, he had found three possibilities: Allied Air Transport, out of Monticello, New York, Expansion Transport out of New York City, and International Air Freight, Inc., out of Boston.

No matter what Gage did with the rest of the money, he would have used some of it to provide a back door, in case he needed to penetrate the border of a country without using commercial airlines or risking the International Customs' attention drawn by a private flight. It was his soldier's nature, driven into him from spending half of his life in the air or on a ship, flying and jumping, always at war.

From the relentless conditioning of always fighting someone, and knowing that the old life might return one day to haunt him, he would have a door, something that would allow him to slide back into a warrior's life if the desperate need ever arose, even if it was only for a last-stand suicide run at revenge.

But Expansion Transport and International Air Freight were both extremely large corporations, too large, even, for Gage's investment. He wouldn't want to be involved with something so big that he couldn't control it. And they were listed for the greater New York and Boston areas.

No, Kertzman thought, shaking his head, that wouldn't work. He looked at Allied Air Transport, saw that it was a small air-freight company created in 1989. Then he considered the location: Monticello, New York.

Kertzman knew the terrain of northern New York. Monticello lay on Interstate 17, a scant 10 miles from the Catskills.

Kertzman caught the wind, saw the track. *That's it.*

He was almost certain. It had to be. The Catskill Mountains. A million acres of undeveloped forest with mountains and wilderness trails that Gage could retreat into. He could use his Special Forces skills to evade an army in there, if he had to.

Kertzman sighed. Yeah, that's where he would be holed up. Somewhere in the Catskills, close to his main business with a wilderness to his back. Even as he thought of it, Kertzman realized how he might be able to bypass Gage's warning flags in the first two or three false identities. It was a long shot, but it looked like the only shot he might get.

"Yeah," he said quietly, unable to confine his emotion to cold thought alone. "It might just work."

But there was a problem. The NSA, because he had told Radford and Milburn to focus on airlines, would be running their own ploddingly methodical investigation. Soon the agency would be stomping all over Allied Air Transport, setting off every alarm in the corporation, alerting Gage to the fact that the government was closing in on him. Gage would hang tight for a while, until the investigation got closer. Then he would retreat for another, more isolated location, maybe somewhere in northwestern Canada, to some last-chance stronghold with deep cover. Something in the back of Kertzman's mind warned him that if he missed this chance, if he let the NSA blow it before he could find Gage's hideout, he'd never find the former Delta commando at all.

Expressionless, Kertzman set the report down with the same casual, disappointed air that he would use if someone were watching him. Then he leaned back, staring at the desk, at the cold cup of coffee, wondering how long it would be before someone else in the Agency tripped Gage's alarms.

It might not happen for a couple more days. Then again, it might happen in a couple of hours. There was no way to know, for certain. There was even a chance they had already done it.

Kertzman exhaled a deep breath. He'd have to do something, stall the NSA from approaching Allied Air Transport. But what?

Slowly, as he stared morosely at his littered desk, a plan suggested itself.

Use a false lead. Give them something to focus their energies on. Then use the time to run this guy to ground before anybody gets wise.

After a moment Kertzman sighed, nodding. If he was really, really lucky, it might even work. But he needed a week. He needed to put them on the wrong trail for at least a week to pull it off. Even then, he'd have to go through the back door of the investigation to get to this guy. It would be touch-and-go. But it could be done. Carefully, he began to work out the details. He was so deep in thought that Radford's appearance in the doorway startled him.

"Found anything?" he asked.

Radford was already halfway across the room before Kertzman recovered his composure. He dropped his feet to the floor, cast a despairing eye over the scattered reports, frustrated.

"I might," he said, indifferent. "But it sure ain't 'cause you pretty boys are helping me." He looked up sharply. "What are your people doing over there, Radford? I thought ya'll were supposed to be a bunch of hotshot investigators!"

Radford sat down heavily in a green metal chair, gazed somberly at him a moment. "Look, Kertzman, we're working, OK? What do you have that we don't?"

Kertzman sniffed, moved his head awkwardly. "I think I know where he might be."

Radford was intrigued, sat upright. "Where?"

Kertzman tossed the report to him. "I told you to concentrate on airlines, didn't I?"

"Yeah." Radford had already opened the report to scan the corporations.

Kertzman continued, "Turn to page 234. Second column. Expansion Transport. New York."

Radford found the listing. He looked up. "How do you know?"

"Everything is happening in New York. All the shootings. Gage needs a home base. He needs a place for equipment. And he's probably got his money invested in an airline. A place he'll stay real close to." Kertzman nodded. "That's it. Has to be. I'll stake everything I've got on it."

Radford studied the page again. "You know that there's two more airlines on here?"

"Yeah, I know," Kertzman said casually. "But they ain't what we want."

"Why?"

"They're too far away from the city."

Radford thought about it. Kertzman couldn't tell whether he agreed or not. After a moment the NSA agent raised his head, spoke in a tone of uncertainty.

"Why does that make any difference?"

Kertzman shifted. "Gage will live close to his business. He'll need to be close in case things burn down in a hurry and he has to run hard. And he couldn't have driven from the city to Boston or Monticello the other night without getting caught by a cop. The car was too noticeable. Shot to pieces, windows shattered. Wrecked. There was probably a thousand cops between New York City and either one of those other places that would have picked it up."

"Maybe he ditched it," offered Radford. "Maybe he had another one."

"I don't think so."

"Why?"

Kertzman sighed. "Radford, if he had another one, why would he risk using a car that was registered to the airline? Or registered at all? And if he ditched it, why haven't we found it by now? We would have, you know. Easy. But we haven't because he took it with him. That means he drove it." He shook his head. "No. That car was all he had available. And while he might have driven it to a safe house somewhere in New York without getting caught, there was no way he could have driven it outside the city without being seen. I'm an ex-cop. I know. It ain't possible. Too many cops ain't got nothing to do at three in the morning except look for drunk drivers and hit-and-run suspects."

Radford seemed to have nodded. He studied the document. "Alright. Now what do you suggest we do?" he asked. "What's the best way to close in on this guy?"

"Go in slow," Kertzman began. Then he waited a minute, staring hard at the NSA man, obviously deep in thought. Then, "Have you ever hunted a coyote?"

Radford rolled his eyes. "Please, Kertzman."

Kertzman raised a hand, gesturing. "No, now, you'll enjoy this one," he added. "Let me tell you how it's done. 'Cause this boy is a lot like a coyote. He's gonna be hard to track."

"We are not *tracking* him, Kertzman. We're trying to arrest him."

"Yeah, well, whatever," Kertzman said, continuing. "This is how it's done."

He leaned forward in his chair, creating the atmosphere of the hunt with his brightened eyes, gesturing hands, and poised bulk. "The coyote is the wiliest animal you'll ever hunt in the woods. Wilier and smarter than a wolf. Quicker. Even smarter than a bear 'cause the coyote understands men a lot better. Out of all the animals in the Dakotas, like the grizzly, the wolf, cougar, or buffalo, the coyote is the only one who's managed to survive since the Old West." He hesitated for dramatic effect. "And do you know why?"

Dismally, Radford shook his head.

"'Cause he's learned to adapt," Kertzman continued. "He watches. He studies man. The coyote knows man almost better than man knows himself. And he's a demon to hunt. If you're huntin' one in the summer, when the ground is hard and you can't find any hot sign or scat, you'll have a real hard time."

"Yeah." Radford nodded. "I can see how all this relates."

"Just give me a minute," Kertzman added. "It gets better. You'll be glad I talked to you about it." He nodded. "'Cause this boy is a lot like a coyote, you see. Now, normally, he would run in a pack, like his old unit, Black Light. But I think he's mostly alone now. So he's going to react a lot differently to a threat, just like a coyote reacts differently to a threat when he's alone, and not with his pack."

Radford looked at him with that. "What do you mean, differently?"

"A lone coyote will respond a lot calmer, a lot slower, to danger. If a coyote is in a pack, they'll all just run away from you. It's the pack mentality. But if he's alone, he'll let you come a lot closer, and he'll move a lot slower."

Radford stared a moment, almost interested. "Why?"

Kertzman shook his head. "I don't know. They just do."

Radford released an exasperated sigh.

"Anyway," Kertzman continued, "if he knows you're tracking him, and he will, then he'll keep leading you around. Watching you. Studying you. Trying to find what you're all about."

"*Watching* you?" asked Radford.

"Yeah. Watching you. He'll lead you out across a grassy plain, or up to high ground. Every now and then he'll turn and study you, see how you're moving. Then he'll move another way, testing you, wearing you out. He'll do that for a long time, maybe all day, until he thinks he knows what you're all about. Then, if you're still with him, and he's gettin' scared, he'll head down into a coolie."

Radford was silent a second. "A coolie?" he asked abruptly. "What's a coolie?"

Kertzman seemed offended. "A ravine," he said suddenly. "It's, uh, like a chasm, or a little gulch or something. I don't know what you easterners call it."

"OK." Radford nodded. "I got it. A coolie."

"Anyway, he'll head down into a coolie. And that's where it'll get tough. He'll go to ground. You'll have to hunt him close. And when you finally get a chance at a shot, it might be a lot closer than you'd like 'cause you might step on him before you see him. Of course, if there's a cave or something, he'll go down into it and then you'll have to go in after him. It can get tough."

Radford was utterly motionless. "So... what are you saying?"

"I'm saying that this guy is not going to make any sudden moves, not even if you're close. But he's watching your every step. And if you do get close, he's probably going to do something to escape that is almost unnoticeable. Something casual, hard to identify. He knows his terrain, knows how to escape and evade. He won't attract attention to himself, won't be noticed. But, as soon as he thinks it's safe, he'll slide out like a ghost. And then he'll be gone, Radford. *Gone.* And that's going to be the end of your little investigation. If this guy hits the backwoods, if he heads north into upper Canada where there ain't nobody, not even Canadians, then he's gone for good. You'll never see him. I'll never see him. He'll live off the land with a horse, a thirty-thirty, a knife, and a box of shells."

"So what do we do?" Radford asked, clearly disturbed.

"Do background checks on everybody working at Expansion Transport. Everybody. Go in real quiet, real slow. No questions, no investigators. No nuthin'. Do everything through the records, the computers. Keep our distance so he can't see us. If you turn up a dead end on someone, concentrate on that ID. Find out if it's false. Just remember to do everything real quiet. That will be the secret to catching him."

Radford was looking at the report again. "You know," he said, absently, "there are probably over eight thousand people working at this company. Background checks are going to take at least two weeks, maybe three. That's if we use the entire NSA staff and the FBI indexing of fingerprint terminals. Of course, this much work is going to tie up all of their terminals. The FBI won't be happy."

"So what?" said Kertzman, raising his eyebrows. "Let it take two weeks. I'm certain he's there. I know he's there. I can feel it. Tell Carthwright I'm absolutely positive. And it's better that we close in on this guy sudden and catch him quick than fumble around and let him see us coming. Then he's gone for good. And you'll have to pay the price for losing him. 'Cause I told you to go slow."

Radford started. That had touched his heart. "Well, I don't plan to fry because of *this* guy, Kertzman, I'll tell you that." He stood, moving for the door. "We'll do it this way. It might take a little while. But at least it's a start."

At the door he hesitated. "Hey, Kertzman."

Kertzman looked up.

"How can somebody just vanish for years at a time?"

Kertzman shrugged. "Easy."

"How?"

"It happens all the time, Radford. There's been people on the FBI's Most Wanted List for twenty, thirty years, and the FBI doesn't have a clue. And those aren't even people who know what they're doing. They can't even hold Gage's coat. He's trained to get lost, and stay lost. He can manufacture phony ID, and he's probably got dozens of undocumented false IDs from his days in the Agency. He can be whoever he wants to be. He's got the money to set up one false identity after another, and establish flags in the first several layers to alert him if someone's poking around. This guy is a pro, Radford. He's not going to make a mistake."

Radford stood in silence a minute, staring at him. "But you said he's not perfect. He'll make a mistake somewhere."

"Yeah," Kertzman allowed, slowly, as if his pride were challenged. "Somewhere."

"Good," Radford replied, nodding. "Because this can't go on much longer. Heads are going to roll if it does."

TWENTY-NINE

It was a white, bitter winter cold, and it seemed like it was all there would ever be; a still, silent, depthless cold force that starkly smothered the hills surrounding the cabin.

Sarah took another sip of coffee, stared through the wide, plate-glass window towards the treeline, where two small distant figures, barely visible, moved easily through the barren stand.

Sandman stepped up beside her, holding his own steaming mug. He had just come in from the cold, having taken a turn at guard duty.

"Cold," he boomed heartily, laughing. "Cold out there. Ain't fit for man nor beast."

Sarah glanced at him, smiled, cozy in her black flannel shirt that she had bought on a discreet trip into Monticello. She'd also purchased an extra pair of jeans and boots. It was warm, rugged clothing, fit for the forest, or the cold. She focused again on the treeline. It had been three weeks. Gage had come around within two days of Sandman's injections of antibiotics and the saline IV. In another week, she had removed the sutures, over 200 of them. Now, two weeks later, he had begun moving over the hills with Chavez, patrolling, seemingly as strong as he ever was. But something was different with him, ever since he had healed. Sarah's face hardened in concentration as she studied the faint form on the hills, leading the lean shape of Chavez, moving with grace through the gray stand of timber.

Sandman was speaking. "You alright?"

"Sure. I'm fine. How do you think Gage is?" She hoped that her question wouldn't arouse suspicion in his mind.

"Oh, he's gonna be fine," Sandman said. "He's as tough as they come. And his cuts weren't that bad. Like you said, it was that venous cut on his forearm that did the real damage, threw him into shock. Anyway, I never did see a man so hard to kill. He's been through stuff that was a lot tougher. At Norfolk in '82 we went through drown-proofing at advanced scuba school. Now *that* was tough. They tied our hands behind our backs, threw us in a fifteen-foot pool, told us to survive. If we could. No gear, no airtanks, no nuthin'. Stay alive, they told us. For *six* hours. We'd kick our way to the surface, get a quick breath, then sink right back down to the bottom again cause we couldn't use our arms to tread water. Gage was right there, stayin' alive, laughin' about it. He'd look at me on the bottom of the pool, smiling. We'd hold our breath as long as we could, kick to the surface again, get a quick breath, sink to the bottom again. For six hours." He shook his head, whistled softly. "The instructors told us it would make us drown-proof. Unkillable. 'Cept a couple 'a guys drowned. The DIs brought 'em back, but they were out of the unit after that. That's how it worked. If you died, you were out of the unit. No second chances."

Sarah laughed. "It sounds tough, alright."

Sandman nodded. "Yeah, and Qualifying Week in Delta was tough, too. Runnin' thirty miles a day. Just miles and miles and miles of runnin' in them big ol' heavy boots and fatigues. Enough to drive a man insane. Less than two hours of sleep a night for seven days in a row. Crawling through the mud all day long. All night long. No bath all week. We had bugs in our ears, hair, everywhere. They wanted to find out what we were made of, if we could pull off missions. Each day was worse than the last. They made us wear red helmets so that if we died in the mudfields they could find our dead bodies." Sandman paused, looked at her expressively. "Who could come up with something like that? You know, that was crazy." He waited a moment, considering his own question, continued. "Anyway, after that we had bomb defusals. *After* we'd been awake for seven days, *after* we'd run over two hundred fifty miles without a break, *after* cold and heat and every other kind of misery was forced on us. If we messed up defusing one of them weird little bombs and blew ourself up, then we were out of the program. It didn't matter that we hadn't slept, that we'd just run two hundred miles, or that we hadn't had no good food." Sandman's face grew even more animated with the memory. "Noooo! And it wasn't, like, if we wanted to try it again, we could get another chance. No, they only gave you one chance to defuse this thing that was probably designed by a rocket scientist." He waited a minute. "Man, it was tough. Everybody, even Gage, was 'bout half-dead. Even ol' Chavez was draggin'."

Sandman hesitated a moment, a rare thing. "Ol' Chavez," he added after a pause, "he cracks me up. He smokes cigarettes like a chimney and he can run all day long. And he takes these little bitty steps." Sandman started to shuffle with the words, as if to depict the image, then stopped, his right leg stiff and awkward, before continuing. "Yeah, he uses these little bitty steps, his tiny ol' feet just flying, and he can run all day long. Still, he could run us all into the ground. I couldn't believe it. Never seen anything like it. Never."

Sarah wondered how long Sandman could keep talking without running out of something to say.

"Well," he added suddenly, surprising her with what followed. "I guess I'll get some rest before I go out there tonight. I've got first watch and we only got three hours before dark."

"Thanks, Sandman." Sarah turned towards him. "Thank you for everything."

"Ah, ol' Sandman's just here for the fun." He smiled and winked. Then he turned, limping into the back of the cabin.

Sarah felt completely alone. She had long lost sight of the shadowy figures in the woodline. Gage had told her that he owned almost 100 acres of the wilderness area, enough to assure him of continued solitude. So she knew the two men could be anywhere in the ridge, or even further back, towards the road. She heard another sound behind her, turned and saw Malachi setting down a load of chopped firewood. With a stiff fluidity of movement that only barely revealed his advancing years, he stacked the wood beside the fireplace, then looked up, smiling, and moved toward her. He dusted bark and woodchips off of his thick woolen sweater. She didn't attempt to hide her troubled fear.

Malachi nodded and reached down to take her in his arms. She rested her head on his shoulder.

"Something's wrong with Gage," she said softly, voicing her fears for the first time.

"Yes," the old man replied, holding her. "I know."

Sarah eased away, shook her head, crossed her arms, and turned to stare out the window. "I'm worried," she said. "What do you think it is?"

"No one can know for certain," Malachi said. "I would think that even he does not know what it is."

Sarah turned her head slightly to look at him. "What do you mean?"

Malachi glanced at the woods. "I mean that something has changed within him. Or it might be said, something within him remains wounded, or broken. His body is fine. He has healed. But his soul is still wounded. The true injury he suffered was far more than physical."

"But he's a fighter," Sarah said steadily. "That's what they've made him. He's trained to never give up, to never quit, no matter how bad it gets. It was driven into him by the kind of conditioning that kills people if they don't have the strength to overcome. Sleep deprivation, pain overload. It's all just a form of brainwashing, to make people what you want them to be. Fighters. Soldiers. The military is an expert at it. That *made* him a survivor. And he's the best there is. He's fought his way back from death a hundred times."

"But anyone can lose strength, Sarah," Malachi said with a gentle concern. "Even Gage. He has known the kind of pain that men die from, and everyone has a limit to what they can endure. You must remember that he is only a man. A strong man, a hard man, to be sure. But still only a man. He knows fear, like anyone else."

Sarah held a concentrated gaze on the hills. "He's searching for something."

"Yes, he is," Malachi said. "He is searching for what he is. He hasn't given up, yet. I know. I am watching him."

"He's so quiet," she whispered.

"Yes."

Sarah's eyes narrowed. "I thought he might just be tired, or exhausted. But it's more. It's a depression." She waited, searching for the proper word, grimaced with compassion when she found it. "It's fear."

Malachi nodded, silent.

She shook her head, teeth clenched. "No. I won't let him do this. I've got to try and reach him, somehow. Because I know he won't stop. He's still going to go against these people, after the manuscript. But if he's lost his edge, if he's lost his confidence, he won't stand a chance."

"Use wisdom, Sarah," Malachi cautioned, gazing down. "True answers to our fears are never simple, or clear. Pain and hardship are the rule of life, even for children of faith. A troubled spirit is rarely healed easily. In time, I believe, he will find both himself, and his courage, again. But it will come when it will come. If you choose to help him find his way, be careful that he does not also come to fear that you have lost faith in him."

Sarah's face was grim. "I understand. I think I know how to deal with him." She paused. "Do you think he may have just been injured too many times?"

"I know that each man has a limit." Malachi's face reflected an uncertainty. "But we cannot know, for certain. I know that Gage is still fighting, in his silent way, to find what he has lost. That is why he is with Chavez, in the hills. Chavez understands. He understands how wounds can haunt, how fear can follow healing. They speak little, but Chavez knows everything. That is why he is following, and Gage is leading. He does not want to push Gage. He wants Gage to set the pace."

Malachi looked at the sun, only a couple of hours from sunset. "Remember that life is often a dark and wounding journey. We bleed. We suffer. It is the price we pay to remain alive. The more we love and live, the more we will suffer. That is why great love requires great courage." He waited. "But Gage is, perhaps, tired of wounds, and no one can fight for him. It is something he must do within himself. By the strength of his spirit, he must resurrect his will to overcome."

Sarah shook her head, a lonely silhouette. "But why now? He was hurt a lot worse than this in the desert, and he came back strong."

A long silence joined them, and Malachi spoke again, a strange air of sudden understanding in his words. "Perhaps..." the old man began, gazing at her with a gathering certainty, "Gage has never possessed reason to fear. Perhaps Gage has never known fear of death because he has never valued life." He paused, focusing on her. "Or love."

Sarah closed her eyes.

"Yes, perhaps it is love that truly wounds us," Malachi intoned, his words deep and purposeful. "And perhaps it is love that heals."

Frowning, Sarah opened her eyes, staring with a steady concentration into the dusk. She nodded slowly.

"I hope so," she whispered.

• • •

Methodically rechambering the Colt .45 and flicking on the safety for a fast first shot, Kertzman laid the semiautomatic on the hotel room desk in front of him. Then, by reflex, he moodily glanced at the hotel door and window, making sure the lock was secure, the curtain completely closed.

On the road for five days, he had collected real estate documents from Sullivan, Ulster, and Delaware counties, all records centering on a time period six months before and after the founding of Allied Air Transport in Monticello. He had a lot, and he was convinced that, somewhere in the records, he would find what he needed.

Radford had paged him earlier in the day to advise him on what was happening in the NSA computer room. They were still checking and cross-checking identifications and personnel records of Expansion Transport. So far the NSA staff had discovered that almost 50 of the employees were currently wanted on local or federal warrants, had stumbled across evidence that Expansion management was overbilling clients, and had uncovered a host of other minor indiscretions of the law. It had even found ten employees who had used false IDs. But every print search on the suspect employee yielded an eventually positive identification through the Henry Classification system of the FBI computer program.

No match yet for Gage.

And nobody, absolutely *nobody*, as Radford had stressed, in the management or ownership level of Expansion was found, in any way, to have any background indiscretions. During the call Radford had seemed somewhat gloomy and unhappy about the drudgery. But Kertzman was enthusiastic, cheered him on for the good work.

He laughed out loud as he remembered the phone call.

Just a few more days, he thought. *Because I'm closing in on this guy. I'll find out who the bad guys are and who the good guys are. And if you don't cooperate, Gage, I'll fry you, too.*

Before Kertzman, spread across the table, laid a wide mass of records revealing land purchased for 1990, including dates, plots, road numbers, and descriptions as well as the current listing of ownerships.

Face scowling in concentration, Kertzman leaned forward in the cheap armchair, the image of a gorilla in a blue working shirt and dark brown corduroy pants. He tried to imagine himself in Gage's position; a renegade Delta Force commando bent on protecting himself, needing a safe house, solitude, a place to hide out for the long run.

Land, he thought, he needed a good-sized chunk of land. At least 50 acres of it. Probably more like 100 or more. And he'd want some distance, no neighbors, no possibilities of cameras in windows. He'd need gullies, ravines, and hills surrounding him so that he could go tactical. But he'd also need a little flatland immediately around the house, a little clear space so he could see them coming. Kertzman had already purchased topography maps according to home sites, and he'd planned to check the purchased land against the topo charts to shuffle any unsuitable locations lower on the list.

With resolute calm and a hot cup of coffee beside him, Kertzman picked up the first batch of records, perused the listing of land purchases for Delaware County. Then, with amazing speed, he began to write them down, rearranging the land purchases with the largest plots first, copying them in descending size for the one-year period. It was a lot; 153. He repeated the procedure with Sullivan and Ulster counties, methodically listing each plot in order of size, from largest to smallest in descending order.

Four hours and six cups of coffee later, he was finished. He could have accomplished a lot more a lot quicker, if he had used an

Agency computer, but that would have violated the rules of his greater plan, exposed his moves. So he did it the old-fashioned way. And in his own, stubborn self-reliance, he enjoyed it.

"Finished." He leaned back from the desk, rubbing his eyes tiredly. It had been a long time since he had done anything this methodical. It was like the old days, when he was just a grunt highway patrolman in South Dakota, finishing paperwork on top of paperwork with no end in sight.

He stared wearily at the 45 legal-size pages of listings.

You're wastin' time with this, boy!

The thought stung Kertzman. "No I'm not," he said aloud so that he'd hear himself say it. Maybe in time he'd believe it.

Frowning, he leaned forward again and began to check the listings of past purchased against current ownerships, discovering who still owned the same plots that were bought in that period of 1990. In the end, he had a list of 25 plots of land that were over 100 acres in size still in the possession of the same owner. There were 40 listings for plots over 50 acres, and the remaining 20 listings were for plots less than 50. Any plots smaller than 20 acres could be ignored.

"That ain't gonna be you, partner," Kertzman whispered to himself. "You want some room. You want to be able to use the terrain, to choose a dozen different lines of retreat."

Kertzman realized that if Gage had arranged another purchase of the land from one identification to another since 1990 it would delay his success at tracking the Delta warrior down. But he was betting Gage hadn't resold the land to another identity. Buying and selling was an activity that violated...*Procedures to Escape and Evade.*

Kertzman recalled the Special Forces training manuals he had studied on the flight from Washington to New York, copies of the same manuals Gage was issued when he was training in the early eighties.

That's where Kertzman had first seen the phrase: Standard Operating Procedures to Escape and Evade.

Escape and Evade—Never move in a straight line. Never become visible. Never attract attention. Move as far as possible as fast as possible, then find concealment and don't move again. Never do anything you don't have to do.

There was more in the training manuals. A lot more. With dazed fascination Kertzman learned methods for creating illegal incendiary weapons out of coffee, sugar, soap, potassium, rubbing alcohol, or turpentine; weapons that could be made quickly and with little preparation from standard kitchen products but which would explode like napalm and burn even under water. He learned how to improvise lethal boobytraps from locks, telephones, whistles, flashlights, doorknobs, and even candy bars. And he learned more about camouflage than he ever believed existed.

Kertzman was already familiar with the concepts of using terrain, shadows, and foliage to conceal shape and cover sound. But, while studying the manuals, he learned how to use an enemy's visual depth perception to conceal movement, how to use double slopes to throw the sound of a rifle shot, causing the sound to come from an area several hundred yards away from the actual point of fire.

He learned new methods for locating water in the desert (by studying the birds in the evening), for sewing wounds shut with human hair, and for nocturnal navigation by the stars. And there were techniques teaching how to eat substances that would make a normal person vomit (pinch nose, close eyes, chew with water, and swallow quickly), how to move on dry sticks without making a sound (set the foot down, heel to toe, upon the sticks and in a direction parallel with the sticks), and how to utilize the red-cone, green-cone color receptors of the eyes to detect motion in the dark, instead of simple visual acuity (stare fixedly at the ground parallel with the moving object. Do not look at moving object, but keep object in peripheral vision, allowing cones to monitor movement by distortion of shading).

Kertzman found every secret of ancient and modern combat that man possessed. It was an encyclopedia of both arcane and high-tech methods of killing, the perfect path through war.

Finally, when most of what he was reading was only sliding off his back, Kertzman had set the manuals back in his briefcase, amazed at the knowledge provided to these elite fighting units.

Kertzman shifted, disturbed again by the thought of how dangerous Gage could be. Then he turned his attention once more to the real estate records. Plot by plot, he studied the properties on the topography map, selecting sites which offered good terrain for defense; terrain with hills, gullies, ridges, or sharp inclines. Some of the plots centered around the Ashokan and Roundout Reservoirs, popular tourist attractions busy with people.

No, thought Kertzman, too many people. You want isolation. No chance of any recognition.

Fifteen plots of purchased land ranging from 100 to 300 acres stretched from east to west across a section, Highway 206 to Highway 28. Some were located in isolated, backwoods lakes like Alder, Beecher, and Balsam. Terrain elevations became increasingly steeper as land moved east. Some of the steepest elevations were in the area of Doubletop Mountain, which capped at almost

4,000 feet, low for a Western State but a respectable elevation for this high on the East Coast. An hour later Kertzman had a specific list of high probables, sites he would begin to explore in the morning.

Morosely, Kertzman stared at the list. Now for the hard part.

Checking out ownerships would be difficult without arousing suspicion. He could question a few neighbors, a couple of sheriff's deputies, see if he couldn't pick up a sign, a mark that might give him what he needed. But right now he wasn't even certain about what that might be. Probably something obscure. Maybe a neighbor who had no idea about the mystery man who lived next door. A sheriff's deputy who remembered sporadic complaints of rifle fire at a particular location. But Kertzman doubted it. No, this guy would be careful, real quiet, but not so quiet as to arouse suspicion. Neighbors would know him as just another vaguely friendly but private person, and checking with cops could go either way. They might know something, but cops liked to talk. That meant that word could get around that someone was asking questions. And if Gage got wind of a hunting party, he would be gone in the blink of an eye. A ghost.

In the morning, as routine, he would check phone records.

Everybody had a phone, even Gage. It wouldn't take much time, and there might be phone records from Allied Air Transport to someone on the property list. It was worth a shot.

Kertzman stared at the papers a moment longer. His eyes burned. It had been a long week, a long day. He had a lot of work to do in the morning. Wearily he rose and walked to the bed, turned off the light.

Outside, the sounds of traffic, the distant drone of a siren.

He sniffed. Caught the faint odor of something stale and sickly sweet. It smelled cheap.

One day he'd leave all this behind, walk away from the lies, the deceptions, the games, and the power. He'd find his home again in the mountains, find what he'd lost in the city walls that had smothered him for too long.

It was a comforting thought, being alone in the high country, the cold wind at his back, blue sky everywhere. But he wouldn't find it tonight. Tonight he had a job to do, and he was locked in by honor to finish it. If he didn't, there would be nothing for him to find in the desert or the hills or the high country. For in the end he'd only have what he took with him, what he took away from this madness.

Honor. Duty.

A man's got to live with himself.

Slowly Kertzman took off his boots and laid down, not bothering to remove his clothes. He was glad he had called Emma earlier in the night, had comforted her in her loneliness, had told her he would be home in a few days. But she had still sounded somehow sad. She was tired of so many years of traveling, of him living on the road, investigating, away from home. But it would soon be over. After this. Then they would move back home, to the country. Where they belonged.

Kertzman placed the Colt on the nightstand and removed his hand, waiting a moment. Then he reached out suddenly, groping for a split second before finding the checkered handle, the safety, flicking it down. He gripped the gun, familiarizing himself with the abrupt action.

He rested for a moment, imprinting the movement in his mind before initiating the safety and laying the Colt down again, allowing himself to relax.

As his eyes closed he fell instantly into dreams of the forest, and hunting, seeing himself on a cold white ridge in the close morning dark, watching a trail through a scope, waiting patiently for the beast to come up the path in the first faint light of dawn.

THIRTY

Slashing, leaping, and circling in a form of deadly ballet, Gage moved forward and back, twisting, catching, and releasing. Suddenly Chavez's knife was torn from his hand, spinning like a wheel to land in the dirt.

Chavez nodded, grunted, and picked up the knife, which was still in its sheath. And they began again, sparring, slashing with the sheathed weapons, moving and fighting as if the blades were exposed.

Sarah watched, sitting on the woodpile beside the house. Almost 24 hours had passed since she had spoken with her father about Gage, and neither of them had mentioned it again. Sandman was preparing to go into the hills, his usual maneuver with dusk, for first-shift guard duty. But for the moment he stood beside Sarah, shouting instructions to Gage and Chavez.

"Don't try for a trap!" Sandman shouted at Gage. "You're always tryin' for a trap! That's what gets you hurt! Let it happen! Don't try to make it happen!"

Teeth clenched, Gage slashed upwards from the waist. Chavez grunted explosively, twisting to deflect Gage's forearm with his own, slashing in again as Gage jerked his arm back. The sheathed blade missed by a foot and they were circling again, keeping careful distance.

"Explain this to me," Sarah said suddenly to Sandman, who immediately seized the opportunity.

"You see," he began enthusiastically, gesturing to describe his point, "you got seven angles of attack. High, middle, and low from each side. That's three on each side. The seventh angle is straight forward. When Gage moves to Chavez's right, he's cutting off three of Chavez's best angles because Chavez is righthanded. That means Chavez has to bring his arm way out to use those three right-side angles to cut. He won't do that. It'll open up his defense. He needs to keep the blade up close, in front. So he has to turn with Gage, or back up and reposition, or something, to get his angles back. It's constant movement, or distance."

Chavez slashed. Gage's free hand followed the blade, caught the wrist, and with his forearm and a quick twist, sent Chavez's sheathed blade pinwheeling through the air again. Chavez nodded, as if he approved of the move. Then he picked up the knife and they began again.

"That's called a trap," Sandman replied without looking at her, keeping his eyes on the sparring. "Gage trapped his hand, disarmed him. Gage is good at it, but he looks for it too much. He always did."

A moment passed.

"A trap is a lot simpler when you're fighting someone who doesn't know what he's doing," Sandman added, still studying the movements. "But Chavez is good. Just in the last thirty seconds Gage tried for two more, and Chavez cut him both times."

"Not really cut," Sarah said, knowing it didn't need to be said, but not able to help herself.

"No, no, just playin'," Sandman replied, smiling at her for a second, then sobered again. "Gage is movin' a little slow, not like he should. Usually he'd be all over Chavez." He paused. "Maybe my boy ain't right yet. Might be hurtin'."

Sarah waited a moment, then, "How good would someone have to be to cut Gage up like he did?"

Sandman shrugged. "When we was in regular Special Forces, they'd get into these knife contests, sort of like a duel but nobody would get killed. If you killed your opponent, you lost, and you lost face. And that was what really mattered. They didn't care about dying. They cared about reputation. And the only way to really win a contest was just to make your opponent stop fightin'."

Sarah narrowed her eyes. "How did they make each other stop fighting?"

"Blood loss," Sandman said, eyes widening. "Shock. Whatever. I never got into one, myself. But Gage got into them all the time. He had a reputation. People was always challengin' him. We'd be in a bar or somethin', and that weird, jabberin' Filipino trash talk would get started. Or sometimes the hotshot knifefighters on the islands would hear that we were in town and they'd hunt Gage down for a little match. He never turned one down." Sandman closed his eyes and grimaced, visibly emotional with the memory. "Man! Them fights was nasty! And fast, boy! Faster than you could see! Blades flyin' everywhere. Blood hittin' the floor, gettin' on your shoes. It was mean. Sometimes the fight would go a minute, and sometimes it'd last for ten minutes. They'd make them shallow cuts on each other until one would go down. If you weren't good enough to cut without really injurin' the other man, you lost the contest. Or if you passed out from shock or somethin', you lost the contest. Gage never lost. He liked livin' on the edge, in more ways than one." He seemed to ponder a thought. "He's changed a lot, you know. You wouldn't 'a known him in them days. He wasn't . . . *right*. Like he is now. I really wasn't that close to him, then. I liked him, but he scared me. That was before Israel, and what happened. But I was out of Black Light by then. Both me and Chavez."

Sarah had wondered about that. "Was that the name of the CIA tactical team?"

He nodded, watching Gage and Chavez.

"Why were you and Chavez out of the unit?"

Sandman sniffed, replied, "I was sent to the house after I lost my leg down south. Chavez left in '89 after he lost his eye."

Sarah focused on Sandman's bitter expression. "How did Chavez lose his eye, if it's not too rude to ask."

Sandman shrugged. "Nuthin' special. He got hit with some phosphorous. 'Bout like usual. Happens to everybody sooner or later. When it's got your name on it, it's got your name on it. Say good night."

A coldness embraced Sarah's heart. "You guys are so calm when you talk about these things. I don't see how you do it. It's sad."

Sandman laughed, breaking the unsettling tension. "Sorry 'bout that. It ain't 'bout a thing. Just soldier talk." He turned to her suddenly. "Hey, you worried? Don't worry. Gage is an expert with a knife."

Sarah shook her head. "I don't understand your world, Sandman. I don't know what it takes to be a soldier. All I know is that I put two hundred stitches in Gage after he came back because somebody had almost killed him in a knifefight. And you say he's an expert with a knife."

She turned her head to stare fully into Sandman's curious face.

"Well, I didn't see the other guy," Sandman muttered, looking down for a moment. "So he might 'a looked worse. But . . . I know it ain't possible to get *too* much better with a knife. Gage knows all the techniques, even the really *weird* ones, all the angles. He's an expert at bridgin' the gap. At closin'. He's fast. Strong. Reflexes like lightnin'. He's a natural at it. Ever since our first days of training, it was always what he was best at. Nobody could touch him. It was, like, a gift from God or somethin'."

He waited so long to speak that Sarah was worried.

"Whoever beat Gage ain't real," he added quietly, with a trace of worry in his voice. "I know Gage. I've seen him do it all. And there ain't nuthin' mortal that could do that to him." He seemed to finish, turned away. "I don't care and I don't know who the other guy is. But I know...he ain't real."

Sandman didn't proclaim his regular round of jokes about the cold as he turned away. Sarah watched him walk limply, and somewhat sadly, across the grass, moving towards the hills. She wouldn't see him again until midnight, when Chavez went out to relieve him.

Malachi and Barto were in the house preparing supper. And Sarah waited while Gage and Chavez finished with their sparring. Finally, they were done, and Gage sat down beside her, sweat glistening on his face and neck, but drying quickly in the cold wind. She watched as Chavez lit a cigarette, walked past her to pick up one of the semiautomatic rifles, went inside. She smiled, amused. After a week, she had still not heard him say one word.

Experimentally, Gage flexed his right hand, moving the fingers, closing them one by one into a fist, opening, testing. Sarah noticed that the incision along his right forearm was healing. The stitches had been removed, leaving slightly noticeable, blue-tinged markings on either side of the incision.

"How do you feel?" she asked casually.

"I'm OK, I guess. Probably a little slow."

She nodded. "You look pretty good to me. You've healed up well."

Gage laid the sheathed blade onto a book. She glanced at the title: *A Book of Five Rings*. An arcane depiction of an ancient samurai was on the cover. The image was scowling, holding a long sword in each hand.

"What's the book?"

Gage shrugged. "Just some research I was doing."

"On what?" she asked, allowing the situation to guide itself.

"I had a hunch about the guy I fought," Gage replied steadily. "I guessed he had studied classical kendo. I thought I recognized one of his techniques. I was studying up on it in case I meet him again. I want to get a better feel for his style."

"What's the technique?"

"Fire and Stones Cut," he replied carefully. "That's what it's called. It's supposed to be done with a long blade. A katana. But I think that this guy is taking old sword techniques, those that concentrate on slashing, and he's adapting them to fit the size blade he's using now. It's a difficult thing to do because a lot of sword techniques will never translate to a shorter blade. But some of them will. The stabbing and slashing techniques are adaptable. But the cutting techniques are difficult to adapt because you need a long edge, and they don't work with a tanto unless you're real strong in the wrist, the forearm."

Sarah didn't have the foggiest idea what a tanto was, but she realized that it was the kind of knife that Gage's opponent had used. Yet she also sensed the faintest lessening of his internal distance as he spoke, and she encouraged him to release a little more, approaching him on the ground he knew best.

"How does this Fire and Stones Cut work?" she asked with only the slightest hesitation.

Gage shifted his right shoulder, as if to release tension or fatigue. Sarah remembered that she had removed over 60 sutures from the area over his right shoulderblade.

"It's a cut that's performed when two blades clash together," he replied, easily. "Without dropping the blade or drawing it back, the samurai pivots his entire body, feet off the ground, all his weight into the arm, and swings the blade in a tight half-circle." He twisted his body slightly, moving his torso to describe the movement. "It's a real quick power move, designed to take advantage of a close situation. That's how I got this cut across my shoulder. It was so fast that I didn't have time to react. Our blades met and he pivoted. Instantly. It was... lightning. I went down and away and he missed, but not by much. He was good. The best I've ever seen."

Sarah swept back a lock of windblown hair from her eyes. "Sandman told me you were unbeatable with a knife."

Gage laughed. "Sandman says lots. There's no such thing as unbeatable. That's a concept that people hold who don't really know a whole lot about the psychology of fighting. Some guys are stronger than others, yeah, but everybody has weaknesses that even a poor opponent can take advantage of. And no matter how good you are, everybody has bad days. Emotions play a big part in combat. So many factors, like emotions, adrenaline, training, and mental attitude are all colliding at unreal speeds. Emotions and adrenaline can really mess you up if you're not in a state of constant mental preparedness. A combat mode."

"Is that the way it is with you?" she asked, genuinely curious. "Sort of a constant combat mode?"

Gage nodded somberly. "After a few years it comes natural. I'm always running combat scenarios through my head. Like, what would I do if this or that happened? What is the best angle of defense or attack if somebody comes out of nowhere with a weapon? What cover do I have? To stay alive in this business you have to make the right move when the right move is there. If you don't have it together mentally, you'll make a mistake when that moment comes. It's the constant combat mode that keeps you alive. There's not much room for anything else."

Sarah leaned forward, wrapping a long arm around her raised knee. "It must be tiring."

"Yeah," he replied. "It's tiring. And it gets old." He paused, staring at the ground, a distant look. "Simon taught me that there is more to life. A lot more. But now I'm back in my old world. And it's hard. I don't know if I'm tough enough for it anymore. I . . . don't really want to be here. But I'm locked in—"

"You're not locked in," she broke in quickly.

Gage cut her a sharp look. "Yeah. I'm locked in. 'Cause I'm gonna finish this. I'm going to get that manuscript. If it kills me." He paused for a second, added dejectedly, "And I think all of you might need to make some good contingency plans, because it's probably going to."

Gage was afraid he would fail all of them, Sarah thought, and maybe he was also afraid he didn't have the nerve to again fight the person who defeated him in New York.

"How good are these people?"

He raised his eyebrows a second, released a sigh. "I can't speak for all of them," he replied steadily, "but Sato, the Japanese, is a master and then some." Gage shook his head, a gaze of shock. "He's just . . . *unreal.* I've never seen anybody like him. He's fast. And stronger than anybody I've ever gone up against. He's got perfect moves. Perfect technique. Eyes that stay on target, no matter what. And his weapon is long enough to give him a distinctive advantage. It looked like an extended tanto. Maybe a twelve-inch blade with a six-inch hilt. Without even trying he could sever an arm or a head. It would be nothing."

Sarah's gaze strayed across *A Book of Five Rings* and the large knife that Gage had laid on the cover, the broad blade still concealed in the sheath.

Casually, she gestured to the knife. "What is that, exactly?" she asked. "It must be special."

Two weeks ago Sarah would have considered a knife just a knife. But exposure to these men had changed her. Now she realized that virtually every weapon these super-soldier warrior-guys used had an almost scientific purpose behind it, and, according to them, required an almost encyclopedic level of knowledge and understanding to use effectively.

Until now she had not voiced her incredulity, but she had listened with a slightly concealed amusement as Sandman and Gage had earlier launched into a long and tedious discussion over methods for insuring the best defense of the cabin. And she had hidden a faint smile as Sandman insisted on the superiority of security methods named after . . . Jomini? In any case, it was an amazingly

complex discussion over flanks, support positions, cover for movement, retreat, or maybe it was pursuit (she could never tell which),
and the topographical advantages of attack or counterattack.

She remembered how she had jumped pleasantly into the
middle of the discussion. "Why doesn't somebody just go up on the
hill and keep a lookout?"

The question provoked a shocked stare from Sandman, though
Gage had laughed. It even seemed that Chavez had laughed, though
she couldn't be sure. After that she merely listened, learning, and,
strangely enough, had slowly come to appreciate the genuine complexities of what they were doing.

Still, Sarah wrestled against the wound he carried within him.
No matter what, she didn't want him to think she doubted his
abilities. At all. He needed to believe that she still held him in the
highest respect, the highest confidence.

It was a tightrope.

He smiled vaguely at her question. "Why do you say it must be
special?"

Sarah laughed. "Because whenever Barto or I ask, 'Hey, what's
that,' we never get a simple answer. It's never 'just a rifle,' or 'just a
gun.' It's either some kind of Winchester double-something with a
bull barrel and who knows what inside it, or it's some kind of space-
age quasi-nuclear bomb that will burn up anything on earth." She
gestured to the knife again. "So what is it?"

Gage smiled, then reached over and picked up the knife.
"You're not going to like it."

"Why?"

"Because, despite the fact that most people realize the world
needs police officers and soldiers to defend them from threats, they
don't want to know how it's done."

Sarah watched him steadily. "I can stand it," she said. "In fact,
you'd probably be surprised at what I can stand."

Gage laughed, looking at her for a long moment. His smile was
tender, affectionate. He picked up the knife.

"Maybe so. I guess I'm the one that doesn't handle it so well,
anymore. A knife reminds me too much of how I used to be. Too
many of the mistakes. Just...too many of them."

Only a moment, and Sarah reached out.

"You know...we've all got a past, Gage," she whispered, her
fingers finding a hold in his shaggy hair. "Just...let it go. Don't let
it haunt you like this. You're better than this."

His face softened, their eyes meeting. Slowly he touched her
face, moving his hand down her skin. His eyes held a longing in
them, as if he had been waiting for this moment.

She leaned forward, forehead to forehead, their faces inches apart, their eyes closed.

"Just let it be," she murmured.

He released a sharp breath, something like a groan, then his entire face set, hard and bitter. He couldn't find it in him, she saw, couldn't let go. Not now. Even though he wanted to, some kind of iron control kept him from releasing himself to her.

Together they rested, close. Sarah was silent for a long time, trying to find a way through. Finally, though, her gaze had strayed to the knife in his other hand.

"Do you think it will come to that?" She gestured to the knife.

He frowned. "I hope not. I'm going to try and keep away from it because he's better than I am. A lot better. And he knows it. I was just a soldier. I was good at this type of thing, but not like him. This guy lives for the chance to kill with his blade. He's pure." He paused. "I got this out because I'll need every advantage."

"Can't you just shoot him?"

Gage laughed. "I tried that last time. Sometimes things don't work that way. You can run out of rounds. Guns can be unreliable. They can jam. You can lose them. Sometimes it comes down to stuff like this."

In some strange, internal way, Sarah crossed the line to be with him. "So, tell me what's special about it."

Gage shook his head. "Some consider it a prototype of the ultimate fighting knife. It was made by a guy named Jim Hammond who lives in a little town in Alabama. There's an art to creating a blade for fighting. And this guy is probably the best in the world at creating fighting knives, and this was probably the best blade he ever created. Maybe the best anyone ever created. It's supposed to exceed all of the tactical requirements for the perfect edged weapon."

Sarah gazed narrowly at it. "Show it to me."

Gage leaned over, lifted the sheath, solemnly unsnapped a strap. Then he removed the blade, inch by slate-gray inch. Sarah reached out, and Gage put the blade in her hand. The heavy steel blade appeared to be well over a quarter-inch thick for its entire length, even at the finely razored point.

"Overall, it's fourteen inches long," Gage told her.

She studied the blade. "Is that long?"

"Your blade needs to be one inch longer than your opponent's," Gage replied, pointing to the black hilt. "The hilt is designed to give you two more inches of reach than the average knife with the same size blade."

Slowly, trying to get a sense of the world as Gage knew it, Sarah gripped the handle more firmly, imagining using the knife for fighting. Instantly her index and middle fingers slid, quite naturally, into grooves cut into the bottom of the hilt, near the guard. She turned the knife, gazing at the finger grooves.

"What are those for?" she asked, holding her hand to display the grooves forged into the hilt.

"Drawing," Gage commented. "When you cut, you pull the knife away at an angle, using your thumb and those two fingers for direction. The finger grooves provide better control. It's...like carving, or swirling the blade. If a man can keep his head in the chaos of combat, he can do a lot more damage pulling the blade away than he can on initial contact."

Sarah waved the knife in the air, felt the almost perfect symmetry, the effortless ease of control, and she realized that there was, indeed, a terrible beauty in the blade. She could understand its perfection. But the entire concept of fighting with this weapon was horrid, even appalling. It was unbelievable what men could do to men in the cause of war.

Sarah frowned slightly as she studied the weapon. "Does this thing have a name?"

Gage laughed shortly. "I don't know what Jim calls it now. The guys in my old unit called it 'Dragon.'"

"After you?" she asked slowly.

Gage shrugged. "I guess. I'm not sure. But...it's not really important." He touched a flat, minutely serrated section cut into the top of the thick blade, near the upper part of the hand guard. "This is where you place your free hand for a power sweep. You hold onto the hilt with your right hand, and place the heel of your left hand on this flat section and sweep from left to right in a vertical slash, pushing out on the blade with your left hand. It reinforces the move and gives you twice as much power as you'd have with one hand. A power move. This knife could cut a man through the ribs, both lungs, and the heart with one slash. It's double-edged for almost its entire length, which makes it perfect for stabbing. But the design also makes it perfect for slashing and cutting. And it's heavy enough to easily sever an arm or a leg." He was silent a moment. "It puts me and the Japanese on even ground."

Sarah twisted the blade in her hand. Already, she was comfortable with it, and the thought amazed her. "It's strange," she remarked, absently, "how much thought men put into killing each other."

Gage stared somberly at the blade, then looked off towards the darkened ridge.

Sarah spoke quietly, felt her heart and breath catch with the question. "Can you beat him?"

Silence.

"I don't know," Gage replied, eyes narrowing with the thought. "If I hurt him badly enough, he'll try for *Ai Uchi*."

"*Ai Uchi?*"

"Mutual death," Gage said simply. "It's a samurai concept that dates from feudal Japan. Basically, it's a tactical move to strike a death blow while receiving a death blow. For him, *Ai Uchi* would be a great victory. Take a deadly blow to give a deadly blow. *Ai Uchi*."

Upon the ridge, a cold wind howled through gray unseen trees.

Sarah lowered her head, heard the words again and again in her mind.

"*...Ai Uchi...It would be easy...A great victory...Mutual death...*"

Gage was silent, and she longed to reach out to him to comfort, and to be comforted. But then she stiffened, remembering that surrendering to deeper feelings would only complicate things. It would distract him. And he had enough distractions.

Gray eyes softening, Gage watched her face. She raised her head, gazing back at him, hiding nothing. After a moment he smiled, somewhat sad and tender. She reached out to lightly brush back his hair from his forehead. He seemed to share her thoughts. He leaned closer to her, wrapping an arm around her shoulders, whispering into her ear.

"Don't be afraid," he said softly. "We'll be alright. I'll bring an ending to this, somehow."

Sarah leaned her head on his shoulder, feeling the moment, and nodded slightly. One hand went up to find his arm, and she held him in silence. The gray, familiar cold swept down from the barren stands on the surrounding hills. And Sarah heard the wind raking limbs; a dry, whispering chorus.

Gage was silent. But, from his weary demeanor, and his slightly bowed head, she knew that he was worried, worried that perhaps he was outmatched, facing a force he could not defeat.

Enough, she decided. *Enough of this. Sadness and doubts and fears won't help. Only action can help. This only makes us feel worse.*

She leaned back, slid down from her perch on the woodpile, reaching again for his arm.

"Come on. I'll bet dinner's ready."

Gage nodded, rising to his feet. "And I bet Barto has already eaten it."

She laughed easily, slipping her hand into his.

• • •

Alone, Gage stared at a pale, haggard moon, ignoring the cold night wind that embraced him, alone with thoughts even colder.

Slowly, stiffly, he rubbed his hands together, feeling the thick bandages around each wrist that covered the last thin wounds his hands had sustained in combat with Sato. Impulsively, he tugged at the straps, loosening the gauze.

At the first exposure of the sensitive skin to the night air he hastened the movement, finally freeing his wrists and hands completely to the coldness. He stared at his healed hands, curling the fingers, testing, clenching and unclenching.

Emerging like a ghost from the dark, Malachi was suddenly and quietly beside him. Gage hadn't heard the approach but revealed no surprise. He had already learned that the professor could sometimes move with the casual silence of an Indian in what seemed an unconscious stealth.

Malachi smiled at him, casual and relaxed, then leaned against a porch beam.

"It's a good night." Gage turned slightly to lean back against the opposite post.

Malachi laughed. "Yes. I have forgotten how much I missed the night sky." He paused. "It was part of my greatest pleasure in archeological digs, particularly in the Negeb, where the sky is never more beautiful."

"I guess you've seen just about every place there is to see," Gage said finally. "You've traveled a lot. Probably even more than me."

"Oh, yes," the old man answered with a smile, "but nothing changes, really. It has always amazed me to see how familiar all the distant countries of the world can appear. The Carpathian mountains, for instance, in Northern Romania are virtually identical in size and design to the Appalachians of North Carolina. And in Israel the plains of Giliead are the same as the eastern deserts of Arizona. The world is not so dissimilar, you know, from where we stand. Nor is history, for that matter. There is nothing new, even in this situation, that has not happened before."

He fell quiet a moment, studying the terrain.

"Like this, for instance," Malachi continued easily, his gaze sweeping along the ridge. "The terrain here reminds me of the Valley of Elan in the Shephelah, where one of Israel's greatest battles took place." He gestured toward the hill. "It was a battle of military might against a single man's faith. And upon that ridge stood Goliath, the greatest warrior the world had ever known."

Gage shifted to look at the ridge, somehow drawn in by the old man's mesmerizing authority.

Malachi pointed gravely to the center of the ridge, concentrating.

"All of Israel trembled at the feet of the giant, Israel's most feared enemy. Standing over nine feet tall, he was customarily armed with an iron sword, a unique and superior weapon for that era. And to make him almost invulnerable he was armored within a long breastplate of brass and bone and leather that weighed almost two hundred pounds." Malachi lowered his arm again, stared at the ridge a moment as if he could behold the haunting vision. "He had never known defeat."

Gage stared at the ground, slightly to the side and away, where the darkness was deepest.

"It was an epic battle between David, a simple warrior, and Goliath, almost a god among those who surrounded him. But the battle did not begin in that contest. No, it began years earlier, when David had chosen to worship the Hebrew God. And it began when Goliath chose to serve Dagon, a demon." He was silent a moment. "No, it did not begin in the valley. It only ended there, in the plain between the two mountains. But the true battle had begun years earlier, when each man had chosen the road he would walk in life, setting themselves on the path where their destinies would collide."

Casually, as if the rest of the story did not matter, as if it were a small and inconsequential tale shared without meaning by two friends, Malachi pushed his hands into his pockets and lowered his gaze to sweep the glade.

"It's an old story, and I'm sure you know the rest," he said easily, abruptly looking down with an old man's solemn, steady gaze.

"David took his head, in the end."

Tired, muddy, and angry, Kertzman sat a hot cup of coffee on the dash, stared sullenly at the charts propped precariously and crookedly against the steering wheel. During the day he had tried six different locations, all of them large pieces of property, heavily wooded with deep ravines, the perfect tactical ground.

He had found nothing. Just six middle-age or retirement-age couples living out the good life in the Catskills. Kertzman had methodically, ploddingly, checked them all out, one by one. Parking his car at a distance and stalking cautiously through the woods, he used the topography map for reference until he located the houses. Then, standing in the cold or lying atop a small hill, he had watched through a pair of 7x50 Tasco surveillance binoculars, reading a 366-foot field of vision at 1,000 yards.

A range-finding reticle in the binoculars provided him with a digital readout of distance, informing him whenever he moved closer than 100 yards to any of the homes. That, at least, had given him some small satisfaction. Because it told him that he had managed to make a positive identification of all residents at over 300 feet, mentally checking occupants against the pictures of Gage, Malachi Halder, Sarah Halder, or Bartholomew O'Henry that he had memorized.

He hadn't wanted to move any closer to the homes, risking a chance detection by the occupants or the hungry attention of guard dogs. He certainly didn't want to endure the ordeal of making explanations to any county sheriff's deputies. Mainly because anything he said would make it back to Washington before nightfall. And as far as the NSA knew, he was supposed to still be in New York City.

Allowing them to know his exact location would reveal his true strategy. So he had moved slowly, carefully on the homes, keeping his distance until he could eliminate an estate from his list. Then, with his Vietnam-era stalking instincts in full glory, he had slid back through the woods to his car, moving stubbornly on to the next site.

Not surprisingly, the phone company offered nothing from the listed homes; no telephone calls to Allied Air Transport, Professor Halder's house, his daughter's apartment, or to anyone else even remotely related to the situation. And, although Kertzman was not surprised, the disappointment caused him to shake his head in frustration.

This guy didn't leave much behind. And he was getting tired of finding nothing.

On top of that dead end, checking the estates one by one was turning into a time-consuming activity. And he was bone-tired. Kertzman told himself that in a few minutes he would head back to the hotel, get some sleep, do it again tomorrow. But he was plagued by the worry that he was wasting his time, that he had gone in the wrong direction.

Patience, he thought. *You're going to have to earn this guy.*

Tomorrow. He nodded with the thought. Tomorrow. He'd check four more locations. Maybe five.

Patience.

• • •

"So what are we looking at?" Barto asked. "I know it's a mixture of Latin and German words, with a few numbers. But it's a simple code. And they're the hardest to break."

"I know," Gage answered, pointing to the marks on Simon's letter. "The Greek with hyphenated numbers refers to the Latin edition of the Old Testament book of Job. Each book of the Bible has a different language designation. Job is Greek. Genesis is Spanish. Revelation is English, and so on. The first number is the chapter, the second is the verse, the third is the number order of the word in the sentence. I can find the word without any problem, but I have to use a dictionary for the translation." He paused. "Sometimes that Latin part screws me up. So many different endings to words. I wish Simon would have come up with a better way of doing this. But he was really worried about his messages getting discovered. He wanted something difficult to decipher."

Sarah sat at the table, watching them work. Gage had pulled a German dictionary from a bookcase and was checking words while Barto leafed through an English edition of the Old Testament. Gage had told him that a Latin edition of the Bible was on the shelf. Barto said he didn't need it and continued the translation with his memory, mentally rewriting the English into Latin to discover what word was needed.

"Wait a second," Barto said after 30 minutes.

Gage looked up. "What?"

"There's a Latin article for 'at' and then a four-digit number, with a letter."

"That's a direction," Gage answered. "When you have a four-digit number and letter after that, it's always a direction. The Latin is just to confuse things. But the letter is always reversed for the true direction. 'N' means 'South.' 'E' stands for 'West.'"

Sarah waited patiently, watching as they worked together on the cryptic note. Gage thumbed back and forth through the dictionary, checking and rechecking the words.

She stretched her arms, looked at Malachi reclining, reading the Bible while they worked.

She smiled faintly at the old man, noticing how noble he seemed under the light of the reading lamp. The sight caused her pain as she thought of how terrible their situation was, how far they had come, and how far they had yet to go before they might know any decent life again.

She looked at Gage, intent in his task of deciphering. Though he seemed unaware of her gaze, she knew he was always aware of her, the way she looked, the smallest mannerisms. She loved him for it. And then she felt a fresh wave of pain as she wondered how great a price he would pay to defend them. She remembered the power of their enemies, how they had murdered Simon, terrorized Rome, and finally pursued them into these mountains. It seemed inconceivable that anyone could overcome such an awesome measure of organized power.

Resisting the depression, she looked again out the darkened window. Somewhere, poised in the dark with the long sniper rifle and nightvisor, or nightscope, Sandman waited, watched. He would stay there, patiently and silently, until midnight when Chavez would relieve him. Then Gage would relieve Chavez at dawn, and Sandman would take again to the woods at noon, relieving Gage. In the late afternoon Gage would patrol with Chavez, letting Sandman rest before his evening watch began.

Sarah had grown accustomed to the unaltering routine. She had ceased to worry about any of them, even Gage, so inured was she to the sight of loaded weapons and tactical discussions and the survivalist attitude of these hardened ex-soldiers.

Trying not to seem obvious, she studied Chavez, who stood beside the kitchen counter, methodically cleaning his M-16. The rifle was disassembled, parts laid carefully on the counter, and the silent Mexican was stoically cleaning and checking the pieces as he cleaned and checked them each night, a routine that had not varied since he had arrived.

Chavez moved like a machine, unceasing in his methodical dedication. And Sarah noticed that he was always careful to have another fully loaded, fully functional weapon beside him while he was cleaning the rifle.

Out of all of them, Chavez was the most unceasing. He reminded her of a watchdog, always wandering the house, the grounds, the hills, even when it was not his turn to stand watch. Sometimes he would join Sandman on the hill in the early evening and wouldn't return until the next morning, cold and wet from the brutal winter night, working through both shifts.

Sometimes, when he did seem to need rest, he would sit in the chair beside the fire, the large black M-16 at his side. He would never stare into the fire, though he seemed to enjoy its heat.

Clearly, he was even more obsessed about security than either Sandman or Gage, but he never spoke about it, or about anything else, for that matter. His was a silent concern, a dedication he released by action, spending much more time in the woods than in the house.

Sarah had long ago concluded that none of them were comfortable in a building. They preferred to be outside, using the woods, the terrain, as they called it, to their advantage. They considered a house a liability. Sandman had said that no building on earth was defensible, and quaintly referred to the cabin as a "death-trap."

Gage was more relaxed about it, not as compelled as the others to remain outside. Though in the past few days, even when he was resting, he was never without the Hi-Power that he had carried in the Hall of Ancient Languages.

"OK," Barto murmured after another hour. "I think I got the Latin."

Malachi turned his head, rose from his chair to approach the table.

"Yeah, I got the German," Gage replied. "Let's put it together and see what it looks like."

In a weird blend of numbers and letters the message seemed to take shape. Gage shifted words around for five minutes, seeming to change them by feel rather than by any legitimate deciphering.

"No," he muttered, "that's not what he meant... It would be this... He does that a lot... I'll put this... here... There, I think that's it."

Barto stared at the message for a moment, his lips moving without sound.

Sarah leaned forward. "Well? Are you going to share it?"

Barto glanced up, wide-eyed behind his glasses. "Oh, yeah," he mumbled.

He looked down again, reading,

"In the arms of the Father, the Abomination sleeps. Yet, by the grace of our Lord, it shall be destroyed. Remember, God will not be mocked. You must travel South from Merano to Ortles. And find the north path up the slope. At the level of clouds, you will find the family crypt of Santacroce against the wall. Roll away the stone, enter the grave, and you will find the prophecy. Destroy it, my son. Destroy it. God will not be mocked. I will pray for you with such passion as I have loved you. Be well. Remember..."

Quietly Barto laid the message down, sat back.

Gage said nothing. His face was set in stone.

Even Chavez had ceased cleaning his weapon. He hadn't looked up, but the Mexican was frozen in an unnatural stillness of intense listening, of concentration. The room seemed heavy, almost smothered, vibrating with an intensifying atmosphere of sadness.

Gage closed his eyes, leaned his head back.

"Yes..." whispered Malachi. "It would be the perfect place..."

Barto turned his head. "Where?"

"It is the old country of Simon," Malachi said. "It is near Bolzano, where he was raised. Beside Bolzano lies the small town of Merano, and south of it rests the mountain of Ortles. It is in the Italian Alps. It is not a particularly high or majestic peak. Not a site for tourists. And for the most part it is ignored. It is only twelve thousand feet high. And in ancient times it was well traveled because it allowed access to the river path that led to the Valley of Po, and from there to Milan. Though I have never walked the mountain myself, I know from Simon that its inhabitants are very secretive and have, for centuries, claimed specific caves on the north side as family crypts. It is an ancient tradition, and the Italian government has ceased feuding over the matter. From this message it is clear that somewhere on the north face there is a familiar path. And at the level of the clouds, perhaps at four to six thousand feet, is the family crypt of Santacroce. On that path. And within that crypt we will find the book."

Malachi turned and walked to the window, staring out. His shoulders allowed a slight sagging that almost frightened Sarah, though from what she could see of his profile, he maintained his rigid strength.

Gage opened his eyes, took a breath. "I'll leave tomorrow night," he said. "I'll make the necessary arrangements in the morning. Chavez and Sandman will stay with all of you while I go after this book."

He nodded, reaffirming. "Then we'll put an end to this."

• • •

Even though he was exhausted, Kertzman forced himself to go through the routine procedures for sanitizing, for shaking any surveillance on the way back to the hotel. He drove for 40 minutes, doubling back a half-dozen times, taking an occasional side street, an alleyway, checking for vehicles that stayed with him.

He saw nothing.

Finally, weary from a long and fruitless day, he arrived at the hotel. Moving steadily but slowly he got out of the car and walked toward the door, leaving the papers in the car. He held his door key in one hand, the .45 in the other, concealing it inside his coat pocket. He planned to open the door, then move the papers inside a few moments later with subsequent trips, always keeping his hands relatively empty.

He was too old a war horse to be caught shambling across the parking lot, both hands hopelessly filled with ridiculous paperwork while some idiot hitter walked up to him and put out his lights with something like a bull-barrel Ruger—a favorite of professionals because of its superb accuracy and natural sound suppression.

No sir, thought Kertzman, not me. *If they want it, they can work for it.*

He opened the door and carefully checked out the room. Then he moved back to the door, and in moments unloaded the car. Finally, with one last look across the parking lot, he closed the door behind him, relieved.

· · ·

With the bored expression of long-term surveillance, Robert Milburn took another sip of coffee. He looked at his watch, noting the time.

Carl, the German, looked back at him. "It seems that Mr. Kertzman is turning in for the night, ya? Is that what you think, Mr. Milburn? Or perhaps Mr. Kertzman, the great hunter, is outfoxing us." He laughed.

Ali, the giant Nigerian, also laughed brutally at the joke.

Milburn blinked, said nothing. Stoically he continued to stare at the distant hotel door that Kertzman had just shut.

Parked on the distant side of the lot, the surveillance van was unpleasantly crowded with him, Carl, and the Nigerian. Milburn didn't know where Sato was, but he knew that the Japanese would not miss another opportunity at Gage. He would be close.

Milburn had only barely survived the nightmarish car accident, leaping clear before the vehicle crashed into the embankment.

Badly injured with four cracked ribs and a dislocated shoulder, he had been treated at a very private, very expensive hospital. Confidentially. He was using painkillers to get him through the rest of this.

Later that same night, after Milburn had returned to the safe house, Sato had also come back with Stern, cursing repeatedly that Gage would die. Horribly. But Milburn had noticed that the big Japanese moved with an unusual stiffness, his ribs heavily bandaged, the arrogance slightly subdued.

Earlier, before Kertzman had left New York, Carl had planted the microwave locator in Kertzman's vehicle. And during each of Kertzman's excursions into the forest during the day, Sato had followed. Fading carefully into the trees, he had followed at an extreme distance.

Caution was the rule. For even Sato recognized that Kertzman was crafty, especially in the woods. He was forced several times to retreat to a distance where he could not even keep Kertzman in visual observation. But when Kertzman would return to his vehicle in a relatively short period of time, they knew this meant that the hunting foray was unsuccessful.

They also knew that Kertzman was well onto something and might find their prey before the week was through.

Milburn leaned his head back against the seat, seeing again and again the image of Gage lying bleeding and beaten in the backseat of the Cavalier before the LTD had driven them off the road. Something had snapped inside him at that moment, though Milburn had revealed nothing. But in that moment he had actually considered turning on his employers, had contemplated smoothly drawing his Beretta and firing a round through the Russian's brain.

Money wasn't worth this, he had thought. Nothing was worth this.

Then the LTD had appeared out of nowhere and they had gone together into the embankment. He had leaped clear before the head-on, escaping serious injury. And, standing in the open, in full view of the mysterious driver of the LTD, he watched while Gage was pulled, unconscious, from the backseat and piled into the car. The bearded driver wasted no time clearing the scene, looking strangely experienced at that kind of thing.

Once, while the fat man was lifting Gage from the Cavalier to the LTD, Milburn absently touched the handle of his Beretta, considering how easy the shot would be. But enough was enough. The sirens were still three miles off when the LTD pulled away from the embankment. Milburn watched it leave, laughing.

Afterwards, obeying orders from D'Oncetta, he had joined the surveillance on Kertzman. Because everyone from D'Oncetta to Stern to even Sato seemed to believe that the stone-age cowboy would eventually run Gage to ground. And for the moment they had decided to wait, and watch.

Milburn hoped that Gage was buried so deeply that Kertzman would never find him. But he knew, or felt, that the end was coming.

Gage packed a black dufflebag with clothing and an assortment of weapons, much the same as he had done before the trip to New York, except he included the specialized fighting knife—the Dragon.

"It will be cold on that mountain," Sarah commented, studying his equipment. "You're going to need mountaineering gear."

Gage smiled, nodded. "I'm taking crampons, boots. And I've got North Face gear that will protect me from the weather. Anyway, I won't be there long. A quick trip. Up and down. Get the book and get out. I should be airborne again in thirty-six hours."

"You're going to need sleep."

"I'll sleep going over, sleep coming back. It's a seven-hour time difference. I'll fly out late tonight and get there early tomorrow afternoon by their time. I can make it to Ortles by nightfall. Then I'll find the path and go up. I'll do all the work through the night. Less chance of discovery."

"How will you find the tomb?"

"Well, I think the path will be easy to find," he replied, concentrating. "Has to be, or Simon would have said more. And Malachi was right. The tomb will be at four to six thousand feet. There's a full moon, so I'll find it easy enough. And I've got the nightvisor for anything else. I'll have plenty of light for the job."

Sarah watched him stuff a pair of Asolo mountaineering boots into the heavy canvas bag. Crampons followed, and a small ice ax.

"Where'd you get all this stuff?" she asked, impressed.

"I did some training on the Eiger," Gage replied. "It was only a two-week thing. But a lot of climbing. A lot of battle scenarios on the rock." Gage cocked his head, a movement of remembered fear. "Now *that* was scary. High altitude combat is different. Ballistics are different. There's no room for evading. I wouldn't ever want to do it again."

Gage continued to check and load equipment. Sandman and Chavez were in the hills together. They would continue to rotate shifts until Gage returned.

"Something's been bothering me." Sarah's remark received Gage's immediate attention.

"What?" he replied, alert.

"You said you used to sanction people," she said carefully. "You said you were part of a special unit, Black Light, that was used to assassinate people. But we both know that intelligence agencies are real careful about that kind of thing. And you thought that some of the missions were personal for someone inside the government. Like with those two Geneva bankers you were ordered to sanction in Beirut, right before your team was ambushed. You even told your supervisor that you thought Black Light was being used for something besides national security."

Gage stared at her. "Yeah. I said that."

"Why?"

"Because too many of the hits didn't make sense," he answered, unblinking. "Not in terms of jurisdiction, or even intelligence priorities. The targets weren't defectors or terrorists or drugrunners. They weren't foreign assassins planning a hit against one of our people. They weren't players at all, as far as I could tell."

Sarah placed her elbows on her knees. "So what do you think the missions were about, exactly?"

Gage fixed on her intensely. "I'm not sure. What are you thinking?"

She shook her head. "I don't know yet. But there's something. I just want to hear a little more."

He waited a moment. "Alright. The Geneva sanction was an investment banker. The two Geneva sanctions I refused to do were also investment bankers. I hit a few OPEC members. They were movers, financiers, but they only had the vaguest connections to any intelligence groups. They were people with power, but they weren't real players. More like watchers, investors. They were powerful in their own way but not in intelligence or counterintelligence."

"What countries did you work in?" she asked. "Where did these people live?"

Gage stopped loading the bag, stood watching her. After a moment, his gaze wandered the room, remembering. "We ... hit a couple of money targets in South America. They moved a lot of gold. Then we hit in Argentina, moved through Mexico City. We did a lot of surveillance in the Middle East and Europe. We even hit a few oil money people funding Al-Fatah, and the PLO, in Beirut. Then we went down and hit somebody in San Paulo. And, like I said, we did the investment banker out of Geneva. All the deaths were made to look accidental."

Barto had wandered over.

"Why did you move around so much in South America, Geneva, and the Middle East?" Sarah asked.

Gage shook his head. "I don't know. I just took orders. Like I said, in those days I didn't really care that much. I just did what I was ordered to do."

"Who gave you the orders?"

A pause.

"My supervisor," Gage answered, staring at her, finding his way in it. "A guy named Robert Milburn. He relayed the messages from the DCI."

"The DCI?"

Barto chimed in. "The Director of Intelligence."

"By the way, Milburn was in New York," Gage added.

"Your old supervisor?" Sarah's eyes widened with the question. "The one who betrayed you in Israel? The same guy who set your team up for the ambush?"

"Yeah," Gage continued. "But he's freelance, now." He shrugged. "I don't know if anything is related. Might be. Might not be. In this business you run into a lot of old *pals*. And a lot of times they're on the opposite side."

On the far side of the room Malachi had turned, stood listening.

"Don't you think that's unusual?" Sarah asked. "Isn't it strange that you would run into Milburn?"

After a moment Gage replied, "Yeah. It's strange. But I don't know what to make of it."

Her intensity was complete. Mesmerizing.

"Alright," she said. "Then let's forget Milburn for a minute. Let's talk about the sanctions. What if these assassinations weren't political and they weren't personal? What if they were for something else altogether?"

Gage absorbed the thought, waited. "Like what?"

"Well," she began, "what did all these places have in common? Why did you hit targets in South America and Geneva, Argentina and Ontario? Let's say, just for argument, that it was all part of a larger plan. What did all these big money people have in common that would benefit someone? What do financiers in Argentina, Ontario, Geneva, and San Paulo have in common?"

Gage concentrated. "I don't know. Do you?"

She nodded. "It's simple. They've got *money* in common. They're all rich. That's what ties them together. It's so simple it's hard to see."

Barto sat back against the table. "Can you remember the specific cities you worked in?"

Gage focused on him. "Johannesburg. Beirut. Leningrad. Moscow. Ontario. San Paulo. Buenos Aires. Soweto. Pretoria. Durban. Cordoba. Geneva. London...a lot of work in Colombia..." Gage paused. "That's about it."

Barto nodded.

"What is it?" Gage asked.

Sarah looked away, concentrating.

"Just an idea." Barto glanced at Sarah. "Soweto and Durban are two of the major towns in South Africa for processing mining ore."

"Mining ore?" she repeated.

"Gold," he said. "And Pretoria and Johannesburg are where a lot of the heavyweights stay who control the mining operations."

"Two of the people I sanctioned were into heavy construction," Gage said slowly. "Movers. They might have been into mining."

Sarah rubbed her eyes for a second, head bowed in concentration. She looked up suddenly. "Aren't Geneva and San Paulo major international exchange points for the gold market?"

Gage held her questioning gaze for a moment, then turned slowly away, to the bright, sunlit window. He walked over, stood looking out through the glass. Training prompted him to move away from the uncurtained opening; it was an easy shot for a sniper. But at the moment he didn't care. Something was coming to him, something horrible. Awakening, he began to look at his old life for the first time in almost four years, finding the courage to put it all together, exploring the depths of what he had truly done. Far better than they, he saw the mosaic.

"Alright," he continued grimly, "let's go through it again. Forget the legitimate sanctions for a moment. Let's say that those were for justifying Black Light's existence for the Intelligence Committee. Let's focus on the hits against financial people." He paused. "What does South Africa, South America, Ontario and Russia have in common? Gold, right? They're the largest gold-producing countries in the world."

He turned to look at them both.

Barto nodded.

"Just one thing," Sarah added. "The United States is also a major gold-producing country. They still dig up a lot of it out in Nevada and North Dakota."

Gage shook his head. "We never worked in America. So let's forget America for a moment. Let's just concentrate on what we've got. If a number of international bankers and gold movers died, who would benefit?"

"Whoever wanted their empires," Sarah answered.

"Right," Gage added. "And how would a person inherit these empires?"

Barto leaped in. "By buying heavily into a company's interest beforehand. Then, when the big guy dies, that person gains a controlling interest. It's the perfect plan. Buy big and when the owner dies this mystery guy's wealth doubles in value, maybe even triples, because the owner's share is no doubt divided up into smaller portions, automatically making his one of the largest. A fortuitous, accidental death doubles the amount of this person's influence in the gold market without changing the amount of gold he actually owns. It's a stepping stone to possessing more, setting the price, controlling the market."

"But why gold?" asked Sarah. "Why not stocks and bonds?"

"Because stocks and bonds are just paper," said Barto. "They're not immune to recession. Gold is the *really* old-fashioned way of building an empire."

Gage nodded grimly.

"Right..." Barto continued slowly, also nodding. "That's it. Accumulating gold is the recession-proof way of gaining economic power. And the oldest. A person can do it quietly, without attracting attention. Except for a privileged few, nobody even knows your name. But among those who know, the people who really count, this guy's a major player, a real force. Somebody who can make things happen in any country in the world."

Sarah looked at Gage again, gaining his attention. "So let's say that this person wanted to use force to make it all come together. Let's say that this person wanted a really elite team of assassins who could eliminate his competition, or his enemies. Let's say that he wanted to make sure that nothing would come between him and his dreams."

Gage frowned. "He would need an assassin," he said solemnly. "Except assassins can make mistakes. They can get caught, or killed. And then it would all come home. Unless this smart guy hired a government hit team to do his dirty work for him. Then nothing would come back on him. Even if things went wrong, he wouldn't take the fall."

No one said anything for a moment.

Sarah's green eyes locked on Gage. "If he did that, then he would be safe," she said. "Whatever government he used would take all the risk."

Gage stared out the window again. The sun was high, bright, and somehow starkly disturbing. "It's the perfect plan."

"But how could it happen?" Sarah asked. "How could a unit of our government be used for this kind of thing?"

Gage laughed bitterly. "Easy. This nation is obsessed with secrecy. After a while, secrecy itself becomes the enemy. It becomes too broad an umbrella. People become so concerned with protecting it that they're scared to lift covers and see what's hidden beneath. And other people, the dirty ones, use that tendency as a weapon. Remember, use lies on lies, like I said before. Destroy evidence, file false reports, mix truth with untruth. Make it so complicated that nobody can ever truly figure it out. And the truth is just lost. It's easy to do. People can speculate all they want. But they'll never really know."

Gage nodded at his own words. "And now it all comes together."

Barto and Sarah stared at him. Gage turned back toward her. She shook her head.

"It can't be that big," she said.

"Yeah," he answered, "it can be. Even bigger."

Tension in the room was almost corporeal.

"OK," she continued, "maybe it is. Then let's assume that this megalomaniac used your old unit, Black Light, to set this plan in motion, to eliminate his competition so he could corner a large portion of the gold market. What does he plan on doing with it?"

No one had an answer.

Then Malachi spoke, for the first time. "A man who would perpetrate this crime would be a madman," he intoned. "And madmen always have the same dream. To conquer. To command. To forge a new world from the dark fire of their dreams. To destroy all those who stand in the way of their dominion."

Silence.

Gage spoke. "That would be a difficult thing to do."

Malachi shook his head. "Not so difficult, no," he answered. "Nothing created by man is outside the dominion of man. And perhaps there is something else. Perhaps it is no coincidence that your former comrade, Milburn, is involved in all of this, Gage. If this man, Milburn, betrayed his country and attempted to dispatch both you and your old unit in Israel, he is a traitor. And traitors seldom betray twice. Once a man has turned against his country to serve another government, or power, he usually remains with that power, knowing that he has cut himself off from much of the world in his treachery, and he does not wish to lose what little he has gained in the loss. If Milburn had already betrayed our government before the incident in Israel, it is likely that he serves the same interest today." He stepped forward. "I would even submit to you, Gage, that the same enemy that misused your old unit, the same enemy that destroyed your team, is the enemy that hunts us now, working for the same ultimate purpose."

Gage stared at the old man, his gray eyes glinting, dead.

The air grew tense.

"Yes, probably," Gage said, after a thoughtful silence. "And that means that I helped to build the organization that is attempting to kill all of you. It...means that I had a hand in...everything." He turned away. "I killed for them," he continued, "worked for them. Stole for them. I even..."

Sarah stood. "Gage, don't—"

"—killed Simon for them, in the end," he added slowly. "I gave them everything they needed to do the job. All the money, the power. Whatever it took."

He nodded, frowning.

"So be it," he added. "I built it. I'll burn it down."

Hunched against the cold wind, Kertzman slid a pair of thick woolen socks over his boots. The socks, coarse and heavy for sub-freezing weather, were perfect for the task he had in mind. But, even so, it was a tight fit.

Finally, after struggling for five minutes, Kertzman managed to twist and pull until the wool completely covered the heel and sole of his leather boot. Then he stepped away from the car, moving into the forest.

A soft rain had fallen during the night, leaving the forest floor muddy and wet. Kertzman took a dozen steps through the brush and low grass, turned and looked at his tracks.

Muffled and indistinct, the footprints could hardly be read on the wet ground. The socks wrapped around the boot had muzzled the imprint of the heel and sole in the muck. Instead of a clear imprint, there was only a soft, indistinct space that seemed to vanish even as Kertzman stood watching it.

Perfect.

Kertzman smiled, an unsightly gash in his prizefighter face. He had picked up the trick from one of Gage's Special Forces training manuals. It amused him to see that it actually worked.

He turned to move further into the brush. It was already past three in the afternoon. He had checked four places so far today; this was the last. The winter day was shortening, the sun already descending.

This location, the ninth on his list of high probables, was an isolated 100-acre mountain estate shredded with ravines and crevices until it ended with a flat, level glade near the top of the ascent.

Kertzman liked the look of it. It was a good place to make a stand. But the forest was exceedingly thick, hard to move through without a lot of noise, so he had risked driving his rented Buick midway up the road before sliding carefully onto a rutted trail near the summit. He had left the car in the brush at the end of a deserted trail, parked on private property but far from view of the estate's main entrance road. He considered it a relatively safe risk, and it saved him from over a mile of ravines and briars and some of the thickest brush he had encountered on the East Coast.

With his binoculars, a 45x Tasco Spotting Scope, and the Colt strapped tight to his right hip, he started forward. A brown camouflage hunting jacket protected him from the biting cold wind as he began a path towards the estate atop Panther Mountain.

• • •

A brooding silence.

Gage stared at the duffle bag. After a long time he shifted, looking away.

Sarah saw it all alive in him, the darkest nightmares of his life, howling and haunting, shredding him. She shook her head, moved to say something when the radio crackled with static and the distant voice of Chavez.

Gage picked it up.

Sarah heard Chavez talking quietly on the other end. Gage listened, his gray eyes keen and smoldering, suddenly holding an unnatural stillness.

He keyed the mike. "Stay there," he said sternly.

He walked to the wall, removing two lever-action, Western-style rifles. He tossed one to Barto, kept one for himself.

"You know how to use a Marlin .30-30?" he asked. "It's fully loaded with one in the pipe. You've got eight rounds altogether."

Barto pushed a button on the right side of the weapon near the hammer. He nodded, eyes bright, and Sarah guessed that in the past two weeks Sandman and Chavez had taught Barto to use every weapon made in the world.

"Figure I do," he answered.

Gage was already moving for the door. "Stay inside and lock the doors. Shoot anything that doesn't look like one of us. Sarah, stay on the radio. Channel three. I'll raise you in a few minutes. Everybody look sharp."

He was gone.

Sarah snatched up the radio and turned, saw Malachi at the front door, bolting it. She ran to the back, finding a terrible home in how things worked in this world; an environment could be cherished peace and relaxed freedom in one moment, stark terror and bloody, horrible death in the next.

• • •

Kertzman had covered only a small distance, and with agonizing slowness. The ground was soft, easy to move on, easy to stalk upon. But he was haunted by a disturbing, mist-shrouded presence that seemed to creep beside him in the cold woods, a threatening half-seen shadow.

Twice he turned, his hands groping, automatically drawing the Colt as he glared into the surrounding stand. And though he saw nothing, he wasn't encouraged. He knew that his eyes weren't what they used to be.

But he didn't need his eyes to know that something was wrong. For days, now, it had felt like someone was trailing him, though he couldn't see anything. Rather it was an old stalking instinct, a leftover alertness from the days when he was a real hunter, instead of a hunter of men. No, he couldn't put his finger on it, but he could feel it; a vaporous, spectral sensation that clung to him in the mossy silence. He was convinced that something was there, but it remained hidden in the mist-shrouded woods.

Scowling, Kertzman moved forward with the .45 in one hand, not bothering to reholster after drawing the second time. He tried to remain even more aware of his surroundings. He still had at least another 200 yards to go before he could see the house.

Slaglike face mean and menacing in the fading afternoon light, he glanced constantly about, haunted, feeling the companionship of ghosts. And, in the oppressive, unreal quiet of the forest, he remembered Stephenson's words.

"...*A superior race of man...A man born to rule, to conquer, to crush down the weak...This man and the men around him will become Lords of the Earth...The ultimate beast of prey...*"

He held the .45 tight in a sweaty hand, his thumb on the safety, ready to throw it down.

• • •

Gage found Chavez squatting in the brush beside the road holding the gray, parkerized fully automatic M-14 at port arms with the casual alertness of a true combat veteran.

With Chavez there was never any excessive movement, no posturing or quickness. Everything was slow and measured, the movements of a man deeply inured to combat, who had long ago mastered the necessary skills for war and who fought now in a comfortable zone of familiar energy-saving economy of ease.

Gage came through the brush, low, using the wind to half-mask the sound of his movements. He wasn't worried about Chavez mistaking him for an enemy. Chavez was too wary, he would know from the steady rhythm of Gage's strides that it was no hostile approach.

From experience they both understood that someone on a stalk moves only two to six steps at a time, then pauses, waiting, watching, before moving another two to six steps, and never more. It was easy to use the wind to cover the sound of less than six steps. But it was also done that way because animals typically moved in short bursts before stopping.

Developed for hunting either men or animals in heavy brush, the stalking technique was invented to duplicate the manner by which animals moved in the woods, partially in the hope that a sentry or another animal would mistake the steps of human beings for beasts.

Until it was too late.

But for now Gage moved a stride every two seconds, constant, not waiting for the gusting breeze to cover the sound of the crackling leaves beneath his boots. That was the wilderness telegraph to Chavez of who he was, and Chavez never even turned to look at him as he approached. Rather, the Mexican continued to scan the brush in front of him. Gage crouched beside Chavez in the bush, both of them carefully concealed.

Chavez's single dark eye gleamed with a relaxed, deadly concentration. He pointed to a mud puddle in the road. No words.

Gage followed the lead, staring at the puddle, and recognized the sign. Rain had fallen during the night, and the puddle was filled with two inches of water. But on the uphill side of the puddle, the side leading *toward* the cabin, tiny rivulets of water were pooled in some tread marks, much more than on the downhill side.

Gage nodded.

It was clear. A car had driven through the puddle since the rain. The tires had pushed the water ahead of the vehicle as it drove through, and as the tire left the puddle the water had rushed back towards the depression. But as always happened, more of the water had pooled in the tread marks where the tire *had left* the mud puddle, than in the tread marks where the tire *had entered* the puddle.

It had been almost a week since any of them had gone into Monticello and returned, so it was not their track. Someone had entered. And not left.

With a glance at Chavez, Gage moved forward and across the road. Quickly but quietly, spending as few seconds as possible in open view, he quickstepped across the mud. Reflexively, Gage flicked off the safety of the Marlin as he moved.

He had chosen the lever-action .30-30 because it was one of the best bush rifles available. It provided a much better round for the forest because the heavy 240-grain bullet wouldn't be deflected by brush, limbs, or even small trees, but would smash through minor obstructions and hit what it was aimed at.

Gage recalled the Marlin's specs by reflex, running it through his head, according to procedure as he moved forward in a crouch.

The terrain didn't allow a shot at any great distance. That was one of the reasons Gage had purchased this piece of land. It wasn't conducive for sniper fire as it provided no long spaces, only a lot of high terrain. And firing a bullet uphill or downhill was a lot more difficult than even most professionals realized.

Shooting downhill, the bullet always drops far more than expected, and rises a lot more than expected when fired uphill. It was a nebulous, strange enigma of sniping, and could throw off even the best shooters.

Moving carefully along the tire track, Gage found the car, a light brown Buick parked discreetly on the old logging road. Gage walked down the passenger side. Chavez took the driver's side.

It was empty.

Bending close to the ground, Gage looked for tracks. Saw none. Chavez was also bent, using the car engine for cover, watching the surrounding trees.

They each understood their jobs. Gage was the best tracker, and because he had already begun to search for signs, Chavez would automatically assume responsibility for rear guard.

So, Chavez would guard while Gage hunted. Later, when Gage grew tired, Chavez would take point and Gage would guard. But for now it was Gage's and he bent low, studying the ground.

Nothing.

He frowned. *Got to be here. Ground's wet, good for tracks.*

He peered closer, studying the grass. Saw some slight bending, not enough for a sign. So he moved out from the vehicle, studying the rocks, forgetting the grass. Forty feet out from the car he saw it.

A small rock, less than the size of his thumb, held a thin dark smear of mud on top of it.

Jungle instincts moving in him, Gage sniffed, feeling the wind, the forest, sensing the air for change, any lingering presence. But the wind was gusting. He could discern nothing.

Scowling, he looked uphill toward the summit. His mind was on automatic...

...Pick the path that you would prefer...Imagine that you want to move towards the cabin...You want the path of least resistance ...Something quiet...As few briars and bushes as possible...

Scanning, he saw a break in the bushes, moved towards it, bent and saw nothing. Crouching, reaching out with one hand to steady himself, holding the Marlin low and parallel with the ground in the other hand, he crept forward. Chavez followed directly behind him at the standard cover position, 15 feet of separation between them. Neither of them made a sound as they moved, except that of the unavoidable crushing of wet grass beneath their boots.

Gage was frustrated, finding nothing, but he continued to move, not knowing what else to do. He stayed low, studying the terrain, the rocks.

Then he saw the pebble. Almost so small as to be unnoticeable, it was pushed into the soft mud. Gage looked up, eyes open and absorbing, reading the forest. Slowly, silently, he held up his free hand in a fist, slightly and to the side. He turned his head minutely to make sure that Chavez saw it.

Chavez was gazing at the hand.

Gage held up one finger.

Chavez nodded once. Then he began scanning the forest again.

Gage moved forward, tracking, finding the almost indiscernible; a crushed blade of grass, a pebble pushed into the mud, or mud picked up by something soft and scrapped further up the trail on a piece of wood or rock. It was difficult, time-consuming work. The sun dropped lower as they moved, Gage leading, eyes on fire with a blood-cold wind in his face.

• • •

Kertzman laid prone on the hill, gazing down at the cabin. No movement. He had watched the lodge, a surprisingly modest and rustic structure for so expensive a piece of property, for over ten minutes. But despite his uneasiness he saw nothing out of the ordinary.

And that's what disturbed him, even more than the feeling that something was clinging to him in the forest. This was obviously the home of someone who didn't care about luxuries, the home of a soldier, a survivor. And a lack of movement always worried him.

Dark smoke drifted faintly from the chimney, but the windows were shut, the doors closed. No cars were visible, although a large log garage was built next to the cabin, a small hallway connecting the two buildings. The garage was expansive, almost as large as the cabin itself, easily large enough to hold three cars and a lot of equipment.

Cold crept from the muddy ground through Kertzman's coat, his shirt, soaking his chest. His elbows were wet with mud while the taller grass, dried by the constant breeze, waved around him.

He was confident that he couldn't be seen from the cabin, not unless someone looked directly at him and studied the area for a few minutes. He was still over 100 yards out, not moving.

Slowly, a plan began to dawn. He studied the terrain, measuring. If he worked down the ridge he might . . .

A twig snapped behind him.

Instantly, by a reflex that surprised even him, Kertzman kept himself from reacting.

A quick man would leap at the sound, spinning. A good professional would roll, drawing his weapon. But Kertzman was in the combat flow now, sharp and alive with fighting instinct, and he didn't move at all. Because in the space of time between when the sound reached his mind and his body could react, he identified the noise.

It was not natural or accidental. Nor was it animal or the muffled, subdued snap of the wind breaking dry limbs. Rather, it was sharp, clear, and close, a purposeful message. The presence was right behind him, had come upon him without any sound until it had chosen to announce its arrival.

Experience told Kertzman that he was in the sights. He didn't question it. Didn't blink. He knew it would be impossible to roll and clear before whoever it was simply squeezed a trigger.

Heart pounding, breath fast, Kertzman waited, the cabin forgotten, everything forgotten except the presence behind him.

"You can stand up," a man said.

The voice was calm, disturbingly familiar with the nature of the command. It was a voice at home in the dangerous arena of men at war.

Kertzman put his hands to the side, flat against the ground, began to rise.

"That's good," the voice said. "Real slow. Keep your hands where I can see them."

Kertzman stood, turned slowly.

Stared into the face of Jonathan Gage.

Kertzman's gaze dropped to the rifle, a lever-action .30-30 leveled evenly at his chest. He was recovering, but was still winded from the surprise, the shock. Gage looked much like his photograph but leaner. He was dressed in blue jeans and a blue T-shirt, with a waist-length leather jacket. He wore ankle-high leather hiking boots. A haggard paleness in the face suggested to Kertzman a distinctive weariness, or fatigue.

Kertzman blinked, focused, thinking furiously behind his stone-faced gaze. It was a situation he hadn't faced for a long time, and he'd forgotten how fast the mind can work. Instantly he scanned the forest behind Gage. Saw nothing. It appeared that the ex-Delta soldier was alone.

Kertzman decided to trust his instincts that the soldier was as confused as he was.

"I'm a federal agent, Gage," he said sullenly. "You can check my ID."

The gray eyes revealed nothing. Kertzman couldn't be sure of anything. "I'm telling you the truth."

Somber but with faint amusement, Gage nodded. "I figure."

"I need to talk to you."

Gage laughed shortly, almost friendly. "I figure that, too." The rifle gestured to Kertzman's waist. "Open your coat. Just do it real careful. If you're a federal agent, you know how it's done."

Kertzman opened his coat, turned his side slightly so that Gage could get a clear look at the .45.

Gage nodded, smiled.

"That's quite a hogleg you got there."

Kertzman could tell that Gage purposefully allowed a slight trace of respect in his tone.

"I'll take it," Gage said. "For now. And don't get crazy about it. You can have it back later if you're really who you say you are. I give you my word."

Kertzman reached carefully for the .45. Saw Gage's hand tighten almost imperceptibly on the .30-30. He removed it from the holster and held it out, butt first.

"Just toss it."

"It might discharge," Kertzman said gruffly.

Gage smiled, laughed lightly. "It ain't gonna go off, partner. Just toss it."

Kertzman tossed it to the grass at his feet.

Still keeping his eyes on Kertzman, Gage bent, picked up the .45. He held it in his right hand, dangling it towards the ground while keeping the rifle leveled with his left. Then he knelt down, motioned with the rifle for Kertzman to follow the movement.

Kertzman followed the command, expressionless. Watched Gage lay the rifle across his knees, almost careless. But Kertzman knew the man wasn't careless.

To the ignorant, Gage appeared relaxed, almost indifferent. But Kertzman knew the relaxed stance was simply the practiced guard of a man who knew exactly how much tension was required for a moment, a man who wasn't ruled by his emotions but by a cold passionless mind that had long ago perfected every skill necessary for physical combat. Kertzman knew if he tried to pull a hidden backup weapon, which he didn't have anyway, he'd be dead before he could clear leather.

"Alright," Gage began carefully, "show me your ID."

Kertzman removed it, tossed it to him. Gage caught it and flipped it open, scanning quickly. He tossed it back.

"I know you don't believe me," Kertzman began. "I know you've got ID, too, that says you're a federal agent, and a CIA agent, and everything else there is. But I'm really a federal agent. I'm an investigator with the Pentagon, but I'm temporarily reinstated with the Bureau for this case. I came here to talk to you, Gage. I'm not here to hurt you. Or them."

Gage's eyes gleamed, impressively dangerous. "Who's them?" he asked.

Kertzman's face was impassive. "Malachi Halder. Sarah Halder. Bartholomew O'Henry."

He waited a moment to see Gage's reaction. There was none.

"You need to trust me, Gage." Kertzman grew bolder, knowing that truth was his greatest ally. "Do you see a rifle? No. All I got is that little ol' peashooter. For protection. I didn't come to fight. And I'm no hitter. I came to find you, to find out what's going on. We need to talk." Kertzman waited for that to settle. "You can believe me or not."

Gage's face revealed a tendril of doubt. Kertzman knew he was a man accustomed to making split-second life-and-death decisions about whether people could be trusted or not. He waited, allowing his cooperation and courage to speak for him.

Gage's eyes scanned the woods beyond Kertzman.

"There's nobody but me," Kertzman said coarsely, throat cold with wind. "I came by myself."

Gage smiled, nodding. "Yeah, I can see that." He waited a minute before speaking again. "You're in no-man's land, Kertzman. You're not supposed to be here."

Kertzman wasn't sure what that meant. He hesitated, deciphering. When Gage said nothing else, Kertzman's natural attitude began to assert itself. It was an impulse that he didn't try to suppress. Because in the back of his mind, just in case Gage *did* decide to pull the trigger, he wanted to die with his hackles up.

"No man's land?" Kertzman growled. "What does that mean?"

"That means you're off the beaten path, old son." Gage laughed. "It means you've got no backup. And that means you're doing something you're not supposed to be doing. The Bureau wouldn't send one man in here to do surveillance on me. That is, if they knew I was here. Or even if they *suspected* that I was here. They'd send fifty agents or more. Special Response, probably. But you're here all by your lonesome, taking a big chance, trying to find ol' Gage. Hoping you don't get killed doing it. And that takes guts and something more." He paused. "What do you want?"

Kertzman didn't hesitate. "Somebody's set you up to die."

Gage's wary gaze narrowed over an accepting smile. "I figure."

"It's somebody inside."

Gage studied him. "And who might that be, Kertzman?"

Kertzman shook his head. "I don't know. Not yet, anyway. But they're coming and they mean to see you and everybody else in that cabin dead. So we'd better talk before they get here, figure somethin' out."

Gage was silent. Then suddenly and without warning, Gage tossed Kertzman the Colt. Kertzman caught it, staring, awestruck at the leanly muscular soldier as he slowly rose to his feet. Kertzman also stood, glaring at the Colt, at Gage.

"I could be a shooter, Gage."

Gage laughed. "You ain't no shooter, Kertzman. I know what you are. You're lost. 'Bout like me." Gage walked past him. "If you want to talk, come on down to the cabin. We'll talk."

Kertzman turned and watched, astounded, as Gage walked down the hill, towards the cabin.

"Gage," he said, feeling the weight of the .45 in his hand. "You're being pretty careless."

Gage stopped and turned, peering carefully at Kertzman. A whispered laugh escaped him. Kertzman recognized it as the sound of a man too long on the edge.

"No," he said, suddenly serious, eyeing Kertzman carefully. "I don't think so."

He turned and walked away.

Kertzman stared after him, blinking stupidly. The Colt dangled in his hand as the soldier moved slowly down the slope. Everything collided in his mind; suspicions and questions, doubts and certainties, as he searched for where the truth lay hidden in the nightmare.

Kertzman started forward, knowing that his first step down the hill was the first step into the heart of this madness.

Kertzman had heard it all.

It was midnight, and he had listened for over six hours. He understood what had happened to Gage in the Negeb, had put it all together from the professor's townhouse to the seminary to the Cathedral of St. Thomas. And then back again to a mansion in Westchester, New York, where Gage had witnessed Father Simon's murder.

Bartholomew, or "Barto" as they called him, was an eyewitness to much of it, with Malachi and Sarah Halder corroborating the additional facts.

Sometimes, in their eagerness to confide to a true law enforcement officer, they had spoken at once, but their stories never contradicted each other.

It wasn't the best way to catch up on things. Usually, it was best to question everyone separately and then check statements, not allowing multiple witnesses, or suspects, to keep a story straight. But this crew had plenty of opportunity to build an elaborate lie before Kertzman arrived, and the usual methods of interrogation had pretty much lost their usefulness.

Anyway, Kertzman knew he was a pretty good judge of character. And he calculated that the solemn, dignified Malachi Halder would not lie.

Gage made a telephone call, postponing his flight to a location in Italy where the manuscript was hidden. He wouldn't say where, and Kertzman didn't push.

The manuscript was the only thing that kept Kertzman continuously off-balance. It seemed to be the central element in this affair but he couldn't accept the significance of the book.

Together, like some kind of secret conclave, they sat around the kitchen table. Gage kept the rifle close, and Kertzman kept his .45.

Barto held a Marlin across his lap, surprisingly at ease with a weapon. And two of Gage's old buddies from Black Light were in the hills, watching.

After midnight, when there was nothing left to say about the series of events, Kertzman turned again to the subject of the manuscript. He looked at the professor.

"Now, Professor Halder," he began, as courteously as possible, but not knowing where, exactly, to go with it, "just why in blazes is this old book so important to somebody? It don't figure to me. Not at all. It's not worth men dying for, is it?"

Malachi Halder maintained a somber and steady air. "Men have already died for it, Mr. Kertzman," he said. "For two thousand years men have died for it. You see, the book is said to contain a prophecy, a valued prophecy, and supposedly contains the name of the Beast, the Antichrist. It began in the fiery days following the destruction of Herod's Temple in Jerusalem. An aged priest, one of the old masters of Egyptian sorcery who commanded a particular allegiance from the demon-god Set, recorded the name and the year of birth of the Beast, the biblical Antichrist, in a manuscript. But the scribe supposedly died soon after penning the prophecy, and the manuscript was lost. Countless emperors and popes and kings have searched for it, from Constantine to Hadrian. Legend held that it was last seen when it was sent from Rome by a centurion, bound for an unnamed city deep in Egypt, possibly Alexandria, where it was to have been hidden away for two thousand years by a secret cult of Set. But the manuscript never reached its destination. So from the days of Titus Flavius Vespasian, Emperor of Rome in 70 A.D., the followers of Set have searched to reclaim the prophecy which will reveal to them the name of their king, the God-Man who will come and bring the entire world into dominion for them." He gazed gravely at Kertzman. "Yes, for two thousand years blood has been shed in search of this manuscript, Mr. Kertzman. No one could ever find it. Until now. Until Simon and I unearthed it in the Negeb, and surrendered it to the power of Clement."

Kertzman stared at the old professor, mouth agape. No one spoke, or moved. Kertzman shifted, a hulking and strangely primordial image in the small kitchen chair. Then he blinked, his massive fists clenching, unclenching nervously.

"Uh, alright, Professor, I can follow that," he said hesitantly. "But, uh, if these people are just priests and stuff, how can they be makin' all this happen? It looks to me like we're dealin' with some kind of, uh, assassins, or somethin'. I can't tell yet, but it looks like these people have started a private army, made up of the best fighters, or soldiers, rather, in the world. How does any of that fit in?"

"Even in times of antiquity the followers of Set and Dagon were the ruling elite of their societies, Mr. Kertzman," responded Mal-achi. "They were wealthy, well-bred, commanding chairs in govern-ment and world affairs. Many controlled international trade. Others were great military leaders, generals, or conquerors. Even while others were priests, scribes, teachers, and historians. And since the beginning they have used their positions to control the masses by intellectual and economic oppression, or by the sheer and brutal persuasion of violence. What is occurring today, in this situation, is nothing new. It is simply the way our enemy conducts his affairs. There are always years, or decades, of inactivity, yes. But when a strong leader emerges, he typically attempts to form a private army of the so-called enlightened or superior beings who will enforce his dreams. And, now, they do indeed have a leader who has built a force of these men, these . . . murderers . . . who are supposed to be the strongest of their kind. And they are willing to do anything to claim the manuscript, so that they can prepare the way for him."

Kertzman leaned forward, eyes darting, hairy gorilla forearms resting on the table. "Uh, you know, Professor, this leader, whoever he is, sounds to me like some kind of Satanic John the Baptist."

Malachi grunted, a short laugh. "Not so farfetched as some prefer to believe, Mr. Kertzman."

Kertzman studied the dark night through the cabin window. After a moment he looked back, focusing on Gage. "And what do you have in mind to do?" he growled.

Gage shrugged. "Get the book. Destroy it. Finish it."

"There's been enough killing, Gage."

"Yeah, Kertzman, there has. That's why I want to put an end to it."

Kertzman thought for a moment. "It's a suicide run," he said.

Somber, Gage said, "It's about time, I guess. I've got debts to pay."

Kertzman bunched forward, changing tact. "You're talking about taking this thing international, Gage. That could get messy."

"I'm still going."

Kertzman paused, his face an unreadable granite slab. "All I have to do is call Washington," he said finally. "And your plane will never land."

"It doesn't have to land," Gage replied.

"Alright," Kertzman added, "then it would never reach Italy."

Gage allowed a half-smile. "But you ain't gonna do that, Kertz-man."

"Why's that?"

"Because you're in this, too. And you need time to figure it out. You make a big move, and you're exposed. This whole thing is exposed. And you still don't know who your enemies are."

"I might not have any enemies. You might be the only one with enemies."

Gage stared at him. "Maybe."

A heaviness punctuated the silence. Gage continued to hold Kertzman's gaze.

Kertzman waited almost three minutes before he spoke. "Well, you're right," he said, stone-faced. "I'm not gonna try and stop you."

Gage allowed a faint expression. "And why not?" he asked mildly.

"Because nothing happens without a purpose, hotshot," Kertzman said, glum. "Not in Washington. And not in a case like this. I was chosen to do this for a reason. They wanted me to lead them to you. And it's not because I'm a great white hunter. No. They wanted me to do this for a real reason. A political reason. And I still don't know what that is, any more than I know who's behind all this uptown. So until I know the score, until I know who the players are, I ain't gonna tip my hand." He nodded. "Let 'em keep guessin'. I'll leave 'em hangin' until I figure this out."

Malachi spoke to him. "That is wise, Mr. Kertzman."

Kertzman nodded, not taking his eyes off Gage. "I figure."

A large limping shape rushed through the doorway, moving fast. Kertzman's hand was on the Colt as Gage brought the rifle up.

"We got big-time movement!" Sandman yelled. "They're jamming the radios. Somethin' mean is goin' down!"

Gage was on his feet, hands flat on the table, leaning forward at Kertzman. "Your people?" he asked angrily.

Kertzman shook his head. "No. Nobody knows I'm here. But we can't be sure. They might be federal. How you gonna know? And you can't fire on a federal agent. I won't allow that."

"I don't intend to," Gage said between gritted teeth and threw the .30-30 to Kertzman, who caught it without effort, working the action. A long brass bullet was ejected from the port onto the table. Kertzman picked it up and slid it back into the magazine.

Gage snatched up the MP5 from the black duffle bag, slid two extra clips under his belt at the small of his back, and took the bag with him as he moved.

"Secure everything!" he shouted, running towards the corridor that attached the cabin to the garage. "Sandman go high! Kertzman, you've got the cabin!"

"Close those doors!" yelled Kertzman, alive with it, feeling it.

Sandman limped toward the back door as Barto stood by, ready to shut it. Kertzman yelled after the big black man, "Don't fire on nuthin' unless you know it ain't a federal agent!"

Sandman threw up a hand, took two steps towards the door when a gunshot exploded in front of him. He shouted, clutching his chest, and fell across the kitchen table to collapse onto the floor.

"Gun!" roared Kertzman.

At the explosion Malachi had also jumped back, shouting, and even as Kertzman had yelled the old man fell, collapsing over a chair.

Screams.

Kertzman grabbed the kitchen table, even as Barto slammed the wooden door and leaped back. Then, twisting explosively, Kertzman hurled the table across the small room to crash against the door.

In the space of a second, as the gunshot had exploded outside and he reacted to the sound, Kertzman accelerated into a mindset he hadn't known in over 30 years, a jungle combat mode with reflexes quick, brain operating on adrenaline, and eyes bright, reading everything around him instantly and in lucid detail.

Whirling, he cast a wild glance across the room to see Sarah Halder, eyes on fire and teeth clenched. She had snatched up a pistol from the counter and was crouching in the kitchen, aiming the gun towards the front door. He saw Bartholomew against the far wall, holding the Marlin tight... and Malachi Halder... flat on the floor... clutching his bleeding side.

Four simultaneous blasts tore through opposite windows of the cabin, covering Kertzman in an explosion of glass and wooden splinters that flew across him, through him.

Enraged, Kertzman yelled and spun, firing from the hip with the .30-30 to shatter a distant table lamp.

Whirled back. "Kill those lights!" he roared.

Barto shouted incoherently and spun, sweeping his hand wildly down over the kitchen light switch.

Casting them into darkness.

"Father!" Sarah Halder screamed through the darkness.

A moment of silence, frantic shuffling. Movement outside. Kertzman's eyes spun from one window to the next. Cold swept in from the outside, deep and sharp in his lungs.

"I am...alright, Sarah," Malachi Halder gasped, a choking sound of pain in his voice. "I am...hurt. But I am...alright."

"Kertzman!" Sarah screamed, enraged. "What do we do? Where's Gage?"

Kertzman shook his head in the darkness, feeling the familiar steel of the rifle in his hand. He did not respond to the question. Silence was their only advantage. Silence and darkness. He crouched, listening, and felt wind blowing through the window. It was going to get a lot worse. Those weren't federal agents out there. No federal agency would open fire without warning.

It was a hit team. And he was in here with two amateurs who would be a liability before they would be any help. Gage would be moving around outside, where he could use some of that special warfare training to do some damage. And Kertzman knew that every exit would be covered, every window, every door.

For the briefest second, and with a flicker of sympathy, Kertzman thought of the black guy, the one they called Sandman. The big man hadn't made a sound since he was hit.

One down.

Kertzman remembered that Gage was supposed to have another buddy in the hills—the Mexican. But he might be gone, too, Kertzman thought bitterly. If these people were smart enough to jam radios, they were smart enough to remove a sentry without making a sound.

What had he walked into? Or, more importantly, who had he led to this place?

Kertzman stifled a curse, shaking with anger and adrenaline, his fist tightening on the steel barrel of the .30-30. He promised

himself that somebody would die for this, oh, yes, yes indeed, somebody would surely die for this.

The breeze blew steadily in from the window. Kertzman glanced
back at it, saw nothing outside. It was as black as the inky gloom
that cloaked the interior of the cabin. He held a steady tension on
the trigger of the Marlin, kept it pointed towards the opening, and
glanced towards the other windows. Barto shuffled in the dark for a
second, then silence.

Sarah Halder had said nothing more, but she hadn't moved,
either. And the old man was down. Maybe dying.

A car engine roared in the garage.

The darkness above Kertzman moved, shifted.

Danger!

Something moving...

Grenades!

. . .

Gage raced into the garage through the connecting hallway,
the MP5 leading. He put on the nightvisor as he hit the darkened
end of the corridor and thumbed the selector to fully auto.

He went into the garage low, scanning left to right.

Nothing.

Gunfire exploded in the cabin.

He whirled back, teeth exposed in a snarl, and decided instantly that he would have to get outside, quick, if he were to
change the situation. He turned towards the LTD, his mind scanning through tactics, blitzing through dozens of defensive measures in seconds before locking in.

*...Assume all exits to be closed...Create confusion, chaos...
Get out fast to break the perimeter...Use the vehicle for cover...Get
outside them and force them to defend...Speed, speed, speed...*

Gage snatched open the door of the LTD and leaped inside,
automatically reaching out to find a grenade in the dufflebag. His
brain was combining tactics, turning a defensive position into an
offensive attack.

Seconds flying.

*...Chavez doesn't have a nightscope, so he can't acquire targets
in the dark...You've got to create a light source outside for target
acquisition...Get outside and set off flares, no, wait, you don't have
any flares in the car and there's no time to search so use something
else, any source of light is enough...Go!*

Gage pulled the pin on the phosphorous grenade, fired the
engine of the LTD.

He floored it.

Closed, the garage door provided only the briefest resistance as the three-ton vehicle smashed into the wooden planks. The door exploded into jagged black shards and Gage was outside, sliding sideways on the gravel.

He threw himself down sideways in the seat, felt rifle fire rocketing into the vehicle from every direction. He didn't try to steer but kept it to the floor, angling slightly to the right.

Seconds gone!

Make it happen! Make them go defensive!

The LTD's rear window blew out beneath rifle fire.

Enough!

Gage estimated that the car had spun 40 yards. He would reach the treeline at 60. He jerked the steering wheel to the right and slammed on the brake, sliding sideways, spinning the automobile to create a ballistic break.

He threw the door open, heard rifle fire, and then he was out with the MP5 and the dufflebag, low beside the car. He tossed the phosphorous grenade into the front seat and sprinted the 20 yards to the woodline, moving right as bullets shattered the trees behind him and the LTD exploded in a mushrooming blast that cast the entire glade into a violent and roaring white light.

• • •

The wind above Kertzman moved, a black patch sailing through the air. And that's when the object hit the wooden planks beside his feet. Instantly a half-dozen additional small objects hit the floor around the cabin.

"Grenades!" yelled Kertzman.

Deafening light!

Kertzman's coat was blown open by the savage concussion, his face scorched by the stunning shock wave.

Blinding! No fire!

The explosions were stun grenades. Survivable but everything was happening too fast. Kertzman swayed at the blasts, rocked by the concussion, then somehow heard, beneath it all, a door kicked open and men rushing inside in the darkness.

Kertzman almost fired a shot in the dark and then his finger froze on the trigger, an almost-gone control resurrected instantly that prevented him from shooting until he could acquire the target.

He blinked in the dark, trying to see a shape.

And a sledgehammer hit him between the eyes.

Kertzman cursed, stunned, as two men leaped upon him. One grappled with the Marlin while the other wrestled to imprison his neck and shoulders in a headlock. He howled and pulled the trigger of the Marlin. Thunder and fire exploded between Kertzman and the man in front of him, but the shot went into the ceiling, and the intruder grimly refused to release his iron grip on the rifle stock.

Together in a hulking, grotesque mound of straining arms and hands, they twisted, spinning, in the dark. Then something massive hit Kertzman behind the neck.

Stunned.

Kertzman almost collapsed before he recovered, roaring, and surged with a scarlet rage. He whirled, hunching his shoulders to protect his neck. Frantically, breath blasting from his clenched teeth in a hissing curse, Kertzman pulled again at the Marlin and, even beneath the explosion outside the cabin, he felt the wooden stock crack against the twisting grip of his opponent.

Descending hatefully, iron thunder in blackness hit Kertzman again in the back of the head, an earthquake that struck deep with a crashing, tree-trunk forearm. Groaning and then shouting in rage, Kertzman released the rifle to the second man to throw him back, and his right hand swept down, finding the Colt at his waist. Pulled it out.

A huge forearm snaked around his neck, choking, lifting Kertzman completely off the ground. Kertzman quickly moved his arm across his chest to shoot behind his back when a two-handed vise closed on his right gun hand, crushing it with a merciless grip.

Enraged, Kertzman growled wordlessly but thrust the Colt towards the man in front of him, the man who had grabbed his gun hand. Kertzman twisted against them both, heard the man in front cursing in a thick Oriental accent.

The big man behind him hissed in anger and tension, while he squeezed, putting pressure on Kertzman's carotid artery to take him down with oxygen debt.

Defiantly, his entire body trembling under the stress, Kertzman surged to move the gun barrel, inch by inch, towards the Japanese, who continued to squeeze his gun hand in a savage contest of brute strength. Jaw locked tight with the effort, Kertzman pulled inwardly in a volcanic effort, and moved the gun barrel closer to the chest of the Oriental.

Heat and red pain and Kertzman felt himself quickly submerged in a conquering landslide of fatigue.

Breath hot, strained and thin. Pain exploding inside his gun hand. Bones breaking.

Too old . . . for this!

Don't give up!

Kertzman strained his one arm against the Oriental's two arms, moving the Colt inch . . . by . . . inch!

Kertzman fired a shot.

Missed!

But the explosion, so close beside them, shocked his two combatants. Together they twisted violently, screaming, trying to throw him down. Kertzman roared against them, staggering, face contorted with effort and surged again, wrenching the .45 toward the Oriental's shoulder and firing even as something cold slid across his forearm.

Razor sharp.

Kertzman shouted in agony. The Colt fell from his deadened hand and the giant threw Kertzman to the floor.

He landed in a heap, groaning, feeling quick blood loss from his wrist. His right hand had lost all feeling and he quickly grabbed his forearm with his left hand, felt heavy blood spilling out of the wound.

Lights. At once the cabin was illuminated again.

Groaning, Kertzman rolled to his side, teeth clenched in pain, trying to find his footing. He turned, saw the room as it now stood. Through the front windows Kertzman saw a car burning in the front yard.

Gage!

Exhaling explosively, Kertzman looked up at the giant, a black man, incredibly muscular and almost seven feet tall but appearing even larger because of the oversized ballistic vest he wore on top of the black fatigues. The giant was sweating, glaring angrily at Kertzman and breathing heavily. He held a nightvisor in one hand.

Kertzman scowled at him, looked away and saw the large Japanese, dressed in somber black clothes, moving quickly and efficiently across the room. He held a long, bloodied knife in his right hand and a nightvisor in the other. He stopped at the kitchen table and in quick, efficient movements gathered all the papers, including Father Simon's letter. Kertzman remembered that Gage had destroyed the uncoded version revealing the manuscript's location.

The Japanese lifted the papers, reading quickly but carefully. Then he looked at the back door where another man stood and shook his head.

"They have destroyed it," he said somberly. "We must bring them."

Sweating profusely in the cold night air, breath hard and deep with pain, Kertzman swung his slightly unfocused gaze across the room. At the closed back door, standing over the unconscious body of Barto, was a tall, older man wearing a brown tweed overcoat. Kertzman couldn't tell if Barto was dead or rendered unconscious. His big chest didn't seem to be moving. The tall man had a hand on the light switch.

"Why didn't you just kill us?" Kertzman growled at the man, obviously the leader.

The man smiled benignly. "Do not presume that this situation will necessarily end in further bloodshed, Mr. Kertzman. The plan was to take you all alive. There is no need for unnecessary alarm. In fact, there is even the chance that none of you will die." He paused. "Except Gage, of course."

Kertzman said nothing. The man had given him the standard reply: Tell them something that won't alarm them further. Kill them all when it's convenient.

He looked toward the kitchen to see a muscular, blond-haired man standing over Sarah Halder. She was holding her mouth, her hand and lips bloodied. She was hurt, possibly hit in the face to dislodge her grip on the pistol. But she was stoically silent, head bowed, not making a sound.

Kertzman rose to his feet, hell in his eyes.

"Sorry about all this, Kertzman," a man said.

Kertzman turned, recognizing the voice and cursing the name as he saw the face. His words contained a terrible and deadly edge as he spoke.

"Hello, Milburn," he said.

Gage leaped across a blackened tree trunk that appeared abruptly in his path, hit the ground, and moved sharply left at the sound of his boots on the dry grass, instinct directing him.

Shadows. Wind.

White moonlight streaked over him through the splintered trees.

Reacting instantly to the light he crossed back to the right, ran low through the night for 20 seconds, covering 100 yards in a tight half-circle to gain an angle of attack toward the rear of the cabin.

He stayed deep inside the trees to avoid target identification by a perimeter guard, scanning tactics as he moved.

...Superiority of numbers only endures as long as there is order...Create chaos!...The simplest means for a small force to disorganize a large force is by sniper attack...Kill twice at a shooting nest before moving to the next...Move fast to create a combination of chaos, terror, and attrition...Destroy their order to keep them from forcing a way into the cabin!

He selected his initial sniper nest, instantly angled toward it. He moved close to a narrow but deep ditch that allowed a close, parallel retreat from the back of the cabin. The ditch led east to a small knoll; a secondary sniper nest. He would choose a third, and a fourth, each nest selected for the availability of a covered retreat and quick repositioning for continued fire.

Attrition! Win by attrition!

Moving fast, shadows flying over him, Gage spun left again, thorns raking his face. He ignored the pain and the blood and fell silently onto his chest as he neared the tree line, sliding forward.

Crawling the final few yards with snakish slowness, he eased into the tall grass beneath the last tree at the edge of the glade, instantly bringing the MP5 up for single-action target acquisition.

Empty.

Alarmed, Gage focused on the cabin, saw frantic movement through the windows.

Inside! They were already inside the cabin!

He groaned, saw a figure stalking toward the back of the cabin. It was crouched, moving through the shadows. Hissing a silent curse, Gage was instantly on his feet and running forward. He switched to fully auto as he crossed the clearing, quickly and quietly.

The front of the cabin was bathed in the white phosphorous fire that had consumed the LTD. He used the long shadow cast by the cabin for cover, closed on the silent figure.

He caught the scent of gasoline, realized that the tank of the LTD had already blown. A quick glance of the entire glade revealed no cars, no intruder vehicles.

They had entered on foot.

An ambush.

Sandman hadn't seen them until the last moment because of the thick woodline. Not even the infrared nightvisor could read through a forest. And Chavez had probably not seen them at all as he had not taken a visor out with him earlier in the day.

It took Gage 30 strides to reach the cabin, and he made no sound with the final steps, boots landing on the balls of his feet with a leaping, silent run. Somewhere in the closing distance, he couldn't be sure of the precise moment, he recognized the shape. Even before it spun and Gage caught a glimpse of the disfigured face and the patched eye, he knew who it was.

From a combat crouch Chavez whirled and leveled the M-14 at him.

Gage raised the MP5 in the air, his left hand empty and high and continued to close the gap. Chavez dropped the guard and turned back quickly toward the cabin, gazing carefully in a window.

Chavez looked over at him, calm and calculating, held up a fist, two fingers raised. Then he drew his hand across his chest in a quick gesture.

Symbol: *Explosive door entry. Cross over once we get inside.*

Gage nodded, fell to the side of the back door, crouching, sweating in the cold, struggling to bring his strained breathing silently under control.

Then he almost shouted in rage, leaping up from the crouch as Sarah screamed.

*   *   *

Kertzman surged forward, shouting.

But the giant grabbed him, slamming him against the wall. Milburn raised his Beretta, holding a cold aim.

Kertzman glared sideways. In the kitchen, the blond-haired man was using a silver roll of duct tape to attach the bore of a sawed-off double-barreled shotgun to the neck of Sarah Halder. The roll went around her neck and both barrels once, twice, three times, locking the bore tight against her spine.

"Schnell!" the blond hissed to the others.

The Japanese stepped forward, moving with the disciplined calm of a man accustomed to violence and the heightened emotions of violent conflict. In seconds he had used the silver tape to attach the German's hand to the sawed-off handle of the weapon. He cocked both barrels.

"We are ready," said the German coldly.

Despite a lightheaded weakness that caused a soft focus at the edges, Kertzman concentrated on Sarah Halder. She had closed her eyes, set her mouth in a grim line. He knew that she was wrestling courageously to control a sheer terror, and she was succeeding. He nodded, admiring.

Then, face rigid, he looked down, studying his wounded arm. It was not a fatal injury. It was almost impossible to die from a slashed wrist, or even two slashed wrists, for that matter.

Usually a wrist injury, even if it was a deep cut that caused actual arterial bleeding, would simply bleed a person's blood pressure down to a point where blood did not exit the body any longer. But the body would retain enough fluid and glucose in vital organs to maintain life. It was an instinctive biological defense mechanism. Shock would come, yes, but not death. Kertzman wanted to forestall even the shock so he quickly undid his belt, wrapping it around his forearm slightly above the elbow.

He blinked sweat out of his eyes.

He worked quickly, heard Sarah yell out in pain as the German jerked her to the door.

"Now we go outside!" the man hissed into her ear, leaning forward.

Sarah's eyes were still shut, and her lip and nose were still bleeding.

Headlights flashed past the front windows.

Kertzman glanced outside, saw a four-door rolling to a stop. Quickly, a man got out, walked through the glare of the headlights, around to the front of the cabin and came inside. Kertzman immediately recognized the walk, the silhouette, and the identity, had even expected it. His emotions had already passed through anger to hatred to a smoldering cold control before the man entered the front door.

Jeremiah Radford, point man for the NSA investigating team, stood in the doorway a moment, surveying. He looked past the frowning and strangely stoic Milburn, locking on Kertzman. He laughed.

"You're really in it this time, Kertzman," Radford said jovially. "Washington is going to give your dead body a medal when this is over. You'll be a hero." He laughed again.

The Nigerian spoke. "This is no moment for humor."

"Oh, I think it is." Radford smiled, taking out a Smith and Wesson .45.

Groaning against the pain, Kertzman ignored him and tightened the tourniquet around his arm. He glanced cautiously down, saw no weapons close. He hadn't worn a backup.

"You're done this time, Kertzman," said Radford. "It's the end of the road. But don't worry. I'm going to make you look like a hero. Do you want to know what the cover story is going to be?"

Kertzman's slag face was impassive. He blinked sweat.

Radford laughed. "I'll tell you anyway, great white hunter." He walked closer. "You tracked Gage to this mountain. Then you called me for some backup because you didn't want to involve the locals. Security problems, all that stuff. You know how it is. They'll love that. Probably give you two medals. Anyway," he continued, "we came in real quiet, planning to just do some surveillance. But we stumbled into a trap. You and I got captured by the super-soldier. We found out that Gage had already killed the woman, her father, and the fat boy. Surprise! Gage was behind it all! Can you believe it?" He winked. "I can't."

Kertzman's voice was dry, cracked. "It'll never work, Radford."

"Sure it will," Radford said. "Gage kills them all. Then you and I find him, get captured, go for our guns. There's a big shootout. You, unfortunately, get killed. Gage gets killed. Your dead body is mourned by nobody. I get promoted." He smiled. "It's beautiful. Who's going to know? It's the perfect plan. Gage takes the fall for everybody."

Kertzman lowered his head, face tight with pain, and jerked the belt tight at the right elbow. Then he tied it off and, exhaling with the agony of his wound, stepped toward the kitchen.

The tall man beside the back door leveled a black semiautomatic pistol at him. And Radford stepped closer, raising the .45.

"Be cool, Kertzman," the NSA man said. "All good things come to those who wait...or something like that."

Milburn, the ex-Delta soldier and Gage's former supervisor, stepped out the back door, gazing into the darkness with a night-visor. Kertzman saw him shake his head.

"Your people have messed up, Stern," Milburn said to the tall man.

Kertzman notched it: *Stern*.

"You have the nightvisor!" said Stern. "Search for him! He is there!"

Milburn laughed, bitter. He spoke with contempt. "A night-visor doesn't mean anything against somebody like Gage, Stern. He knows how to beat it. You won't see him until he blows your brains out." He paused, laughing shortly. "What was all that about how your people are the ultimate soldiers? The perfect predators? I'd like to hear that again."

"Do as I say!" said Stern. "Find him!"

Milburn removed the nightvisor, stared solidly and scornfully at the tall man. "Your people were supposed to trap Gage *inside*, Stern. They didn't. Now he's on the loose and I guarantee you he's going to do some real serious damage. *Real* serious." He looked around the room, cold, adding, "Some of you are going to die."

"We have other contingency plans," said Stern, recovering. "We are not fools, Milburn." Then he looked at the German. "Carl, bring her!"

"Leave her alone!" Kertzman shouted.

"Relax, Kertzman," Radford said, thumbing back the hammer. "What you say doesn't count anymore. Not that it ever did."

The German moved towards the back door with Sarah Halder, followed by Milburn, the Japanese, and Stern.

Kertzman's mind raced for something to stall them. "Gage is out there," he said lamely.

Stern hesitated, turning to face Kertzman with aristocratic British calm. Kertzman thought that he seemed like a man professionally trained to handle catastrophes.

"Yes, Mr. Kertzman, he is," Stern replied. "And if he does anything precipitous, his beloved will die." Then he smiled evenly, opened the door.

Helpless, Kertzman watched as the German went outside first, moving Sarah in front of him as a shield. The Japanese followed, with Stern and Milburn in the rear.

Clumsily, suddenly faint, Kertzman fell against the wall, slamming his good hand heavily against the fireplace mantle. He breathed deeply, trying to get equilibrium. And he glanced around once more.

Barto and Sandman were unmoving. Malachi Halder stirred, as if in pain. And through a red haze Kertzman heard Radford speaking again.

"Don't make it worse, Kertzman," he continued. "It's over. It's been over."

Kertzman focused on him, mumbling, "You sold out, Radford. Sold out your country. That's why they picked you ... for the job. So you could sell us out ..."

Radford laughed, a grunt of contempt. "For God and country, huh, Kertzman?" he asked. "You really are a simpleton," he added, leaning forward. "There's no such thing as *countries* anymore, Kertzman! Do you actually think that governments care about political objectives?" He shook his head. "That's the dark ages, man. This is the new world! Now there's only money. Lots and lots of money. And it can do anything. And it doesn't matter whose hand it comes from. It doesn't matter if he's Republican or Democrat or a Communist or a Chinese drugrunner. If you've got the weight, you can call the shot." He stared a moment, suddenly more serious. "Any shot at all."

Kertzman's face was stone.

Radford shook his head. "You're a dinosaur, man. It's probably good that you die before you see the truth. It would drive you insane. They say there's a merciful god. He probably wants to kill you before you see what's really going on." He laughed. "Yeah, that's it. A merciful god who's gonna do you in. You believe in right and wrong, honor, God, country, all that. And look where it's got you." A pause. "Well, let me tell you something, partner. There's no such thing as right and wrong. There's just decisions. And none of 'em are wrong. You do whatever it takes to get to the top. You steal, you push 'em into the street, you sell 'em out. Only the strongest survive. That's the rule of the jungle, pal. And this *is* the jungle."

Radford continued to talk, but Kertzman was no longer listening. Something had caught his attention, something subliminal. He waited, hoping to place it.

Sandman.

The big guy had fallen beside the kitchen table, his hands automatically clutching his abdomen as any wounded man would do, and Kertzman had not seen him move again. But now Sandman's right arm was stretched on the floor, the hand poised close to the left ankle.

Kertzman knew what was coming.

The Nigerian had gone back to the kitchen table, couldn't see Sandman. Only Radford had a clear view. So Kertzman turned into him, menacing, distracting, when he heard shouting outside.

"Gage, we have the woman!"

• • •

Coldly, Gage held the German in his sights, the front targeting blade of the MP5 fixed steadily between the blond man's eyes.

When the back door opened Gage had slid quickly and silently around the corner of the cabin, with Chavez retreating in the opposite direction. There was no time for communication, no time to signal. They would have to wing it. Now, prone in the shadows at 50 yards, he furiously calculated the next move. He didn't know what position Chavez had taken and no time to find out.

Hostage situations were always extremely volatile. Negotiation was the hard rule unless there was a clear shot. But this was no ordinary hostage situation. Negotiation wasn't an option because there could be no defusing of the situation, no persuasion. And killing the German wasn't an option because violence might cause him to pull the trigger of the shotgun.

A no-win situation.

If Gage hit him, even between the eyes, which he was certain he could do at this distance, the German's dead weight would still pull the single action on the shotgun, probably on both barrels.

But a single rule came to Gage as he lay prone in the darkness, the MP5 still centered on the German: He would not surrender his weapon.

No matter what they promised, no matter what they threatened, he would not surrender his weapon. Because as long as he was moving, as long as he could still strike and react, there was a chance he could create a new situation that might free Sarah.

"Gage, come out!" the tall man shouted. "It is over! I will give you ten seconds! If you do not show yourself in ten seconds we will kill her!"

Gage concentrated.

"Gage!" the man shouted again. "Do you hear me!"

Gage felt the rage, the heat, and he decided. *Create a new situation!* Shutting down all emotion, Gage stood, instantly visible and instantly menacing. Then, to everyone's apparent shock, he walked quickly toward them, the MP5 in one hand, the Hi-Power in the other.

"Stop where you are!" the tall man shouted, pointing a semiautomatic pistol at him.

Gage smiled savagely.

Advancing.

"Stop!"

Gage laughed.

His fingers tightened on the triggers.

THIRTY-SEVEN

Gage stopped six feet in front of the tall man, raising the Hi-Power in his right hand, pointing at the face.

"Stop or she dies!" the man shouted.

With his left hand Gage raised the MP5 and pointed it toward Sato and Milburn. All three of them had leveled pistols at him, holding eye-sight aim. The fourth man, the German, shouted something, shifting quickly from side to side.

"What are you gonna do?" Gage said, angry.

"Throw down your weapon or I will kill her."

Gage laughed. "Then kill her."

Shock was evident in the tall man's face.

Sato laughed out loud.

"And then one second later I'll kill you," Gage said. "You've lived too long as it is."

The tall man hesitated, blinked. "You'll die too, Gage," he said, caught a quick breath.

Gage thumbed back the hammer on the Hi-Power. "Like I care."

Sarah made a faint sound, a choked-off cry of panic.

"Alright, alright." The tall man motioned with his free hand. "Let's calm down. If we can only . . ." He looked at Sato to finish the sentence.

"Don't!" Gage shouted.

The tall man froze, moved only his eyes to stare nervously. Utter stillness.

"Before you die, I want to know your name," Gage whispered.

The tall man's eyes were focused on the barrel of the Hi-Power but he seemed to grow steadily calmer, recovering from Gage's suicidal move, finding balance in it.

"My name is Stern."

"Well, Stern," said Gage, "Sato's good, but he ain't that good. I'll kill him and you too if he makes a move." He nodded curtly. "Try me."

Stern watched him. "Yes, but you will not get Carl or Milburn, will you, Gage? You will shoot me, yes, and probably Sato. But Milburn will kill you. It is unavoidable. And than Carl will kill the woman."

"Maybe," Gage replied, placing a name on the German without removing his eyes from Stern. "But that won't mean a lot to you because you'll be in hell."

Inside the cabin a loud argument erupted between Kertzman and Radford. It sounded as if it were on the verge of further violence.

"Very well," said Stern quickly, the air crisp with an electric tension. "How do you wish to resolve this?"

"Let her go. We'll work out the rest later." Gage said it more quickly than he intended, regretted it instantly. It revealed nervousness, weakness.

"No," said Stern evenly.

Abruptly, in the darkness beside the cabin, Gage saw a faint shadow move, low and quiet, toward the back of Carl.

Chavez.

Gage took another step toward Stern, drawing sharp attention to himself. "Last chance, Stern," he said. "Let her go."

Stern smiled, shook his head. "No. She is our insurance, Gage. Our plans have not worked as well as I had intended. But I know you will not interfere as long as we have her with us. We will be taking her father, as well."

Milburn shifted, and Gage focused on him.

"Did they pay you enough for this, Bob?"

"It's just money, Gage," Milburn replied, tired. "If it wasn't me, it'd be somebody else."

"Why'd you set us up to die in Israel, Bob? Why'd you set the whole team up? Was that about money, too? Do you know how they did it?" Gage's voice became angrier with each word. "They cut us to pieces! Sammy and Brock and me and the rest of the team! We never stood a chance! Everybody died. Was it worth the money, Bob?" He didn't wait for an answer. "Who did it? These people? Are these the people who told you to sell us out? Are these the people that got rich off Black Light?"

Milburn shook his head. "It wasn't my call."

Gage laughed harshly. "And whose call was it, Bob? Who did Black Light really work for? Tell me! Who got rich off all that blood?"

"It's way beyond you, Gage," he answered. "Let it go."

"Too late."

But Gage felt the situation turning away from him. His finger tightened on the trigger of the Hi-Power. A half-ounce more of pressure and it would end. For all of them.

He centered on Stern. "Time's up. Let her go or die."

Stern shook his head. "No, Gage." He smiled. "You are, as the Americans would say, bluffing. You will do nothing that precipitates her death."

The argument inside the cabin got louder.

Chavez moved closer to Carl's back.

Four more steps; four more steps and Chavez would be on the German. Gage knew how Chavez would execute the maneuver. He had done it a hundred times, himself, in training.

The standard method for disarming someone with a single action weapon was to slam your hand down in the space between the cocked hammer and the firing pin before the offender could shoot, while simultaneously grabbing the underside of the weapon with your other hand. Automatically, with the attack, the offender would pull the trigger. But with a hand or finger placed between the hammer and the firing pin, the weapon would not discharge. It was a move that required the speed and accuracy of a snake. Once someone gripped the weapon, it could not be released until the offender had been killed.

Chavez could pull it off, but as soon as he grabbed the weapon Gage would have to instantly kill Carl, and then try to take out Stern, Milburn and Sato in one sweeping burst.

But the German had to be first.

A wave of hidden panic passed through Gage, a stark trembling fear. And his mind recognized the truth, stressed it over and over again until his higher consciousness was smothered by it: There were too many of them.

Gage knew he couldn't make the shots alone, and Chavez wouldn't be able to help because he would be preoccupied with holding the hammer back on the shotgun.

Calculating the move, Gage knew without doubt that he would have time to take out the German, a half-second to acquire and fire the shot. But the light was bad here. Even at six feet, Gage could barely discern outlines. Of course, Sato and Milburn would be in action instantly, even as he killed Carl. Gage estimated that the Japanese would move as soon as Chavez came around Carl to grab the shotgun.

Locking down on his control, Gage ignored a panicked sweat, concentrated to keep his face completely calm. His eyes focused intently on Stern but he was prepared to switch instantly to Carl.

Chavez moved again, silent and low to the ground, directly behind the German.

Three more steps.

"We're leaving," said Stern, backing up. Carl also moved back.

"No!" shouted Gage, swinging the Hi-Power toward Carl.

"Wait!" yelled Sato.

Together they froze in position.

As calmly as a snake feasting on dead prey, the Japanese turned slowly, leveling a Desert Eagle .44 semiautomatic pistol at Chavez, who still stood three paces behind Carl.

Gage grimaced.

This was unreal. By some kind of uncanny intuition or peripheral gift of sight, the Japanese had known all along that Chavez was behind them, and had waited until the last moment to reveal it. He had toyed with them, all of them.

Chavez turned to Sato, gazing at him with a despising contempt, straightening. The M-14 was slung across his back. His hands were empty.

Still holding the large black semiauto on Chavez, Sato turned to Gage.

"Don't do it." Gage raised the MP5 to shoulder level, centering on Sato. "I'll burn this down."

Sato laughed out loud.

Stern turned to Carl. "Put her in the car!"

Gage moved but felt the situation on the brink and hesitated. Deep inside he knew his next move, his last move. He opened his mouth to speak. "If you—"

Gunfire exploded inside the cabin. Stern shouted and fired at Gage.

Sato fired at Chavez.

Gage dropped instantly to the ground, firing both weapons as fast as he could pull the triggers and then he was rolling, firing as the ground beside him erupted volcanically in flames and fire and explosions with men screaming in panic and fear.

• • •

Kertzman leaped to smash a bull shoulder into Radford even as Sandman pulled the backup weapon from his ankle and rolled, firing a round into the gigantic Nigerian.

Screaming, Radford was thrown back by the collision and the .45 discharged to the side.

Missed!

Kertzman's uninjured left hand crashed down on the semiauto, straining, wrestling to tear it from Radford's grip as gunfire exploded in the kitchen.

With a wild roar Kertzman tore the gun from Radford's hand, savagely overpowering the NSA man with sheer brute force. Then he swung an elbow back, smashing into Radford's face. Shouting wildly, Radford stumbled back, grasping convulsively at his face and Kertzman whirled, leveling the .45 at the Nigerian.

Sandman fired four bursts from his prone position on the floor, and the Nigerian cut loose at him with the AK-47.

Kertzman fired.

With the first shot the Nigerian staggered, howling. Spun around by the thunderous impact of the bullet, he stared at Kertzman in shock before he screamed, raising the AK-47.

Sandman fell back, limp.

Enraged with a cold and experienced aim, Kertzman fired again.

The Nigerian stumbled back, his ballistic vest exploding at the impact of the .45 caliber round. Kertzman pulled the trigger two more times.

The second shot blew the vest open on the right side, a lung. The third shot hit high in the chest, nailing the Nigerian to the wall. The barrel of the AK-47 had dropped off aim, was pointed at the floor.

Kertzman heard nothing, saw nothing but the hulking form in front of him. He shouted, all else forgotten or ignored, and took an extra half-second for a solid sight-picture alignment. With almost surreal concentration he fixed the front blade of the .45 over the center of the Nigerian's chest, even as he stumbled away from the wall, raising the rifle again.

A standard police rule from his days as a state trooper raged over and over in Kertzman's head with blood-white adrenaline: *Shoot until the aggression stops... Shoot until the aggression stops... Shoot until the aggression stops.*

Kertzman pulled the trigger.

Deafening blast. Knew he'd hit.

Mist erupted from the Nigerian's chest with shredded white ballistic material and the giant stumbled, swaying. Kertzman held aim, counting the one round he had left in the clip, watching for the final result.

Shoot until the aggression stops... Shoot until the aggression stops... Shoot until...

Staggering, the Nigerian fell to his knees.

Kertzman, blood hot, raging, stared wide-eyed.

The Nigerian hesitated a moment, as if hovering between hell and earth, before pitching forward onto his face. The AK-47 clattered to his side.

Kertzman glanced at Sandman, saw the bloody, massive wounds caused by the rifle, the silent and still form. But he was adrenalized and mentally shattered by the combat, had no energy and no emotion left for thought. Groaning, he rose from one knee, swinging the .45 toward Radford.

But the room was empty.

He grimaced, would have cursed the NSA man if he could have found breath. He glanced around, saw that the front door was open; the car that had driven up during the standoff was gone.

Suddenly a wave of dizziness swept across Kertzman, and he bent, losing focus. Black swept in from the edges but he resisted, fighting it. He raised his head, hands on his knees, struggling to think. But his blood was burned out by adrenaline, his thinking flowing with the speed.

Routine!

Don't try and get creative!

Just go by routine, he thought. *Secure this place and call for backup. Don't try and think. Just go by routine!*

First, secure this place!

But I'm almost empty. I need a tactical reload.

Radford's Smith and Wesson .45 wasn't compatible with the extra clips he had hidden in his boots. So Kertzman scanned the room, remembered his Colt .45 falling to the floor, someone kicking it across the room toward the . . . kitchen.

Kertzman saw it, there on the kitchen floor. Nodding, he grinned, feeling a familiar, suicidal abandon, content that he would at least kill one more of them before he was put down.

He knew he should have felt fear but he didn't. Pain had burned all emotion, all thought, down to a single place: He didn't care anymore.

He removed an extra clip from his boot and staggered across the room, past the silent Sandman and Malachi's unconscious body. As he moved, he tried to analyze what he could analyze of the past few moments. After the car drove up, Sandman had drawn his hideaway, firing, and then there was firing . . . outside!

Kertzman clenched his teeth, groaning in agony, recognizing, now, what the sounds outside the cabin were. He had vaguely registered them during the firefight, but his mind was already fully occupied. Now, though, he had a moment to think, and he knew: There was a shootout between Gage and the rest of them.

Reaching the .45, Kertzman bent, groping numbly with a bloody hand. He ejected the half-spent clip as he straightened, slammed in a new one.

Tactical reload.

Now secure this place. Call for backup.

He moved to the back door and killed the light switch, cursing himself for not doing it earlier. Then he stepped outside, scanning. White lights from the still-burning LTD cast the back of the cabin in shadow.

Sweating, breath rasping, Kertzman eased weakly, faintly, along a logged wall toward the garage. He had only taken half a dozen steps when he stumbled over it.

Dizzy and already off-balance, Kertzman fell heavily, pitching clumsily forward to crash in a heap. Landing noisily on his side, he shouted in pain, struggling desperately in a billowing internal fog not to accidentally discharge the Colt.

Stunned, he lay in silence for a moment, breathing deeply, tired, so tired. Then curiosity and concern sparked him and he roused what remained of his strength, rolling, groping in the dark to find what he had fallen over.

A coat . . . a body.

Kertzman peered through the dark at the face.

A Mexican.

Kertzman didn't know him. Then he heard a slight sound behind him and he rolled, the .45 leading.

Prone on the ground, eyes slowly adjusting to the dim light, he gazed steadily about.

A moan.

Kertzman saw the shape in the darkness; another man lay on the ground. As he watched, the man moved slightly and rolled onto his side. Eyes wide, Kertzman searched the shadows for anyone else. Saw nothing. Sharp with the moment, he moved forward, easing into a perfectly smooth 20-year-old jungle crawl that he executed despite his fatigue, one arm sliding over the other.

With the first touch of his right forearm on the grass, needled slivers of hot fire lanced the open wound. Kertzman grimaced, blinking sweat, stifling a moan. In moments he was over the second man. He peered at the form and rolled him onto his back.

Milburn. Shot through the chest, but still alive.

Kertzman couldn't tell how long the ex-CIA man would last, but it looked bad. Slowly, Kertzman brought one foot underneath, staggering, and rose. He stood for a moment, still dizzy, feeling the blood on his arm. He shook his head, fatigued, feeling the madness, endless and out of control.

Movement behind.

Kertzman whirled, the .45 going out to eye-level and his finger tightening.

But the man was too close and too experienced with soldiers caught up in the heat of combat for that. Kertzman never managed the shot as a strong hand closed on the Colt, twisting to instantly dislodge it from his weakened grip.

Gage.

Breathing heavily, sweat glistening on his face and neck, in a second he had dropped the hammer of the Colt and handed it back to Kertzman, who received it in a mechanical grip.

"They're gone," Gage whispered hoarsely. "They took Sarah. And they're gone." He shook his head, focusing on the Mexican for a moment before speaking again.

"I'll kill them for this," he rasped hoarsely.

Gage's right hand tightened into a bloodless fist, trembling. His head was bowed, his voice a hushed, choking oath. His eyes glinted, red. "As God as my witness," he whispered, "I'll kill every one of them for this."

Kertzman pointed to Milburn. "He's still alive."

Looking sharply, Gage instantly crouched over Milburn. After a moment he reached out to shake the CIA man. Milburn opened his eyes, focused with a supreme effort.

Silence.

Gage leaned down further, speaking loudly. "Who are they, Bob?"

Milburn's gaze was unseeing, distant. His voice was less than a whisper, the eyes half-closed. Kertzman thought he caught a hint of emotion in Gage's face as he waited for a reply.

"You can't...beat 'em, Gage," Milburn whispered. "Nobody can...beat 'em...*Nobody*...They ain't...real."

Face impassive, Gage waited.

"They're.... some kind...some kind 'a...supermen..." He shook his head. "Supposed to be...like gods...or something...A sixth order..." He coughed blood.

Moments passed, and Gage waited, growing more still. Kertzman thought he perceived the slightest lessening of the former Delta commando's stance.

Milburn stirred. "I'm sorry, buddy," he said finally, shifting. "I...got lost...in it...Got lost..."

Gage tilted his head slightly, inhaled heavily, exhaled. After a short silence he spoke, so quietly Kertzman could barely hear the words. "Me too, Bob."

Gage waited, his head still tilted, as if he were looking at Milburn in a strangely softer light. "Just rest, Bob," he said quietly. "Just rest."

Pained, Milburn blinked, stirring suddenly, struggling to rise. Gage pushed down, gently but firmly, on the shoulder. "No, Bob," he said. "Just rest."

Milburn coughed, leaving a bloody, blackened froth on his lips. He stared at Gage as if he were a supernatural being. "It was me," he said brokenly. "I sanctioned...the old man...the priest."

Gage nodded, his face a mask of pain. "I know," he replied.

Milburn seemed to cry, moaned. "Find D'Oncetta," he whispered, lifting his head. "Find the priest...D'Oncetta...and you'll find the woman...He's at...the Hassler...Rome..." Convulsing, coughing again, Milburn rolled onto his side. And in a moment was utterly still.

Gage continued to clutch Milburn's shoulder, unmoving. Then, finally, he stood.

Kertzman moved to say something calming. But no order of thought would come to his mind, his logic shattered by pain and fear and the terror of combat. He shook his head, thinking only of...*madness...just madness...no end to it.*

"C'mon, Kertzman," said Gage, stepping forward to grasp him lightly under his injured arm. "You're hurt. Malachi's hurt. You need to call this in. Make it official."

"I've got less than twelve hours to get the book," said Gage. "They'll break the code by then, or they'll give Sarah something to make her talk."

Kertzman stared numbly. "You think she'll talk?"

Gage nodded, a frown turning his face. "Yeah, she'll talk. She won't be able to help herself. She won't talk easy. But she'll have to talk, in the end. They'll wear her down."

Kertzman turned his huge, squared head to stare at Malachi.

The old man was lying, pale and unmoving, on the couch, still unconscious. Blood loss had drained him to a state of near lifelessness. But Kertzman thought that, with proper medical care, he might live.

Gage had quickly respliced the phone lines where they were cut and called for two ambulances and sheriff's deputies. He told them that the injuries were caused by firearms. Nothing more.

Meanwhile, Barto had recovered, slowly and groggily. Gage had checked the big guy's eyes and head, saw that he was hit low on the left side of his neck, on the nerve cluster. It had caused instant and painless unconsciousness but had also left a mild concussion. For the moment Barto was resting, dazed, in a chair.

Sandman was dead, and Gage had solemnly covered him with an Army G.I. blanket.

The dead Nigerian still lay in a pool of blood, exactly where he had fallen.

Kertzman and Gage ignored him.

"What are you going to do when you get the book?" asked Kertzman tiredly, holding a hastily bandaged right forearm with his left hand.

Gage sniffed, finished packing the dufflebag. "Exchange."

"That's going to be rough."

"I know."

"You ain't got no backup, Gage."

He nodded. "I know."

"There's still three of them, plus Radford."

Face an icy mask, Gage tightened the strap of the duffle. "I'll deal with it."

Kertzman was expressionless. "You can trust me, you know. You should know that by now. I ain't one of them."

Gage looked up. "Yeah, Kertzman, I trust you. You've proven what you are. But you can't go with me. We got dead guys here and there's gonna be questions out the wazoo. You're gonna have to handle it."

Kertzman looked absently at the door, raised his eyebrows faintly. "How much longer before they get here?"

"Fifteen minutes," Gage said quickly. "It takes a while up here."

"And the deputies?"

"I don't know. It depends. Third shift is small. They might be on something else. Might take half an hour. Or they might not be doing anything at all, just waiting for a call. It might be soon. But they'll probably try and get some backup from the troopers before they come in. That'll add a few minutes."

Kertzman nodded, face pale. He mumbled, as if an afterthought, "What happened outside?"

Setting the dufflebag on the table, Gage removed the Hi-Power from his waist, ejecting the clip.

"Sarah was in the car," he said. "We were in a standoff. Stern, the leader, took a shot at me as soon as that scene started in here. I fell back, trying to take out him and Sato."

"The Japanese?" Kertzman growled, eyes vacuous and mouth slack with pain and exhaustion.

Gage nodded.

"Pay him back for me."

"I will," Gage said, with a terse nod, and raised his head suddenly, listening. "They're coming."

In the distance, Kertzman could hear the faintest sounds of sirens, a lot of them. They were far away but coming fast.

"Anyway, I went to the ground," Gage continued. "I tried to take out Sato with the MP5. But Stern was firing down on me and I had to look at him to hit him with the Browning. It was pitch black out there. I missed, I think. And then Bob got hit. Somehow. I don't know who did it. It could have been anyone. But I think..." He shook his head, trying to recall it all. "...I *think* that Bob turned and took a shot at Sato. I can't be sure." He paused, took a breath. "It was a wild scene. Just a point-blank shootout in the dark. I'd forgotten how hard it was. But Stern got away with Sato. They were in the car."

"You didn't get the Japanese at all?" asked Kertzman, almost angry. "Didn't even wound him?"

Sirens were closing fast.

Gage grew tense. "No. I missed. But I won't miss next time. Chavez was hit right off. Sato killed him. He...didn't stand a chance. Didn't have a weapon in his hand. Then, as Chavez and Bob went down, Sato was moving. I went around the building after him, but the car was already headed down the driveway. I couldn't take a shot into the vehicle."

Kertzman nodded. "I know."

"By that time," Gage continued, "the shooting had stopped inside. I knew it was over, whatever it was. So I came back to the house. I worked my way to the front door, couldn't see you. Then I came around to the back."

Sirens seemed to be converging on the driveway entrance, almost a mile away.

The county deputies would come in with extreme caution, slow and tactical, not eager to walk into a firefight between drugrunners or worse. The ambulances would only come in when the scene was secured by local police.

For at least three minutes, officers would debate different approaches, deciding who was in charge and who would take the heat if things went bad.

Kertzman gazed at Gage's bag. "How you gonna get out of here?"

"South trail." Gage slammed a fresh clip into the Browning. "It leads to a shack down by the highway. I've got a Harley there. I'll be in Monticello in less than half an hour. Cargo transfer flight is on standby. Then I'll be airborne."

Gage focused, suddenly concentrated. "You gonna be alright with this?" he asked. "It's coming down on your head."

"Oh, yeah, I'll be alright," said Kertzman, eyes dead-tired and filled with pain. "I'm gonna drag the local FBI guys down here. The whole scene is going federal, and the locals will be glad to get rid of it. We're gonna fingerprint the dead Nigerian there 'cause I know he's somebody. Just like ol' dead Milburn out there is somebody." He shook his head angrily. "I'm used to this, by now. I've almost figured it out and now I'm gonna drag it into the daylight. I'll be in Washington in a couple of hours accusing Milburn and Radford of treason, a cover-up, murder, kidnapping, the whole shebang. And I'll be looking to place the blame on somebody higher. I haven't quite got proof, yet. But I've got a suspicion. There'll be a lot of scrambling. I'll drag the NSA into it, the CIA, the Justice Department, and maybe even the White House. There's gonna be jurisdictional fights and everybody's gonna be accusing everybody else of wrongdoing. And they'll probably point the finger at me, too, accusing me of who-knows-what. But I'll be in their face at the same time, accusing them of worse. It's gonna be hot." He paused, licked dry lips. "It don't matter none. It's time for somethin' to shake loose."

Gage nodded.

The distant sound of sirens had stopped.

Gage walked to the front window, eased a curtain back to gaze out. He stared into the darkness for a minute. "They're coming up the driveway," he said. "Real slow. No code."

"That's how it's done," Kertzman mumbled. He waited a moment, eyes bright and narrow with concentration. "I'd like to meet you in Rome. Before the showdown."

Gage moved to the table, picked up the dufflebag. He stared back at Kertzman, and over the big man's shoulder he saw, through the open front door, at least three deputy cars and a New York State Trooper unit stop in the driveway, barely visible inside the light. Gage heard the doors shut, glimpsed uniforms moving around, approaching slowly. Shotguns and revolvers and automatics were displayed. Last in line, he saw the white and red outline of an ambulance. No code equipment on any vehicle that he could see.

Pure tactical.

He looked at Kertzman. "You ain't had enough, Kertzman?"

"It ain't over," Kertzman said, the customary gruffness in his voice. "I ain't had enough. That's an American citizen, and a woman, that those pigs took. And I've seen a good and decent old man shot down in front of me. Not to mention your two friends." He paused, face tightening in hard lines. "It's been a while, since that. No, it ain't over. And I ain't had enough. Not yet."

"What about your chain of command?"

"The only thing they got to be afraid of is me."

Kertzman's face grew more expressive, ultimately and fearlessly committed to the words. "Somebody's gonna pay for this. Somebody big."

Gage felt as if he were floating in the moment. "You watch yourself, Kertzman. It's out of hand. Way out of hand." He hesitated. "It always was."

Kertzman stood up, stepped forward.

"You meet me in Italy, boy." He pointed a finger from a broad, scarred fist at Gage's chest. "You meet me in Italy, and we'll finish this thing together."

Debating, Gage paused.

In the distance he saw men with shotguns flanking the sides of the cabin, angling around to the back to seal off the building. Standard procedure.

No time left.

He nodded.

"Alright," he replied. "Check into the Medici Hotel on the Via Vittorio, Rome. I'll meet you there at midnight on Friday. Two days from now. But be there." He leaned close, face only inches from Kertzman's. "I won't wait for you, Kertzman. If you're not there by midnight on the day after tomorrow I'll move without you. So don't let them intimidate you with paperwork. Don't let them control the situation."

Kertzman nodded. "You don't worry about me, kid. Just get the book for the exchange." He hesitated, eyes wide with a sudden thought. "Wait a second. We don't even know who these goons are. How are you gonna set up a meet?"

Gage's eyes were gleaming, vengeful and narrowed as he turned away. Moving with deathly poise, he stepped into the darkness.

"I'm going to visit a priest," he said.

Sarah kept her eyes closed, listening. She remembered waking, and as if in a fog, she remembered speaking, but she couldn't recall what she had spoken of, or to whom.

It seemed like a distant, surreal dream experience, a childhood nightmare that had left an imprinted moment of terror so real it was branded upon her conscious mind. She couldn't recall much of what had happened to her in recent days, but she felt the ghostly tendrils of a drifting fear, like tattered clouds clinging to the side of a cliff, and she recalled ... danger, yes, and men with guns ... killing ...

Father!

Sarah took in a pained, sharp breath, rolling her head to the side. She was lying on something soft. Carefully, finding a desperate but complete control, she opened her eyes.

Veiled light.

Shadows.

Gray somber hues outside the curtained windows.

Moving stiffly, Sarah raised herself to one elbow, gazed around.

She was in a small bedroom, fully clothed, her right forearm lightly bandaged with a strip of white gauze. Instinctively she touched the taped adhesive, eyes narrow, remembering.

The cabin, fighting, blood, terror ... Gage ... gunfire and Kertzman ... and Father ... hurt.

She closed her eyes, bowing and shaking her head at the memory. Malachi had said that he was alright, but she knew he was badly injured, perhaps even dead by now.

Emotional pain blended with physical fatigue to smother her mind in a gray-black wave of swelling exhaustion. So much had happened, so fast.

She looked at her wrist. Her watch was gone. Mind awakening, she searched the room. No clock. She might have been unconscious for one day, or three. There was no way to know.

Grimacing in pain at her stiff muscles and joints, she moved quietly off the bed, walking awkwardly to the door, listening. She reached out to place a hand on it, tentatively, wondering.

It opened.

Sarah stepped back, breath catching.

A tall and distinguished man, the man from the cabin, entered, leaving the door open behind him. He approached her, his gaze kind and gentle, the demeanor of a gracious and considerate host.

"Good evening, Ms. Halder," he said.

• • •

Gage buried the chute beneath a rock, checked himself for injury. Found none.

Remarkable, considering the landing.

He had pulled a HALO at 200 feet, and six seconds later he had crashlanded, hard, sprawling wildly down a narrow ridge, still carrying much of the momentum from his 10,000-foot freefall before the chute canopied. But he had avoided the larger rocks that would have broken a leg, or his back. Now, shielding his eyes against the descending sun, he estimated the time remaining before nightfall.

Two hours. Maybe less.

It would take another three hours to reach the mountain, five hours to climb to the tomb. He could reach it in early morning, if everything went well.

Gage pulled the straps of the backpack over his shoulders, hitched the waistbelt tight, then the sternum strap to hold the shoulder straps in place. Mentally he ran a final inventory: Hi-Power on his left ribs, three extra clips strapped to each ankle for a total of six reloads; MP5 inside the backpack with five extra clips; six antipersonnel grenades, two stun grenades. A pound of C-4 and three detonators were also in the black Lowe backpack. The knife, Dragon, was sheathed and duct-taped to his right thigh, the pocket of his pants cut out to allow quick retrieval of the weapon. The nightvisor, fully powered with two extra battery charges, was within easy reach inside the pack.

He wore heavy North Face mountaineering gear, and the internal frame pack held the gloves and facemask that he planned to use at higher altitudes. Crampons and a small ice-ax were strapped to the outside of the pack for easy accessibility, and a small medical kit was inside, with suture materials and adrenaline and morphine injections prepped. Also, he had packed an extra change of civilian clothes and boots, two extra pair of woolen socks, one day's worth of climbing food, and a pack of Energy bars.

Gage didn't plan to do any serious climbing, but he had prepared for it with a handful of pitons, carabiniers, chocks, and a 150-section of rappeling rope. If he was forced onto the rock face in a high-incline combat situation, at least he would be able to deal with it.

Famished and exhausted after the confrontation at the cabin, he had managed to eat two meals and snatch some sleep on the eight-hour flight, knowing he would need the energy. He had awakened one hour before the jump to complete a last-minute routine equipment inspection. And now the standard rules for covert operations blitzed through his mind, despite his will, training asserting itself.

Equipment. Take care of your equipment.

Gage shook his head; it was enough.

Focusing, he looked at the snow-cloaked mountain in the distance, a pale stark fear gripping him. Something told him that the odds were long, exceedingly long, that he could pull it off. He was in a bad zone, maybe the worst he had ever seen.

New York, at least, was fairly neutral territory, no clear advantages to either side. But this was their home ground. He had no support, no backup, no way for a quick extraction. He had no guarantee that Kertzman would even make it for the final showdown, no guarantee that he would be able to provide cover during the exchange. Already, the Pentagon cowboy might be neutralized by heavyweights in the State Department, or Justice. He might even be in jail. There was no way of knowing what had come out of the fiasco at the cabin.

Gage shook his head, tried not to think about it.

When Kertzman had insisted on coming along for the showdown, Gage had, at first, not even considered it. But now, alone in a foreign land after almost four years out of the flow, he wanted the backup, needed the backup. Now, he couldn't imagine going into the final conflict without Kertzman's presence.

Once more, he measured the distance to the mountain, as it laid by foot.

Long, he thought. At least 15 miles. And 15 miles in these mountains would seem like 50 in the flatlands.

But he had jumped as close to the mountain as the pilot could get without arousing attention. The last-minute flight plan carried him almost directly across Merano, where he bailed. Then the DC10 landed minutes later at Bolzano with its misdirected load of farming equipment. After refueling it would take off again for a layover in Germany. Gage would call when he needed a pickup, but there would be a two-hour delay.

He had never used this system before, but it was working beautifully. It cost him a fortune to put it in place, but he had done it, with money he took from a runaway program that was doomed from the very beginning to end in betrayal and scandal.

Gage had seen it from the first days, before he even signed on. Although he never anticipated that many of the missions would build an empire that he would one day attempt to destroy, he had always known that the program was too blacked-out for him to ever walk away from. He had discovered too much, questioned too much, and controlled too much for the Agency to let him go. Ever.

So he made plans, carefully and cunningly ferreting away a few hundred thousand here and there. And as the heat picked up and Iran-Contra began to get out of hand, tendrils of investigation spiraling everywhere, he discreetly liquified all of Black Light's assets in delayed closings, building himself a back door.

Then Israel. The last mission.

If it had waited two more weeks, he would have been gone. Vanished.

But it was too early to go under. The check-stops weren't yet in place. Loose ends still dangled that could lead to a thread of information, a number or name, which might lead to another, and then another. And then they would have found him.

And now it had all come home.

Gage gazed pensively across the sky, the mountain. The river cut across the landscape with a vivid blue sheen, electric within iridescent flame.

He frowned, staring, felt the moment inside him.

He had come so close to escaping. So close. And now he was inside it again, deeper than ever, battling the most powerful enemy he had ever faced. And the game was against him. But he would play it out to the end. Because he wasn't fighting for his country. There were no orders, no nations. Not this time. No, this time he was fighting for something more. Something that meant more.

They had called him here, he knew.

And he had answered them, descending the mountain to meet them in the desert, where the battle would be waged, the blood shed. And he knew, too, that life and death had brought him to this hour, to claim a freedom too long overdue. While deep in his soul, where desperate peace made war against guilt and regret, he knew it was finally time.

Time to put old ghosts to rest.

• • •

"I hope you slept well."

Stern poured Sarah a glass of wine.

Despite a dry, rasping thirst, Sarah ignored the wine, kept her gaze focused on Stern. They had moved to the central and largest room of the sprawling estate house. Through the large windows she could see well-kept grounds, grassy despite the cold, professionally manicured.

Carefully, she shifted her eyes about the room, attempting to analyze the decor. It was a combination of rich and finely crafted work, with a trace of American culture. But it wasn't American. It was European, decidedly European.

She couldn't discern the country. Maybe Italy, or Spain. It was difficult to decide because of the confusing mixture of color and tone.

She turned her mind away from it. For now, it was enough to know she was in Europe.

"Why am I here?" she asked coldly.

Stern smiled graciously. "For safekeeping, Ms. Halder."

Remote and intense, Sarah held him in a cold gaze. "You killed my father," she said.

Stern paused, stepped closer. "No, Ms. Halder. Your father is alive."

She had no reason to believe him. Her thirst was overwhelming now.

"What have you done to me?"

Lifting his eyebrows, Stern looked at her curiously. He set his wine glass down with a polished poise.

"Strange," he remarked casually, "that you would experience aftereffects from the medication. Perhaps it was the combination we were forced to utilize. But in any case, the physical sensations will wear off shortly, and then you will feel normal again."

Contempt controlled by a hard will passed beneath the mask of Sarah's face. Her voice was analytical, without emotion. "What did you give me?"

"Oh, a combination of various injections," Stern replied politely. "Nothing you would recognize." He shook his head, a condescending indulgence in his tone. "Certainly nothing you should be concerned about."

But Sarah *was* concerned. She remembered learning in nursing school about a drug that intelligence services used to coerce illegal confessions. "Was it Sodium Pentothal?"

Stern laughed. "Oh, no, Ms. Halder. Nothing so brutish as that. We are refined people. Sodium Pentothal is used by cretins of the CIA or KGB. We are beyond that."

He enjoyed his own amusement for a moment, folding his arms and staring placidly at her.

Sarah held her ground, refusing to react to either his amused manner, his courtesy, or his arrogance. She had asked a question. She let it stand.

Finally, Stern seemed affected by her coldness. "If you must know," he said, "you were given approximately 130 CCs of Dipravan by intravenous drip. But you refused to speak. So we were forced to inject a rather heavy dosage of Ketamine with Valium. And, interestingly enough, you still refused to speak. In fact, you became somewhat, ah, how shall I say, *hostile*." He chuckled. "You are quite a fighter, Ms. Halder. Very strong. Even when sedated."

He paused, as if remembering. "I must admit that I have never beheld such a rigid and unyielding unconscious will. But in the end, after we injected you with a near lethal dosage of Amidate, you did, indeed, begin to crumble. And you told us all that you knew."

Sarah blinked, expressionless.

"I suppose," Stern continued passively, "that any physical discomfort you feel is from your physical attacks, your wrestling against the restraints. Usually there are no side effects from the medications. That is why we use Amidate. But, then again, it is rare that we use it in such an overpowering, continuous dosage. So I was not certain as to what to expect. In any case it was, unfortunately, a necessity. And in the end, somewhat dangerous. You would have reached unconsciousness, but we administered an amphetamine line to keep you lucid enough to continue speaking."

Sarah's mouth was a grim line, her eyes glistening with pale green ice, and she suddenly seemed to grow more distant from the man in front of her. Her hands were empty, her stance relaxed, and she held Stern in a calculating, despising gaze. A wave of emotions flooded through her, hating and degrading, but she shut them down, one by one, until she felt nothing.

Imposing, Stern stepped closer. "It shall all be over quickly, Ms. Halder. The situation is beyond us, really. We are mere players in this drama, and we only act our roles."

Her eyes blinked once, slowly. She looked through him. "Why don't you just kill me?"

Stern laughed, motioned for her to recline on an opulent, dark green couch. But she ignored the gesture, and he shook his head, revealing his disappointment.

"Ms. Halder," he said, with a faint trace of embarrassment, "do not force me to be . . . indelicate. We are both inured to this situation. There is no need for unseemly or contemptible behavior."

Abruptly, Sarah smiled. "Give me a baseball bat, Stern, and I'll show you unseemly."

Shocked, Stern regarded her with a suddenly chilling presence. "I see that you have no superior poise within you," he said slowly, advancing steadily. "No presence of mind to behave with the courtesy often reserved for these situations by people of character. So I shall treat you as one of the inferior minions that you truly are."

Shifting her eyes, Sarah searched for a weapon.

"There is no escape, Ms. Halder." He halted a short space from her and clasped his hands with quiet dignity behind his back. "You shall remain here until we find the manuscript. If Gage reaches it first, you shall be our guarantee that he delivers it to us. That is the reason I have allowed you to live until now. There is no other."

It took iron control for Sarah to continue her composure. *Gage is alive*, she thought. *He's alive!*

"And," continued Stern, "to be brutally honest, I confess that I reserve no compassion for either you or your father. By your own decision you entered a world where you did not belong, a world that is ruled by men of far greater faculties." He tilted his head, as if discerning her terrible imperfections. "Also, I am inclined to warn you not to attempt an escape. You will be severely pained by the experience."

A contemptible smile touched Sarah's face. "You can't stop him," she said quietly.

Anger suddenly masked Stern's lean face, but a disciplined, professional control instantly overcame it. Yet the emotional content of his stance intensified his presence, making him seem both more remote and more threatening in the same moment.

"But I *have* stopped him, Ms. Halder," he said severely. "I have stopped him many times. And now Gage is completely alone, and, as the cliché says so perfectly, a man alone is easy prey. He has no one to fight beside him. Even Kertzman, the consummate hunter, is deluged in Washington amid cries of scandal." He paused, raising empty hands in a mocking, searching movement. "Now there is only Gage. A single, desperate man waging a private war against a monolithic force he cannot even begin to understand. Tragic, is it not?"

"Not as tragic as it's going to be," said Sarah. "For you."

Silence between them.

"You have sublime hopes, Ms. Halder," Stern said, his gaze unfriendly. "To be sure, Gage is an exceptional man. Your nation trained him well, sparing no expense. But it is too late. We know where the manuscript is buried."

Sarah searched his face.

Stern laughed. "Allow me to hazard a guess," he said with a benign smile. "The tomb of Santacroce?" He laughed again. "Well, now the dance is almost over. Soon we will have the book, and then the end game shall begin."

"And then you'll kill me."

"Oh, no, Ms. Halder," Stern replied. "Order must be maintained. First, we will tell Gage where you are imprisoned. You see, it is much easier to trap someone than it is to hunt them. We will wait until he comes for you. Then we will kill him. Only then will we kill you."

A cryptic silence.

"Do not be mistaken, Ms. Halder. Gage will die, just as you will die. You see, I understand him, and I know that he will be defeated because he is doomed to be defeated. He is doomed to die in the metaphorical black void from which he crawled, and from which there has never been any escape for him. It is his destiny, you see, to die as he has lived, fighting in the shadows, lost in the darkness of unseen wars, surviving like a wild beast within a sanctioned secrecy that is both his punishment and his reward.

"Yes, I know him well. Gage is an animal, Ms. Halder. He is a man utterly controlled by his base nature. Whether his motivation is revenge or guilt or love makes no difference to me. I do not even care if his motivation is to find redemption, or penance, as someone suggested to me. I am only certain that he is not a superior man. He is weak with sentimental emotion and foolishly trapped by an archaic moral standard for right and wrong that should have been abolished from the world centuries ago. It is obsolete. And his devotion to it shall, quite frankly, be his undoing."

In rigid silence Sarah listened, and when Stern finished speaking, she waited. Then, from high inside her being, she felt something coming to her heart, demanding voice.

"No," she said, "you don't understand Gage at all, Stern. If you did you'd be far more afraid than you are. It's not revenge he's after. It's not...*penance.* It's more. Much more. And it's beyond you. Beyond all of you. And there's nothing you can do to stop it."

"Are you Kertzman?"

Kertzman turned, fixed bloodshot eyes on a familiar, gray-black rectangular FBI identification. He looked at the man who held it. Sullen, he nodded.

"I'm Special Agent William Acklin." The man folded the ID with a practiced, gentle gesture and slipped it back into the side pocket of his dark blue coat. "I'm out of the Washington office."

Kertzman didn't bother identifying the clothing. Even at first glance, it was obviously a mid-range department store off-the-rack coat and slacks. Nothing special. A working man's suit. He focused on the man.

William Acklin was six inches shorter and a good 80 pounds lighter than Kertzman. He had a broad, long face with a high forehead and light brown, short wavy hair. His large, blue-gray eyes were open and honest. He smiled nervously at Kertzman, seeming to notice the huge bandage wrapped around Kertzman's right forearm that left only the hand and upper arm visible. Acklin glanced down at the arm, said nothing for a minute.

"Well?" said Kertzman harshly, focusing at him. "What is it?"

"Uh, well," Acklin began, shuffling, a serious tone to his voice, "I probably need to talk to you, Mr. Kertzman." He hesitated, seemingly embarrassed. "You know, the use of force investigation is underway. A hearing will be scheduled. That's just standard procedure. But we do need to talk, I believe."

Kertzman nodded, irritated. "Yeah, yeah, well talk already," he said. "I been listening to talk all night. I been attacked by every Bureau guy in Washington and New York. Even Justice has gotten in on the act. What do you have to add?"

"Well," Acklin began, "I've read the reports and all."

"Is that so?" Kertzman asked abruptly.

"Yes, sir," Acklin continued. "But I've verified some things, based on the statements given to you by Malachi Halder and Jonathan Gage, that I think you need to know about."

Acklin shifted a little, gazed up at Kertzman with a suddenly even, gentle eye.

Kertzman returned the look, strangely disturbed. He sensed that something about the quiet little man should be feared and profoundly respected, though he couldn't place what it was. Acklin wasn't, by any means, an intimidating person. But something lent the FBI man an almost invisible air of profound authority. He felt that, beneath the surface, Acklin was a whole lot tougher than he seemed to be.

Kertzman reached into his shirt pocket, removed a pack of Marlboros. Nodded. "So ask," he said, lighting one.

Until last night Kertzman hadn't smoked in ten years. But with state, local, and federal law enforcement cars backed up to the cabin for three miles, with confused ambulance attendants and dead bodies and the collective crimes of a massive conspiracy coming down on his head, Kertzman decided to buy a pack off a young New York Trooper. He had smoked them through the hard ordeal of questions and more questions, through veiled accusations of incompetent procedural methods that went way beyond veiled and, even, legal, and finally through two extremely tense question-and-stare matches with a senior agent of the New York State FBI Office.

Stubbornly, Kertzman had covered his own ground from first to last, going toe to toe in nerve-racking verbal battles with every heavyweight that came onto the scene, gruffly defending himself while simultaneously protecting everyone who was, at least, *mostly* innocent. But it was difficult, with endless interpretations of possible crimes and thoroughly comprehensive government policies crisscrossing before him, to lay a convoluted minefield; he negotiated with the most extreme care.

He had almost escaped responsibility for causing the shootout. But in the bitter end, jurisdictional disputes, chaos, and the lack of someone to truly accuse caused the heat to come back to him, by default. It helped to have the dead Nigerian to blame, but he wasn't enough. The State Department didn't want a foot soldier. They wanted a name that could take the fall for a conspiracy that had appallingly emerged into the daylight. And neither Milburn or Radford was significant enough. It had to be somebody bigger.

Like Kertzman himself. But Kertzman wasn't about to let that fly. He stopped it point-blank, threatening anyone who threatened him until the insinuation was choked out by intimidation. Still, the government wanted to put a lid on this, and they wanted someone to sacrifice, someone they could slay as a blood-offering on the altar of public consumption.

Carthwright was big enough, had the weight, but no one was willing to actually *accuse* him of anything. He was too big a name.

It was inferred by a nebulous FBI official that, since Milburn and Radford were on loan from the NSA, under Carthwright's control, they could have been following orders from Carthwright to kill the hostages. But, in all fairness, Kertzman had no genuine proof that Carthwright was guilty of orchestrating the plot to have him killed at the cabin. It seemed likely, yes, but that could also be a red herring, as Stephenson would say. And testimony to back up the theory would be a problem, especially with Milburn dead and Radford missing. Kertzman realized that all he had were his instincts, a cold track. And it was hard concentrating on that aspect of the case amidst the heat descending on his head for the fiasco of the shootout itself.

Criticisms were endless. He should have notified Special Response if he thought the situation might go tactical. He should have, at least, called for backup agents to monitor the situation. He should not have endangered the lives of Professor Halder and his daughter with reckless behavior. It went on and on.

Kertzman refused to back up. He'd done what he'd done, stood behind it. It hadn't ended well, but that wasn't his fault, and it was over now, as far as he was concerned. The only remaining question was whether Carthwright would back him because the NSA supervisor was still in charge of the investigation. Deep inside, Kertzman had no idea whether he would or not. It was still too early to tell. In any case, it was a mess, and the Bureau didn't want any details of it leaking out, especially not names.

Recalling the Bureau's takeover of the scene, Kertzman reluctantly gave credit where credit was due. Yeah, they had cut off all official lines on the situation. But, for the most part, it was a futile gesture. The locals already had part of it; they were the first on the scene, knew basically what had happened, who was involved, the rest. By noon of the next day, Friday, news broadcasts were uncovering some of the details, verified through reliable and "anonymous" law enforcement personnel. Special reports were shown in hourly intervals, adding a higher strain of tension to an already tense situation. With each announcement or investigatory report, more pressure came from the top to find someone to blame.

Kertzman understood the process. It wouldn't end until guilt descended on an appropriate name. Then the papers would print, a quick conviction would punish the guilty, and those who had covered themselves well enough could resume their well-protected, golden careers.

Everything that Kertzman had documented, every statement by Admiral Talbot, Carthwright, Radford, and Milburn were included in the official reports. And the statements did, indeed, make Carthwright look bad. In fact, it looked like the NSA man was covering for someone within the Agency, or covering himself. Still, though, no one had made a move against him. Not yet. And no one *would* make a move until they possessed ten times more evidence than they needed.

Kertzman didn't regret filing any of the reports. So far, the statements were all that protected him. If certain unknowns in the Bureau were allowed their free will, Kertzman would have already been charged for a mixture of profound policy violations and a combination of federal crimes from abuse of process to illegal search to felonious misuse of governmental authority. As it was, according to policy, he was supposed to be suspended from duty pending an investigation by the FBI's Shooting Review Board. But that, too, was delayed in light of the more complicated aspects of the situation that went beyond law enforcement and into national security.

Kertzman had laughed at that; national security concerns could override anything.

But Kertzman sensed that there was some kind of reluctance to drop a full measure of governmental wrath on his head. He sensed that a major player was covering him, defending him. Maybe it was Carthwright. Kertzman couldn't be sure. But he wanted to find out.

One thing was certain; he needed to put this thing to bed as quickly as possible because he still had a flight to catch.

Kertzman grunted, blew out a stream of smoke, focused on Acklin. "I'm waiting, Acklin. Talk."

The FBI man stepped forward, a submissive gesture. "Well, it seems, Mr. Kertzman, that you still have much to do."

A pause.

"What does that mean?" Kertzman grumbled. "Right now I've got FBI yahoos telling me I ought to be in jail for the way everything went down."

Acklin nodded, polite. "Yes, yes, I see. But I wouldn't pay much attention to them, Mr. Kertzman. Mr. Carthwright is completely backing you up at Justice. He said you had his full authorization to do whatever you felt the situation required. He said that he believes all your accusations against Milburn and Radford are true. He says that he believes they did, indeed, commit the crimes. And he told Justice that if they wish to place the blame on someone, they can place it on him. No one is willing to do that."

This was truly amazing. It took Kertzman a second to absorb it. Acklin stood in polite silence.

So it *had* been Carthwright. Covered him solid.

"When did Carthwright back me?" Kertzman asked after a moment.

"Since it began, I believe," Acklin responded. "I suppose, too, that Justice was somewhat, uh, alarmed by what I told them."

A moment of curious silence.

Kertzman almost smiled. This was getting more interesting by the second. Things were shaking loose all over the place. Never any telling what a good hair-raising shootout can do for a government investigation.

"And what did you tell them?" he asked.

"Uh, well, I read the full reports when they were faxed in this morning. I work in the Washington office—"

"Yeah you told me that."

"Yes, anyway, Mr. Kertzman, I began looking into the angle of someone profiteering from the actions of Black Light, as you alleged in your reports. And I discovered a few things. So this morning I called Justice and told them that I had incontrovertible evidence that an element inside the CIA was guilty of violating National Security Intelligence Directive Seven, concerning the Agency's right to conduct certain covert affairs on American soil. And these persons, these high-ranking persons, have, uh, also probably violated National Security Intelligence Directive Ten, which regulates the authority of the Agency to participate in money-making enterprises which cause a prejudiced financial profit for select civilians."

Kertzman's cigarette hung forgotten in his hand. He stared at Acklin.

"So, Mr. Kertzman, I also told them that senior officials were implicated in the . . . uh, scandal, I called it. And I told them that you have evidence and knowledge of the situation which might prevent untoward embarrassment to the President of the United States and Congress . . ."

Acklin paused, as if considering. Kertzman tried to recover, tried to hide his amazement. He nodded.

Finally, the FBI agent finished. "Oh," Acklin added in a kindly voice, "I told them that a, um, Bay of Pigs-type, uh, debacle, I called it, might be prevented by keeping you on the investigation for a few days."

Kertzman waited a moment, then laughed out loud in a sudden, uncontrollable burst of humor. His prizefighter face split in a mean-looking smile.

"Just who are you, Acklin?"

Acklin smiled. "Oh, no one special, Mr. Kertzman," he continued humbly. "But, for some reason, the Washington office received full reports on last night's incident, addressed to my attention. I read your background reports and the incident cases from the shooting and took it upon myself to begin checking computers for information that might verify allegations that Black Light was used for profit-making.

"I want you to know, Mr. Kertzman, that this wasn't originally my case. I'm not sure why I received copies of the report. But when I investigated your allegations earlier today and found some things in the computer to back it all up, I was allowed, so to speak, into the situation."

"And who allowed you?" Kertzman asked, suddenly more serious.

Acklin nodded. "Why, Mr. Carthwright allowed me in," he said, pausing. "He was reluctant, I might add. He said to stay clear of pursuing the gold allegations. He still believes the case should focus on a rogue element of the government trying to control foreign policy through Black Light. He believes, I think, that the angle of profiteering is unsubstantiated. But he did, in any case, allow me into the operation to assist you. You need an assistant, anyway, Mr. Kertzman, now that Radford and Milburn are gone."

Kertzman made a mental note to call Carthwright as soon as Acklin left. He squinted through a long, silent, studied drag on his cigarette. Then he released it in a meditative calm, patiently watching the FBI man.

"I appreciate what you've done, son," he continued, purposefully and plainly respectful. "I've needed a little help. Tell me what you found on the angle of the gold."

"Oh, I didn't really find solid evidence to link Black Light's official operations to the deaths," Acklin added, shuffling. "That's why Mr. Carthwright told me to ignore it. But there is considerable *circumstantial* evidence to support the gold theory. And if Gage is still alive, and willing to verify my theory with his testimony, we might be able to find the guilty party behind all of this, bring indictments. Immunity has been offered to Gage, if he will come in and testify."

Smoke from the Marlboro hovered in the still air, half-masking Kertzman's narrowed gaze. "I'll bet that took some doin'," he mumbled.

Acklin nodded. "Yes, sir, it did. Justice wasn't cooperative. But Mr. Carthwright was adamant about granting the immunity. He has some influence, you know. And he is eager to see the case brought to an end."

Kertzman blinked, silent for a moment. He was trying to follow Acklin, but he was tired, not catching every detail. The sudden appearance of a front-line guy who was actually fighting for him had relieved some of the electric tension that had kept him wired and awake. Through eyes burning in fatigue, he focused again on Acklin.

"Alright," he began, clearing his throat. "Tell me more about what you've got."

Acklin produced a folded sheet of paper from his coat. "Yes, sir," Acklin said quickly, stepping forward, handing it humbly to Kertzman.

Kertzman opened it, read a list of names. Some he recognized as major financial movers in America. A lot of the names were foreign. He didn't know them.

"What's this?" he asked gruffly, exhaling a long stream of smoke from the Marlboro.

"A list of dead men, sir," Acklin continued. "Those are persons who died at time periods and in certain cities where Black Light was assigned an operation."

Something hit Kertzman on that. But because he was so exhausted he had to think about it for a moment. Finally it came to him.

"And how were you able to pinpoint exactly where Black Light operated and when? If they doctored the records, the paperwork, how can you be sure of where they were?"

Acklin seemed pleased with himself. "Well, actually, sir, a computer printout of military and civilian travel logs also arrived on my desk this morning, with a cover letter explaining which flights were used by Black Light, and the means of verifying. It appears that the printout is a legitimate travel record of the unit. I'm using it to draw the timetable, to link Black Light with probable covert operations. But we'll need Gage to confirm."

Kertzman didn't like it. "And you don't know where this package came from?"

"No, sir." Acklin shook his head. "The papers were sanitized, no headings."

"How did you get incident reports of what happened at the cabin?"

"They were faxed to me from the White House, sir."

Not good, thought Kertzman. But he couldn't figure it. Who was Acklin that he would receive this package of reports? Who had sent it to him? It didn't make sense, but it *appeared* to be Kertzman's good fortune because Acklin may have actually run something to ground. Still, though, it bothered him. But after a moment he decided to leave it alone. Come back to it later.

He studied the list. "Black Light was busy," he said dully.

"Yes, sir," Acklin continued. "I'm beginning to build a scenario over the financial institutions that were affected by their activities."

Kertzman nodded, still studying the list. "How are you linking the travel schedule to probable hits?"

"By computer, sir," Acklin replied humbly. "I wrote a program to do the searching and compiling for me and then I released it into the system through the CIA Cray linkup. The Cray pretty much has access to everything: obituaries, newspaper articles, television broadcasts, financial reports, gold transfers, and takeovers. Mr. Carthwright gave me permission to use it. All I had to do was give it the commands." He nodded at the paper. "By tomorrow we should have a list of suspect organizations that profited directly from Black Light's probable sanctions."

Kertzman nodded, stared at the list.

Acklin continued eagerly. "You see, it appears that Black Light was a type of rogue military adventure against the American civilian sector, and the entire world, for that matter. This is a list of wealthy individuals whose empires were, upon their deaths, basically absorbed by an unidentifiable organization. I can't place, yet, who is behind the organization. But I will. For the time being let's just call it 'Company A.'"

Kertzman nodded, sighing. His bandaged right forearm throbbed. The medication he'd taken earlier in the day was wearing off.

Acklin, the computer wizard, didn't seem to notice his discomfort.

"My theory is that 'Company A' was built from Black Light's activities by using assassination to disintegrate existing financial empires, and then using different agencies working for 'Company A' to control the pieces of the former organization."

Gazing dully through a spiral of smoke, Kertzman mumbled, "And how did they do that? How do you control a company by killing somebody?"

"Well," Acklin answered quickly, eagerly, "'Company A' would buy heavily into a financial empire and when individuals, who happened to hold a majority interest were, uh, *sanctioned*, 'Company A' would automatically assume a controlling share. Naturally there would be a redistribution of the deceased's wealth among others. But it would be in smaller shares and therefore less influential. Also, we must remember that financial power, like anything else in life, Mr. Kertzman, is often an extension of personality. With a certain strong personality gone, it was much easier for 'Company A' to gain control over the respective company."

A hesitant step, and Acklin stood closer. He held Kertzman with an honest gaze.

"Death, Mr. Kertzman, is how this empire did business. Assassination, in a sense, was an essential element of the takeover. This empire could not have been created without it." He paused. "Gage has committed grave crimes, it's true. But he was also operating under the auspices of someone inside this government who passed the orders down to Black Light. He was an arm of our secret military, obeying orders as he was trained to obey orders. Until he refused, of course, as your report indicated. Then someone attempted to kill him and the other members of Black Light. And now it is clear that Gage has turned against his former supervisors. Which provides us the perfect opportunity to bring this situation into court and punish the guilty. But we must succeed in bringing Gage in for testimony."

Kertzman sat back, face expressionless, eyes dead to the world. He rubbed his forearm on his thigh. The incision, closed with 35 sutures, was beginning to ache.

Acklin continued, "This, at least, is what the circumstantial evidence suggests to me. I admit it is a complicated theory."

Kertzman roused himself. "Who inside the government profited?"

"I don't know, yet." Acklin stepped to one side. He was almost nervous, but not quite, and Kertzman began to perceive that the FBI agent's passive presence was the cloak for something more. "I am still tracing the gold trail back through holding companies, trust funds, corporations and such. Whoever did this is an expert at laundering and hiding money. Like I said, it may take another two or three days."

"Do you think you'll have enough for a conviction?"

Acklin shook his head solidly. "Not without Gage."

"Why?"

"Because we must first prove that Black Light *did* indeed commit these sanctions. That will require Gage's honest and complete testimony. Without that, we have nothing but conjecture."

Kertzman flicked ashes from the Marlboro to the tile floor. "Are there any more surviving members of Black Light?"

"No. Gage is the only survivor. Wilfred Chavez, the Hispanic-American who died at Gage's cabin, and Pearson Thomas, who you knew as Sandman, were the other survivors. Only Gage remains."

Kertzman understood. "I like the idea. I think you've got something." He nodded. "You're on the team. I'll tell Carthwright to give you clearance." A pause. "What's the word on Radford?"

"We haven't located him, yet. The Soviets deny they have him. Which, of course, makes everyone believe they do. But I can't tell you any more than that."

Kertzman laughed brutally. "Alright," he added, a wave of weariness in his voice. "We'll find him. Sooner or later. So what's next? You seem to have given this a lot of thought."

Acklin bowed slightly as he continued, held his hands clasped. "Well," he began, "Ms. Halder is obviously missing, and the Bureau is working the situation as a legitimate kidnapping—"

"They *should*," Kertzman broke in, angry.

"Yes, sir," Acklin continued, unperturbed, "I made that clear. Now, Mr. Carthwright has allowed me to work for you, and though he's told me to ignore the gold theory, I believe it should be pursued. So I suggest that I pursue the gold through the computers while you attempt to find both Ms. Halder and Gage."

Grunting, Kertzman nodded.

Acklin shuffled, spoke again. "In all candor, Mr. Kertzman, I do hope you can bring Gage in. If he doesn't testify, we'll never get convictions for whoever was responsible for Black Light."

Kertzman drew a deep, long drag on the Marlboro, released it, searched Acklin's eyes. "I'm going to do what I can," he said. "But Ms. Halder is my top priority right now."

Gravely serious and unblinking, Acklin continued. "Yes, sir, I understand. She is everyone's priority. But I believe if you find Gage, you will find her. I understand, after talking with Professor Halder and Mr. O'Henry, that she and Gage were rather close. So I'm certain he will go after her. On his own."

Kertzman nodded, eyes dull with pain. "Yeah, that's a safe bet," he responded quietly. "If I find him, I'll probably find her."

Acklin was silent, then, "I suppose that, when you decide to go after him, you would prefer to work alone."

Calculating, Kertzman watched. Then he nodded curtly, but with a gentle respect.

He liked Acklin, but he wouldn't take him along, not on this. Because this really wasn't about business, and it would probably end as badly as any situation could. Kertzman had no doubt that it was his last assignment. Nobody could work again after something like this. Acklin didn't need to be in any deeper than he was.

Acklin followed Kertzman's nod, and his blue-gray eyes were suddenly keen. "Yes, sir, I understand. I think that it's good for you to work alone." He paused, searching for words. "Too many people can complicate things, Mr. Kertzman," he continued, after a moment. "Sometimes... it can be hard to know who to trust. The secret behind these tactical operations is to always... keep it simple."

That phrase. *Keep it simple.*

Kertzman's hunting eyes glinted, suddenly tense and still. He gazed down at the smaller man. "Yeah," he rumbled slowly. "I heard that phrase before. Keep it simple. Reminds me of somebody else I know."

Acklin didn't move. A faint smile seemed to come to him slowly. "Yes, sir," he added politely, openly. "That's an old phrase that we used in the 10th Special Forces." He waited. "Keep it simple. Always keep it simple. Then there's not much that can go wrong."

Kertzman nodded slowly, understanding now, why Acklin was so willing to help Gage, knowing it in his gut, where it really mattered.

"That's funny," he said dully. "Gage was in the 10th."

"Yes sir. The 10th back in '80 was a tight outfit. We had unit integrity, loyalty. I guess we still do."

Cold.

Ice in freezing wind enveloped him, sheathing him in glistening clear rivulets that cracked and splintered with every movement.

Wind gusted, howled.

Gage shivered, tried to relax, resisting the impulse to fight the trembling. He knew that if he stiffened up he would use more energy, only get colder, so he breathed deeply, tried to control his physical reaction to his surroundings with his mind.

Crouching on a slanting, icy boulder, hidden by the shadow of a deep overhang, he studied the path before him.

Marked by a single, deeply carved obelisk that indicated a neglected graveyard, the path descended from the main road into a narrow cleft, a jagged crevice not more than 400 feet long and steep on both sides with freezing black cliffs.

Gage had half-suspected that the initial trail over the mountains was one of the forgotten trade roads used in ancient times for hauling cargo to the Valley of Po, primarily used now for hiking. He was right. It was an easy climb to 5,000 feet, a wide and well-used walking trial. He had quickly located the thin path to the tomb; it angled right, a short descent that led to the ancient family crypt of Santacroce.

Focusing, Gage switched on the nightvisor.

In the generous illumination of amplified moonlight, he gazed down the trail and into the relative darkness. The overgrown path ended at a large tomb, a darkened door with a single narrow column on either side.

He expelled a long breath through his black face mask. Then he turned his head, his mind calculating an approach to the tomb while his eyes searched the distant road behind him for the faintest betrayal of man-made light, or movement, in the distance.

His senses reached out around him, feeling the night and cold, open to any shift of wind, any distant sound or the faintest noise. It was a trained effort to let his animal instincts loose, to allow the lower mind, the sharper mind, to guide and direct. This instinctive power was almost lost to civilized man, but during the years of brutal conditioning in jungles and mountains, Gage had learned to resurrect it or die.

After being beaten by the Japanese in New York he had realized fear, simple and pure. And it had crippled him, in a sense. But from experience he knew that enough time in combat, with enough fear and enough pain, could cripple anyone. Only those who were never alone in the black cold night could say they were never afraid of the dark.

But he had come through it. No, he was not the same as when he went into it, but he had endured the worst, waited until his mind had returned. Then when Sarah was taken, it moved him the final step, back to the fight.

Nothing could explain it.

It was simply a phenomenon of action, a phenomenon that he didn't understand himself, and he didn't try. He had come through it, and that was enough. To go back and look at it would only resurrect it. And for now, he had a job to do.

Crouching, cold wind moving over him, Gage felt the night.

Howling winter.

Ice and snow and dark.

Predators, hunting him in black winds, death.

Home.

Eyes glinting in the moonlight, he felt everything alive within him, flowing together. There was no wasted movement, no pause. In his mind and heart, thought and action were one; a pure and primal state of being.

Face in shadow, Gage laughed.

He was back.

In darkness he poised on the rock, deathly silent and still, listening, watching, open to everything. But the night was quiet and close.

Turning his head, he gazed carefully into the distance, down the road he had ascended. He knew that, soon, they would be coming, might be already on the road. Probably, it would be Sato and Carl. But it might be more.

Or, then again, they might have already been here and gone, leaving behind a careful trap.

Turning his head back to the path, Gage released one hand from the suppressed MP5 slung across his chest, switched the nightvisor to thermal imaging.

On the inside of the screen, the readout indicated a starlight luminosity of fifty-four percent. But the heat imaging index was flat and unresponsive, registering nothing, reading nothing but cold.

The thermal imager could detect residual body heat down to one degree Fahrenheit. Under proper conditions it could even find the heated imprint of a human hand on a claymore or a granite wall. Sometimes, in the past, he had used residual heat to identify tripwires and bombs that couldn't be seen by simple luminosity.

Residual imprints left behind in this weather wouldn't last long, not on cold steel nearly frozen by the icy wind and sleet. It was unreliable. He would have to use another tactic.

Carefully, silently, Gage eased down from the rock, holding the weight of the MP5 primarily by the sling draped over his shoulder, pointing it with his left hand, descending to the trail. He moved slowly forward, eyes focused slightly in front of his feet. He kept far to the side of the path, his back to the wall with his right hand down at his side, palm facing back.

In this manner he could slide forward, step by silent step, presenting only a side view of his body. And, without looking, he could stay close to the rock by the feel of his gloved palm touching the wall, positioning him automatically at the edge of the path. Meanwhile his eyes constantly searched the ground at his feet for where a tripwire might be tied off.

Steadily, he moved forward.

It was far easier to detect a tripwire where it was tied off than across the path itself. His eyes stayed locked on the trail at his feet, always searching. Occasionally, he glanced up, searching the walls for a sniper. It was unlikely that a sniper could lay in that cold for any length of time, waiting for a shot. In this weather it was a reluctant method for ambush. Still, by habit, he looked up anyway, covering everything, leaving nothing unexplored.

He remembered the words of an old sergeant...

"Soldiers never look up. They never look up and that's what gets them killed. In 'Nam they would hang the claymores in trees, wipe out an entire platoon. Always do what ain't natural, son. Always do what ain't natural."

Gage continued forward. As he glanced up he saw that the walls were steeper, smoothed from long erosion by water, sheathed in ice. Impossible to climb.

The narrow, treacherous path would probably be the only way into the crypt. And, by the looks of the steep and icy condition of the walls, the only way out.

Beneath his black face mask, he frowned. *Not good.* He could be trapped in here too easily.

Slowly, slowly, he moved down the path, poised with the MP5, occasionally holding in place to look steadily ahead, or above, scanning the shadows with a combination of nightvision and thermal imaging. But he saw nothing. Finally, after 100 careful steps, he stood before the tomb.

Silently he crouched, holding a steady position ten feet from the entrance.

Darkened, the doorway was open. Gage tried to penetrate the corporeal shadows with the visor, but even the luminosity imaging couldn't see where there was no light at all. He narrowed his eyes, peering, but nothing was visible. He slid silently forward, removing a maglight from a sidepocket of the Lowe backpack. Then he took off the visor, turning on the flashlight.

Immediately the steps of the crypt, slate gray in dusty granite, were visible before him, angling downward to dissolve in a smooth gray granite floor. But, while the interior of the chamber appeared smoothly chiseled, the tunnel walls leading down were jagged and uncut, pitted with dozens of impenetrable, deep shadows.

Peering, Gage searched the dust on the steps, found no sign of tracks. There was some slight disturbance, perhaps three or four weeks old, but none since then.

Movement!

Gage whirled and lifted the MP5.

A thin tangle of dry weeds blew across the path behind him, tumbling.

A tense breath escaped. Breathing hard, he poised, searching the shadows.

He had automatically thrown down the safety of the weapon, his finger tightening on the trigger. He scanned left and right, searching with the flashlight.

Nothing.

He felt the panicky urge to rush into the tomb, get the book, and be gone.

He grimaced. *Patience, boy!*

"Take it easy," Gage whispered to himself. "Don't get spooked ...Don't let 'em rush you...Be cool...Be cool...Do it right."

He turned back to the entrance, dropping the MP5 on the sling. Then he reached out and snatched up a single, long dry weed from beside the open portal. With a quick twist he broke it off near the ground, leaving a two-foot section in his hand.

Carefully, he eased down the steps, gently and slowly sweeping the weed in front of him, downward, up, downward, watching to see if the thin reed hit the tripwire of a trap not visible to the light. He held the light in one hand, the weed in the other.

It grew colder as he descended into the tomb. But it was a still, unnatural coldness, unlike the night cold of the air outside that moved and swept over him in dark gusting winds. No, the tomb held a coldness that hung, solid, in the air, deathlike and disturbing with an unearthly, somber sensation.

He moved forward, step by step, crouching, sweeping gently with the weed while using the maglight to illuminate more and more of the tomb as he descended. In moments he was in the mausoleum, gazing at the carefully sealed graves.

Staring about in the shadow and narrow light, he saw that the underground chamber was at least 100 feet long with the oldest, largest tomb centered at the opposite end, its marble slab slightly askew.

Still searching the floor with the weed, he moved slowly forward until he stood before it. He reached out with a gloved hand, pulling the loosened marble slab aside. The icy stone moved slowly, creakily, grinding marble against the rough cut granite of the wall. As the grave opened itself to him he found, finally, the horror he had sought.

Gage's face was solid in a frowning mask, and his cold eyes narrowed, menacing and measured, staring into the crypt.

Darkness in skeletal bones, it was there; a thick and dusty dry manuscript hauntingly clutched in spidery white arms beneath a grinning skull dead to the Earth for 500 years.

• • •

"May I provide you with anything?"

Sarah ignored the polite tone, continued to gaze remotely out the window of the mansion. The sun had descended quickly, too quickly, suggesting mountains. But she had no clear view from the window, couldn't be certain.

Slowly, she took another sip of tea. She had made it herself in the kitchen, a kitchen conspicuously devoid of knives and cutting utensils.

Gradually her thirst was satisfied, but as the dullness in her joints worked out she had become aware of a painful hunger. She tried to ignore the sensation, following some primitive instinct to remain independent.

Stern attempted to be gracious. "Are you certain that I cannot bring you something? You must be famished."

Sarah laughed in hostile amusement. "You sure are polite, Stern."

"Oh, yes," he responded. "Certainly, there is no need to be uncivil. What must be done will be done. That is beyond us. But we should try and remain decently disposed until such a time, don't you agree?"

Sarah took another sip of tea. "No. I don't agree."

He received her comment with an interested, studious expression, sat down at the opposite end of the table, holding a cup of tea that he had made for himself.

Sarah watched him stir the tea, moving the water gently with a silver spoon of obvious value. It was amazing, she thought, how much wealth was evident in the furnishings of this residence. But the house didn't appear to be anyone's home. It was simply a house, a place for business. But without asking she knew the structure was inescapable. The windows and doors had complicated electronic devices that substituted for normal locks. And the windows seemed thicker, double paneled, like those on airplanes.

Finally she spoke, an indifferent tone. "So did your people run Black Light, too?"

He laughed. "Black Light? I don't understand."

Sarah smiled bitterly and closed her eyes, leaning her head back against the wooden chair. She shut her eyes tighter, concentrating. A strange expression rose in her face, released from somewhere deep inside, ascending, transforming her features gradually from pain to anger to a bitter and powerful resolution.

She spoke quietly. "Tell me what you believe, Stern."

He raised his gaze to her, released a tired sigh, questioning.

"Go ahead," she continued, a faint bitter edge to her voice. "I want to know. I'm curious."

Stern stirred his tea. He retained an amused and superior smile, condescending and indulgent.

"What I believe is what I believe, Ms. Halder. I do not think that it would hold much interest for you."

Sarah opened her eyes, focused on him completely. "Oh, I'd find it interesting. Believe me. Because I think you're a fool. And you're too old to be a fool. You should be a wise man, Stern. You should be a teacher. But you've wasted your life believing lies, ridiculous philosophy. Stupidity. And life is too short for that. Life is too short to know anything but the truth."

He seemed amused by her taunt, still reluctant to talk but curious despite himself. "And you presume to know the truth, Ms. Halder?"

Eyes steady, Sarah nodded. "A little."

Stern nodded politely, looked at his tea. "Beliefs are not a subject for polite conversation, Ms. Halder. And I reluctantly perceive that you are already skeptical of my moral and judgmental qualities, so obviously you have quantified my beliefs as an aberration."

"No," said Sarah, in a strange tone. "I'm willing to hear any argument."

He laughed. "Except that I will not argue with you, Ms. Halder. I believe as I believe. That is that. And, I might add, I am a soldier. So I will do as I must do. Life is not a simple journey of beliefs, Ms. Halder. It is a struggle for survival."

She stared again out the window, holding a mocking smile.

Stern laid one arm, relaxed, across the table, watching her. After a moment, however, he seemed annoyed by her presence.

"Very well, Ms. Halder," he said at last, with an indulgent smile. "Let us test your wisdom."

Sarah waited.

"I believe," he began, "in strength. I believe in the strong rising above the rest. I believe, Ms. Halder, in the selection of species."

Sarah interjected, "Then you're nothing but a predator, Stern. An animal."

"Oh, not at all, Ms. Halder," Stern's voice was pleasing. "Unlike a beast, I also believe in perfect achievement in art, in literature, in music. In beauty. So it is not mindless predation. There is strength, intellect, and beauty." He smiled, challenging her. "Yes, I believe in perfection in order to glorify a freer, higher state of being and, even, immortality. However, unlike you, or Gage, I do not believe in destructive guilt or the self-immolating paralysis of a bankrupt and archaic moral bastille where you can neither please your God nor escape Him, and therefore only makes you weak in the process. No, I believe in true freedom, freedom of the cosmic spirit that makes one strong. I believe in the unity of a man's beliefs with his natural desires and actions. I believe that a man must create and create it to perfection, whether it is character, society, or the world. I believe that a superior man may rise above the infantile delusions of a Dark Age culture entombed with moral standards long since proven void of eternal substance. I believe, Ms. Halder, that what is eternal is man himself. And that only what man creates by personal perfection and his will shall last eternally. That is what I believe, and where my faith lies. I have never heard an argument that might stand against it. You may not believe as I do. But you cannot refute my argument. As your own ministers profess, every final step must be a leap of faith. In one direction or another."

Sarah was silent, meditative. A smile came to her slowly. "Guilt can be a terrible thing, can't it, Stern?"

"I would not know."

Sarah looked up, a frowning gaze. "It must be convenient to be free from moral restraints. And guilt. And sin. It must be nice to do whatever you want to do." She paused. "To satisfy all those impulses and instincts without judgment or restraints."

Stern shook his head, smiling slightly, as if to a disobedient child. "You intimate," he replied calmly, undisturbed, "that I believe as I do to escape the burden of guilt which cripples so many like yourself."

"I'm not crippled by guilt, Stern. I'm merely aware of it, sometimes. There's a difference. That's sort of a tired argument, isn't it?" Leaning forward slightly, Sarah turned to him. "But to be precise, I don't believe guilt is your motivation. I believe *you* are your motivation."

"I, Ms. Halder?"

Sarah nodded.

"How so?"

"As far as I can see, all your arguments do one thing," she said. "They permit you to do as you please."

Stern leaned back, smiling benignly. "How arrogant of you," he said in a polite, mocking tone. "But you cannot know my mind, Ms. Halder. You do not know what I am thinking, or why I believe the way I do. You can find nothing to refute my argument so you vainly and insultingly accuse me of manufacturing my philosophy to justify my actions against some inner moral law imprinted on my eternal soul. You infer that I believe as I do so that I may do as I wish."

Sarah remained poised. "That's about the size of it."

Stern laughed again. "These conversations are always so sadly, tragically pathetic and nonsensical," he continued. "And they always end in the same, pedestrian manner. Do you truly think I have not heard this argument a thousand times before? No, Ms. Halder, I have heard these things many times. To your surprise, I am considered quite skilled in critical reason, in philosophical thought, and in what you would call theology. Long ago I came to believe that the entire concept of a merciful God was the desperate ravings of sad, deluded people." His arm reached out in a gesture. "Look around you, Ms. Halder, and tell me, do you see any evidence of a merciful God?" He waited. "No. That is because there is no such thing. I have lived, and I have seen men who conquered by the strength of their mind. I have seen men who conquered by the strength of their wealth. But, though I have searched high and low, I have *never* seen evidence of someone who conquered, or even *survived*, because of a merciful God. I have seen only the contrary. I have seen endless rows of men and women who placed all their hopes in God, only to die bitterly in the end, starving, sick, and financially broken, greatly preferring death to life. No, Ms. Halder. Your God is a dream, or He is insane. Only an insane God or a Dream-God would allow so many to die so horribly. In any case, He would not be merciful. Personally, I believe that the Christian God is the dream of people who are unable to live autonomously, finding their way by intellectual argument and reason."

It was Sarah this time who laughed aloud. "The reasoning of intellectuals?" she asked. "Isn't that an oxymoron?"

Stern allowed that he was amused at her amusement. But over his thin smile his gaze was calculating, distantly angry. "You laugh," he said.

"Yes," she replied, another laugh. "You amuse me, Stern."

"How so?"

Casually, Sarah leaned forward, elbows on the table, hands clasped. Her presence seemed to suddenly intensify, somehow focusing a power that made her green eyes harden, impenetrable but penetrating, quick, acute. It was the face of a scholar, a scientist.

"Tell me about some intellectuals you admire," she said in a toneless voice.

Stern paused. Then he sniffed, moved his chin a hair forward. "In philosophy I admire Jean-Paul Sartre. He was—"

"A drunk," Sarah finished. "And a coward."

Stern blinked. "He wrote—"

"Of existentialism," Sarah said. "Define significance and strength of life by action. Except he was too cowardly to lift a finger against the Nazi occupation of France in 1942. He spoke against German occupation, but he shamelessly hid himself from the SS and wrote meaningless plays while the *uneducated* French Resistance fighters died defending their country." She waited. "He was a sick man."

Cold, Stern hesitated.

"Give me another one," said Sarah. "I'm hungry."

A tense silence.

"In poetry," Stern began slowly, "I admire Percy Bysshe Shelly. He believed that imaginative poetry could recreate society to a higher state of being."

Sarah nodded studiously. "Yes," she agreed. "Ah, let me think, how does that go?" She closed her eyes, concentrating, opened them again to look at Stern, speaking pedantically, "'We want the creative faculty to imagine that which we know; we want the generous impulse to act that which we imagine; we want the poetry of life.'"

Without a pause she continued, "Shelly supposedly wanted to transform the world through intellectual beauty. And since he thought that artists were the most beautiful people in the world, intellectually, he thought they should lead the revolution. Do away with religion! Let the strong and beautiful direct us all! Away with the concept of God! Let the human mind, by itself alone, be the measure of everything right!"

She laughed again. "Shelly refused to believe in any absolute moral standards, so he set up his own," she continued. "But like most intellectuals he changed his moral standards whenever they became inconvenient. He valued honesty, but when money was tight he stole from everybody he knew, forged their names on bills that he owed, and left his friends in crippling debt. Remarkable, isn't it, what intellectuals believe?"

Amused, Stern stared at her. "So you intimate that the existence of God is necessary in order to set up an absolute moral standard, a standard outside of man that will place limitations on man's actions? You are saying that only in this way can there logically be order?"

She smiled. "Could be."

"Yes," Stern agreed. "I have studied this. But I don't believe it, Ms. Halder. Many people find it servile reasoning. In the first place, nothing in the universe demands any moral order whatsoever, so why should man be any different? What supposition ever decreed that there must be absolute moral standards at all? Your entire argument rests on the supposition that is, in itself, unsubstantiated."

"And yet you have morals, Stern."

"Yes. They are my own."

"And what if someone disagrees with you?"

"Then we shall be in conflict."

"And how will it be settled?"

"By dialogue, hopefully. And, if not, there are many other means. There is always the will to power."

Sarah stared at him. "I guess you think Hitler's final solution was a good idea." Her tone had a grim and terrible hardness.

He laughed. "To someone who believes that only the strongest should survive and that there are inferior races of people, it makes perfect sense, doesn't it? However, I believe that Hitler was far too limited in his view. He should also have included many other peoples besides the Jew and Christian and Slavic peoples."

Silence. Sarah stared at him. "You're crazy," she said slowly. "You're nothing but a murderer, Stern. All you really have are your illusions."

"Many of the world's leading intellectuals agree with me, Ms. Halder."

"And many don't, Stern. And many never will. All you have is a gun. That's your real god." She paused. "But I'm willing to bet that it's not enough."

Stern appeared unfazed by her comment. "By the way, Ms. Halder, what do you believe?" he asked.

Sarah stared at him for a long moment. "To love mercy, to do justly, and to walk humbly before my God," she said.

"A pity," he said slowly. "I would prefer to trust my life to the strength of my own arm than to the whim of a mad God."

Sarah nodded. "Then by your own words...you stand condemned."

"As do you," he said.

. . .

Carthwright, dressed in black and gray, resembled a vulture, and was waiting, staring pensively into the huge, empty marble Memorial when Kertzman arrived.

Early evening had cast the park in a gray twilight hue that left a thin amber streak over the Potomac. As Kertzman passed the steps towards the shadowy figure standing beside the pond, he noticed the distant scattered clouds, thin with a harsh winter, that hovered over deep red spiraled towers of a nearby cathedral.

Massive and gloomy, hands hanging in the cold at his sides, Carthwright watched the colossal image of Lincoln as Kertzman stepped up beside him. He didn't turn to Kertzman as he spoke. "I am glad to see that you're well," he said.

Kertzman nodded. "I'm alright." He waited a second. "I've just finished talking with Acklin. He told me about the deal. Does he have it straight? Does Gage have immunity if he comes in?"

Carthwright nodded slightly, and for a long time. But Kertzman had the impression that he really wasn't thinking about the question.

"Yes," he replied finally. "Yes, he does. As long as he gives his full testimony. Under oath. And he'll have to be willing to testify at proceedings, if it's necessary."

"Then I think I can bring him in," Kertzman said.

Carthwright smiled. He turned up the collar of his black cashmere coat with his black-gloved hands. Kertzman got a flash of a delicately thin golden watch on his right wrist, a black cufflink.

An expensive taste in small things. By reflex, he filed it.

"I'll be leaving in the morning." Kertzman blinked against the wind. He needed sleep, needed it badly, but he had to finish this first. Then he'd stop by and see Barto and Malachi and head home. His flight to Rome left early tomorrow, an eight-hour hitch from Dulles International to Di Vinci Airport.

Carthwright received the statement coolly. "Be careful, Kertzman. Something is afoot." He hesitated. "Too bad about Milburn and Radford."

"They were lost from the beginning," Kertzman said gruffly, coldly. "It was coming around." He paused. "A long time coming."

"Yes, perhaps," Carthwright agreed. A gust of sudden wind disheveled his blond hair. "And, now, what is next?" he continued. "Few people would guess it, but I admit that this situation is almost out of my control. A shooting where one federal agent is forced to kill another is a delicate thing."

"I didn't kill Milburn."

"No," Carthwright agreed. "But you were on the side that did."

Kertzman frowned. "Anyway, I thought Milburn was retired."

"No," Carthwright replied. "He wasn't retired. Nobody retires from this game, Kertzman."

The words hung in the air. Brutal face appearing mean in the gray evening light, revealing nothing. "I've truly pushed my influence on this, Kertzman." Carthwright stuck his hands casually into the Armani overcoat. "How much longer 'til you can bring him in?"

"Forty-eight hours," said Kertzman gruffly. "Maybe three days. No more."

Carthwright shook his head. "That's too long."

Kertzman didn't move. "It ain't gonna be no quicker, I can tell you that. *If* he comes in at all." He paused. "But I think he will. He wants to do right, get free from this. I don't think he even cares about immunity. He'll probably come in, anyway."

Carthwright's face was tense. "Alright. Bring him in as soon as you can. But I want you to know that I can't keep the lid on this much longer. Pretty soon they'll replace me, and there's heat coming from . . . sources . . . that are going to hurt you and me, both. I can promise you that." He paused. "Is Acklin working out?"

"Yeah, he's working out," Kertzman replied. "Black Light was a for-profit company from the get-go. Somebody made a lot of money. And I don't mean Gage. It has somethin' to do with gold, takeovers, all that stuff."

Carthwright blinked, indifferent. "Yeah, I know the scenario," he replied. "I told Acklin that I didn't think there was anything to it."

Kertzman was studious. "Uh-huh. He told me. Do you know who delivered that package of information to Acklin?"

"No," Carthwright replied, "I don't know anything about the travel logs. I understand the fax came from the White House, but it was sent from the West Wing. Anyone has access to it. But somebody with weight obviously wanted Acklin working on the case because he's an old Special Forces buddy of Gage. I found out that much on my own." He shrugged. "I saw which way the wind was blowing. I didn't try and fight it. Once Acklin had done his home-work, I was justified to let him in, anyway. I figured you could use the help now that Radford and Milburn are gone." He paused. "What are you going to do about the gold angle?"

"Pursue it," Kertzman answered, without hesitation.

"I don't think you should."

Kertzman searched him. "Why?"

A heavy sigh. "Because there's nothing there, Kertzman. This is about foreign policy. I'm sure of it."

"I'll put your opinion in the report."

"Whatever," Carthwright said pensively. "But I want it on record that I think the crux of this is foreign policy."

"Alright," said Kertzman. "But I'm still going to search out the gold angle. If nothing's there we'll go back to foreign policy. But I think the money is the key." He waited. Carthwright didn't say anything. "We're going to find out what companies are behind some of these takeovers. Then we'll find something that will lead us to a name, somebody who could have run Black Light through a flunkey like Milburn. That'll be enough to justify a more specific investigation. With luck, something will shake loose and we can get some charges, an indictment, everything else. Our job will be done. Conviction will come down the road, but that won't be our respon-sibility. Justice'll do it. First we have to find a name. A head honcho. The rest just comes from shaking the tree."

"Do you think Milburn did it? Could he have been the top man? Or Radford?"

"No," Kertzman said. "Nobody would ever buy that. It would be convenient to blame Milburn because he's dead and can't defend himself. But he's a lightweight. It wouldn't fly. He didn't have the weight to set it up or keep it hidden. It had to be somebody higher. Somebody with power. Radford was never a real player. He was a gofer. A bootlicker. Whoever was running him is probably the man we want. Might even be a couple of people." He hesitated. "Could be anybody."

Carthwright just stared at the Memorial.

Kertzman studied him. His voice was old, mean. "Do you know something I don't know?"

Carthwright was turned slightly away. Kertzman thought his face was focused, intent.

"No, Kertzman, I don't know anything," Carthwright said finally. "Just trace this organization back, find out who's behind it all, and get this over with."

Manuscript wrapped in plastic and stashed deeply within the Lowe, Gage was halfway down the trail and moving fast to clear the treacherous trap created by the crevice when he saw the light.

It had been the first, farthest touch of a familiar glow that had traveled past the entrance of the graveyard in the moonlit night, and then died.

He understood instantly.

Headlights!

Headlights were coming up the wide mountain road, killed as soon as the driver spotted the entrance to the tomb; the mark of someone who did not want to be seen.

With a breath, Gage was in combat mode, wind delivering to him the sounds of the engine that carried in the cold and then, also, died. He bent his head a split-second, not hearing it within the icy walls but he *knew* the automobile was coasting now, the engine dead, closing silently on the entrance to the tomb.

Thirty seconds! You've got thirty seconds to get out of this crevice!

He ran, having turned already, back towards the tomb.

...When trapped by a larger foe, lure them into an ambush ...Move with them, not against them...The more desperate the situation, the more you need a single decisive blow...Fire is the quickest means of destroying a superior force.

Gage was at the crypt, down the stairs.

They would have reached the entrance to the graveyard by now. And they wouldn't take as long to come up the path as he did. No, they'd come careful, but faster, more confident.

Gage expected Sato and Carl, the German. Also, maybe, Stern and Radford. Two for certain, maybe four. At best, he had two minutes before they reached the entrance of the mausoleum.

Gage ran across the underground chamber to the tomb of the forefather of Santacroce.

Two minutes! Move!

Slinging the MP5 across his back, he reached out and grabbed the marble slab, moving it back into place. He left it barely open, jerked off the black backpack.

Stored for easy access, the grenades were in the top of the Lowe. Gage removed them all, placed them in the bottom of the sarcophagus. Then he broke off half a pound of C-4, mashed a portion of it inside the marble lid, half at knee-level and the rest at chest-level. He left two phosphorous grenades on the floor, outside the tomb.

Quickly, he knelt, glancing furtively, nervously, over his shoulder at the entrance.

Don't look at the entrance! Concentrate on what you're doing!

Reaching up with both hands, he shut the door even more until only a few inches remained open. Then, straining, he reached through the narrow opening, seconds flying, stuck a detonator into the lower portion of the C-4, and another.

Never trust a single detonator.

Pulling out his arm, he closed the sarcophagus another two inches, moving quickly while his hair prickled at the grinding, grating sound of marble and stone. He closed it until only a thin narrow blackness was visible.

Thirty seconds gone! Do it fast!

He had to kill the flashlight immediately. He turned to memorize the layout of the tomb, then reached, turning off the light to cast the mausoleum into total darkness.

Finish it!

Fighting a frantic impulse, he removed the pin on the phosphorous grenade, knowing he couldn't remove it, one-handed, once the device was wedged inside the tomb. Then, with infinite caution despite his panic and the sweat that drenched his face in cold, he reached inside the tomb, carefully wedging the grenade tightly between the door and the granite wall, low, near the floor.

If they did not make a thorough search, it would be difficult to see. And in the most delicate portion of the operation, he released it, feeling softly at the lever to make sure the pressure was secure.

Discipline! Discipline!

Gage blinked sweat from his eyes. It held. Lever in place.

Now get clear!

Moving with a slow, disciplined but relentless efficiency, face tight in exhausting tension, he inexorably removed his strained arm from the narrow gap. In a second he was clear, rolling and instantly hoisting his pack in a smooth motion.

He moved across the room, remembering the layout, estimating that they were at least halfway up the trail, probably using nightvision.

It was too late to leave the tomb.

Gage was across the tomb, having already decided the rest of his strategy. He felt until he found a sarcophagus, close to the stairway. Instantly he pulled at the sealed door, straining.

Marble in granite. Immovable. It wouldn't budge.

Mind heated, sweat stinging his face, Gage drew Dragon, finding a familiar hold on the 14-inch slab of sharpened steel. Despite its intended purpose as a pure fighting knife, it served as an effective tool for prying, hacking, and cutting.

Risking everything and with no choice, Gage jammed the tip of the blade into the narrow wedge between the marble door and the granite wall and strained, pulling until the quarter-inch thick piece of stainless steel bent, and bent even more with the groaning effort.

Nothing.

Teeth clenched, Gage twisted the blade against the marble seal, prying, pulling with desperate, savage strength.

A whispering gasp escaped his grimacing face, his brow contorting with the effort. All strength in it, he placed a booted foot against the wall, straining, straining, pulling with the sustained power of his legs and back. Finally, after a long trembling tension that racked his entire body, he felt the marble seal crack, splintering. Panting and exhausted, spent by the long and unendurable strain, in a second he had broken it, opened it.

Without a moment's respite he slid inside, shoving the backpack ahead of him, at his feet. Squeezing himself into the close confines of the narrow space, he pulled the door toward him.

Tight! Too Tight!

He couldn't get the door closed.

Gage pushed back, felt the skeletal form, ages dead, pressed against his back.

No time for emotion! Do something!

He half-turned in the sarcophagus and savagely swept a forearm down on the skull and ribs of the skeleton, splintering and shattering the dusty bones that collapsed in a heap at his feet with an explosion of dry dust.

Gage choked on the dust, held back a cough, and turned again, pulling the door shut, sealing himself in the grave.

Forever. It seemed like forever.

Gage held still, his breath quiet, subdued, listening to the darkness outside the tomb. He couldn't shift because of the dry bones that embraced him, the dust of death hanging over him, inside of him.

He closed his eyes.

In his left hand, close across his chest, he clutched the MP5, switched already to a fully automatic mode, safety off. He had retained one of the phosphorous grenades in his coat. He would use it to cover his retreat. If he had the chance.

Time, silence and time; death, dust, the grave.

He shut off his mind, his emotions, becoming one with the tomb, using everything he had learned, everything he was taught when they forced him to lay for days and nights in a thin shallow hole on the desert floor, covered only by a gauze of camouflage.

Patience; that was what it required.

Patience to lie for weeks, watching, while nothing happened. Patience that could drive a man insane—to lie utterly unmoving and concealed, monitoring an occasional, random troop movement in the far distance while centipedes and ants and scorpions crawled across him.

Silence, stillness, and Gage finally perceived a sound, a presence, outside the tomb. The shallow breath in his chest hovered, unreleased, as he opened his eyes. Using all his senses, feeling what could not be seen, he tried to become one with the tomb itself.

Until . . . pale light.

A fragment of light passed beneath him, a soft touch that Gage sensed as well as he saw. He released his breath carefully, his heart racing, thumping violently in his chest in the silence, the strain of his position.

It came back to him, alive, fearful; the trauma of lying so close to the enemy, the strain of lying motionless in the dark, watching the shadow silently shift, move . . . so close, unaware of him, searching for him.

And, like before, he was amazed that the thunderous beating of his heart did not reveal his position. Dimly, he recognized the familiar tension in his body, tried to relax but knew he couldn't. His hand tightened on the grip of the MP5, his finger curling, even tighter, around the trigger. He blinked the sweat out of his eyes and gritted his teeth, jaw tight, a self-caused oxygen debt building in his system, prompting him to draw a single, harsh breath.

Sound carries farther in cold air.

He waited, counting to himself.

Chest hurting!

Need air!

Gage fought it, resisted with every last measure of will, holding as still as death in the arms of death. Dust, smothering him.

No more!

They'd passed the entrance by now, would be moving toward the tomb. Gage closed his eyes and slowly, quietly, drew a shallow breath. It wasn't enough, but he felt slight relief immediately.

He pictured it all in his mind, reading the primary and secondary blasts; the phosphorous grenade would ignite three seconds after they shifted the lid of the grave. The explosion would simultaneously ignite the C-4, shattering the marble top for a secondary, shrapnel explosion, lancing the entirety of the underground chamber from one end to the other in severing white fragments of stone. It would have a killing effect, while the last two grenades, placed into the bottom of the tomb, would also detonate the C-4, also spraying the room with steel and stone.

Gage calculated . . .

. . . Wait four seconds after the explosion to move . . . Phosphorous will be everywhere . . . Avoid it . . . Don't step in it . . . It'll get on the boots and nothing will put it out . . . Five steps to the stairs, hit the ground running and get out of the crevice . . . Drop the last phosphorous grenade in the path to cover retreat . . .

Seconds passed.

Gage waited.

Nothing.

Too long!

They found it!

Gage listened intently, trying to search the darkness. But he heard nothing, no sound of marble creaking at the far end of the mausoleum, no calm voices discussing methods for defusal, no sounds of frustration. Nothing.

He waited longer, panic rising

And whether it was instinct or some finely tuned, unconscious survival mechanism melded to him from 1,000 combat missions, Gage would never know. But he realized that his trap had been found. The game was up and he instantly decided: Suicide move!

He slammed against the marble slab, brought the MP5 up, firing blindly left to right, sweeping the chamber as his mind registered all the options, the dangers, and blind zones.

...Outside: there's no way to know, could be anything waiting...Stairs: hazard, clear them fast and firing...Inside: cover the entire chamber in a burst, moving to the door.

Sato!

Carl and Sato stood at the open tomb, rising, drawing weapons. It didn't matter how they did it.

Nothing mattered but escape.

Gage swept fast and low, the MP5 ejecting a long stream of brass in continuous fire, the suppressor and chambering action of the weapon deafening in the underground chamber.

On the far opposite end of the mausoleum granite exploded and splintered at the shattering impact and ricochet of the rounds.

Gage glimpsed Sato rolling low and away from the pattern of fire, Carl falling back awkwardly, and it was all together, happening with his steps to the exit in a single chaotic scene.

Almost before the marble slab hit the floor Gage was at the stairs and then he was on the third step, firing over his shoulder blindly as he leaped up.

A deafening roar from inside the chamber and a granite step exploded beside his leg, slicing something across his thigh.

Shot!

Gage shouted, took another step, and pulled the pin on the phosphorous grenade, tossing it back. He didn't hear it hit the granite, didn't turn back as he leaped wildly through the entrance and into the moonlight. He hit the ground, clearing the portal, and then the explosion erupted beneath him, filling the cavern with hateful fire.

Gage rolled, dazed, his leg numb.

Don't take a break! No time!

Drenched now in sweat in the freezing wind, he shuffled a step, felt his leg coming back to him. No time for thought but he knew what had hit him: a wild shot had struck the steps and either a bullet fragment or a slice of granite had cut across his thigh.

Already, with the way the vaguely familiar numbness was holding steady, he knew it was not a serious injury.

Beneath the ground, Gage heard the cavern burning, rumbling. He had not yet heard a secondary explosion. But it would come, he was sure. The phosphorous would soon heat the chamber to an unendurable temperature, burning everything, including the C-4.

Gage turned, running under a stronger leg. He moved quickly down the trail, the machine gun at chest-level.

Tactical reload.

He ejected the two-thirds empty clip, slammed in another with a 50-round capacity. He had almost reached their vehicle when he heard the screaming.

Whirling back, Gage saw two burning figures dash up the stairs, touched by white fire of the phosphorous. Screaming in rage, one of the shapes took three lightning quick steps, jerked off his coat, leaving it burning in the snow behind him.

The other one rolled briefly on the ground, attempting futilely to put out the phosphorous when the first man ran to him, jerked off his coat as well and cast it far to the side.

Then the tomb exploded with secondary explosions, rocking the crevice and frozen ground. Gage felt the cliffs around him tremble. Snow drifted lightly from the slopes.

The second man had rolled out of sight, far from the tunnel entrance. The other had advanced toward Gage but was knocked down by the shock wave of the secondary explosions. He now struggled to his feet.

Amazed, Gage stared.

Smoking, outlined against the white burning background of the tomb, the shape slowly stood, volcanic, enraged, staring at Gage down the length of the path.

Sato.

Gage leveled the MP5, releasing a long burst. But even as he straightened his arm to fire, Sato leaped off the end of the path behind the narrow wall, avoiding the first fierce blast that shattered snow in a wide white mist.

Frustrated, Gage lowered the weapon. He knew he'd missed. His first impulse was to finish it, to advance back down the path.

Finish it!

He debated.

Clearly, Sato was not badly injured. Carl was in worse condition but could probably still fight.

Obviously neither of them had panicked at the first explosion, had deduced that their only chance lay in vaulting the pool of burning phosphorous. And that is what they had done. But they were hurt, now, and probably had only their handguns.

Sato would have the tanto and the Desert Eagle. He didn't know what Carl would carry.

Gage measured his chances.

It was the most profound rule of combat that made him advance back into the crevice, something he had learned by experience but that was also driven into him at the general strategy course in Virginia at the National War College: *Mere endurance is not fighting. You must destroy the enemy's ability to wage war. Always victory comes from this. Do your enemy harm at every opportunity. Do him damage in a general way. Always.*

Sato; the enemy's most powerful force.

Gage's eyes narrowed, cold, a frown turning the corners of his mouth: He was willing to sacrifice to take down Sato. Carl would be a bonus.

He started forward. *Time to end this game!*

He didn't need the nightvisor or the flashlight. A soft white glow from the burning tomb illuminated the dead end of the crevice. It warmed the walls, melting some of the ice. Even from a distance of 100 feet he felt the heat.

Holding the MP5 at a shoulder firing position he moved steadily down the crevice, close to the wall, scanning up, down, across, eyes never locking, watching for both image and movement in the flickering white light.

Stealthily, resolutely, Gage reached the end of the crevice, passing the corner carefully ... carefully.

Ice smashed into his head as the granite beside him exploded at the impact of a round.

Gage rolled, knowing the impossible origin of the shot as he came up, firing the MP5 on fully auto to blast the top of the ridge in a haze of gunfire and then he leaped back, firing still.

Sweating, breathing hard, Gage tried to understand.

The top of the ridge! How could they have gotten to the top of the ridge?

Narrowly, Gage risked another glance at the high darkness on white snow. Saw nothing.

But they were there. Watching. Gage could feel it.

... No way to climb the ridge in this hole without coming under fire ... Retreat ... Find another way ... But it'll take some time to retreat and find another way up the cliff ... So make them think you're staying! ... Keep them in position!

Gage fired another burst from around the wall.

A vengeful volley of return fire hit the granite, missing him by inches, and then Gage was running, retreating quickly down the crevice, scanning for a fast unroped climb to the top.

"There has to be a way," he whispered harshly, breathless between clenched teeth.

He reached the back of the crevice, passing their car, a dark-colored 4x4 Jeep, and moved right, scanning. He had already seen the southern side of the ridge on the way up; the wall was too steep, too covered in ice for a fast climb. But 50 feet up the northern ridge he found a chimney, icy but broken, a good climbing hole.

Mounting the nightvisor, switched to luminosity only, he entered the chimney, climbing with both hands, the automatic slung across his back. In two minutes, gasping for breath in the thin air, he was at the top, 60 feet above the trail, the same height Sato commanded. He emerged from the chimney covered with freezing mud and snow, breath heaving with gloved hands black from scrambling on the rock.

Ignoring his fatigue, Gage brought the MP5 around for shoulder fire, moved forward. Reflexively, night hunting rules requiring it, he switched the visor to dual luminosity-heat imaging.

A creeping, balanced step; careful, soft. Snow crunched underfoot. Unavoidable noise. Gage hesitated.

He moved forward as cautiously as possible, finding rocks for placement, bent low, scanning. He tried to ignore the disturbing heat that had suddenly developed, stifling him inside the mountaineering gear.

Twenty steps and he was hot now, sweating badly. He felt the impulse to hurry. He shut it down, holding back on speed, grimly maintaining a rigidly unyielding noise discipline.

Thirty more steps and he saw them; the distant, bright red-yellow glow of two human shapes poised carefully on the lip of the canyon, gazing down into the pit where the graveyard lay.

Motionless, they were both crouched.

Gage realized they had not seen him, were still looking into the pit.

He waited, focused: no emotion, no excitement, just cold killer instinct controlling, homing in, feeling the heart of his prey. Carefully, slowly, inch by inch, Gage brought up the barrel of the MP5 for front sight-target picture alignment.

Can't move closer. Snow makes too much noise . . . like thunder.

He concentrated, preferring to take down Sato first.

Bathed in the thermal imaging glow, both men were identical. Gage couldn't discern which was Sato. He hesitated, debating. Then, as rules and training required, he made a quick decision.

He estimated the distance at 280 feet, not a long shot for warm weather or on level ground; he could routinely make head shots at 150 feet. But cold air would slow the bullet, drop it. Also, he was shooting across a narrow slice of the pit; the rising heat might cause the nine millimeter bullet to rise with it. Or, on the other hand, the heat could create a tumbling effect, throw the round badly off trajectory.

To add to the factoring, Gage realized they were on slightly higher ground. Physics required that the bullet would rise more than point of aim when fired uphill.

A thousand calculations passed through his mind in the space of a breath; Gage didn't know whether to shoot high, low, or directly on target. He opted for the heat throwing the round up, the elevation factor throwing it up even more. So he aimed low on one of the shapes, just beneath the sternum.

If the bullet rose, he could still claim a possible chest shot or head shot. He held on target, feeling the breeze on his skin, but no wind gusts. Good. He only had to worry about elevation, not lateral trajectory.

Melding to the weapon, he found his hold, using the nightvisor for a flat TV-like image of the target with the front-sight blade fixed on the heart.

He released a half-breath. Held it.

And in the time it takes to freeze movement he had computed the ballistics of the trajectory and the probable angle of the bullet's climb by height, heat, and cold, and in a flowing instant of perfect poise, fired.

Gage knew he'd hit as he brought the MP5 out of recoil and heard the thrashing, the angry shout. And instantly he brought the sights on target again but the second man leaped to the side, rolling.

Gage fired a quick shot, leading him with the barrel but he knew he'd missed as soon he squeezed the trigger.

Then the first man hit, the one who had gone down screaming, suddenly rolled to the side also, finding solid cover behind a white boulder.

No! Missed both!

White adrenaline surged and Gage was moving. He leaped a frozen slab of granite, switching to three-shot, and then he fired another quick burst to prevent them from moving.

Breath harsh, fast, snarling with blood hot with the heat of the kill, Gage closed the distance and was there, firing behind the rock. He dropped instantly into a crouch, scanning, alert, vivid and fired with fear and excitement . . . *alive.*

He looked down, scanning. Tracks in the snow. Blood.

So . . . he hadn't missed, after all. He just hadn't claimed a clean kill. The round had probably hit too high, a shoulder or collar injury. A hampering injury but not a killing wound. Maybe not even crippling.

Dead to emotion, Gage scanned the forest, breathing slower, slower still. He used the moment to recover his pulse, slow his racing heart, removing the adrenaline from his thought processes as much as possible.

No thermal images registered on the nightvisor's luminosity or heat index. Slowly, breath catching, he nodded, understanding; they had already gone deep into the trees, finding cover, waiting for him to follow.

An ambush.

Take your time ... Don't move too fast ... They'll expect you to be excited ... Rushing in ... Do it slow and careful ... Stay alert ... Stay close to cover at all times.

Moving with the thought, Gage was instantly tracking, body bent low, his face up, scanning, holding the MP5 close to his chest. He used the nightvisor's thermal imaging, following the blood through the screen's green-tinted moonlit snow, deep and red and glowing.

An expert tracker uses the land itself, both the infinitely small and the grand scale of terrain, as an ally. Because tracking is more than pursuing; it is an all but lost art where a hunter *perceives* the direction of prey by understanding the creature's physical limitations, its habits, and the movements forced upon it by its surroundings.

Stalking was another name for it, and as Gage moved forward it all came back to him, how it was done, the beauty of it, the feel.

It was most important to know habits; to understand how a creature preferred to move, its instincts, reflexes, and fears.

Gage had learned that anticipation and knowledge were far more important than simply reading tracks. But on this cold killing ground anticipation was at a minimum, maybe even impossible; professional killers were careful to remain unpredictable.

It was made even more difficult because Gage didn't have a true feel for the land, couldn't find that essential overview of imagination that enabled him to map out future movements.

He had studied the terrain in a dimensional sketch before he jumped, just to familiarize himself with the topography. So he remembered some details from the charts. But it wasn't enough. Vaguely, he recalled that a sharp ridge lay directly ahead, and beyond that lay a long steep slope of a glacier, perhaps 1,000 feet down, which ended in a dropoff.

Gage didn't want to deal with that, not in a combat situation. The glacier would be sheathed in ice and broken with hidden dropoffs, hazardous to negotiate. Even with crampons and a rope, it would be a difficult traverse, and impossible to complete if he was receiving or returning fire.

Certainly they wouldn't go that far.

Scanning, he considered the most likely scenario. Almost all men, particularly professional soldiers, when they were retreating, would generally look for the first defensible position to provide a strong counterstrike. A platoon would mount a rear guard, throwing back a steady stream of fire to slow a pursuer's advance. And a battalion would retreat in separate, smaller groups, moving in parallel lines or eccentrically to catch the enemy in a haze of crossfire.

A crossfire, more than anything else, is what Gage expected. He guessed that they would soon divide, moving diversely. One would try to draw him straight on, stumbling through the snow, showing signs of weakness, intimating an easy kill. The second man would work away and to the flank, gaining higher ground for a sniper post. But then again, knowing he would be expecting it, they might reverse the scenario.

Gage paused, shook his head. It could go either way; a guessing game.

A moment passed and he decided that if the tracks divided, he would follow those that led straight ahead. But he would keep his real attention on the flank, searching for a thermal image.

He would try and outshoot the sniper, hitting him first. It was possible, because the sniper, Carl or Sato, would have to come from behind cover before he took the shot.

Step by cautious step, Gage continued into the night. Then, looming before him was the ridge.

Not high, it rose on a gradual incline and was steep enough to provide solid cover for someone shooting from the far side. A good place to make a stand.

Gage hesitated, then moved behind cover, studying the terrain through the nightvisor. To his advantage, the rocky slope provided plenty of large granite blocks for quick cover.

A moment's rest and Gage ran forward for six steps before finding advanced concealment behind a boulder. Then, gradually, sprinting from rock to rock in quick bursts, he continued up the slope, pausing only at the top.

Grimacing with exhaustion, hot, he glanced sideways, catching his breath.

The tracks still ran together, but the ground was rocky, breaking up the signs of flight. The steps near the ridgecrest vanished in a patch of broken granite stones, then appeared again in the snow at the top. Together, the tracks disappeared over the rim. Quickly, moving in a line parallel to the snowy footprints, Gage vaulted the crest, sweeping left and right, and dropping instantly behind a freezing granite slab.

Concealed again, he rested, breathing tiredly, sweating, feeling a sudden and terrifying nervousness. He wanted to shed the heavy coat and backpack, but resisted the temptation, remembering the training at Northern Warfare School.

*If you become overheated, do not remove your utility jacket . . .
Sweat exposed to cold air will cause immediate hypothermia . . . And
if you fall into water, your jacket will delay death.*

It all came back to him, over and over, again and again, the
rules, the exceptions, the way to survive, how to forestall and shut
down cold or hypothermia with drugs and movement, how to find
the path to overcome.

Distantly familiar thoughts passed through his mind. This was
the world, the world of cold and darkness and fear that no one truly
wanted to experience or inhabit; a world that had always separated
him from the rest of humanity; a world of cruelty, terror, and white
trembling courage, of mistakes, regrets, and harrowing death that
left nightmares and madness in its wake.

For a brief second, breath heaving, Gage felt his sweat-soaked
face twist with the pain of his scarred soul; the pain of too much of
this fear and adrenaline and heat that had long ago burned his
blood thin and weak. He felt again the agony of too many nights
like this in the cold, nights where he had forced himself to stalk
grimly and patiently through a withering fear, a maniacal courage
controlling the panic inside.

He paused, scanning. *It's been too much of this,* he thought. *Too
much.*

But, as always, the faces came to him, Simon and Sarah and
Malachi. And the faces of people who had died from the work of his
hands; faces and names of people whose lives were destroyed because of gold and power and an ancient book.

Fear lessened under the force of something else, something
new.

Do what you have to do! Finish it!

Crouching, Gage advanced down the slope, moving cautiously,
every boulder, every slope holding a probable ambush site. The
risks were great now because they had run out of tactical ground.
Gage knew they couldn't retreat past the glacier.

The tracks ended on the edge of the glacier, descending down a
slash in the rock. Gage crouched beside it, peering down cautiously.
It was a sort of half-chimney, exposed on one side and cut deeply
with jagged, frozen rock on the other. He scanned the rocks, saw ice
and snow torn off the boulders from someone's frantic and dangerously unroped descent. The snow at the bottom, on the edge of the
sloping ice wall, was blasted and scattered from a bruising fall.
Below the 40-foot chimney, on a narrow ledge that ran the length of
the glacier, Gage saw bootprints that trailed out of sight. When he
looked closer, he saw a slight glow on dark stone.

Blood.

He frowned. They were waiting for him down there. There was no place left to run.

Something told him to turn back. He was outnumbered and they had selected a dangerous ambush site. But he hesitated, playing out the odds; first, he possessed superior firepower with the MP5, but, then again, they would have him in a crossfire; second, on the narrow ledge, he did not have room to maneuver, and they would have found solid cover, not needing to maneuver; last, they would have first acquisition of target, could claim the first shot.

Not good.

Cold was on him, now, the heat fading with his stillness, and he wanted to turn back, forget it. The tactics were bad, there was no good way to do it.

The manuscript felt heavy in his pack. He thought about the lives it would save.

Don't push a bad situation...Pull out.

But he was too far out to pull back. Overcome by heat and anger, the greatest mistake of men locked in mortal combat, he felt himself going over the edge. He knew something was wrong with it, but in a rare moment of procedure violation, he ignored the warning, moved past the impulse to retreat.

He took out the rope.

The chimney was the only path down the 60-foot cliff and ended at the top of the glacier. Through the nightvisor he saw the steep, ice-glazed slope that slid brokenly out of sight, vanishing into the far distance at least 1,000 feet away, maybe more. If any of them lost purchase on the narrow lip of rock at the top, and began sliding, they wouldn't stop. They would gather speed on the ice, plummeting faster and faster down the glacier until they reached the dropoff which would hurl them into the heart of this ancient chasm.

Gage uncoiled the rope and secured it at the top over a granite pylon. Then he removed the carabinier from his pocket, clipped it to his belt, and slipped the rope through the descenduer.

He locked himself into it, and holding the MP5 in one hand, he eased over the frozen edge to rappel carefully down the chimney. His boots skidded wildly as he touched the wall, and he went to his knees, locking down clumsily on the rope to stop his descent.

Struggling for balance, he found dark footholds in the side of the chimney and tried again, moving cautiously, one jagged step at a time. It was an awkward descent, one hand holding the rope, the other holding the automatic on a steady beat at the bottom of the shaft.

Gage figured they would leap out and begin firing up the chimney as soon as they heard him descending. He was prepared to return fire. Or, possibly, they would let him reach the bottom, then cut loose with a crossfire. Either way, it would be a point-blank confrontation.

He took another cautious leap, four feet. And again. A dozen more leaps and he would be at the bottom. By reflex he glanced up.

A massive figure against the sky.

Arm outstretched, as if offering something, but Gage brought the MP5 up and fired wildly even before he was on target.

Explosions thundered between them with light blinding. Gage let go of the rope. Then falling, he smashed into a rock as the figure at the top fell back, roaring.

Pain and another rock had collided against him and Gage was thrown out, sprawling wildly through the chimney and in a space of time too short for human measurement and too quick for human reaction he saw it all . . . Carl at the bottom on the shaft, lifting the gun to shoot . . . white snow approaching and ice flashing past his face and there was no time for anything else as he smashed wildly into the German.

Stunning impact in Gage's face and the nightvisor was gone in a wild tangle of limbs and then they were in the air, wrestling.

Gunshot!

Gage shouted and brought the MP5 up, but it wasn't in his hand. Then he locked up with Carl and they were sliding down the glacier, sliding, sliding, gathering speed every second and the German fired another shot past his ribs.

Shouting angrily Gage caught Carl's gun hand in his left and spun as they careened wildly down the glacial slope. Then Gage rolled, grabbing the gun barrel with his right hand and twisting it backwards against the German's wrist.

Carl roared as the automatic weapon was torn from his hand and Gage spun again, elbows and fists, and the rope was still with him, tangled around them both.

Then, a thunderous numbing impact launched them through the air. They had reached the bottom. This was death. And then they came down again, smashing together into the slope and rolling at a blinding, incredible speed on the continuing slope.

Forget him! Execute emergency rollover! Now!

Gage slammed his forehead into Carl's face and pushed, separating himself as the German screamed in rage and in a wild moment of clarity, Gage saw the end, the edge of the glacial slope that emptied into night.

NOW!

Savagely Gage tore the ice ax from his shoulder strap and rolled to his chest, slamming the sharpened pick into the glacier.

Bearing down with everything he had, the ax plowed a deepening trench down the slope.

Sliding! Seconds... seconds.

In an incredible descending rush he slowed, slowed. He pushed, hard, jamming the ice ax in deeper, and then he stopped, breath beaten from him in a gut-stunning concussion.

Instantly Gage wrapped his right hand through the wriststrap of the ax handle. But a horrendous impact ripped the ice ax from his hands and Gage roared.

Tangled around his legs and waist, the rope stretched with incredible tension and it was immediately clear: Carl had gone over the nearby edge holding the far end of the rope, was still holding it.

Tenacious. Incredible weight, pulling.

Frantic, groaning with the strain, Gage glanced up wildly and saw that the ice ax was holding, his right wrist burning in the strap. But the pick wouldn't stay long without his weight pushing it into the ice wall.

He reached up with his left hand, clawing and pushing with his feet, but the icy slope was too steep to gain any purchase.

Weight swung on the rope, changing. Grimacing in pain, blood hot on his face, Gage glanced down, saw a hand come over the edge, Carl climbing the rope.

Gage pulled, groaning and straining with every fiber to raise himself for a grip on the ice ax. And in shuddering slow motion he crept up an inch.

Exhaustion struck him in a tidal wave. *Don't rest! Do it now! Do it now or you'll never do it!*

Ignoring the pain, screaming with the effort, Gage pulled again, lifting both himself and Carl a step. His left hand locked on the ice ax.

Wildly he looked down. Saw Carl at the edge of the abyss.

Face disfigured by pain and blood, shoulder tearing with the combined weight, Gage desperately gripped the ice ax with his left hand. With his right hand, he frantically grabbed the Dragon.

Enraged, Carl climbed over the edge of the ravine, holding the rope in both hands. Savagely the German strained backwards, heaving.

The rope drew taunt as a bowstring. *Unendurable!*

"We'll die together Gage!" he shouted in a maniacal rage, a death rage.

Struggling, scrambling, Gage dug one knee hard against the glacier and pivoted, straining to hold onto the ax. He glared down.

Carl hauled back on the rope, laughing.

Gage swung the blade, severing the rope with a touch, and Carl stood in space for a frozen time, arms pinwheeling in the air, face and eyes open in shock.

Screamed.

. . .

Cold came to him again, frosted breath vanishing into the stars in long streams.

Closing his eyes, Gage leaned his head back against the icy rock slab. The outcropping provided a small place to reorganize, to recover.

It took him ten long, scrambling minutes to reach the slab after seeing it from the edge of the abyss. Ten minutes of clutching nervously, dangerously at the icy slope, but he had finally made it, beaten and bleeding, trembling from adrenaline and exhaustion, death creeping in.

Fumbling in the night, Gage found the ends of the rope, coiled it. He found the top half; the end was smashed, blasted, torn, the mark of a heavy grain, low velocity bullet.

Tired, he sighed.

Probably, one of his own subsonic rounds in that wild and sudden blast from the MP5 had done it. He expelled a slow breath, too tired to analyze it. It happened and now it was over. He had work to do. He geared down into the reflexive machine mind required for prolonged combat.

Gage *felt* his body all over and at once, his breath was regular, steady, deep enough; hands were slightly injured, still functionable; chest and back were bruised, twisted, nothing crippling. He noticed his eyesight focusing keenly on the distant stars, everything surreal in its clarity.

He nodded faintly. Everything was good.

He recognized the familiar, sharpened combat sensation; he was in the zone, perfect and fluid, body reacting on instinct, mind in the machine mode with muscle reflex carrying him past the point where thought falls away from exhaustion.

He could do a thousand things now, reflex providing the impulse, the initial spark, then leaving his muscle memory to execute and finish the task while his mind continued to the next level with what energy remained. Moving constantly ahead of wherever he was, like a master chess player forgetting his hands, his mind deeply advanced into the game while his body moved the pieces through only the faintest self-awareness.

Closing his eyes, concentrating, Gage leaned his head back against the rock, checking equipment in his mind. The nightvisor and MP5 were gone. But he still had the ice ax, the knife, and the Hi-Power with six extra clips, plus half the rope.

Most important, the manuscript was secured in the Lowe backpack.

Staring up into the night, Gage calculated his injuries more thoroughly. His face was slashed high on the left side, blood already dry and clotted in the cold. But it didn't affect his sight; there was no swelling on the eye itself.

Let it be. Worry about it later.

Yet, as the moments passed, his entire body felt stiff with uncounted stresses and bruises that probably merited emergency room treatment. But emergency rooms were for other people. He had learned to move beyond torn muscles, stress fractures, and any other kind of similar wound that could break a man down.

Overcome. Do what you do. Finish it.

Thought was shut down and Gage reacted, moving with a corpselike stiffness.

Dry breath burning in his throat, body wet with a condensing, shivering cold, he sat awkwardly upright on the horizontal granite slab; a relatively comfortable resting place on the otherwise treacherous slope.

Wearily he pulled off the backpack, dragging it around in front of him to place it securely between his legs. He removed two Energybars, his canteen, painkillers, and an adrenaline injection.

He chewed the first bar slowly, thoroughly, swallowing each bite with a large sip of water from the canteen. The water was heavily laced with Ricelyte to quickly restore his electrolyte level, improving nerve synapse, fooling his body into believing that it was stronger than it actually was. And slowly, degree by degree, he began to feel more recovered, rested.

Methodically, he repeated the procedure on the second bar, drinking the rest of his water, knowing he would need it; dehydration was a lightning-fast killer this high in the mountains.

Last, Gage inexorably shoved the piercing needle of the adrenaline syringe into the side of his neck, pushed the valve closed to inject the full dosage.

Warm, flowing, and instantly lifting him to a comforting soft wave, the epinephrine increased his heartbeat, restored his energy, and fought back the overwhelming cloud of fatigue.

Gage felt it coursing through him, all over, and he swallowed a Lorcet Plus to take the edge off the wracking pain. The barbiturate would enable him to work the torn muscles and stretched ligaments with less awareness of injury, pushing them far past the point where his body would protest the abuse. It was a dangerous procedure, but in the savage night world of military combat, it was the way men drove themselves past the edge, pushing their bodies to do what couldn't be done any other way.

He waited for the painkiller to take effect, stared down dully. He sighed. Now for the hard part.

Slowly, steadily, Gage began to attach the crampons to both boots; a difficult job because the leather straps were stiff with ice, frozen, unbending. Moving mechanically, he beat the crampons against the rock, breaking the rigidness, and in a long, protracted struggle, finally succeeded in attaching one to each ice-covered boot.

Feeling the drug taking hold, moving more easily with each moment, Gage rose to his feet. He hoisted the Lowe onto his back and attached the shoulder straps.

He gazed up the slope, fastening the belt and mechanically tightening the side-stays of the backpack to minimize lateral twisting of its weight, an act that could throw him off balance on the wall.

Mentally, he went through it; crampons for climbing with his boots, ice ax in his right hand, the knife for the other hand.

Keep three points on the rock at all times . . . Move only a hand or a foot at a time . . . Basic rule: Never move two points at the same time . . . Go slow . . . Steady.

Gage estimated; 1,000 feet and at least four hours to the top. He would reach the ledge in early morning, maybe two hours before sunrise. Sato would be gone, figuring him for dead.

Then he remembered the brutal ten-mile descent into the town, how it waited for him after this long ordeal. And in a strange convulsion of his soul he remembered the desert, the walk under the moon to the tomb where he had died; felt again the pain and death and utter hopelessness. Something whispered to him, deeply, hauntingly, that the strongest part of him was permanently wasted and burned out in that long walk across the desert . . . leaving him forever weaker than he had ever been, before.

"No," Gage murmured, falling weakly forward against the wall, leaning against the glacier, hands on the ice, shaking his head. "No, don't do it, boy . . . Don't let fear beat you 'cause there ain't no life in it . . . Ain't no life . . ."

Gage swallowed dry breath, gathering, felt grave dirt in his mouth, dry and moldering. He looked up again, sight lost in the glistening blue-white ice. Eyes hot, he peered up the slope, searching; ice appeared rougher to the right, the grade at 60 degrees.

He looked past it, to the sky, stars. His teeth were bared, his voice choked. "It's just you, old man," he whispered. "It's you . . ."

A second, and Gage closed his eyes, lowering his head.

Come on ... Come on ... Finish it!

He shouted, face twisting in rage, and swung his arm, spiking the ax sharply into the glacial wall.

Night had faded into a cold silent morning, and the day had passed, itself, in relative silence. And now it was nightfall again.

Stern was gone.

The one called Radford had taken his place, and Sarah sat pensively in a maroon leather chair in the formal living room, staring at him.

Radford appeared angry, vaguely hostile, and stared back. "You have no idea what this has done to my life," he said moodily, his angry gaze never leaving her.

Sarah smiled, laughed lightly. "I hope so." She glanced out the window, towards the sunset.

Her mind wandered over the day. Sato, the Japanese, had come in with the slate gray sunrise, but without the German, Carl.

Sarah watched him pass through the room, caught his single, contemptuous glance, and felt real fear. Then he disappeared into the back of the estate, leaving her staring blankly at the wall where her gaze had fallen from his brooding face.

Since that moment the house had been still, silent.

Through the day she managed to catch brief snatches of sleep on the couch, but restless and worried, slept fitfully. She had not seen either the Japanese or Stern since morning.

She shook her head, leaning her head back, tired. And heard Radford again.

"My life is ruined," he said in a low, mumbling voice. "Ruined. Because of you."

He had been drinking all afternoon.

Sarah measured him, judged him unstable. "You did it to yourself." She carefully brought up one foot to place it on the chair. She rested her elbow on her knee, forearm across her chest, feeling a slight security in the casual physical shield.

Radford rose, walked toward her unsteadily. "No," he said in a strange tone. "*You* ruined my life. You and that book."

Sarah felt a sharp thrill of fear, of energy. Breath increasing, she stiffened.

Radford stopped before her, smiling. "Gage is dead," he said, and laughed, watching for her reaction.

Sarah frowned at him.

"Do you want to know how?" he asked sweetly, leaning forward.

Her face was bitter with resolve.

Radford was amused.

"Sato did him in," he continued and, strangely, seemed to tire of the game. He turned away wearily, waving a hand at nothing. "Dropped him off a glacier. Dead as a mackerel by now, I'll bet."

Sarah had trouble catching her breath, but she didn't move at all with the words. "No," she said, in a low tone. "He's alive."

Radford turned back, eyebrows raised, smiling. "No, he ain't alive. He's deader 'a wedge, as Kertzman would say." He stared at her distantly. "You know," he added slowly, eyes suddenly remote, remembering, "I'd like to kill Kertzman."

Sarah said nothing.

"We had it all set up." Radford moved to a bottle of bourbon and poured himself a drink. He ignored the bucket of ice. The lukewarm whiskey sloshed heavily in the glass.

"Yeah . . . all set up. Let Kertzman find the boy, then kill everybody, blame it on Gage." He nodded to himself. "Perfect containment, they said. And it would have worked, too. Would have worked out . . . real well. Would have ended everything. Kertzman would be dead. Everybody'd be dead. I'd be a rich man, moving up in the world."

He swallowed a long drink, belched, rubbed his chest angrily with one hand. Then he expelled a long breath, regarded her again with a grimace.

"Now Gage's dead, Kertzman's alive, and I've lost my career. Lost . . . my *life*. I'm going to have to . . ." He seemed to lose train on his thoughts, added in a whisper, ". . . do something."

He pulled a pistol from his belt, turned to her. "Kertzman thought I was such an idiot," he mumbled, stepping closer, face flushed. "Thought I was such a fool. But I knew from the first . . . what they were doing to him. I knew they were setting him up."

Radford stared, unfocused, at her.

"Makin' me run all those . . . *background* checks," he sneered, laughing. "Then Milburn told me it was all a facade. Kertzman's game. Orders came down to trail Kertzman, keep him in sight. Everybody knew he'd find Gage, sooner or later. Old Milburn and me, we were in on it. Kertzman was a fool. Stupid old man. But he's gonna die, I tell you that. I'm gonna kill him . . . myself. He ain't . . . nuthin'. Just a lot of talk. Big hunter . . ."

He turned away slightly. "Coyotes," he hissed, "bears and lions and...how does it go? Bears and...lions and tigers and...bears?" He smiled at her, shook his head again. "We ain't in Kansas no more."

He took another drink, laughed.

Sarah focused, locked down her nerve. "You're drunk."

Moving with startling speed and precision, Radford instantly leveled the pistol at her and thumbed back the hammer in a single practiced motion, eyes a deep wavering focus. He smiled stupidly.

"What?" he asked quietly.

Silence; tension.

"Did you say something?" he whispered.

Sarah didn't move, kept her eyes directed at the floor, closed them. She had told herself that she didn't really care about dying, but she still felt a fear, instinctive and uncontrollable.

"You don't understand, woman!" Radford shouted, stepping closer. *"My...life...is...over!"*

Her entire body tightened at the sudden scream.

Radford leaned down over her, shoving the barrel of the pistol to her temple.

Sarah kept her eyes closed, mouth tight.

"You don't understand!" he shouted. "What am I gonna do? I wasn't getting enough money out of this to live forever! What am I gonna do? Go back and talk my way out of it?"

Sarah waited.

"No!" he screamed. "Never! Ain't gonna happen! It's over! What am I gonna do? Live in Europe the rest of my life? I hate this place! It stinks. The people are stupid! I did this for money! But I had a life! I had something going for me and now it's gone because of Kertzman, because of Gage..." Radford shoved the barrel, hard, into her temple. "Because of you!"

Sarah flinched to scream, raising her hands. Beside her, she heard a scrambling and...Impact!

Dazed, she opened her eyes, holding her arms up to protect her face. Radford walked hesitantly away from her, the gun hanging limply, forgotten, in his hand.

Standing beside her was the Japanese, hands empty. Naked except for a sumo-type garment worn around his waist and groin, he looked vaguely like he had been sleeping.

For a minute Sato frowned down at her, then he turned, walked casually to Radford and carefully took the black pistol away from him. Then, with a massive hand, he grabbed Radford's shoulder and pushed him easily to the side. Radford collapsed onto the couch, fell over, instantly unconscious. In the next second the Japanese disassembled the weapon, almost without moving his hands. The gun fell into several pieces. He dropped all but one in a chair, turned back toward her.

Eyes wide, breath wild, Sarah looked at Radford. He appeared alive, his chest rising and falling with each breath. But the Japanese had clearly done something to him, something she didn't understand. Radford didn't look injured; there was no blood, nothing. But he was clearly hit, somehow.

Confused, she focused on the Japanese who stood, unmoving, in the center of the room.

Sarah waited for the Japanese to leave. But he stood quietly before her. Finally, understanding that he would not leave until she met his gaze, Sarah shifted her eyes, feeling alone and frightened with this unsettling force standing beside her. Slowly, she raised her eyes to the face of stern discipline and strength, the blackly impenetrable eyes of pure, cold will.

Lightheaded, Sarah held the gaze, and she understood *his* meaning of strength. Tired, she chose to let it go, looked away. But Sato stood, still staring at her, waiting.

"You were his woman," he said somberly.

It was not a question.

Sarah raised her face with a sudden spark, almost a curiosity. She didn't want to reply. A tension passed between them; held, endured.

"He'll come for me," she said.

Confusion was evident in Sato's narrow gaze for the slightest, flashing moment.

"He is dead," he said in a flat tone.

"No," Sarah said, voice brittle and eyes widening slightly with a shake of her head. "He's not dead. He won't die in this." A pause. "He'll come for me."

Sato seemed amused. "And how do you know?" He laughed. "Your God, does He tell you this?"

Sarah held her silence.

"You know nothing," he said.

Her face was grim. "He's not dead," she said, more quietly.

Implacable, inhumanly disciplined and cold, Sato looked down upon her like a god beholding an unsatisfying, imperfect product of his own creation. For a moment he seemed to ponder her words, yet his presence revealed neither agreement nor disagreement, concern nor pleasure. It was, in its purest essence, a life-force that revealed nothing at all; not fear of death nor love of life nor compassion nor cruelty nor anything else that could be called human.

Never could Sarah have imagined such inhuman control. It was as if, by the power of his will alone, he had forged his body and mind into something more than mortal.

Steady, fighting a trembling, she faced the blackened gaze and the single thought returned; it was all she had.

"He'll come for me," she whispered.

Sato blinked, studying her. "It will make no difference," he said. "I will kill him."

Sarah closed her eyes a moment, tempering herself against the force she faced. "No," she said softly. "You can't kill him. Nothing can kill him. Not in this."

She stared at him. There was nothing more to say.

Sato seemed touched by a faint anger. Frowning, he slowly stepped closer, one hand reaching around his waist to his back. And the hand emerged again with what Sarah knew by instinct was his soul, his essence.

Held in his strong right hand, the tanto was horrible, a blade forged in dark fire, cold death. And as a living force, its razored edge caught a white line of light, capturing it, burning it into her eyes, searing.

The Japanese poised, unmoving, before her. And in the eeriness of the moment his entire body, equally tempered and forged in the black flames of pure war, seemed a weapon equal to the blade.

He stood over her.

"We shall see," he said.

In a truly foul mood, Kertzman cleared customs without incident and moved through the lobby of Di Vinci Airport in Rome, catching the hue of a gloomy winter-gray sky through the late afternoon sun.

Carthwright had volunteered an Embassy CIA man who could usher him past customs with diplomatic clearance and no hassles, but Kertzman had waved it off, preferring as little contact with the Embassy as possible.

He found his bag on the cargo belt and moved past a cadre of white-shirted security men holding Beretta machine guns in the front lobby. He spotted at least 30 civilian police, maybe 40 military.

At the exit of the cargo belt, at least four separated plainclothes cops stood watching, drinking coffee, doing a fairly good job of looking inconspicuous.

Kertzman passed them all, looked at his watch. He swore softly; the entire day had passed with the flight, leaving only five hours till midnight. But he still had time to find the Medici Hotel on the Via Vittorio.

Resisting the impulse to rush, Kertzman moved stoically, resolutely, past three additional beltways in the airport's undersized front lobby.

A man in a blue coat accosted him. "Taxi, sir?" the man asked eagerly.

Kertzman eyed him with a suspicious, vaguely threatening air and walked on. He brushed past four more drivers who solicited his service and stopped before a small man leaning dejectedly at a closed exchange counter.

"You got a car?" Kertzman asked, impatient.

Shocked, the man nodded.

Kertzman dropped his suitcase, took out a Marlboro, gesturing downward as he lit. "Let's go," he rumbled.

Thrilled at his sudden good fortune, the man bent and snatched up the suitcase.

It would cost at least 50 bucks, with a little padding, to catch a cab instead of the train. But he had no patience for trains right now, no patience for ticket punchers or the long walk through the metro to the subway. And, anyway, the United States Department of Justice was paying.

Still smiling, the driver moved hastily out the door with the suitcase. Kertzman followed, scanning left and right with a wary, tired air. He moved outside into the cold wind as the driver loaded the suitcase into an old, beaten beige Hyundai.

In the winter's late evening light, Kertzman stared at the tiny car, the narrow backseat and low ceiling. He shook his head. "Figures," he mumbled.

A voice came from behind him. "Perhaps I can be of service."

Kertzman turned slowly, no expression. "Hello, Sir Stephenson."

Smiling, Sir Henry Stephenson stepped up beside him. He was dressed sharply in a black chesterfield, the collars of a white starched shirt barely visible underneath. His luxurious black overcoat was casually unbuttoned, and his black cotton pants were perfectly creased above a pair of polished lace-up Oxfords.

Stephenson was cordial. Two old friends meeting in a faraway place. "Can I give you a lift into the city?"

Without waiting for a reply Stephenson nodded toward the parking lot. Kertzman turned to see a large black four-door Mercedes with a diplomatic plate pull away from a reserved parking place. It drove smoothly through the broken traffic to stop at the curb.

The driver didn't get out.

Kertzman felt that he was losing control of the situation. He focused on Stephenson. "Maybe I don't want a ride," he said, low.

"Well, Mr. Kertzman, perhaps you don't," Stephenson replied courteously, his voice also suddenly low. "I certainly have no wish to impose on you, my American friend. I only thought we might discuss a rather delicate situation involving a mutual acquaintance. And, just perhaps, as opposed to our last meeting, I might be of some use to you."

Kertzman noticed two Italian, white-shirted uniform police watching them suspiciously.

Make a decision.

Kertzman knew he was in the badlands, where nothing was safe and nobody could be known for certain. It was a place where one had to make instant decisions about who to trust, and where actions spoke far louder than words. Then he remembered that Stephenson was just about the only person who had helped him, so far.

He sniffed, nodded slightly. "Alright," he said, a tone of caution. "But make it quick. I got some place I gotta be."

Stephenson smiled. "Of course." He walked to the cabdriver, who had watched it all with a disappointed gaze. But his expression changed to one of gratitude when Stephenson handed him a large note, speaking quickly. Then, without complaint, the driver placed Kertzman's suitcase in the trunk of the Mercedes.

Kertzman walked to the formidable black car, which seemed to be armored even though he could see no armor. With only the slightest hesitation at the open back door, he climbed in.

Stephenson climbed in behind him, and the door shut with reinforced strength.

Locking.

A winged dragon with red eyes and grinning fangs crouched in the nightmares of Father Stanford Aquanine D'Oncetta, hovering over him, hungry, reaching out with taloned hands, clutching.

Father D'Oncetta sat up rigidly in his silken bed, instinctively bringing one forearm up across his face. Breath hard and fast, he stared wildly into the darkness at the foot of his bed. He was clammy with sweat.

Trembling, he grasped his chest with one hand, felt his panicked, racing heart as, suddenly lightheaded, he gasped for breath.

He scanned the surreal shadows of his darkened bedroom, watching through eyes still thick and heavy with sleep. After a moment he caught a breath, his near invulnerable control quickly asserting itself. Groaning in relief, he looked closer, more confidently, into the shadows.

No, he thought, there is nothing. "A dream," he said aloud. "Only a dream."

Bowing his head, D'Oncetta rested upright hands flat on the soft white silk.

Then D'Oncetta glanced up, finding the nightmarish shape beside him. And for a skipped heartbeat he searched for voice or breath but neither voice nor breath would come and the horror seemed to be choking him.

Black shape in shadow, poised at the foot of his bed, stygian form outlined before the faint light of the distant curtained windows. And D'Oncetta froze; it was no dream.

Slowly, with difficulty, D'Oncetta's keen intellect recovered his racing heart, his nerve. His cunning eyes narrowed slightly, estimating. Casually, he moved toward the side of the bed.

"Don't," the voice said quietly, almost sadly. "This belongs to me."

D'Oncetta ceased moving. He gazed at the intruder with a gathering calm, revealing himself as a man of some courage. After a moment D'Oncetta leaned forward, hands relaxed, open on the sheets. His voice was steady, strong.

"So," he said, undisturbed. "You have come."

A pause of ominous silence. "Yes," said Gage.

D'Oncetta's chin lifted slightly, a thin smile glancing across the tanned face. "And will you kill me?" he asked strongly, no fear traceable in his tone. "Is that why you are here? To kill me?"

The stranger seemed to move, shift; D'Oncetta could not be sure.

"Not yet," he replied.

D'Oncetta's gathering composure contained an element of contempt. "No," he replied bitterly. "Not yet." He paused. "So what do you want? What will be your vengeance?"

Thick, condensing silence.

D'Oncetta saw the black-gloved hands, the hue of a dark leather coat.

Face in shadow, the man bowed his head slightly forward. "I have the manuscript," he said.

D'Oncetta thought that he perceived a hint of fatigue in the dry, cracked voice. "And I am supposed to believe you?"

"You'll know soon enough."

The man seemed to sway slightly, and D'Oncetta thought he perceived the faintest lessening of the strong tone.

"Bring the woman to the Catacombs of Priscilla in the Villa Ada," the man instructed. "At midnight tomorrow. Unharmed. If you want the manuscript. If you don't come, or if I see police or military, I'll destroy the book."

D'Oncetta nodded, leaned forward, fully recovered. "Gage," he began, almost warmly, without fear, "you must listen to me. You must listen to reason. If—"

"Enough," said Gage. "Tomorrow night."

A pause. D'Oncetta nodded again. "As you wish," he replied, unwavering. "But I would impose a request. I do not wish to be with you alone, not after you have Ms. Halder at your side. I do not mean to transgress upon your honor, but I would insist on bringing an escort to insure that I do, indeed, depart from this."

No reply.

D'Oncetta repeated, "I will not meet you alone in the night! I am not a fool! Once you have Ms. Halder, you may commit something... precipitous. If you do not agree to this reasonable request, then you may destroy the book."

A swaying hesitation.

"Alright," Gage replied quietly. "Bring the men from the cabin."

D'Oncetta's face was curious, concentrated.

Cautiously, the stranger backed away, moving slowly, with soft steps. He was halfway across the room, completely lost in the gloom, when the almost indiscernible footsteps disappeared.

D'Oncetta turned his head slightly, listening.

"I know you are still there," he said calmly, driving back the intimidating darkness with the strong tone. "You have not deceived me."

"There was a time..." the voice came back, soft and whispering, "when I would have killed you... for this."

Rigid lines of control in D'Oncetta's face relaxed in a suddenly absorbing thought, or shock. But he recovered quickly, fluidly.

"Yes," replied the priest indulgently, with a priest's patient, understanding demeanor, "but you are not the man you were, are you, Gage?"

Silence.

D'Oncetta's tone reached out again, slightly impatient, faintly edged. "Gage?"

Wind and darkness whispered in the shadowed room.

D'Oncetta's strong tanned hands clutched involuntarily at the silken sheets of his bed.

"Gage?"

. . .

Stern stared moodily at the ocean from the windows of the palatial fortress by the sea, seemingly mesmerized by waves crashing against the cliffs in a gathering, rhythmic force of night.

Stately and composed, the white-haired man approached him from the side, elegant and regal in a long purple robe that swept the salt-stained stones of the balcony. The imperious figure hesitated as he drew near, ice-blue eyes focused and patient, infinitely calm.

Stern looked away from the cliffs, and his gaze settled on the man's aristocratic face. His voice was low and brooding. "Carl is dead, Augustus," he said, waiting. "Sato came in this morning and reported."

Stern looked again, dejectedly, to the ocean. "Gage reached the tomb last night before we arrived," he continued with a sigh. "There was... an incident. And now Carl is dead. Gage is also dead. Or at least I hope that he is dead." He paused, shook his head. "We can never be sure about him. He has survived so much. In any case, I fear that we may have lost the manuscript. Possibly forever."

A momentary concentration passed across the face of the man called Augustus. He nodded solemnly. "A sword may also wound the hand that wields it, Charles," he said. "From the beginning, we were certain to sustain injury. That is the hard rule of war."

Stern looked upon Augustus with respect. "Sato says that Gage slid into an ice-fall with Carl," he continued, morose. "And Gage was in possession of the prophecy." He waited. "Which means the manuscript has gone into the glacier. Lost."

Augustus smiled. "Nothing is lost, my friend," he added. "We must only reorganize for another attempt to claim what is rightfully ours. Remember, Charles, that genius in war is nothing more than the ability to maintain a calm mind in the excitement of conflict."

"Yes," said Stern slowly, and smiled wanly. "I wrote the manual on generalship, Augustus. I know these things. But in reality it is a difficult thing to do."

Augustus nodded. "Difficult, yes, because perception is always accompanied by pleasure, or pain. And the ordinary mind is tragically influenced by both. But we must rise above the ordinary, Charles. We must become more than mere men in order to claim the destiny that is ours. We must not stumble at pain, and we must not fear. Because fear, even as pain, lays the foundation for confusion, and confusion is the mark of the weak."

With consummate composure Augustus stepped forward. "Pain and fear are the masters of inferior men, Charles. They are the curse of ordinary minds, the minds of the defeated, and the foolish; minds that fulfill meaningless, fearful lives and are not missed by the world when they pass. As we both know, that is not our destiny. We were born to rule."

There was a slight relaxing in Stern's rigid stance. He nodded slowly and for a long time. "Yes," he said, "but, still, I fear the book is lost."

Augustus smiled encouragingly. "Great wealth can accomplish great things," he said stoically. "Nothing is lost as long as it is on the Earth. The book shall, in the end, be ours. And then we shall discover the name. Of that you can be utterly certain. Nothing can prevent it. Our intellects are superior. Our plans are infinite. There is nothing we cannot overcome."

Stern gazed at him with a solidifying confidence.

"For example, our original containment plan was unsuccessful," Augustus continued. "But that was merely the original plan. There are worlds within worlds, Charles. There were many, many more plans designed and prepared to serve our purpose, should that one have failed, as it did. It is only a minor inconvenience."

Stern regarded him calmly. "Very well. But the professor and his daughter still pose a security risk, Augustus. They must be dealt with."

Augustus nodded solemnly. "Yes, they must be silenced. But Gage is gone now, so their deaths shall be far simpler to accomplish, and far more merciful. Yet the professor must not be eliminated too quickly or it will arouse attention, and provide some evidence to his wild accusations which no one truly believes as yet. No, we shall wait for a suitable time, until he is released from protective custody. Then we shall do it quietly. And his unfortunate death, as usual, must seem providential." He waited, considering. "The woman, Ms. Halder, will be the most delicate matter. She must be dealt with immediately. And yet I hope that the act, unseemly as it is, is accomplished in a manner that appears quite natural. If possible, it must appear accidental, with witnesses to verify that no malevolent forces were at work."

Stern nodded. "It will be done, Augustus." He waited a moment. "And Kertzman? What shall be done with him? He has discovered a great deal."

Almost brooding, the austere, white-haired man turned his head slightly away, meditatively placing both hands in the front fold of his purple robe. A troubled look passed across the lean, careful countenance. "This man, Kertzman, is he a danger?" he asked.

Silence between them, waves crashing.

"He is a hunter," said Stern. "He arrived in Rome an hour ago. We believe he was planning to meet Gage. But that won't happen now, of course. Still, I don't think that Kertzman will stop his investigation. He is a hard man, and he will continue hunting. For the truth."

Thunderous wind swirled with white slashing mist below the fortress. Augustus nodded. "Death is a terrible thing," he said softly.

Suddenly an elegantly crafted phone positioned on a black rattan table rang softly.

Augustus stared at the intrusive device. Stern was also strangely still. Then the white-haired man picked it up, listening closely, his expression studious, concentrated. After a moment he replaced it, turning back calmly.

"Our friend, Father D'Oncetta, has visited the domain of dragons," he said quietly.

Inhaling a sudden breath, Stern stepped forward. "When?"

"A moment past," replied Augustus.

Stern's control seemed tested by the emotional intensity of the situation. "I *knew* he was alive. I *knew* he would not die. He wants an exchange." He looked at Augustus with the words. It was not a question.

Augustus nodded his head, solemn. "Yes."

"When?"

"At midnight tomorrow," Augustus replied, without emotion.

Stern shook his head. He clenched his fist, half-raising it as if to strike an unseen enemy, and he gazed about, like a man searching for an invisible foe.

Augustus smiled, blinked softly.

"Do not fear, my friend," he said, complete in his enduring calm. "Even dragons must die."

FORTY-EIGHT

Kertzman gazed out over Rome's sprawling city lights that pulsated dimly in the mid-darkness of night. He was all too aware of Sir Henry Stephenson, composed and patient, standing beside him.

"So," said Kertzman, with a trace of gathering anger. "Stern is MI6."

Silence.

"He *was* MI6," Stephenson replied finally, like a man constantly pained to speak with exactitude. "As I said, he disappeared from our operations over six years ago. At first we suspected that he might have defected, as Philby. Then we came to a more thorough understanding of Stern's philosophical principles and we reached quite a different conclusion. Since that time we have searched for him throughout America and Western Europe."

Kertzman didn't look at the Englishman. "But now you know that Stern has gone to work for someone else," he said. His voice wasn't friendly. "And you're trying to find out who. That's why you came to New York. You weren't there to make arrangements for Maitland. You couldn't have cared less about Maitland. You were there trying to figure out what your man, Stern, is up to nowadays."

Stephenson replied quickly and easily. "Yes."

Turning fully to face him, Kertzman's tone became genuinely angry. Hostile. "Does my government have all this?"

Stephenson held his ground against Kertzman's imposing force. Then, finally, he shook his head, noncommittal. "Who can say, Mr. Kertzman?" He sighed. "This profession can be somewhat tedious. But I would presume that, yes, they do know something. I, for one, believe that *someone* knows everything."

Nervously Kertzman clenched his empty left hand, wishing he'd brought the .45. International jurisdictional disputes had interceded, and he was forced to leave his gun in Washington.

Technically, if Gage would come in, Kertzman was supposed to escort him "without incident" to the American Embassy. Or, if

Gage refused to come in, Kertzman was supposed to pinpoint his location and notify the Embassy's resident FBI special agent who would, in turn, notify the Italian police for an official pickup order. The official word was that if Kertzman or any other Bureau special agent used a weapon on Italian soil while searching for Gage or Sarah Halder they would be prosecuted as an American civilian in violation of and under the jurisdiction of Italian law.

In reality everyone knew that there would never be any prosecution of an American federal agent for using a weapon on Italian soil, even if the weapon was used without permission. But the political repercussions would be profound, far-reaching and, though the situation certainly wouldn't come to imprisonment, it would assuredly end in a prompt and sacrificial termination once the agent returned to the States.

But as far as Kertzman was concerned, Sarah Halder was priority, and if he needed to use a weapon to get her back, then he'd use a weapon. If he could get his hands on one.

Gage had become a secondary issue. Kertzman didn't know if the Delta commando would come in, not with the situation as dirty as it was. And, somehow, he felt that Gage wouldn't live long if he did, indeed, come into protective custody. He almost wished that the soldier would take to the high country, get clear of it all. But Kertzman knew that he wouldn't; Gage had to finish this. He had to bring an ending to this part of his life, and the only way to truly do that was to come in, to testify.

And as bad as things were, they would get a lot worse before it was over. Kertzman couldn't remember a time when he wanted a gun as badly as he wanted one now.

He met Stephenson's even composure.

"So why didn't you tell me about Stern earlier?" he asked coarsely.

With a disappointed air Stephenson answered, "Mr. Kertzman, we do not flag our defections and disappearances before the scornful winds of the intelligence community. At the least, it is embarrassing. At worst, it could profoundly injure relationships."

"But you said it wasn't a defection."

Stephenson took out a silver case of long, thin cigarettes, offered one to Kertzman. Kertzman shook his head, took out a pack of Marlboros. Stephenson lit his cigarette with a small gold lighter. Kertzman used a match.

"No," the Englishman said somberly, exhaling. "No. Not a defection."

"Then what was it?" Kertzman rumbled, releasing a cloud of blue smoke.

Stephenson regarded him carefully. "What I'm about to tell you—"

"Yeah, I heard that part already," Kertzman growled, smoke drifting from his nostrils. He spat out a piece of tobacco. "Just tell me."

Stephenson's face revealed a pleasant amusement, but he continued in a serious tone. "For more than twenty years the man you know as Charles Stern was England's top counterintelligence operative for Western Europe and South Africa. During his tenure in MI6 he penetrated virtually every major intelligence network in his section of the globe. An astonishing feat, to say the least. And even more astonishing because he relied so heavily on live sources who could continuously process data for verification, a type of intelligence work, I might add, that is greatly superior to the simple data collection system used by your NSA satellites." He took an almost depressed draw on the cigarette. "All of Stern's work was consummate, and he had the highest clearance. At the time of his disappearance he had risen to the ninth most powerful position in Special Branch. Then he quite simply vanished. Disappeared without a trace while holding the keys to virtually all of our government's most carefully guarded secrets. Not a scandal, mind you, but sufficient cause for a decided panic."

Kertzman listened patiently.

"Upon the alarming occasion of his disappearance," Stephenson continued, "I was assigned the morbid responsibility of locating him, dead or alive. But there were only denials from the Soviets and East Germans. And our informants argued that Stern had not defected. So I began to explore other avenues to explain his disappearance, such as kidnapping by a foreign power, or assassination. Yet nothing developed to substantiate those suppositions, either. Finally, I began to investigate the possibility of a sort of private defection, a self-imposed exile initiated because of some mysterious interworkings of his own mind."

Understanding, Kertzman nodded. Then he pulled again on the Marlboro and released it patiently, letting it drift with Stephenson's words.

Stephenson thrust a hand into the pocket of his black overcoat. His left hand held the cigarette, which he gestured with, abstractly.

"For a time, I was unable to explain why he might commit such an act," the Englishman continued, exhaling. "Then I began a careful perusal of the books in Stern's private library. And I began to understand, or perceive, a distinct pattern of thought; a pattern of thought that led me to investigate the possibility that Stern might have shared certain philosophical ideals with a few of the world's more infamous megalomaniacs, ideals which would have made him...fundamentally unstable."

Cigarette forgotten in his hand, Kertzman held the Englishman's gaze.

"You see," continued Sir Stephenson, "I discovered that the man you know as Charles Stern possessed an almost pathological obsession with, ah, how shall I describe it, the selection of species."

"Superior beings," interjected Kertzman, with a touch of scorn.

Stephenson smiled benignly. "Yes, Mr. Kertzman. You might say that."

"So all that stuff you told me in the church was true," Kertzman asked gruffly. "Stern and whoever he's working for consider themselves to be some kind of master race. Superior. 'Cept their buddies ain't chosen by the color of their skin or hair or their nationality. They're chosen by how good they are at killing."

"As far as Stern is concerned, yes," Stephenson offered, with a nod. "He works only with the purest predators. During past years I have confirmed that Stern heads a secretive private group known as The Sixth Order."

Beneath his anger, Kertzman was confused. "What does that mean?"

Stephenson gestured vaguely with his cigarette, gazed out over the city a moment. In contrast to Kertzman's implacable anger, the Englishman appeared faintly disturbed.

"It is a rather nebulous concept," Stephenson explained patiently. "But, to put it into few words, it is a term taken from modern spiritism."

"Explain it to me," said Kertzman.

Stephenson nodded. "Yes, of course. It shall help you understand what you are facing. And then we will proceed with other matters."

Kertzman glanced at his watch. "I ain't got long, Stephenson."

Deliberate and calm, the Englishman continued, "Stern serves a man who considers himself to be some type of immortal being, a sort of modern Pharaoh who holds, within himself, the keys of eternal life."

Frowning, Kertzman took another drag, then released it with the stolid, ponderous, and thoroughly unfriendly gaze of a dinosaur. "What's this guy's name?" he asked.

"We do not know," Stephenson answered, shaking his head. "We only know that Stern does, indeed, serve this man." He continued, "This man, whoever he is, has established seven orders for mankind so that man may reach his own state of godhood, each stage being slightly more enlightened. The first stage, or the first order, is total ignorance. The second stage is the beginning of knowledge. The seventh order is when man can transcend, ah, flesh, and reign as a type of god." He paused. "Now, the sixth order, of which these men are known, is considered to be 'perfect man.' Perfect physically. Perfect mentally. Perfect psychically. Perfect spiritually."

Kertzman was unimpressed. His voice was brutally sarcastic. "So let me guess. These guys are supposed to be perfect."

Stephenson didn't laugh. "Oh, more than that, Mr. Kertzman," he replied with a steady and serious gaze. "They are part of a special group known as The Sixth Order. And the men in this group are considered perfect soldiers, perfect assassins."

"And this Sixth Order is this nut's enforcement arm, right?" growled Kertzman.

The Englishman nodded.

"And how many guys are in this little group?"

Stephenson shook his head. "Five, not including Stern. His inclusion brings it to six."

Kertzman moved ahead of it. "There ain't six no more, Stephenson. They've lost three, for sure. The Russian, the Nigerian, and Maitland."

"Yes," the Englishman agreed. "Only three remain. Stern, Carl Zossen, the German, and the Japanese known as Sato."

Struck by the name, Kertzman asked, "What's the story on the Japanese? Where does he come from?"

After a slow draw on the thin cigarette, Stephenson replied, "He was a counterterrorist for the Japanese Secret Police, working mostly against the Koreans or Chinese. But unlike most of his countrymen skilled in similar methods of warfare, Sato has always shunned working for *Yakuza*. He considers himself to be above an *Oyabun*. Until recently he has served only his country, so records of him are still highly classified and incomplete to our sources. But to be reasonably objective I must say that he was quite accomplished at virtually all forms of terrorism and counterterrorism. He was also highly paid by his very grateful country. Until he became involved in this particular form of spiritism, moving his talents beyond the arena of international industrial sanctions. His obsession with this, ah, enlightenment, is quite extreme." He paused. "As are his methods."

Stephenson's gaze strayed to Kertzman's bandaged arm.

Face impassive, Kertzman waited.

"So that you might estimate how formidable a foe he truly is," continued Stephenson calmly, "I can tell you, rather accurately, that Sato has committed no less than one hundred fifty sanctions in his time. Now, mind you, not all of them were initial targets. But because he prefers to use, ah, how shall we say, rather *primitive* methods, he is usually forced to get within close physical proximity of his target. Which necessitates the removal of numerous security personnel, and so forth." He shook his head. "It becomes quite tedious to recount."

"Forget it," said Kertzman, indifferent. "Let me finish what you were going to say." He took a deep breath, stepped forward. "Some spiritual psychopath, identity still unknown, has this army of so-called supermen killing people all over the world because they want this manuscript. They believe that this thing reveals the name of the Antichrist." He paused, shook his head. "This guy is obsessed with it. 'Bout like Hitler was obsessed with ancient artifacts that would give him some kind 'a power over the Allied forces. And Black Light was used by Stern and his boss to build their financial base, in case they could prepare the way for this... whatever it is. Just like Stern has probably used the military units of a dozen other countries for the same thing. He just paid whoever it took, got the orders cut to do the hit, and passed it to the military. It only worked 'cause soldiers don't ask no questions. They're trained to take orders, do their job. They didn't know that someone inside their own government had sold them out, was using them to build an empire for a psychopath."

"Yes," Stephenson agreed easily. "I believe that you have correctly summed up the situation."

Kertzman stepped forward, angry, growling. "Well, I hope you don't mind me saying it, Stephenson, but it sounds to me like Stern and whoever he's working for are *crazy*."

Stephenson was undisturbed. "Without question," he said. "However, that does not change the fact that Charles Stern is a great danger to the defense of the Realm. He must be apprehended. Because we suspect that if he is not soon stopped he will begin some type of systematic repression, inspired by this lunatic who is his employer, against the nation of Israel. Possibly, it could even lead to nuclear threats inspired by the orchestrated cooperation between Middle Eastern countries that would be forged from this ancient manuscript." He waited. "In this situation, Mr. Kertzman, time is most certainly not on our side."

Kertzman nodded. "Yeah," he said, "I know this part." He waited to decide what he wanted to ask. "And now you want me to help you bring Stern back in from the cold."

It was a statement. Not a question.

Stephenson nodded, utterly dignified. "Yes. I ask you for this single favor. I have been honest with you, and I would like for you to return that courtesy."

"And how, exactly, do you want me to do that?"

Stephenson stepped forward, earnest. Kertzman didn't move.

"It is a simple request, really," Stephenson said. "I understand that the American, Jonathan Gage, is attempting to obtain the manuscript that Stern and his employer seek so badly. Also, I understand from my sources that you are planning an exchange, the manuscript for the woman. I merely ask that you telephone and advise me where you will be making the rendezvous so that I may attend. I will not interfere until after the exchange. I give you my word that I will not jeopardize your plans. Perhaps, I might even be of assistance in some small way."

Kertzman nodded, cold. "You must want Stern pretty badly."

"Yes," the Englishman replied. "We do. He must be taken for interrogation." He took another draw on the cigarette, released it steadily, unhurried.

"And if you can't take him alive," Kertzman said, "you're gonna kill him. In fact, you would probably prefer to kill him because if you take him alive you'll have to figure out what to do with him. It'd turn out to be a long-term problem. Too many questions. Too many people who can disagree with your methods." He paused, eyed Stephenson up close. "That's the real plan, ain't it Stephenson? You're gonna kill him."

Silence followed Kertzman's words. Stephenson waited, composed. "Yes," the Englishman said, finally. "That is the plan."

Kertzman took it in, saw how far things had gotten out of hand. Old comrades killing one another. No arrests, no apprehensions. No questions.

He shook his head, half-turned away. "Well, at least you didn't lie to me," he said, looking at the city again. "And that's good. 'Cause I knew the answer, anyway."

"I know," said Stephenson.

Kertzman laughed shortly, without humor.

"Yeah," he continued, "I figure you do." Then he shook his head again. "But I think I'll pass, Sir Henry. I only drop a man in self-defense. And, then, when I have to. I ain't no hitter. And I ain't gonna set nobody up to get hit."

He stared at Stephenson for a moment, as if he were searching for what he wanted to say.

"I'm grateful for what you've told me. I owe you for that. But I don't bend over backwards for nobody. Never have. Never will."

Suddenly, even as Kertzman uttered the words, Sir Henry Stephenson seemed struck by something else, an idea, or inspiration. He gazed at Kertzman for a long moment. Then he slowly nodded, murmuring.

"Yes, of course," he said, turning away from Kertzman. "That would be it ... I see ..."

"What do you see?" Kertzman asked, in no mood for games.

A pause, and Stephenson looked back at Kertzman with an abrupt and unusual compassion. "How is it, if I may ask, that you were chosen to hunt down Gage, Mr. Kertzman?"

"'Bout the same as always," Kertzman said. "I got volunteered."

"Because of your integrity, I presume."

Kertzman's face revealed nothing. "That was the line they used."

"Yes." Stephenson's gaze grew distant. "Of course."

Kertzman took a step forward, eye to eye. "I'm runnin' out of patience, Stephenson."

The Englishman's fortitude was unmoved. He studied Kertzman with a mesmerizing steadiness. "I would like to ask you one more question," he ventured.

"Make it quick," said Kertzman.

"First, I must tell you that I know of Black Light. I know of Radford and Milburn and Carthwright and, even, Admiral Talbot."

"I figured," Kertzman said, without blinking.

Stephenson laughed. "Yes, I suppose that you would. In any case, when you agreed to take this assignment from Carthwright, when you agreed to discover who was running Black Light, you obviously told them that you would document everything. You warned them you would protect no one. Absolutely no one. Even if it led straight to their desk, so to speak."

It didn't sound like a question. Kertzman wasn't sure how to reply. "Yeah," he said finally. "I told them I'd document everything. I told them I'd nail whoever it led back to. Even them."

Stephenson nodded. "Of course you did. Because you are a man of genuine integrity. A man, even, of *unyielding* integrity."

A silent, focused stare from Kertzman. "What are you thinking, Stephenson?"

Bowing his head slightly, Stephenson looked at the ground for a moment. "You must allow me some credit, Mr. Kertzman," he began, looking up again. "I am, as an old OSS man would put it, 'a perfect spy.' It is both my craft, and my love. You, however, are primarily a hunter. You are not attuned to the subtleties of this world, as I am. So you could not be expected to see it. Not in the beginning, at least."

Kertzman began to get a terrible feeling. A question came to him, but he couldn't ask it.

"Let me tell you how it happened," said Sir Stephenson, kindly. "I know, already, the basic scenario. The NSA needed a man who could hunt Gage. You, as a consummate hunter, were deemed a good selection for the job. But there are other men who are also good hunters, Mr. Kertzman. So why did the NSA select you for the job, and not one of them? That is the question you must first ask. And quite probably, you did. And you were simply told that you were the best available man."

Kertzman nodded slowly. "Go on," he grunted, emotionless.

Stephenson's gaze strayed toward the city lights, and back. He seemed to be recalling a vast panorama of experience and trade-craft, weaving it together in a mesmerizing dialogue.

"Your superior, Carthwright, told you that the situation was extremely grave. Further, he told you that someone occupying a significant post within your government was possibly the sinister force who misused Black Light for his own personal gain. So you began your investigation. Your primary objective was to locate Gage. Your secondary objective was to locate whomever had misused the unit. As it happened, you did eventually find Gage's safe house. At this point you also discovered that someone within your own division had betrayed you. However, against what fate might have decreed, Stern and his men, who were also hunting Gage, failed to kill all of you. So, whoever it was that was trying to contain the investigation and confine the blame to Gage alone failed. And you refocused your efforts to find out who had truly misused Black Light."

Stephenson shuffled a step, studied Kertzman. "Let us begin with basics, Mr. Kertzman." He paused. "Who attempted to kill you at the cabin?"

"Stern," said Kertzman.

"Yes. So it has, of course, occurred to you that Black Light was run by Stern, and he was under orders from someone to contain the situation with Gage?"

"Yeah, I've gone past that already," said Kertzman.

"Yes, of course you have," Stephenson replied. "So you've obviously surmised that Stern and his...master...were the force using someone within your government, and by extension using Black Light, to build their financial empire."

"Uh huh," Kertzman grunted. "I'm just trying to find out who it was." With the words, Kertzman began to arrive at a terrible conclusion, nothing he had ever anticipated.

"Now, at this point, after the situation at the cabin, the investigation began to take a new and unexpected turn," Stephenson said.

"More than likely, evidence was mysteriously uncovered that cast the light of guilt onto a new head..."

Kertzman remembered Acklin's package.

"Yes," said the Englishman mildly, as if he were teaching a history class, "but it was not someone you did not already suspect. No, this guilt was thrown onto the head of someone that you did, indeed, suspect. It might even be someone who knew that you would do whatever you had to do to find the guilty party. Someone who knew, without question, that you would never allow any personal feelings of loyalty to interfere with your unyielding integrity. Ideally, it was someone who, on several occasions, warned you explicitly to stay away from a certain area of the investigation, an area where evidence would lead the investigation back to him." Stephenson nodded with his words, spoke more slowly. "Yes, someone who knew that you would document all of his hampering efforts to prevent the investigation from following a certain line of inquiry that would lead, without question, directly back to him. Making him appear even more guilty."

Kertzman waited in a subdued, awful silence.

A long drag on the cigarette and Stephenson resumed in a knowing, patient voice. "Yes, you documented everything, Mr. Kertzman. You documented every stonewalling action, every misdirecting comment or hampering effort, just as you told them you would."

Kertzman closed his eyes.

"Just as they *wanted* you to do," Stephenson continued. "It was for this purpose that you were truly selected for the job. They knew that you would not allow personal feelings to interfere in your dedicated, single-minded pursuit of truth. They could, in a sense, bank on your integrity to support their efforts, where another man might fail them by concealing information, or even overlooking something that would have incriminated his superiors." He paused, continued, "However, with you, they knew there would be no danger of that, that you would follow the tracks of guilt to the last man, even to the desk of your beloved supervisor."

Shaking his head, Kertzman saw the perfection.

"You see, Mr. Kertzman, it is the craft of a spy to use an adversary's own, ah... *casual nature*, if you will, against him. For you, this means that your adversary would use your own unbending integrity to serve his purpose."

Kertzman released a deep breath, half-turned his head away, remembering the words.

"Make sure you document everything..."

And,

"I knew we could count on you..."

Carthwright.

Kertzman understood, at last, why they had picked him: He was the perfect man for the job. So stubbornly determined not to be broken, not to bend backward, he had documented all the denials, all the misdirection, just as they knew all along that he would, had planned on it. He had even seen it, *felt* it, from the very beginning, had sensed that something was wrong, but he'd never understood it.

He had looked for something complicated, something buried. That's why he'd never seen it. It never was buried, never concealed. From the very beginning, it was too easy to see.

Hiding in plain sight.

Carthwright.

A head high enough to take the heat, heavy enough to call the shots. But still a fall guy, set up from the very beginning to make the sacrifice.

"Don't mess with these people, Kertzman... Stay away from the money... There's nothing there... Stay away from the money... There's nothing there..."

The perfect plan.

And, like the perfect fool, he had done exactly what he was supposed to do to make it work. Kertzman knew now what name Acklin would eventually find in the computer search, knew where it would end, even as he knew that it was a sacrificial move. And their sacrifice would work. It would work because he had *made* it work by documenting every action that would have stalled the investigation, and had even moved beyond it to the place where they always intended for him to go.

Sullen and angry, he looked at Stephenson.

The Englishman smiled. "Yes, Mr. Kertzman. I would surmise that there is no one who is truly on your side."

Kertzman couldn't think of anything to say.

"And yet," Stephenson added, "I believe that Mr. Carthwright is a valuable man. More than likely, he would be a costly sacrifice. And their game is not over. If you and Gage still happen to fall under a sanction, I'm sure other containment plans can be initiated which will save the career of both your supervisor and those around him." He debated. "Carthwright would normally be reserved as an extreme sacrifice for an extreme emergency. Surely, both Gage and you remain primary targets."

Solemn, Kertzman nodded. "Yeah," he said quietly. "If they can still kill me and Gage they might be able to pin it all on him, despite everything I've written in my reports. But if Gage survives, it'll all fall on Carthwright. For containment. It'll never reach who's really guilty. It'll never reach Stern. Carthwright will take it all and live with it."

"Yes," said Stephenson, finishing his cigarette, squinting. "I imagine that he will. Just as I imagine he will do his best to see that you are dispatched before this is over."

Kertzman sniffed, taking it all in. He looked at his watch. One hour till midnight. He released a weary breath. He felt cold, sweaty and grimy from the long flight.

"Alright," he mumbled. "I appreciate your help. And I'd like to pay you back. But it still don't mean I can set up a hit on Stern." He paused. "I am what I am, Stephenson. And I ain't no killer."

Stephenson smiled. "I understand," he said. "We must all live by our personal code of honor. But I am certain that you will encounter extreme violence when you attempt to make the exchange. I am convinced that Stern and his Sixth Order will attempt to kill all three of you."

"Yeah," said Kertzman, tiredly. "I guess. But there ain't nuthin' I can do about that. I'll have to play it by ear. 'Bout like everything else I been doing." He took two steps towards the Mercedes. "I got to get to the hotel."

"Mr. Kertzman?"

Kertzman turned back to see a large black revolver in Stephenson's hand. The gun was being handed to him, butt first, Stephenson holding the barrel.

"For the exchange," said the Englishman.

Kertzman looked down at the gun, saw the blue-black sheen in the moonlight. He wondered how many guns he had held in his life, how many men he had killed. He felt tired.

Stephenson waited.

Kertzman saw, and felt, it all, the fatigue and the pain... Sarah Halder screaming in horror...Gage, alone and hunted, waging a desperate war against these forces...Sandman on the floor ...Barto...Malachi.

And here he was, caught in the middle, feeling like an old man trying to find his way through a darkened labyrinth of lies. Being used. Being fooled. Doing more harm than good.

Losing. He wondered how much longer he could keep it up.

He gazed steadily at the gun. Stephenson's hand was dead calm.

A man's got to live with himself.

Frowning, nodding, Kertzman reached out with his uninjured left hand, folding calloused fingers around the smooth, polished blue steel.

One last time.

. . .

Kertzman stared at the balcony doors, closed and curtained, from the inside of his third-floor room at the Medici Hotel on the Via Vittorio.

Midnight. He'd made it, but not by much. In silence and shadows, he waited. Alone. He looked at his watch. Again.

"Midnight," he mumbled. "I know I got it right. I know he said midnight."

A droning ring sounded at the desk.

Face rigid and suddenly tense, Kertzman gazed at the black telephone.

It rang again.

For the briefest moment he hesitated, feeling the tempting and life-preserving impulse to walk away. He hovered over the decision. A moment more passed, and Kertzman walked to the desk, sat down heavily in the chair.

Another ring.

A scarred hand reached out and picked it up.

"Yeah."

"Listen quick," the voice said. "You're under surveillance. You've got to move fast."

Kertzman's face was instantly concentrated. Gage's voice sounded strange, brittle, seeming to come from the depths of something dry and hoarse.

Kertzman grunted that he understood.

"Go north on Vittorio on foot. After five blocks you'll come to a park. The Galoppatoio. Go straight down the middle past the two big bronze statues of whoever those guys are. Just walk to the other side. Go down the alley. I'll meet you there."

"Yeah. I got it," Kertzman rumbled. "But make sure you meet me. I've come too far to miss out on this."

The line went dead.

Kertzman stared at the phone for a solemn, heavy minute. Placed it carefully on the hook. He sniffed, face frowning in deep emotion, hot with a fear that he couldn't quite put down.

This was far out, as far out as he had ever been, and, even now, he wasn't sure what had compelled him to go to the edge. Maybe something had snapped inside of him at the cabin. Maybe it was vengeance at being used and set up. Or maybe it was simply because he was old and tired and pushed too far.

Whatever, it had come to this place, to this dangerous and lonely place.

And there was always something else...

A man's got to live with himself.

Kertzman stood up and walked to the bed, grabbing his coat. Finding comfort in the commitment of movement he walked toward the door, relieved that the waiting game had finally passed.

He stepped into the hallway, locking the door behind him. Then he walked quietly down the dark mahogany corridor. He considered the stairs and decided against them. He kept moving toward the elevator.

He was disturbed by something as he walked forward, his mind resisting even as it crossed over him in a mocking wave.

Too quiet. You're too quiet.

And it was too early for stalking, too soon for the kind of silence that comes with the hunt.

Kertzman realized it even as he reached the elevator. He knew the reason, and he tried not to think about it as he pushed the elevator button, his other hand creeping up to find a casual, empty hold on the .44 in his belt.

It whispered to him.

Fear.

• • •

Kertzman exited the lobby through the wide double glass doors and was on the street, moving with purpose, crossing the Via Ludovisi and the subway.

Then, out of nowhere, Gage was moving against him. Descending into the subway tunnel, relaxed and quick. Gage cast him a narrow nod. Then Kertzman had turned, too, casually, stepping quickly down the stairs, following.

He didn't look back.

Below, Gage moved through the subway turnstile as the train was loading but walked down the trestle, away from the open doors. He was ahead of Kertzman, who hadn't slowed, still hadn't looked back.

At the end of the underground station was a red metal door that Kertzman knew would be locked. But Gage opened it without hesitation, vanished inside.

In ten seconds, sweat clammy on his back, Kertzman also reached it, turning as he went through to cast a quick, furtive glance back down the trestle.

Coming fast through the turnstile, head turning to scan and locking instantly on him, was a strongly athletic man in a three-piece suit and dark coat. Kertzman didn't recognize him from the cabin. The man paused for a second, saw Kertzman staring at him, froze as if caught.

Kertzman turned away, glimpsed darkness inside, and quickly closed the door behind him.

A moonlit howl marked the mist that swept in white winds across the darkened cape, while far below the cliffs the sea foamed alive in the slashing tide.

Silently at the cliff edge, amidst the wind that moved the misty air, the old man stood; alone and lonely, forlorn in the quiet grave-yard of the coast where only the sea claimed a proud domain.

He watched with quiet solitude as the mist rolled over the waves that struck the shore in a deepening, gathering rhythm, as if to enlarge its imprisoned domain.

Frowning, the man stared silently into the raging sea.

He was old, yes, very old, and it came to him that he had lived too long, and seen too much, but not yet had he seen nature overcome itself. Not yet had he seen the sea claim dominion over the strand, nor the night-light rise to rival the dawn.

Nature remained consistent, each force as unchanging as the level of the sea or the expanse of the sky; it could never be altered or transformed, not by the power of human will or desperate dreams nor even by the bold and ageless fantasy realms of man.

The wrinkled, weathered lines in the old man's face deepened in a frown. No, the sea had never overcome the shore and never would. And the world was more fortunate for it, for many things were imprisoned in the sea; yes, many... many things.

Soft movement.

Gazing down at a grave, the old man half-turned his head to the sound, saying nothing.

A voice from the gloom was respectful.

"A ruler should be the last to arrive at a tryst, Holiness. Not the first."

Clement said nothing.

Atlantean in poise, emerging from the fog like an ancient god striding forth, loosed from the mists of time, Augustus walked forward. Clad to the waist in a thick black vestment, he strode steadily up the small hill, his dark cape billowing in the darkness, moving with the wind.

Turning fully, Clement faced him.

Calmly, regally, Augustus emerged into the moonlight, aquiline features placid and serene beneath the straight white hair that swept back nobly from the high forehead. As he came forward Clement saw the tastefully crafted black pants, loose and vaguely militaristic, with high, tight-laced boots of soft, luxurious leather.

Silent, respectful, Augustus halted before the old man. The moon lit the silver clasps that secured his heavy black cloak.

Augustus gazed down upon a gray-shadowed moss-covered grave. Seeming to forget the old man before him, he bent, reaching down to touch the tombstone with a strong, gentle hand.

"How appropriate that we would meet here," Augustus said softly. "And how tragic the cause of our gathering."

Clement was silent.

"I am reminded of the beginning," Augustus continued. "When you were the priest in yonder church along the shore, and I was the apprentice. When I searched only for truth, and you lived only to serve." He paused. "Before we became enemies, Clement. Before we came to waste our power and our lives in this foolish struggle."

Clement's face was suddenly moved, gently emotional. But Augustus failed to notice. He lifted his head to gaze at the moon, now full, white, and low.

"A tragedy," he added, gazing at the white glowing horizon of night, where the moon merged with the sea, "that we were both so unyielding."

Clement's voice was soft. "The only tragedy, Augustus," he replied, steady and deep, "is that you long ago ceased to search for truth. And I long ago ceased to truly serve. We were blessed in both intellect and will, and we might have changed the Church, and even the world, for good. But we lost our way and made our lives a ruin."

"Nothing is lost, Clement." Augustus shook his head indulgently, undisturbed. "We have a new beginning, a new chance to find what escaped us."

Clement laughed shortly, sadly. "Fantasies, Augustus. I come here to speak to you of life, and death. And you speak to me of fantasies. Is this where your great search and your proud wisdom has brought you?"

Augustus smiled. "Reality is more than men realize, Holiness. They say faith is the substance of things hoped for, the evidence of things unseen. Well, I would tell you that reality is the substance of dreams, of will and the untapped powers of man." Augustus stepped forward, his face brightening. "And it is no illusion, Clement! Reality is not the simple-minded metaphysical way of the world, nor the way of meaningless superstition, nor the way of the dying Church. No, my friend, I have found the true and unlimited path to freedom, to everything eternal!"

Clement shook his head, face tightening in pain. "You are mad, Augustus."

Augustus laughed. "Madness to madmen may be reason, Clement. So which one of us is sane, and which, mad?"

Turning away slightly, Clement gazed down at the distant surf. "Even gold grows dim in the darkness."

"I am not the fool, old friend, as you claim," vaunted Augustus. "I know the truth, and I am free by my own divine will! And, if I find the book, we shall all be free. It's true, Clement, that long ago I ceased to follow the Church because the Church ceased to follow the truth. I have never regretted that choice. And hubris has remained my foe. I am not proud or overreaching to my own destruction. And I will not deny what I have found." He stepped forward even more. "I know the truth, Clement! I know the truth without God or devils or pagan rituals. I have been to the other side!"

A sudden wind lifted the short white cape around Clement's neck. "You want what you cannot have, Augustus."

"Not so." Augustus raised his hand, gesturing to the sky and the stars that whitely dotted the dome of darkness. "All that there is, is there, Clement, so that it can be known. The Cosmos is all that is, and it is there so that we may know it. There are worlds within worlds, my friend. I am telling you the truth."

The old man's voice was resolute. "The secret things belong to God."

Augustus laughed lightly. "Not any longer," he replied softly. "There is an end to all things. Even God."

Clement paused, head bowing above a bitter face, the face of a father remembering the death of a son. "Augustus . . . my poor, deceived Augustus," he began slowly, looking up again. "When was it that I destroyed you? What did I do to lead you down this path of madness? Was it in exploring ideas that were beyond you, at too early an age? Was it in not being more circumspect in my reasoning? In using too many Jesuit twists of logic in our early words?"

Looking away vaguely, Clement shook his head. He closed his eyes, opened them again with a sigh. "I cannot say. I cannot remember. My sins are my sins. It is enough." He centered his gaze again on Augustus. "I ask you for the final time. Will you not turn from this task? Will you not surrender your claim over this ancient book?

I know that you do not yet have it, and I cannot allow you to claim it. If you continue, I will be forced to stand against you."

Augustus shook his head. "The book shall be mine, Clement."

"No, Augustus. It is evil. It is not just a man! It is a beast! And you are deceived into believing that it is Almighty God!"

Augustus stood squarely before the old man. "Clement, hear me. He is *not* evil! How can anyone who brings unity be evil? He is good. He is the ultimate superior being! He is God without the mystery! And we must prepare the way for him!"

Persuasively, Clement leaned forward. "Augustus, hear reason from me, for perhaps the last time," he began. "Because after this night you will hear no more. Lines will be drawn. And you will defend yourself against me. If this book were merely philosophy or even ancient literature I would release it to the entire world. Even Simon, whom you killed, would have had no opposition to that. But it is more, Augustus. It is much more. It reveals the family lineage, the time and place where the Beast shall be born. It reveals his very name. Some, if they knew his identity, would prepare his kingdom beforehand, so that he could even enlarge upon the monstrous persecutions which God will so mysteriously allow. Others, such as Israel, if they knew of him, would attempt to slay him. But he cannot be slain by the arm of man. For it is written that he will rise from the sea and conquer, and, yes, for a time he will unite the world in peace. But the peace shall mask his evil, and serve *his* purpose! And when the peace has passed he will make war against the saints. But he will not overcome until the Messiah returns. That does not mean we cannot stand against him to prevent what suffering can be prevented, to save those lives that can be saved! Listen, Augustus! You must see the reason in this! The Beast is evil but he is wise. Wiser than us. And he has deceived you into believing these illusions! Hear me, old friend. You are deceived!"

Clement shook his head with the fervor of his words. "We *cannot* be in league with the devil, Augustus! It is an abomination. Listen to me! Repent from this! Find your old way! Perhaps there is still hope for you. Perhaps your sins are not mortal. Destroy this book and forget. Yes, forget and let us pray together, now, tonight, as we prayed together when you were only a child and I was your confessor, and God may yet receive you. Because if you do not, then you will be serving the Abomination. In your foolishness you will strengthen his empire. You may even hasten his dominion over what he has no right to claim! So listen to me! The book must be destroyed! Even as I should have destroyed it years ago, after it was resurrected by Simon. But I was sinful and cowardly and resisted what I knew was right. Now, though, I will not fail. I will *not* let you have it. The manuscript must be destroyed. At any cost."

Augustus seemed unfazed. "I am not convinced that you could make war against me, Clement. My powers are great, and protected. It would take many years for you to affect my empire at all."

For a long silent moment, Clement stood, breathless from his petition. His eyes searched the determined face before him. Then he nodded, weary, with pain in his voice, his face. "So be it," he whispered. "Then I shall take years."

Calm, Augustus's steady gaze centered on the old man.

"Better to be a living dog, Clement," he said slowly, "than a dead lion."

"And better, yet," Clement replied, releasing a sad laugh, "to be a living lion."

Augustus's face was grim. "I tell you again, Clement, the book is not evil!"

"Look at your hands!" roared Clement, ignited suddenly to step forward in a startling display of immense and volcanic anger. "You are destroying yourself, Augustus! There is blood on your hands! Listen!" He flung out a robed arm. "Simon's blood calls to you from the Earth! I can hear it! You search for truth, but your search has caused you to destroy the lives of the innocent! Is that not evil? Is it not evil to grind down the lives of the weak? Look at what you have become, Augustus! A murderer! A medieval warlord, like Genghis Khan, or Hitler, with a mercenary army! Your words are noble, but your actions reveal what you truly are!"

"Desperate times require desperate measures, Clement." Augustus stepped back. His ice-blue eyes revealed the first, faintest lessening of composure, of doubt that flashed across the visage like lightning, and was gone. Hesitantly, he continued, "I...had no other option. You would not surrender the book."

"As I said, Augustus. It was not yours to possess."

Augustus stiffened. "And was it yours, Clement? Was it yours? Was it Simon's? Whose?"

Clement said nothing.

Recovering, Augustus gathered himself. "I *will* have the manuscript, Clement!"

For a long moment, the old man was silent, seeming to debate and resist some impulse within himself.

"So be it," he said, finally. "But if you claim the manuscript you will worship at the feet of the Beast. So I cannot allow you to possess it, even if only for your own sake. I will resist you until I die."

Fully composed, though his face hardened, Augustus sighed tiredly. "Enough, Clement," he said with a hint of pain. "I see there can be no peace between us."

Clement agreed. "No, not peace. Not between us. Not as long as you murder and oppress to claim what is not yours."

A long silence held, intensified, and lingered between them. Clement's gaze was stone, implacable and unyielding. And Augustus in quick degrees solidified a rigid control, becoming equally as implacable, and unyielding.

Cold wind passed between them, and clouds hung between the earth and sky, casting a gray night-shadow.

"Remember this," said Clement. "The law shall always stand against the lawless. The peaceful shall always stand against the violent. The righteous shall always stand against the wicked. It is the way of all things. So there will be no ultimate victory for you, Augustus. The Beast will conquer and make war, but he shall not rule. The Christ, whom you worshipped as a child, will not allow it. And, despite your fantasies and your madness, you have no eternal dominion that will shift the power to your side. So there will be conflict, even as there is conflict in the sea rising against the shore. The sea will never overcome, nor will the shore yield."

Augustus nodded, thoughtful. "And what will you do?" he asked.

"What I must do."

"That is no answer."

Clement frowned. "No. But it is truth. And truth is enough. It is more than you have offered."

Augustus retreated cautiously a step as the wind silently lifted his black cloak, caressing the darkness behind him. Warily, with distance, he eyed the old man before him.

A bellowing wave crashed upon the strand.

Roaring.

FIFTY

Gage taped a fresh bandage on Kertzman's forearm. Kertzman had trashed the other during their long run through the sewer system in Rome.

As Gage finished, Kertzman looked around at the safe house: a deserted, square, yellow two-tier building on the distant outskirts of Rome. He had no doubt that he would never see his hotel again.

Gage had rented the place from some farmer. It smelled like it might have once been used as a slaughterhouse; no heat, no electricity, no running water. It was old and dilapidated, had no phone, no windows, and probably not even an address.

Kertzman shifted in the old wooden chair.

Escaping from the subway station was far simpler than Kertzman had feared.

First, a long but uncomplicated run down the maintenance tunnel to the rail system itself, then over the rails and into another tunnel that ended at a large underground drainage pipe, a sewer. Then down the pipe to a manhole cover that exited onto a street somewhere downtown.

Gage had already acquisitioned a car, and, after sanitation procedures to lose any possible surveillance, they drove back to this place, arriving in the dark of early morning.

Tired, Kertzman sighed. It had been a long night. A long couple of days.

His arm itched, and, frowning down, he resisted the impulse to scratch his bandage. His forearm and a portion of his hand were still numb. The Japanese had sliced him deep, severing muscle, tendons, and a major nerve.

Two nights ago, on the night of the shooting, physicians at Monticello Medical Center had told Kertzman he would probably regain partial use of his hand, but little of the feeling. The nerve wouldn't heal, they said, but would "fuse" in time, so there was no way to predict how his hand would eventually function.

Concealing his disappointment, Kertzman had grunted indifferently at the diagnosis. But he had taken it hard and felt it hard. Steel had sliced again through him, another wound from the Japanese.

Gage finished changing the forearm bandage with an expert, methodical familiarity. Bandage and gauze, strips of tape moving over a butterfly tie that helped the sutures hold the wound closed. Experienced with wounds, his hands moved swiftly, gingerly, without the roughness expected from a professional soldier. He softly applied the final strips of tape, smoothed it down.

"That should do it, Kertzman." He rose to turn tiredly away. "That's good enough to hold you." He waited a second. "Do you still want to go through with this? You're hurt worse than I thought you were. You're only going to have one arm."

"Yeah," Kertzman grunted. "I want to go through with it. I want to finish it."

Gage watched him. Kertzman saw the wheels turning.

Gage began, "You're—"

"Going with you to finish this," Kertzman said gruffly, bluntly. "Okay, I'm hurt worse than you thought. So?" He paused. "Look, I need your testimony but I ain't gonna force you. You been through enough, and I don't think you'll live long if they take you into custody. This thing is even dirtier than I thought. There's still too many spooks running around who can save their hides by having you pushed into the street. No, I'm here to get Sarah Halder, take her back. So we might as well work together. We could both use the backup." He looked at Gage steadily. "After that, you can do what you want. I'll cover you as long as I can. They're offering immunity, but that's up to you. There's a fall guy set up, but I don't know who really ran Black Light, and neither do you. Frankly, I don't think we ever will."

Reaching out with his left hand, his good hand, Kertzman lifted a steaming cup of coffee that Gage had heated on a small stove. He took a sip, held the cup in his hand. "Who do you figure that guy was who came through the turnstile after us?" he asked.

Gage almost smiled. "No way to know." He leaned back and seemed to search an image inside his mind. "He was on somebody's squad, but there were at least two different teams and they weren't working together. I saw at least twelve people on surveillance. There might have been as many as twenty." He waited, shook his head. "It was weird. You're a popular person."

Kertzman pondered it. "Probably British. They want Stern. He's a runaway."

"MI6 is hunting Stern?"

Kertzman nodded. "They wanted me to help them take him down. Kill him. They want him pretty bad. A loose cannon sort 'a thing."

Gage shook his head. "I'm not going to trust anybody else at this stage, Kertzman. Too much can go wrong. We'll take Stern down ourselves."

Kertzman took another sip of coffee. "Well, you sure lost all of 'em pretty easy."

"It's easy to lose surveillance when you go underground." Gage loosened his shoulder, as if stretching sore muscles. "But we never would have lost them on the street. Never. We would have had to kill one of them. And I don't want to hurt anybody. I just want those guys to stay out of my way. Anyway, there's no way to know who they were, for sure. Not without bringing one of them with us for some questions. It definitely wasn't an Italian team, but it might have been KGB. CIA. Rome's resident FBI guys. More of Stern's crew. An NSA team. All of them together stepping over each other's feet. This stuff gets so complicated, you wouldn't believe it. But you can assume that everybody is in bed with everybody else. So the general rule is not to trust anybody. Assume everyone is a threat and lose them."

With a pained expression on his face, Gage reached over and lifted a small pill bottle. He took out three capsules, swallowing them with a long drink of water. He leaned his head back against the wall, eyes closed.

Kertzman watched him. "You don't look so good, boy," he rumbled. "What happened?"

Gage smiled wryly, opened his eyes. "I could look a lot worse, Kertzman. I had a little dance with them over who was going to walk off with the book. Now I've got to keep the pain down, or I won't be able to concentrate. Or move." He blinked tiredly. "I guess I've got maybe seventy-two hours before I can't go anymore. I'm hurt pretty bad. And I'll probably get hurt a lot worse before this thing is finished. By then the pain will be too much to overcome, even with drugs." He massaged his shoulder.

Kertzman's eyes widened. "Did you get any of them?"

"One."

"The Japanese?"

Gage shook his head. "No. He got away. But I got the German. We went into a glacier together." He rolled his left shoulder, massaging it with his hand. "He didn't come out."

Kertzman absorbed that for a moment. "That leaves two of them."

"Plus Radford and D'Oncetta," Gage added. "Unless they recruit some new talent."

"They won't get any new talent," growled Kertzman. "It'd be too much of an insult. They're supposed to be perfect. Some kind of religious, spiritual new order or something. A sixth order, somebody told me. They're supposed to be like gods."

Gage stared at him. His eyes were solid, steady, and he smiled slightly. "There's only one God, Kertzman," he said quietly.

Kertzman smiled, nodding. "Yeah," he replied. "That's what I think."

Then, suddenly Kertzman became aware of the old and yellowed manuscript lying on the table between them.

In form, it appeared similar to a scroll. Exceedingly ancient, frighteningly ancient. It disturbed him to look at it, lying there, echoing unknown, apocryphal voices from blood-soaked halls of a dark history. Kertzman stared at it warily, cautiously, like a man who had stumbled over a dead rattlesnake. He gestured vaguely with his injured hand.

"So, can you read it?"

"No," answered Gage quickly, not looking at it. "It's written in Latin. Sarah could read it, or Malachi or Barto."

Kertzman stared at the manuscript for a long time. Then he spoke, slowly and hesitantly. "Do you think that it's, you know, real? I mean, do you think all that legend stuff is true? About it containing the name of the Beast and all that?"

Exhaustion seemed to battle with anger in Gage. His eyes were flat dead on Kertzman. "Yeah, Kertzman. I think it's real."

Kertzman nodded, looked away. He turned his mind from the manuscript, instantly feeling a lightness in his soul, a relief. "The old priest, Father Simon," he began, "he was your friend?"

Gage held his gaze. "More than a friend. He was the only father I ever knew."

Silent, Kertzman waited.

"He helped me," Gage continued. "Without him I couldn't have changed my life. He taught me things. Taught me how to live in peace. He was . . . the best man I ever knew. He was just a genuinely holy person who loved God with all his heart and loved his fellow man, too. He was a simple man, but he wasn't simpleminded. He knew more about philosophy and science and theology than most people ever dream of. But he knew about just plain everyday living, too. He was wise about life. He understood everyday problems, and he knew how to find a way through them. And he was so peaceful, so balanced. It was amazing, just knowing him. And these thugs killed him because of . . . *this*." He shook his head, angry. "Such a waste. And that's all they are, Kertzman. Thugs. Rich or poor doesn't make any difference."

Kertzman nodded, somber. "I'm sorry about the old man." Kertzman stared at Gage. "You think we can put them down?"

"I don't know." Gage shook his head. "They're committed. And they've got a lot on their side."

"But they want to trade for this thing, right? Sarah for the book?"

"Yeah."

"Tonight?"

"Yeah."

Kertzman scanned the room. His eyes strayed over the Hi-Power on the moldy table, the knife, the backpack, and assorted rounds.

"Is that all you got? The nine? That ain't much to back up a scene like this. I got this four-inch Smith from the British. But that ain't much, either. I mean, we're gonna pull a doublecross on 'em. So it's probably going to get mean." He blew out a long, hard breath. *"Real mean."*

"Well, I've got a little more," said Gage. "But it's in a safety deposit box downtown. With some money. It's a safety drop I took out about five years ago. But it's Saturday so the bank is closed. I can't get to it until Monday." He hesitated. "We'll just have to go with what we've got."

Kertzman's curiosity was touched. "I thought all you big-time spies kept your money in Swiss bank accounts."

Gage laughed. "No, Kertzman. All that stuff is too complicated. And it can be traced. No, the best way to hide money is with safety deposit boxes. Distribute a sizeable amount in a dozen safety deposit boxes that are listed under a dozen names. Keep a few weapons in them. I did that in Europe, did the same thing in the States. It's easy. It's simple and there's not much that can go wrong. Pay the boxes up ten years in advance and if you need them, they're there."

Kertzman took another sip of coffee, nodded. "Simple," he repeated, his lips carefully forming the word, as if he'd never heard it before. "Simple."

Gage's eyes were locked on him. He smiled faintly. "You're in deep, Kertzman. Helping me. How are you ever going to get out of this?"

Kertzman's brutish face was unexpressive. "I got a job to do, kid. That's all there is."

"But now you're saying that I don't have to go back, right?"

Voice flat and honest, Kertzman grunted, "Not if you don't want."

Gage's eyes narrowed, almost laughing. "Don't worry, Kertzman." He looked away, amused. "I'll go back and give testimony. But I'll have to take immunity because I'll need to stay free."

"Why's that?"

"I'll have to be free in order to make my plan work."

"So that's how you're going to do it," he mumbled, deadpan. "Keep them watching their backs for the rest of their lives."

Gage was steady. "No other way, Kertzman. At first I thought I could rig up some kind of dead man's switch with the manuscript, threaten them with it. But now I think they'd just kidnap somebody else, do another exchange. Now, I think that the only way clear of this is to get both Sarah and the manuscript. Then destroy the manuscript and get myself clear. Then, if any actions are taken in the future..." He paused, looked hard at Kertzman, "and I'll *know* if actions are taken, I'll execute ten times as much against the other side. And they'll know it, beforehand."

Stone-faced, Kertzman nodded. "Sort of like a nuclear deterrent," he mumbled. "Doomsday weapon."

Gage replied, "Sort of. They don't fear laws. They don't fear governments. They don't even fear God. But they fear for their own necks. They won't do anything again as long as they know I'm out there, somewhere, and that I'll retaliate. They provoked me at the beginning of this, when they killed Simon. But they didn't really know me as well as they do now. Now they know I can... visit them. It doesn't matter what kind of security they get. I can get into anything, get past anything. Anyway, the manuscript will be gone so they won't have anything to gain by vengeance. It will only cause them a lot of trouble, and I don't think they want any more trouble than they've had. This has been expensive for them, in people and in money. So they'll lay low and they'll look for me, try to eliminate me first. But they won't find me." He looked down, shook his head. "Nobody will ever find me."

"You got good places?" Kertzman asked.

"A few."

Kertzman couldn't help himself.

"Up north?" he asked.

Laughing, Gage fixed on him.

"OK," said Kertzman. "But you need to be careful. Your whole plan rests on staying low. Hidden."

"That's the easy part," said Gage. "It's the easiest thing in the world to stay hidden." Then his voice assumed a bitter, tired tone. "I just hope I never have any reason to come back."

Kertzman took another sip of coffee. Finally, he removed a Marlboro from the pack in his jacket, lit it. Pensively, he exhaled a long stream of smoke, looking curiously at Gage. "How come you're doing all this?" he asked in a distant voice. "I mean, it seems like it's for something more than old Father Simon. I don't know, really. It...just seems that way."

Gage looked at the wall, his face pale and fatigued with stress. "It's hard to put into words, Kertzman." Thoughtful, Gage shifted, looked at Kertzman with a curious gaze. "I'm trying to find something, Kertzman. Maybe I just want to find a balance, somehow, with some things that are out there. Get clear of some things I can't ever forget. Maybe...I just want to put some old ghosts to rest. Make peace with them."

Kertzman waited calmly. He didn't need to ask questions. Too much time with broken soldiers and broken cops had long ago conditioned him to guilt and madness and the pain of old sins. Slowly he sent two long, lazy spirals of smoke floating up from his nostrils, expelled with a meditative breath.

"Things are coming around, old son," Gage added, after a moment. "You want to know why I'm doing this. Part of it is because of Simon. That's for sure. And it's for Sarah. But...there's something more." He exhaled deeply. "You know, I'm different than I was, Kertzman. I was...a bad person. Didn't believe in anything, really. But I learned from Simon. He taught me how to believe, how to live. Still, I remember what I used to be. And sometimes...it's hard to live with."

"Yeah." Kertzman nodded, compassion in his voice of granite and stone. "I know the feeling. We all got ghosts, kid."

Gage hung his head for a moment, concentrating. Kertzman knew he was trying to find words to capture what he truly felt. Then he leaned back against the wall, stared distantly at the ceiling. His voice was haunted.

"There's probably something else," he said quietly.

Kertzman was struck by the solemnity of the tone. "What's that?" he asked.

Gage closed his eyes. "A debt."

"A debt?" growled Kertzman. "To Father Simon?"

"No." Gage shook his head.

"To who?"

Gage opened his eyes, shrugged. "I've felt it for a long time. There's something I've got to make right, partner. Maybe to myself. Maybe to the world. I don't know. But I've got a debt to pay." He paused. "I know it. I can feel it."

He waited so long Kertzman thought he was finished.

"There's something waiting for me out there, Kertzman. Has been, for a long time. I did some things, and now the consequences are out there. I created it, set it in motion. And now it's come home. Come home to me."

Gage became suddenly quiet, as if the words had unexpectedly captured something, had unexpectedly *agreed* with something inside his own mind. He seemed solemn, serious, faintly satisfied.

Hulking and unmoving, Kertzman blinked. His eyes were open, focused, and he rumbled, "Out in South Dakota we call it 'a reckoning.'"

Gage seemed to consider it. "A reckoning?" he repeated quietly. "A reckoning." He hesitated, eyes slightly widened. "Yeah, I guess it is."

"So...I know what you mean," Kertzman said, after a moment. "But I think that it's...it's gonna cost you. Might cost you a lot."

Gage shifted uncomfortably. "No other way, Kertzman. I was called to this, in a way. I guess you could say it was...meant to be. And I'm not going to lay down this time. And they're not going to quit. If I die, I'll know it was right. And if I live, somehow I'll know that I'm clear, at least inside myself. I'll know that I faced up to something that has followed me for years. I won't have it over me, anymore." He nodded quietly. "And that's enough. To live or die with. It'll be...enough."

Agreeing, Kertzman leaned back. He noticed the building was warmer, warmed by the late-morning sun. Suddenly the faint aroma of something old, moldering and stagnant, was in his nostrils. The cigarette had burned down, forgotten, in his hand. Sniffing, he stubbed it out. Absently, he scratched his right arm. The wound, and a large area of his forearm, felt numb, but not from painkillers. It felt permanently numb, like he had received a shot of Novocain directly into the incision. He knew that the nerve damage would be slow healing, if it healed at all.

Tenderly, Kertzman flexed his injured right hand, felt the tendons where they were sewn together; a dull, tightening fire of pain. He released the tension, resting a moment. Then he flexed his left hand, simply for the primitive pleasure of it, feeling the strength, thick rough fingers folding against a calloused hand with a broad thumb laid across; a sledgehammer fist, massive knuckles leading beneath weathered, scarred skin. He stared at the fist, squeezed it tight, holding its force with the strength of a hulking forearm and bicep. Owning it.

His mind turned away.

"Tonight," he said, blinking. "Is the Japanese gonna be there?"

Gage was watching it all.

"Yeah," he replied, steady. "He's gonna be there."

Kertzman nodded, frowning.

"Good," he said somberly. "I'd like a piece of him."

Brutal head bending, he looked across, fist relaxing to rest lightly on his bandaged forearm.

"Just a piece."

A shadowed wind carried cries of distant hounds through the night; hot, hunting beneath a cold moon. There was a scent of rain, the feel of thunder in the air.

Gage glanced up at the sky, then frowned at the five shadowed shapes approaching across the darkened distance; silhouettes moving closer, coming up the deserted pathway beneath the skeletal shadows of trees.

Sarah moved in front, Sato beside her. Gage stepped forward, walking down the path that led toward the catacombs. He zipped up the short leather jacket, preparing.

Zoning, every instinct and skill keen and focused, he suddenly stopped, standing ready, relaxed. The Hi-Power was at his right hip, hammer back with the safety on for a fast first shot. He didn't look to the woodline at his right, where Kertzman stood, hidden.

Nearer, they came. Sato moved Sarah slightly off to the side, away from Kertzman's position.

Stern advanced, D'Oncetta beside him. Another man, the one from the cabin that Kertzman had told him about, called Radford, stood on the other side of Sarah.

Gage stared at Stern, who stopped ten feet away. The tall man scanned the woodline with a practiced alertness, the gaze intense but forced to assume a nervous indifference.

"So, Gage," Stern said politely but suspiciously, "shall we quickly resolve this situation?"

Gage almost smiled. And just for communicating intent, he focused on D'Oncetta a moment, allowing an intimidating hostility to beam across. D'Oncetta held his ground, implacable and in control, above it all.

Watching Sato peripherally, Gage looked back to Stern as he spoke. "Let her go."

Sato twisted Sarah's arm, and Gage caught the glimpse of black metal in his hand, glistening in the distant city light.

Thunder rumbled overhead. Wind swept a cold mist, early rain, across them, swaying Radford where he stood.

Stern was open, blinking. "I would like the manuscript, first," he said reasonably. "That is the customary way in which these unpleasantries are finalized."

Gage shook his head, eyes narrow, face hardening.

Sato started something.

"Don't!" Gage said with a violent focus. "I'd just as soon kill all of you and her, too. I don't care anymore." He stepped to Stern, attempting to direct the emotional tide of the situation with his will. "Release her or the manuscript burns! I'm not alone."

Without looking away Stern's arm immediately pointed at Sato. "Release her," he said quickly.

Sarah staggered away, clutching her throat where Sato had gripped her. She took a step toward Gage, face open, breathless.

"Stay," Stern said tersely, pointing at her.

She froze in stride, mouth grim, looked at him with a cool hate. For a moment Gage thought she would disobey and it wasn't time yet. He held up his hand.

"Hold on, Sarah!" He focused on Stern. "If you don't want to lose the manuscript, let her go!" He took a quick breath, calculated a firing pattern.

"First, the manuscript!" Stern said.

D'Oncetta stepped forward and Gage saw Sato move towards Sarah.

"Stern, this is not what it seems!" D'Oncetta began. "He is—"

"*Be silent,* priest!" Stern hissed with seeming hatred, half-turning his head. "I *know* what he is doing! You will do as I say or I will kill you myself!"

Gage's hand sweated, but he didn't move his fingers. He blew out a slow, focused breath.

Sarah called out, "Gage, don't let them have the manuscript—"

A quick step and Sato was almost on her. In a blink Gage drew the Hi-Power with his right hand, holding down on Sato. But he was too late, the Japanese too close to her. It wasn't a clear shot.

Gage snarled, flicked the safety down, a startling sharp crack in the wind. "Go ahead, boy!" he yelled. "Do something! You've lived too long as it is!"

"Wait!" yelled Stern, glaring angrily at Sato, drawing his own pistol at Gage. "Wait! Wait!"

"Get away from her!" Gage raged at Sato. "Get away from her or die! You got one second!"

Face twisting, enraged, Sato took a narrow step back. He held the automatic low, pointing at the ground.

"We have released the woman, Gage!" Stern yelled. "Where is the manuscript!"

Gage kept his eyes on Sato. "Let her get clear!"

"No!"

"Alright, Stern, then let's burn it down!" shouted Gage, smiling. "I'm tired of this!"

"I will not let the girl go!"

"Yeah, uh huh," Gage said angrily, lower, still focusing on Sato. "Then maybe you need some incentive."

Over 100 feet to the side, a flame suddenly leaped to life, hot, orange-white fire reaching into the air. A gust of wind blew over them, a sheet of rain that passed. In his peripheral vision Gage watched Radford draw a weapon. He calculated a firing pattern.

Fire fast from left to right...Get Sato first...Then Radford ...Stern...One shot for each man on the first sweep and then go back to finish them with two more shots on the second sweep.

Stern stared, angry and confused, at the fire which, Gage knew, was blazing inside a large, ten-gallon drum. Kertzman would be standing beside the drum, holding an old and cherished manuscript high for all to see.

"No!" screamed Stern, stepping convulsively toward the fire.

"Let her go, Stern!" shouted Gage.

Stern staggered back and forth, as if he couldn't decide which direction to take.

"Let her go!"

Tension spiraling out of control.

"Alright, alright!" screamed Stern. "She can go! Go! Go! She can go!"

"Run, Sarah!" said Gage.

Instantly Sato stepped forward behind her, raising his automatic, aiming for her back. "No!" he yelled.

Gage almost fired at the move. His finger removed every ounce of pressure from the trigger, tightening; a half-ounce more pressure, a touch almost too small to measure by human feel, and the Hi-Power would discharge. But the range was too great for a sure head shot, at least 20 feet, too far...

"Wait!" screamed Stern.

"Burn it!" yelled Gage.

Stern screamed incoherently, D'Oncetta also cried out, and without turning, Gage knew that Kertzman had just thrown a handful of pages into the flames.

Aghast, Stern staggered backwards, and D'Oncetta turned toward Gage, screaming, shockingly emotional.

"Savage!" he yelled. "Barbarian! You have destroyed what cannot be replaced!"

Gage laughed. "You want to see it again?"

D'Oncetta staggered, cast a wild look back at Kertzman.

"Burn some more!" yelled Gage.

"No!" screamed Stern, lifting both hands, regaining a wild calm with a frantic, gasping effort. His eyes bulged with a spiraling panic. "Wait," he struggled to say, "just . . . wait . . . a moment."

Stern gestured to Kertzman with a high, empty hand to hold him from more destruction. Gage didn't look but knew Kertzman hadn't thrown another handful of pages into the flames.

"She can go!" Stern raged, motioning, pushing the words forward with his empty hand.

"No!" screamed Sato. He turned to level the automatic at Kertzman and fired, a single smooth motion that was there, perfect. Gage also fired instantly. The blasts blended together and Sato went back, roaring, hit dead center.

Everything happened at once, and Gage moved with it, firing and moving. Stern's pistol came up. Gage swept right with the Hi-Power and fell backwards firing, firing, white fire and thunder roaring out from him. Chaos. Sarah screaming, Sato staggering . . . away . . . into dark. Stern shouted, staggering, blasting at Gage with an automatic. Gage rolled, shooting, realigning as he moved and shooting as the rounds hit beside him. Then he was on his knee, sighting solid on Stern, firing the remainder of the clip until the slide locked.

Mouth open, Stern stood in place. Then, in slow motion, he dropped his automatic to the ground, fell back.

Radford raised his automatic. Frantic, Gage tore the empty clip from the Browning and yelled for Sarah to run as she leaped into the forest, disappearing instantly. Radford centered on him with the .45 and he knew he wouldn't have time to slam in a new load before the CIA man fired.

Radford laughed, raising the automatic to eye-level. "Game's over, Gage. You're dead."

In that uncanny combat acuity that comes with perfect concentration, Gage knew Radford's shot would hit him dead center.

Thunder from the right.

Gage spun, hurled himself to the ground, rolled. Realizing he wasn't hit, he was up, staggering back, the empty Hi-Power in his hand, scanning wildly as Radford shouted, staggering. Gage glimpsed the familiar bulk coming quick from the shadows, the huge Smith and Wesson .44 magnum leveled.

"Drop it, Radford!" Kertzman yelled. "You got one chance! Drop it!"

A madness, a maddened shaking gaze and Radford laughed.

Kertzman walked closer as he shouted. "Just drop it, Radford! Do it now! Drop it!"

Then Radford cried out something indiscernible, lifted the .45. Kertzman shouted again and the revolver thundered flame. Radford staggered back again, screaming, also firing the .45 at Kertzman.

From somewhere within the woods Sarah screamed.

Gage whirled at the cry that tore through the forest, at the same time dropping the slide on the Hi-Power to chamber a new round and a full clip.

Sarah!

Gage ran toward her scream, more blasts thundering behind him. He ducked, moving under the limbs of trees, running forward.

Scream was to the left, deep inside the trees. But she was clear and running.

Sato!

Gage ran with all his speed, using a panther's perfect balance and movement in lightning-quick leaps and steps through the dark with the Hi-Power held high, teeth bared to kill and be killed. Just get to her!

Don't worry about where Sato is ... When he fires, you fire and close on him ... Take a round to give what you got and you'll get him.

Night wind around him and in a hot tactical analysis he saw a shape on the ground and dropped, scanning, gun out in front with eyes shifting left, right, seeing everything both moving and still; darkness, white shape lying motionless on the ground, small, not Sato.

Finger tight on the trigger tension, Gage moved forward slowly, slowly, scanning, closing on Sarah without looking at her, turning, revolving in the shadows while listening to the leaves whispering around him.

Sirens in the distance, closing.

Gage reached her, knelt quickly, rolled her over. Looked down.

A cruel slash descended from her forehead across her cheek and jaw, a straight diagonal line that razored down her face, slicing the beautiful skin. Blood oozed.

"Oh, Sarah..." Gage whispered, choking, forgetting everything else. "Sarah..."

She was still. Gage felt for the pulse, the heart, caught the faint beat with his own. He caught his breath, fierce and charged with emotion, rage.

She stirred, groaned, and Gage tore off his leather coat, removed his shirt. Then, moaning in remorse, he wadded his shirt as a bandage, and placed the soft fabric over her face. He was grateful it was dark so she could not see herself.

Her lips opened. "Gage..."

"I'm here," he whispered. "I'm here."

Her hand squeezed his, tight. She shook a moment, groaned, lifted a hand to her face. "What...did he do...to me?" she whispered. A cry.

"It'll be alright," Gage said quietly. "You're hurt. But you'll be alright. They can fix it. It's just a cut. Don't worry about it. You'll be fine. You've just lost...a little blood...You'll be fine."

She turned her face into the bandage, holding his hand.

His mind was raging, overloaded.

Get it back together!

Gunshots, a roar, screaming.

Gage spun, crouched, staring back at the path over 200 feet away. He heard the struggle; Kertzman roaring, fighting, cursing and then three more shots, the .44 blasting away in the night, Sato screaming.

Breath hard, face grimacing, Gage listened. "I can't leave Sarah...Can't leave her," he whispered tensely. "Come on, Kertzman, handle him. Take him down...Take him down...Come on."

The sounds continued; a savage conflict.

Gage turned back to Sarah, pulling on his leather jacket. He put her hands on her face, holding the bandage in place.

"Hold this," he said softly. "Just keep the pressure down. It'll stop the bleeding."

She moaned something in reply.

Then, holding the Hi-Power in his left hand, he lifted her. Cautiously and quickly, he moved forward.

Two more shots sounded. And the night thundered with a howl from Kertzman.

Gage froze, listening, heard only silence in the forest, sirens closing from everywhere on the park, the catacombs.

Eyes keen to the dark, reading everything, Gage moved quickly forward, sacrificing stealth for speed, almost running, and then he saw the path, Kertzman sitting upright against a black, wet stone tablet. The massive head was bent; exhausted. Or dead.

"Kertzman!" Gage shouted. Sirens closing from every direction.

Steps!

Livid with rage Gage spun smoothly to fire from the hip, blasting a pattern at the Japanese 40 feet away who leaped wildly to the side for the cover of trees. Gage continued to fire, reflexively tracking the movement, rising with the recoil, the Hi-Power sounding like a submachine gun as it blasted out 14 rounds in three seconds.

Breath hard and tight, Gage paused; clip empty, gun and night hazed in smoke. Frowning, he scanned the gloom. Echoing silence; a ringing stillness.

Gage glared through the wall of blue smoke, his arm still extended with the slide of the weapon locked back. He suddenly heard—Sarah was screaming. Had been screaming.

He hugged her with his right arm, whispering to her.

"Shhh..." he said softly in her ear, keeping his eyes on the shadows where Sato had leaped. She was quiet instantly, rocking slightly, holding the bloody bandage on her face.

Gage heard the steps, somewhere in the forest, Sato moving away quickly, deeply inside the cover of trees. Cold and enraged, Gage ignored the retreating steps and turned to Kertzman, who seemed to hear them as they approached. He lifted his head as they came closer.

Gage saw the thick, bloodstained portion of his shirt, a deep chest wound; a knife wound. Other slashes, glistening wet black, were visible through the heavy arms of his coat. His knee was slashed open, and there was a long shallow wound on his forehead.

Kertzman struggled to speak. "Came up...behind me," he gasped, as Gage laid Sarah down beside him. "He ran off... as you got here." He coughed blood, continued, "Got me good... and he got the book." He groaned sickly, leaning, falling over.

Gage caught him with his left arm, his right arm still supporting Sarah. Grimacing at the weight, he pushed Kertzman back against the stone.

"It's alright, partner," Gage whispered. "You did good. Nobody could 'a done better."

Kertzman leaned his head back, rolled it from side to side. "Got excited," he gasped. "Forgot to burn the rest of the book...when the shootin' started. Came in...had to take Radford. But the priest...got away."

"Doesn't matter." Gage gazed down at Sarah. She was still, slowly gaining more control within her shock. Sadly, she lifted her face to gaze at him with one visible eye.

Suddenly, Gage heard frantic shouting near the Catacombs of Priscilla. He turned, staring into the darkness at the widening beams of a dozen flashlights bouncing in the night. Men ran forward, an army of men.

Italian police.

He looked down softly at Sarah, touching her face. "They'll take care of you," he said. "They'll take care of both of you."

He released her, turned toward Kertzman. "Listen careful, Kertzman. Make sure that they know right away that you are a

United States federal agent! Tell them Sarah's a kidnap victim and a federal witness! Do you hear me? You are an American federal agent and this is state department responsibility! You got it?"

"You bet," said Kertzman numbly, and then his massive head turned, face silvery with sweat, dark with blood. "Are you ... goin' after him?"

Gage nodded and stood, backing away.

"Be careful," Kertzman said weakly. "He won't ... stay down. You're gonna have to ... kill him."

Gage nodded again, backing. "I know."

Sarah watched him sadly and struggled a moment, rising, slowly gaining balance to stand, unsteadily, on her feet. Hesitating in his stride, Gage watched her. In the silence he looked past her, saw flashlights charging frantically in the distance, measured their approach; 30 seconds. He gazed down, smiled faintly, sadly. Turned away.

"Gage," she gasped, a choking cry.

Gage froze, turned back in a single, ghostly stride. Their eyes met.

"Gage ... Come back to me ..."

He nodded. "I'll always come back to you."

Wind at his back and thunder overhead, Gage ran through the night, breath hard and fast, searching. By mental reflex, by training procedures driven into his subconscious, he knew where Sato would go, just as he knew where *he* would go if he were evading, obeying the rules.

Get clear of the area, fast...Break the perimeter...Take the quickest escape route...Move as fast as possible before you find concealment.

To the east! Towards the Via Salaria, the eight-lane street that ran past the park, 200 yards to the right. Has to be!

To the west was the park, and forest, a mile of woodland that could easily be encircled, sealed off, and searched; to the north, more forest, miles of it. A natural trap. Sato would move for the street, would try to break the perimeter of the park as quickly as possible, get clear in the city.

Without breaking stride Gage slipped like lightning under a low-hanging branch, running, and in 30 seconds heard the traffic of the streets. He broke through the trees, slammed in another clip, chambered the automatic by dropping the slide.

He entered a field, instantly dropping low, scanning. He was on a hill that offered a good sweeping view of a half mile to the north and south. Immediately he caught sight of Sato running toward the ravine that separated the park from the street itself.

Gage descended the hill on a parallel course, 100 yards between them, knowing Sato would try to find transportation.

Sirens blaring, three police cars drove south on the Via Salaria, not noticing his approach out of the darkness. Then he was at the ravine, as Sato climbed the slope in the distance and entered the street.

Gage splashed through the ditch and then he was climbing the slope, tired now, breath heavy. He barely made it the final few strides, slowing, climbing, groaning in exhaustion. Finally, he hit the middle of the street, turned to see a commotion . . . Sato stealing something, a van.

Gage spun, his arm lashing out in an iron clothesline tackle, carrying the motorcyclist off the back of his bike. They tumbled together into the street, a chaotic mass, and rolling, Gage broke their fall with his arm.

A roar somewhere north, a gunshot.

"Move!" Gage shouted, pushing the young Italian who wanted to fight until he saw the Browning. In a second Gage was on the bike as a van roared down the street, wild and rushing.

Gage looked up, saw the dark familiar face, and gunned the bike, gaining the sidewalk as it swerved after him. *Missed!*

Gage spun the bike, and then he was pursuing, the Hi-Power in his belt, heading south into the city.

Gage accelerated the bike, gaining on the van. He pulled alongside, but Sato swerved towards him and Gage veered to the left as a vehicle passed wildly between them.

Use it!

Gage accelerated the bike hard, fast and came in at a sharp angle on the van, pulling the Hi-Power and leaning low.

Beyond fear, in that combat zone where everything is slow and real beyond ordinary clarity, he was beside the van again. He aimed low, firing continuously at the left front tire of the vehicle, and in a shredding explosion of tire and wheel, the black twisting mass lashed toward him while the van's gray wheel struck fire from the cobblestones over a thunderous black shape. Shifting, twisting.

A rolling, chaotic crash exploded beside him and Gage hit something, lost it. The bike skidded on the wet street. He struggled a split-second and then laid it down. The van passed behind him, across his tracks in a revolving, shattering mass, and the bike disintegrated before him against stone and black rain, storm.

Seconds of skidding, rolling.

Rolling, slowing.

A stunned stillness.

Gage heard himself groaning.

Oh . . . man!

Stunned, Gage turned over. He was torn everywhere, his right elbow was bruised and he was smeared with mud. Numbly, mind struggling violently to reorient, to focus, he struggled to stand, not taking time for wound assessment. It didn't matter now, as long as he could finish this.

Straining for breath he looked toward the van. Sato was staggering away, clutching his forehead while holding something large, black . . . the manuscript . . . in his hand.

Gage stumbled forward numbly, brain beginning to find itself beneath the shock.

"Sato!" he shouted.

The Japanese turned a moment, hesitating, his face an angry mask. Gage moved another step. Then Sato turned away, running with a slight limp. Gage glanced around. The Hi-Power was gone, lost in the darkness; could be anywhere. No time to search. He moved forward in a gathering run that slowly turned into a sprint. And then Sato, also, was running.

Into the shadows.

Gage had no idea of direction, no idea of street, but he couldn't worry about it. He was beyond procedures now; he was at the top of the plateau, where there were no rules. No rules but those he made for himself.

Sato ran and Gage followed, pursuing at an even pace and an even distance of 50 yards. It was a miler's pace, fast but not sprinting, the strides long and strong, bouncing but not pushing with the energy that burns out legs in an explosive sprint. It was a pace Gage could hold for four minutes, maybe six.

They left the Via Salaria to merge into the darkness of the side streets, running left down an alley, right, taking another deserted street and then another alley, the chaos of the intersection fading, quickly, far behind.

Gage stumbled over something low on the sidewalk and crashed painfully to the ground. He rolled again with the impact and then, gaining his feet, he was up. But Sato was lost from his vision.

Breath blasting, Gage ran.

Black shadow breaking shadow ahead.

Shouting in rage and frustration, Gage leaped forward. The distant movement was too quick to be anything other than what it was; Sato, still running straight but with at least a 100-yard lead.

Gage increased his pace as much as he dared and immediately felt the heaviness begin, the lactic acid buildup in muscles. He couldn't hold it for much longer, knew Sato had to feel the same.

He's human...He's hurting as bad as you...Keep the pressure...He'll break!

Steady, no weapon drawn to weigh down his hands, Gage held the violent pace, pumping his arms to keep a tiring stride; breath racking him in spasms, side stitched with a piercing pain, body soaked in sweat, groaning.

Step by step.

Stride, stride, run him down!...Hold a long pace that he can't match...Keep him in sight...He'll break!

Gage stared ahead through widened eyes; saw nothing, no movement.

Gone.

He broke stride while still moving and tried to focus more clearly on the darkness ahead.

Nothing.

Breath steady, he continued to hold his speed until he came to the place where he had last caught Sato's image.

Alley to the right.

He scanned around, saw nothing. There was no other path for escape.

Crouching, Gage moved into the alley. Moving quickly and slightly sideways to present a narrower target, in seconds he had reached the end; a gate marked by two tall, wide wooden doors, black in the night. His fighting rage heated by the run, Gage glared angrily up the smooth wall. He saw only level edges of night sky, an unbroken ridge of flat building. No sniper outlines.

He turned. Nothing was behind him.

Sweating, breath burning his throat but adrenaline burning his blood, Gage leaned for a second against the door, eyes focused on the bolt that secured it.

He looked closer, slowing a hard breath, expelling it deeply, then drawing another, trying to slow his heartbeats. Sweat blinked in his eyes, and hot perspiration soaked the leather coat. He felt lightheaded. And then he saw the sharp gleam on the bolt, a smooth mark, glistening with a silvery sheen.

He reached out, felt.

Cut. It was cleanly cut; a steel bolt, at least a quarter-inch thick, cut cleanly in half by a single, slashing blow.

Gage leaned back against the door, breathing heavily, and drew the only weapon he had left. Closing his eyes, gathering, he held it across his chest, the 14-inch knife comfortingly broad, heavy, unbreakable with cold strength.

His breath frosted in the night air; warm and streaming. He focused, holding the black micarti handle of the Dragon in a familiar grip, a natural grip. The blade was heavy, but it felt weightless.

Cautiously Gage reached out, pulled the door open. He went through fast, crouching, moving sideways with the blade held high and close, scanning.

Inside, it was almost completely dark. But at the distant wall stood a wide, gray altar, the crucified Christ staring down from above.

It was a basilica, a sanctuary. He was inside a deserted cathedral. Gage waited, concealed within the shadow of a marble column. He looked to the single source of light, and saw the shadowy figure standing, before the crucifix. Waiting for him.

The Japanese stood fully in the light, casting his own darkness, a long pale shadow. And Gage stepped out, instinctively searching the shadows on the left and right for an ambush, but knowing he would find no one.

There was just the two of them, as it was meant to be.

Slowly, Gage walked forward.

Sato tossed the manuscript behind him, onto the altar. He smiled and raised the murderous tanto. Arm fully extended to hold the blade horizontally, slightly beneath his eyes, his gaze passed over the edge to focus on Gage.

Face impassive, Gage came closer.

In normal combat a master knifefighter would never reveal the location of his weapon before he struck; it was his advantage. And, as a rule, a master would never relinquish an advantage. Yet Sato was boldly displaying the tanto, brandishing the blade in an ancient escrima salute not seen in ritual combat for 500 years. But Gage knew what it truly was; a challenge, a commitment, a sacred vow to finish this battle only by death.

And with the gesture Gage knew that he had entered a world that went beyond tactics, beyond techniques, beyond known rules of combat; this was the place where flesh and blood failed, where battles were won by something beyond skill.

Gage stopped 20 feet from the Japanese, a minimum safe distance. His eyes locked on Sato, the blade.

So it comes to this.

Gage raised his blade to hold it horizontally across his face, gazing over the razored edge. His left arm was folded, like a shield, across his chest. He lowered his head, his eyes hidden in shadow. Sweat glistened on his face.

"You're a fool!" Sato hissed, black eyes gleaming like obsidian orbs. His face burned with wild rage, endless strength. "You're a *fool* to stand against me! What do you gain by defending them? Nothing!" He shook his head fiercely, sweat scattering. "You will gain nothing because their deaths *mean* nothing! Will you die for such fools?"

Gage gazed over the blade. Nodded.

With a shout Sato leaped into the open area before the crucifix.

And Gage also leaped forward, blade leading, knowing instantly and without thinking that he had descended into the dominion of pain and blood and cold razored steel where only death wins in the end.

FIFTY - THREE

A flash.

With a desperate twist Gage had leaped outside the tanto that struck a silver arc through the air, tearing a shallow line through his leather coat, and he spun instantly, slashing backhanded to hit Sato across the shoulder.

The Japanese roared at the blow, turning into the blade like a wild beast, and Gage fell back, alive and on fire, ready for anything. He feinted to the left, Sato took it and Gage leaped clear to the right.

Sato adjusted without expression, advancing; enraged, glaring. He didn't look down at his wound, but Gage knew he would be assessing the shallow injury by feel, just as he would have done.

When Sato had taken the nine millimeter round in the park, Gage had assumed that the Japanese was wearing a ballistic vest. But now, with the way his blade had sliced through to flesh, Gage realized that Sato was wearing a ballistic *shirt,* far more pliable and far less resistant against a knife. But Gage guessed that Sato would also have his ribs strapped to immediately staunch bleeding and maintain blood pressure. And, perhaps, to even further armor himself against a blade, the Japanese would be wearing leather gauntlets on his forearms, beneath his coat, similar to the gauntlets worn by ancient samurai.

Gage was less prepared for the conflict, with only the waist-length leather coat. He had even removed his shirt to stop Sarah's bleeding, leaving even less protection against the tanto's razor edge.

Circling to the right, Gage kept his blade alive in constant, swaying movements primarily so that, when he did strike again, the blade's sudden movement forward would be lost for a split-second in its casual, constantly waving motion.

Sato matched his steps and movements in an equal but opposite direction, moving to his right, also, countering the circling action.

He whispered to Gage, taunting. "Did you like the way I marked your woman?"

Gage felt the rage and instantly shut it down, away to somewhere else.

Not yet!

Concentrate!

He'll strike when you've got the steps to your back...He'll try and force you to retreat, to trip on the steps...Get ready...And don't move back...That's what he'll expect...Go lateral...Know your distance from everything without looking at it.

Two more steps and Gage had his back to the altar. Without looking he knew he could retreat six feet and then he'd have to back-step up.

A blinding low feint and Sato closed, Gage slashing down at the forearm as if he had taken the feint, and then he had leaped left, Sato's face following in surprised shock.

Gage lunged, stabbing at a leg, but Sato reacted instantly, whirling, coming off his feet in a spinning backhand.

Too fast!

Frantically Gage twisted down and away but felt the impact across his back. And he realized that he had kicked out instantly at the hit, roaring in pain, to connect against Sato's shins.

Collision, chaos, and they went down together, clutching. Sato, stronger and faster, came down on top, and the tanto flashed down. Anticipating the blow, Gage had already moved to grab Sato's elbow, jamming the arm high. And they struggled in the position, Sato's blade held high by Gage's desperate grip. Then Gage struck Sato with his forehead, stunning the Japanese before he tore away, rolling out of arm's reach to gain his feet. He staggered as he rose, dizzy.

Sato rolled, dazed. And Gage used the moment to bend over, catching his breath. He felt a sharp, throbbing pain in his back; sharp, sharper at each feathery heartbeat.

Hot!

Gathering, Gage circled back for more room to maneuver, for more space to think. He blew out a breath to focus his mind. He was beginning to overheat, the conflict too long, too exhausting.

A sharp pain, and Gage realized that he'd been cut somewhere else while they were on the floor, but there was no time to find it, to measure it. He circled left again as Sato rose up, calm, still holding his blade. The dark face was drenched in sweat but utterly untouched by fatigue or pain. The coal black eyes were coldly focused.

Gage felt a wave of fear.

He's too good, the voice whispered to him.

No! Don't listen!

Do what you have to do!

Analyze the situation!

His reach is longer...So close the gap quick, get inside it...Use speed and feints to confuse your move...He's stronger, don't wrestle with him...Control him...Guide him...Wear him down with feints...Harass him.

Shouting, Gage feinted low, an aggressive move. And Sato took it, the twelve-inch blade of the tanto flashing in an arc across the space where Gage's forearm would have been if the blow had continued.

Gage smiled.

Almost invisibly Sato shifted his weight.

Gage saw it, reacted.

A blur.

Sato was inside with the blinding leap, but in the last moment Gage had seen the weight and balance go back on Sato's rear leg, had understood the movement, anticipating, and he had leaped forward also to meet the Japanese in midair, a stop-hit.

As quick as Sato was, he wasn't prepared to close the distance so quickly, and Gage collided against him, face to face. Then Gage was inside Sato's long reach and he instantly trapped the Japanese's knife arm, hooking it with his left.

Once, twice, Gage's blade flashed inside, roars and screams echoing between them, and Sato grunted explosively at the blows that powered into his chest. Then the Japanese surged, adrenalized with the hysterical strength of pain, and headbutted.

Stunning!

Dazed by the sledgehammer blow, Gage only dimly sensed that he was flung back to crash against the bannister. He ignored the splintered wood, quickly rolled through it to leap away, gaining his feet, circling until he had a visual lock again on Sato.

Upon acquiring a visual lock on the Japanese, still standing 30 feet away holding his wound, Gage felt a wild relief.

Taking advantage, he bent over, resting in a basic karate stance with feet spread wide apart for balance. Then, wearily, he wiped his sweaty brow with a forearm, catching his breath. He placed both hands on his knees, breathing deeply, steadily, hoping that Sato was suffering some damage from the chest wounds.

Clearly, the Japanese was hurt.

There was a long stillness, each man holding position, recovering.

Gage didn't initiate an attack, but chose to let the bleeding take its toll. Patient and alert, he waited. And for an instant Gage searched for words, for something to say, but there was nothing. There never had been.

It was understood; this was gladiatorial.

Sato shifted the tanto in his hand and walked forward. Gage, raising the blade before him in a rightside-forward stance, danced in and out, changing the distance with every step, making it more difficult for the Japanese to bridge the gap.

Sato was stalking slower now, scowling in pain. He shuffled forward in a solid stance, controlling the center of the floor, attempting to cut off Gage's space, to corner him. And Gage moved around him, feinting, dancing.

Suddenly Sato changed, putting his leftside forward, his right hand holding the tanto close to his chest, coiled like a spring.

Gage saw it, leaped in.

Exploding from this stance to spin his entire body in a tight half-circle, Sato swung the blade hard, a Fire and Stones Cut. But Gage was expecting the blow and had already jerked back, knowing instantly that the move was powerful but short-range. The tanto passed him and Gage had leaped inside again, jamming Sato's upper arm against his body to strike over the Japanese's shoulder at the neck. He missed and Sato shouted and jerk-stepped back, slashing down at Gage's leg, and Gage slashed downward also to see his blade tear through the sleeve of Sato's coat....

Hard!

Instantly, knowing something but with no time to evaluate it, Gage reversed the blow as the blade came off the hardened forearm, used the weight of the blade to flip it, and the Dragon sliced down again, from the outside in, hitting the forearm a second time and some frantically computing corner of Gage's mind recognized...

Gauntlet!

Forget the forearm!

Gage saw Sato shift, tried to retreat.

Too late!

Roaring, Sato leaped forward and was inside, and Gage felt the heat as they closed a third time, blades flashing up in a blinding series of blows that struck each man and drew blood. Gage ducked as the tanto came across his shoulders in a blow that would have severed his neck.

Off balance!

Stall him to get distance!

Gage feinted a wild straight-ahead thrust, and Sato froze for a split-second to read it, and then Gage leaped to the side, deluged suddenly with overcoming heat, perspiration.

The sudden blast of fear had shaken Gage, and he lost his concentration. He leaped back frantically, retreating to increase the space, trying to regain his focus.

He knew what had happened.

It was one of those wild panic moments that come in combat when the mind, for no apparent reason, simply goes somewhere else, destroying concentration. It happens suddenly, without warning, and can cost a man his life because it shuts down reflexes and shatters the ability to anticipate, to initiate.

So Gage backed up quickly, knowing that he had only to concentrate for a moment to free himself from it. And while he concentrated, he analyzed his wounds, measuring blood loss, the pale shock descending.

He realized from the dull, deep, throbbing pain that his side had been hit, the shallow wound passing through the skin along his ribs, but not penetrating deep. And his forearm was bleeding, down onto his hand, while his right thigh was blackened in the faint light, aching; a stab wound through muscle tissue, no arterial bleeding.

Hot!

So much heat.

Face drenched in sweat, Gage grimaced at the heat, heat everything now, overcoming, distracting; he heard himself groaning, an unconscious release of pain, his overstressed body refusing to deny what his mind refused to admit.

And yet Sato seemed undisturbed by the heated stress, the hard physical strain of the contest. The Japanese laughed as Gage grimaced. And, implacable as ice, he moved forward.

Impossible!

Breathing out hard to concentrate, to regain his focus, Gage retreated. He clenched his teeth, eyes narrowing, focusing through the mist. His steps were light, but only with effort.

Pain everywhere, blood following.

Six feet separated them.

Gage stepped back, but then, suddenly finding his concentration again, he stopped his retreat, focused once more, and saw Sato hovering, poised at the edge of a lunge.

Gage relaxed, balancing, coming onto the balls of his feet. Crouching, he held his position, all quickness; saw Sato shift to leap.

Inside!

The broad, flashing blade was lost in the blur, and Gage lashed out blindly with his free hand to hit the Japanese in the chest with a stop-hit.

Sato stalled in mid-lunge, spun tight: *blade!*

Hit!

Gage felt it tear through his left shoulder, high and to the side, knew the muscle had taken the slicing wound, and Sato savagely twisted the blade, pulling out. But Gage roared at the bolting pain and spun, locking the tanto in his shoulder muscle, and drove the Dragon out, blasting Sato's free arm aside. His blade hit the Japanese along the side of his face with a spear-point thrust and plowed a channel through the skin.

Savage as wounded beasts, they struck; roaring, cursing, slicing deeply with the blades. And then, gasping in pain, Sato finally tore loose, staggering back to rip the tanto from Gage's shoulder. Dazed, the Japanese retreated a few steps before he fell backwards, tripping. Moaning, Gage also staggered backward from the wounding encounter, blinded by the agony, and then he fell, numb, rolling, lost in depthless pain.

Pain...so much...pain...

Squinting breathless through a red haze, Gage looked up, saw Sato climbing to his feet, gravely wounded but rising, always rising.

Unkillable.

Gage staggered up and fell backwards again, over a bench, before finally gaining his feet once more with a ragged steadiness. And Sato stood in blood, staring, the mouth slack, the eyes empty, seeming to recognize for the first time the true strength of his enemy.

No words were spoken. Each held a respectful distance, measuring, breathing hard.

Gage exhaled a breath, hard, and waited, trying to reduce his oxygen level, to clear his eyesight. A series of slow breaths brought his heart rate under control. His body felt so much pain that his mind had difficulty following all of it; the nerves were overloaded, carrying too much, crossing over one another with messages of deep injury that were getting sidetracked on other deep nerve clusters, ultimately lost in the collision to confuse his mind as to where he was actually hurt.

He nodded his head faintly at the shock coming in, a red bloodless haze, as he recognized the massive overload of pain. Good, he thought, the greater the pain, the more confused the body would become. To a point, it would help him go farther.

Use it!

Gage felt himself centering, his eyes clearing, his balance returning. He stepped backwards, rightside forward, circling slowly to the right.

Sato gazed at him dumbly and reached into his coat pocket, searching, pulling his bloody hand out slowly. Then he squeezed, cracked something inside his fist.

Gage didn't move; he knew. And he watched with a cold, calculating gaze.

Frowning, the Japanese raised the bloody hand to his wounded face, sniffed, sniffed again. Then he stared at Gage as the drug took effect. Gage watched the Japanese's face and saw the energy, the strength returning, fresh and heated, as the seconds passed.

Sato laughed, lifting his hand again to sniff the last of the powder, rising internally, ascending above the exhaustion, the pain.

Gage didn't know what he had taken. Probably a PCP derivative, the worst. He knew that the drug would phenomenally enhance strength and endurance, increase blood pressure, kill pain, and alter the nervous system's ability to perceive injury, or even death.

He's got the advantage! ... Find a way to neutralize it! ... Put him in a position where he can't use his strength!

Mind scanning, Gage glanced behind him, searching for some tactic to neutralize Sato's sudden advantage. And he saw it; a desperate last chance, a final arena for this conflict.

When he looked back, Sato had taken a slow step forward, the knife held out again, waving, threatening. And the darkened face laughed, suddenly oblivious to the injuries and the blood loss.

In pain Gage retreated, luring Sato forward. He blinked to focus, backed more quickly as Sato continued to advance. In seconds he was at the entrance of a stone corridor, Sato only 20 feet away, still advancing, smiling, strength by strength building within him as the moments passed.

Gage backed until he stood well inside the hallway, and Sato advanced into it a dozen paces, also well inside. A single light, mounted low on the wall, was all that illuminated the subterranean tunnel.

Gage stood beside the lamp, glanced sideways at it. And the Japanese seemed to perceive his intent, laughed.

Sato advanced with the knife held tight, controlled and focused. Unafraid.

Fifteen feet.

Smiling, advancing.

Frowning, Gage watched.

Ten feet.

Advancing.

Gage's fist lashed out to shatter the light, plunging them into darkness.

Silence.

Gage moved quickly back to make more noise than necessary, scraping his blade along the stones, and then he leaped forward again, with a quick step to the side, crouching in blood.

Still.

Listening.

He heard nothing.

Gage strained, listening closer, silently twisting his head to turn his ear slightly forward. He almost completely halted his breathing, a difficult task, and he closed his eyes, knowing only the rushing sound of blood inside, his heart pounding, a faint ringing that seemed to echo within him.

Careful to hold silence, Gage turned his head to offer his other ear to the corridor, his sweating face grimacing with the encompassing pain of his bleeding wounds.

Only silence.

Don't move...Don't panic...Don't let him push you...Let him make the mistake...It's almost impossible to move without sound ...Let him come to you...Wait...Wait...Don't move.

Searching hard, Gage glared into the darkness of the corridor, but it was only gloom, utter gloom. Not even the faintest gray shade could be seen in the blackness, only inky blackness. And Gage knew that if Sato had been standing directly in front of him, he could not have seen the Japanese.

Gage tried to feel the air on his face, the stillness of it, the faint movement of it. Hot sweat on his neck and face was sensitive to the cool touch, the faintest shifting of the subterranean stillness. And he used it, glaring into the deathshadow, his face turned slightly for the feel of the current, and to provide direct access of sound to his ear.

Gage heard nothing.

What is he doing!

Where is he?

Panic rose up.

Cold sweat dripping off his face, stomach muscles tight in a crouch with legs dead, trembling from exhaustion, Gage forced himself to wait.

Sweat blinked out of his eyes. And, through his exhaustion, Gage slowly released a single, tightly focused breath, directed it downward, felt drops of sweat come off his chin, his lips.

He closed his eyes, focusing.

Wet leather cold on his skin.

He ignored the clamminess, breathed quietly and shallowly through his nose to slow his respiration, his heart rate. But he didn't know how long he could control it; the oxygen strain was building, intensifying fast. He trembled, holding position, muscles cramping, tried not to move at all because the leather would sound so easily in the stillness.

And the thoughts came to him again.

Where is he?

Did he retreat?

No, something told him, *the answer is no. He's there, waiting. He wants to claim you, to claim the joy of killing you. This is to the death.*

Gage poised in silence, beyond silence, and only silence surrounded him, a corridor of silence, of nothing; darkness. And what he did next was simply done, without real thought, his inner being *knowing,* while his mind watched.

Get him to move!

Not so faintly that it would have been made on purpose but to indicate an accident, the rare mistake of a true professional, Gage purposefully made the slightest, faintest sound, shifting his boot delicately on the stone; a sound that would not have existed at all if someone were not poised in the dark, crouching only feet away, waiting for it, prepared for it.

Then, unmoving enough to become part of the darkness himself, Gage listened, fingers tight on the hilt of Dragon, waiting. And he lowered his free hand in front of him to touch the floor, palm and fingers facing out, feeling the dark air against his blood-soaked hand, relaxed to catch the cool current. He held the position, knowing nothing, frustrated.

He waited, knowing more air would stir on the floor than at any other level.

Still, nothing.

Sweat rained from his face, silent against the stones. He stifled a moan at the agony of his wounds and hoped that the chemicals Sato had taken would cause an adverse reaction, provoking the powerful Japanese to grow impatient and move first.

Maybe.

Gage estimated the depth of the corridor, imagining how Sato would advance. He tried to perceive what was beyond him in the darkness when a sudden, thrill-charged instinct made him freeze.

Gage held his crouch, his muscles instantly knotting in *unendurable* pain at the fatigue, the vivid fear. Something...had happened.

A touch had passed him.

It had been along the floor, but also somewhere else. With his bloody hand he had felt the wind stirred by a close footstep. Whatever else he had felt could not be discerned; it was too faint.

Face freezing in sweat, Gage strained desperately to understand, using every sense to perceive, to search out what it had been.

There!

Close again.

Now, gone.

Gage concentrated frantically, face grimacing in cold, sweating frustration, faint.

What *was* it?

Then he felt, again, the ghostly stirring of air along the floor, and he knew that Sato was close, maybe directly in front of him, searching.

Eyes wide to stare through the gloom, Gage froze in fear and trembling rage, his skin open to the slightest brush of wind. Reflexively, his hand tightened even more on the knife. And he understood suddenly that Sato had, indeed, been closing on him since he had made that first, faint scraping sound. And the Japanese had came upon him without a whisper of warning. Now they were face to face, Sato searching for his exact location so he could launch a final, savage attack.

There!

Something faintly moved a thin ribbon of air, the stirring not strong enough to indicate a body. And then Gage knew it completely and at once, understanding finally the reason for the faint stirring of wind, what it was, what it had been.

A blade.

It was a blade; the cold steel almost at Gage's face, moving slowly through the air, its coldness emanating through the stillness to faintly touch the chilled air which, in turn, brushed the sweat of his skin; a ghostly caress.

Tensing violently against a trembling that threatened the stillness, Gage stiffened. An overpowering panic almost compelled him to leap forward, stabbing blindly, but training instantly shut down instinct.

Cold, nearer now. A whisper of wind.

Sato had moved a silent step forward, slow enough to only barely stir the air. And he was crouched only a step away, was searching the space before him with the tanto.

Gage knew that, on the first faint contact of the blade, Sato would lunge forward, impaling him, willing to match his superior, drug-induced strength against Gage's failing endurance. And Gage knew that if he himself struck too soon and missed a vital area, Sato would simply throw him down and, in series of short, brutal blows, stab him to death.

Sweat-soaked face tight in a terrible tension, moving with imperceptible slowness, Gage cautiously raised his left hand to his chest, holding it close. And his right hand froze in a blood-grip to the hilt of the Dragon, holding the blade low for an upward sweep.

A faint stirring of wind.

Coldness, passing.

Gage's toes curled silently within his boots. And he held a trembling high tension, leg muscles bunching, coiling.

Any . . . *second!*

A razored edge touched his face.

Roaring Gage swept the blade aside with his left hand and leaped forward to stab, and he collided solidly with Sato's massive form and the Japanese went backward before the assault. Gage came down on top on him, instantly trapping his knife arm.

Sato yelled out to throw him off, tried a headbutt, missed. And Gage reversed his knife grip, stabbing downward to plunge the nine-inch steel blade through the ballistic shirt and along Sato's ribs, pushing deep on the blade, wrenching, driving, twisting the steel through flesh and bone to savage a mortal wound. Screaming in pain, Sato kicked him in the chest, hurling Gage back. But Gage held onto the blade as he fell, drawing it free to continue the damage.

Gasping he collapsed to one knee, and through a misty red haze he heard Sato stagger up, stumbling, moving away from him, out of the corridor.

Rising on will and the dying fire of an exhausted rage, Gage stumbled after him. And together they entered the deserted cathedral again, shuffling with exhausted slowness into the gray light. There was only a small distance between them, but Gage no longer cared about distance, no longer needed it: This belonged to him now; he owned it, would finish it.

Swaying, Sato turned, face slack in pain, staring back at him.

Gage waited, breathing heavily, watching. Then with a guttural laugh Sato reached slowly into his bloodied coat to remove another crystal. Beyond caring, Gage waited. He knew what was coming; knew it would make no difference.

It was too late.

Sato cracked the crystal, raised it to his face, sniffed, and sniffed again. Instantly the chemical hit his system, and he shook his head violently, glaring at Gage with fresh strength. He shouted something indiscernible, eyes vivid and bright.

With a wary expression Gage widened his stance, coming onto the balls of his feet. His grip shifted slightly on the blade, tightening.

"Ai Uchi!"

Sato screamed and, with an explosive leap to bridge the gap, he stabbed straight with the tanto to deliver a suicide blow, but Gage sidestepped, slashing down on Sato's unprotected wrist to hit a hard, straight blow.

The tanto clanged to the floor, and Sato staggered forward another step, propelled by the momentum of his thrust before he wildly regained his balance, straightening, glaring at his crippled hand with an unfocused strangeness.

Gage suspected that he didn't even feel the wound; knew he would never stop.

As if in sullen disbelief, Sato gazed back at him, eyes red. Then the massive Japanese blinked angrily and glanced toward the bloodied tanto at his feet, as if measuring his chances. Gage followed the gaze, made no move to stop him.

Sato laughed.

Impassive, Gage blinked sweat from his eyes.

With surprising speed Sato had crouched and leaped forward again, stabbing with the long steel tanto, but Gage had stepped inside the blow, moving with almost casual speed to swing the Dragon from left to right in a two-hand power sweep.

Pivoting hard, Gage felt the blade bite deep into Sato's right side, smashing through bone, and he finished the blow, the fight, roaring and sweeping the blade completely through the rib cage. When the blade hit Sato's left ribs, Gage violently tore it free, on fire with the savage effort, and then they separated, standing close for a moment, leaning with shoulders touching, face to face, eye to eye, before Gage stepped slowly, angrily, to the side.

Sato made a choked, strained sound, then glanced down strangely at his chest, his ribs. Face contorted by pain, he looked up, focusing on Gage.

Gage stood a step away, and his face softened in a strange and exhausted amazement, eyes narrowing in disbelief. It was incredible that the Japanese was still standing. Then the amazed expression was gone, replaced by a bitter and grim resolve, and Gage remembered that he would go as long as he had to go, to finish this fight. But he *would* finish it.

Forever.

A silent, crazed stare and Sato suddenly staggered, falling to one knee. But he still held the tanto in his left hand, and, glaring insanely, struggled to strike again, to fight, to kill.

And Gage stepped close, his face dark with something more than blood. Slowly, he reached out to grab the hair of Sato's head.

His voice was chilling.

"Enough!" he rasped. "There will be . . . an *ending!*"

Gage brought the blade, the Dragon, back on a line horizontal with Sato's neck.

Sato screamed.

Dragon roared.

Winter died.

It was spring, and Kertzman, as strong, as massively imposing as he had ever been, sat patiently on the steps of the Memorial, watching the golden light that waved across the pond.

Across the distance of the river, almost lost in the exhaust and traffic, he heard the fresh sounds of the wild, sounds that called out to him, even here.

It was his last day.

Tomorrow he'd return to the high country where he could track on a high white ridge, the wind in his face, blue sky beside him, beyond.

He was retiring.

Everything was finished: the investigation, the indictments, the plea bargaining. Only sentencing remained for the guilty.

He laughed.

Carthwright.

The NSA man had gone down hard, protesting and fighting just enough to make it seem real. But Kertzman had known beforehand that he would take the fall, in the end. And he did.

Perfectly.

And it had only turned into a minor scandal, after all, with Carthwright alone convicted for using covert military units of the government for personal profit. But murder trials were expected against him eventually for all of Black Light's illegal sanctions. And Kertzman hoped that he lived long enough to see them. But he had a bad feeling about it. A bad feeling.

A sky shadow passed over him, and Kertzman glanced up to catch the spectral image, saw the wide, wild wings spread against a golden sun.

He laughed again, remembering. Rome had ended well enough. None of them were ever charged, or even detained, for the gunfight in the park. Even after Sato's headless body was found in the basilica, there had been no complications. And, remarkably, both the police and the militia had gone the extra mile to ensure that they were treated hospitably. All of them, even Gage, had received the best medical treatment, diplomatic immunity, the works.

And it wasn't because the United States Embassy had intervened, either. Kertzman was sure of that. No, from the very beginning Washington had pulled out, waiting to see what direction the wind would blow before they exerted any influence. Kertzman knew he had suddenly become a liability. Expendable.

He hadn't forgotten it.

Never would.

In the end, though, it hadn't made any difference because they'd been covered by someone else. Someone with power. And although Kertzman could never discover who it had been, he had a suspicion. One day, Kertzman knew, he'd thank him for it. If he ever went back to Rome.

For now, though, there was only this last meeting; a few words to draw lines, set down ground rules for the future. And in the distance, walking calmly down the side of the pond, Kertzman saw him approaching.

Austere and dignified, dressed in a customary, hand-tailored black suit despite the heat, Carthwright came slowly forward.

With dead calm eyes Kertzman watched the NSA man as he neared, finally climbing the steps to stand resolutely before Kertzman. Carthwright stopped a short distance apart, his head on the same level as Kertzman's. Then he nodded politely, looked around.

"This is becoming a habit," he said, indifferent.

Kertzman stared at him a moment. "Thought you might need to know some things," he said, finally. "Before they send you off."

Carthwright smiled. "Of course."

A bag of peanuts was open before Kertzman. Casually, he reached down with his right hand, removing a handful. And he began to crack them as he spoke, watching his hands. His voice was relaxed, as though he were speaking of hunting, or fishing.

"Gage is gone."

"I know," replied Carthwright, with a polite smile. "I understand that he has gone into the witness protection program."

A snorting laugh broke from Kertzman. "His *own* witness protection program," he mumbled. "He's on his own, Carthwright. On his own." He cracked open a shell, ate the nuts slowly. "I'd say he's somewhere in the wild blue yonder by now. He told Justice that he'd just take care of hisself."

Carthwright blinked slowly. Didn't respond.

Then Kertzman lifted his face to fix the NSA man with a dull stare. "He wanted me to give you a message," he continued.

For a moment Carthwright appeared like he would look over his shoulder. He didn't. But his jaw tightened and he stared at Kertzman strangely. His voice was faintly quieter when he responded.

"Yes?"

Kertzman was nodding vaguely with his own words, shifting his gaze between the shells he was breaking and the NSA man. "Gage says to stay away from everybody," Kertzman continued easily. "He says they're family."

A pause.

"Kertzman, surely you don't—"

"Save it," Kertzman growled, deadpan, eyes sleepy and uncaring. "I don't wanna hear it. You just pass it on. Sarah Halder is family. The old man is family. Barto's the same." He paused. "The book is gone. Destroyed. Gage burned it. There ain't nuthin' left to fight for."

Carthwright seemed to sway slightly, his mouth was open. He caught a breath.

"It's over," added Kertzman. He threw a few more nuts into his mouth, chewing slowly, relaxed.

A long hesitation and Carthwright seemed to grow more steady. Casually, he turned his head to gaze slowly to one side, the other.

The warm spring evening was alive with tourists, cops, war veterans paying tribute to the Vietnam Memorial only 50 yards away.

"I don't want to see you again," Kertzman said, commanding Carthwright's attention once more. "Gage don't want to see you again. But he knows how to find you. No matter where you hide." He nodded curtly. "You'd be surprised. So just don't hurt anybody and he won't hurt you. But if you do, he wants you to know up front that he'll take ten times as much from your side." He waited a moment, smiled slightly. "And you'll be the first."

Carthwright revealed his shock. "Look, Kertzman, I can't guarantee anything. People get killed. It's inevitable. There's car accidents, other things. What if—"

"Then you'd better hope none of 'em have a car accident," Kertzman grumbled, sniffing. "It'll be ugly for ya."

"This is *unreal*, Kertzman," Carthwright continued, struggling to recover. "Nobody could live with that. It's—"

"You just pass the message on," Kertzman said evenly, breaking another shell. "That's all you need to know. That's all there is."

In a sudden anger, Carthwright seemed to regain something. And after a pause he stepped forward, exuding an air of aggression, control. "Look, Kertzman, maybe you don't know it yet, but I'm going to *prison!* And I'll be there for a long time! I'm really not in a position to do anything against Gage or anyone else."

"But you'll die pretty soon," Kertzman said in a bored tone, shaking his head. "You won't see five years in the pen."

Kertzman seemed to be agreeing with himself as he continued.

"Yeah, you'll go in, all prettied up, the picture of health." He looked down, reaching for another handful. "And in a few years you'll supposedly die in prison from some weird disease or somethin.'" He watched his hands work the shells. "Then you'll live out the rest of your life on some beach, somewhere. Thinkin' that you're safe. But don't get too happy." He looked up. "He'll find you, if he has to. It'd be best not to start somethin.'"

Carthwright was staring at him.

"You won't fool me again, boy," Kertzman rumbled, a tone of growling granite. "You fooled me the first time, but you'd better remember it cause it'll be the last." He ate a few nuts, chewing thoughtfully. "You let me find the initial tracks in all of this on my own, right from that first meetin'. 'Cause you knew it'd be more real to me like that. Then you let me build the case against you 'cause you knew all along that Gage might just end up stompin' all 'a your supermen into the dirt. And you knew you'd have to take the heat yourself. You tried to set me up to die at the cabin, with Gage. But that didn't work out. Then you sent that travel log to Acklin, along with the reports of the shootout 'cause you knew that Acklin would actually do somethin' with it. You got him building a case." He shook his head. "Yeah, you got Acklin building the case you wanted him to build. Against you. Just like you got me to build a case against you by documentin' all them attempts to sidetrack the investigation." He paused. "If somebody'd look close enough at it, long enough, they'd find the holes. They'd see that it was a setup. Had to be. But nobody's gonna look that close. The White House is just happy to have a head, glad they can close the book on this one without calling in a special prosecutor that could turn this into a headhuntin' party."

Kertzman barely hesitated as he spat out a piece of shell. "It wasn't a bad plan," he continued. "Worked pretty well, I guess. All the damage will stay with you. And you'll end up protectin' whoever it is you're protectin'. Just like you were supposed to do. Just like you'd planned to do, if you had to."

Carthwright was silent, noncomfirming. His gaze was passive, slightly bored.

Kertzman didn't seem to notice.

"There ain't nuthin' I ain't figured out, boy," he added. "Nuthin'. I know that all of you work for some kind 'a psycho. And I know he probably ain't gonna stop doin' whatever he's doin'. But he needs to stay away from everybody in this." Kertzman nodded, a mean hardness in his bar-fighter face. "I can guarantee you that."

Carthwright held his silence. Then, abruptly, he seemed to want to say something. He opened his mouth, staring at Kertzman carefully, before he thought better of it, held his silence.

Dismissively, Kertzman nodded.

"You can go," he said gruffly. "I ain't got no more use for you. You just remember what I said."

Carthwright was already backing away, eyeing Kertzman warily, like a wild dog. When he had retreated three steps the NSA man turned and walked down the steps.

Chewing slowly, Kertzman watched him go, staring after him until Carthwright's tall, dignified black form was lost in the trees.

Kertzman turned his face to the sun.

It was dimmer, and lower, a grayness gaining in the horizon, the sky.

He laughed.

It was time.

•   •   •

Only a hunter could have found him.

Kertzman saw him in the trees, the shadows, poised motionless as a mountain lion; careful, always careful. Quietly, Kertzman walked through the dark mossy silence and gloom, finding a slow path through the overgrown forest and ferns until, finally, they stood face to face again.

Still unmoving, Gage smiled easily. He was leaning against a tree. And for a moment neither man spoke, then Gage shifted, releasing a short laugh.

"You look like you can still hunt pretty good," he said.

"I do alright," Kertzman replied, solid. "It's about time I got back home. I'm tired of cities." He paused. "Been too long."

Gage placed both hands in the pockets of his long, dark green coat. "When are you leaving?"

"Tomorrow morning," Kertzman answered. "When you headin' out?"

"Tonight. I just wanted to say goodbye."

Kertzman's face was brotherly, friendly. "How's Sarah?"

Brightening, Gage smiled. "She's good. They fixed her up." He hesitated, added more quietly, "She's still got a little scar, but it'll fade with time."

"She's a good woman," Kertzman responded, leaning into it. "Maybe ya'll can come visit me and the wife out in South Dakota some time. Bring all the kids with you."

Gage laughed hard. "Maybe we will, Kertzman. But we'll lay low for a while. Malachi is still going to teach at the college, and Barto's going to keep doing whatever he's been doing. Translation work, or something. But Sarah will stay with me. We're together, from here. She won't be going back to the city."

"Good. Is the new place gonna work?"

"Yeah," Gage replied, stepping away from the tree. "It's not in the States. But it's a good place. Better than the last, even." He waited, suddenly more serious. "You got everything straight? You know how to get in touch?"

"Yeah, I got it," said Kertzman. "You just lay low."

"I will."

Gage stepped forward, extending his open right hand. Face serious, he waited.

Kertzman stared at the hand for a moment, then he reached out, carefully, with his own right hand, grasping.

Their hands held strong.

"That's a real mean grip you got there," Gage smiled. "You need to be careful with that."

Kertzman laughed.

"Take care, Kertzman," Gage said.

"You, too."

And then Gage stepped back, turning slowly away. He walked for a step before he suddenly hesitated, abruptly turning back once more.

"Oh," he added, with a single step toward Kertzman. "I almost forgot this."

He stopped in front of Kertzman, removing a hand from his coat to offer a thin object about two feet long and wrapped in brown paper. The coarse paper was tied with a white string.

Kertzman saw it, knew.

Face hardening, he stepped ponderously forward, reaching out with his huge hand to grab it, taking it from Gage's grip. In silence, he studied it.

Gage smiled.

"Just a piece," he nodded.

Kertzman met his gaze, then stared at the object again. And, carefully, he squeezed it with his right hand, feeling the cold steel tanto beneath the paper. And then he squeezed it again, harder, knowing the strength returning to his hand, once more.

He nodded slowly, looked up.

"Good enough," he said.

Together, they rested before the flames.

Gage held her in his arms, covering her against the high cold outside, the darkness that shrouded the cabin in the frozen north woods. Sarah laughed, touching his hand, watching the flames.

"I like this place," she said.

Gage smiled.

"Winter's a long time leavin', this high," he said. "But it's a good place to live. It's quiet. And peaceful."

She nodded, didn't say anything for a long time.

Before them, in front of the fireplace, lay a dry and yellowed manuscript, its pages open, warmed by the flames of the hearth.

Silence.

Gage knew she had read it, but somehow he felt a fear to ask about it. Even so, though, he felt himself staring at the book, heard his own question.

"You read it, didn't you?"

A pause.

"Yes."

He hesitated. "And . . . was it there? Is there a name?"

She blinked, stared into the flames. "Yes."

His arms tightened around her. "Well, at least we've done them some damage," he added quietly. "That always counts for something."

"Yes," she replied, a half-smile. "We've done them some damage. And now he'll have to build a lot of it for himself. It won't be as easy for him."

Finally, after a heavy moment, Sarah leaned forward, arms wrapping around her knees. And her head was slightly tilted, saddened. Gage leaned forward, also, staying close, and he saw her eyes studying the manuscript, the ancient lettering dark and wavering in the red glow of the fire. After a time she reached down, grabbing hold of it, slowly raising a handful of pages before her face. She seemed lost in thought, far away.

Looked back at him, again.

Gage touched her hair, her face, as she spoke.

Her words were mournful, remembering. "So much suffering..." she whispered. "You know, sometimes I think that eternity won't be long enough... to forget what happened here." Her eyes searched him. "And then sometimes I think when all this is finally over, and we reach eternity, none of this will matter."

Gage saw the hurt, the fading white scar that still marked her face, and he knew the deepest scars left by her suffering would heal much slower, if they healed at all. And there were no easy answers. None at all.

"Ain't no answers, darlin'," he whispered and reached up to softly touch her face. "There ain't nuthin' but what we believe, and what we do."

Sarah continued to gaze at him a moment, and then the faintest smile touched her lips, her eyes, also, smiling with the effort. Then she looked back to the fire, a strength shining through the softness, emerging, overcoming the gentleness, the sadness of her gaze.

And, one by one, she began feeding the pages into the flames.

• • •

Hand hard in strength, the man raised the hammer high, brought it down upon the glowing red steel with crushing force.

Heated in the coals until its purity was surrendered to the same holocaust that had forged it, the glowing steel had lost its temper, its strength.

Kertzman laughed, raised the hammer high once more in his strong right hand, his other hand holding the super-heated steel against the anvil. And the hammer descended once more, tearing red shreds from the ancient blade.

Again, and again.

And, though the steel was strong, it could not endure, had slowly surrendered to hammer and anvil and flame, the strength of his own right hand, and something more. And, finally, Kertzman knew he had broken it, had crushed its purity with blow after blow, destroying its soul.

A cold gray wind blew across the black hills, and Kertzman turned to watch a slow South Dakota dawn.

Cold, refreshing wind.

Land, the wild.

He nodded, to himself.

Home.

Gazing down brutally, once more, at the blade, he knew at last that its purity, its beauty, was gone. And he remembered something he had read once, something about how men would take swords and beat them...into plowshares...

He waited, trying to remember, and thought for a moment that it was somewhere...in the Bible.

A vast wind moved over Kertzman with the thought, and it meant something to him. And he wondered about it. And as he wondered he turned his head to look across the deep, cloud-gray horizon, vast and deep and old with wind.

He stood still for a moment, searching.

Maybe somewhere...in the Old Testament.

And then he nodded, yes, maybe somewhere in the Old Testament.

With a grunt Kertzman tossed the glowing red steel into the water, laughing as it hissed in anger, utterly destroyed. And he turned massively away, walked toward the house.

Thought he might look it up.

Acknowledgments

To begin, I would like to thank my beloved mother, who has always provided such critical support at critical times, and who, far more than anyone else, allowed me to complete the novel on schedule. Though I might dedicate a thousand books to her name, I could never truly show my heartfelt gratitude for her selfless assistance, both in this and in countless other moments of my life. Some debts are simply too great to be repaid.

And I thank my wife, Karen, for her patience while I disappeared into my office for long days and weeks and months of writing and rewriting, for her selfless support, for being my most faithful friend and companion, and for being the inspiration for whatever is truly beautiful within the story itself.

To continue, I wish to thank Bill Jensen of Harvest House for his unshakable courage, his unwavering support and friendship, and for standing solidly behind me during those crucial hours. I thank him for freely providing his genius, his vision, and a generous number of his incomparable ideas to greatly enhance the storyline and character development.

And I also thank my good friend, Jan Dennis, of Jan Dennis Books, a division of Thomas Nelson, for his valued criticism and for his brilliant suggestions, which also greatly enhanced the storyline and characters.

In retrospect I realize, more than ever before, that this novel was no mean task. Capturing the world inhabited by America's most elite military commandos while at the same time portraying a compelling moral story was by far the most difficult fictional challenge I have ever faced. And, to its success, I owe a great debt of gratitude to Mark Matthews, who researched the most complex tactics of both foreign and American military personnel, and who provided exhaustive resources on weapons and methods. Also, I thank Chet Williams for his in-depth contributions describing how America's deadliest counterterrorist units are trained and conditioned, and for his technical assistance in operations.

A sincere thanks is extended to Jim Hammond, of Jim Hammond's Knives in Arab, Alabama, for his invaluable contributions in knife-fighting techniques used by Delta Force and Naval SEAL commandos. And I thank him for allowing me to use his specialized fighting knife termed "FleshEater," a weapon designed for and used extensively in America's military counterterrorist units, as the prototype for the weapon referred to as "Dragon" in the novel.

I also thank Stan Moore and Glenn Fincher for their invaluable computer assistance. And I greatly appreciated technical contributions in the area of medical care and treatment provided by Vicki Morris, John Sims, and David Jump. In addition, Trina Spond was responsible for providing methods of psychological testing used by American intelligence agencies for selecting field operatives. And I thank Glenda Rodman for her patient editorial assistance and criticism during the manuscript's development.

I also offer my sincere thanks to all those at Harvest House who contributed to the production of the work including Eileen Mason, Julie Castle, Fred Renich, Barbara Sherrill, LaRae Weikert, and especially Steve Miller, whose outstanding editorial judgment I have always held in the highest respect.

In research, I can estimate that I utilized almost one hundred separate sources of study. However, for the sake of sheer expediency, I will only refer to those that I feel a particular debt.

For factual and psychological insights into modern conflict I relied heavily upon *The Art of War* by Baron Jomini, *The Art of War* by Sun Tzu, and particularly upon *On War* by Carl von Clausewitz. I also found great use for the factual history of the American intelligence community detailed in *The CIA and the Cult of Intelligence* by Victor Marchetti and John D. Marks. And I found *Intellectuals* by Paul Johnson and *On Being a Christian* by Hans Kung to be extremely enlightening; I relied extensively upon both works to understand the often-contradictory modern mind.

Lastly, all military tactics, equipment, and physical methods utilized by the novel's characters are taken as cleanly as possible from current military manuals issued to Special Forces personnel by the United States Government. I remain grateful for the extensive technical assistance, and freely accept any errors as my own.

About the Author

James Byron Huggins has worked as an investigative reporter and award-winning newspaper writer and photographer, spent several years as a homeless person, risked his life repeatedly as a Christian smuggler behind the Iron Curtain, and faced danger on the streets daily as an Alabama police officer.

Huggins sacrificed a career in newspaper journalism when he refused to compromise his values. Working odd jobs, Huggins had saved enough money by 1985 to go to Romania in hope of helping the people of Eastern Europe. Once there he helped build and fund an underground system and risked his life smuggling documents in and out of Eastern Bloc countries. Most recently Huggins left his job on the police force to pursue writing full-time.

Huggins earned his degree in journalism and English from Troy State University. He lives in Alabama with his wife, Karen, and their two children.

CONTEMPORARY FICTION FROM HARVEST HOUSE

A WOLF STORY
by *James Byron Huggins*

Long ago, the inhabitants of the deep woods were given a difficult choice: to follow the Silver Wolf and his Lord, the Lightmaker, or join the secretive forces of the Dark Council. A war rages across the harsh wilderness, and the Dark Council is on the threshold of victory—only a lone wolf, Aramus, stands in their way.

This fast-paced novel portrays the struggle between good and evil—which is more than strength against strength, more than wit against wit. It is a path of endurance and faith....

UNFORGIVEN SINS
by *Joe Dallas*

"If you do nothing," the haunted figure on the videotape said solemnly, "you'll never forgive me for laying a burden of truth on you which you'll spend a lifetime fighting to ignore."

Greg Bishop is caught in the cross fire. A midnight suicide, a tormented believer's plea for help, and a mysterious videotape have put Greg in possession of information that exposes a dangerous faction of the gay community—at the risk of losing his family, his job, his life. ...One dark moment twenty years ago, a moment Greg has tried to forget, has set into motion a chain of events destined to bring back the past...with a vengeance.

RUMORS OF ANGELS
by *John Vincent Coniglio*

The world's greatest legal mind was finally getting the trial he had spent his life preparing for. Will stood ready to challenge the reality of Christ's resurrection—and brand it forever as a myth. A final warning that he was violating sacred ground fell on deaf ears—"The God whose logic you question is the God of the universe.... If I were in your shoes, I would bend a heedful ear to the proclamation of the angels in the tomb that morning."

Startling and unpredictable, *Rumors of Angels* is a search for evidence...a search for facts...and ultimately, a search for truth.